PARIAH

REDUX

Also By Bob Fingerman

White Like She
Minimum Wage
Beg the Question
You Deserved It
Recess Pieces
Bottomfeeder
Connective Tissue
From the Ashes
Maximum Minimum Wage
Minimum Wage, Book 1: Focus on the Strange
Minimum Wage, Book 2: So Many Bad Decisions
Dotty's Inferno

PARIAH

REDUX

BOB FINGERMAN

HEAVY METAL

Pariah first published in 2010 by Tor
This revised edition published in 2021 by Heavy Metal

"The Summer Place" originally appeared in
The Living Dead 2, Night Shade Books, September 2010
"Ink" originally appeared in *Weird Tales* #362, Spring 2014

Cover Illustration by Glenn Fabry
Cover Design by Bob Fingerman
Book Design by Jeff Wong

For more info: www.heavymetal.com

ISBN 978-1-73681-798-8

Printed in The United States by Fry Communications, Inc.

10 9 8 7 6 5 4 3 2 1

Chief Executive Officer: **Matthew Medney**
Publisher & Chief Creative Overlord: **David Erwin**
President & Head of Studio: **Tommy Coriale**
Executive Editor: **Joseph Illidge**
Chief Sales Officer: **Kris Longo**
Publisher, Magma Comix: **Denton Tipton**
Sales & Marketing Manager: **Jeromy Dechant**
Distribution Manager: **Jim Killen**
Publicist: **Cat Nuwer**
Marketing Manager: **Michael Pratt**
Marketing Specialist: **Eryk Puzeck**
Operations: **Martin Wendel**
Affiliate Marketing: **Sean Dyer**
Editor: **Fabrice Sapolsky**
Contributing Editor: **Justin Molhman**
Senior Digital Editor: **Josh Robertson**
Editor, Dir. Editorial Prod: **Morgan Rosenblum**
Digital Editor: **Joshua Sky**
Art Director: **Pete "Voodoo Bownz" Russo**
Production Editor: **Dezi Sienty**
Production Editor: **Taylor Esposito**
Assistant to the CEO: **Maya St. Clair**

For Val,
who always helps me
see things in a brighter context. Love you.

Part One

February, *Then*

Larry Gabler lay there, gasping, bleeding. At seventy-two, he was Abe's junior by eleven years, but at the moment he could have given Methuselah a run for his money.

"You gotta get home to Ruthie," he wheezed as sweat glossed his waxy face.

"Yeah, yeah," Abe said, pouring himself a stiff one from the bottle in his desk, the radio droning the barely coherent reportage of nerve-wracked correspondents attempting to articulate what was happening throughout the five boroughs—not to mention *the entire globe.* Abe took a tentative sip of the whisky, then downed it as he sauntered over to the window to catch an eyeful of uncorked chaos below. As he peered down, three taxis collided, the driver of one bursting through his windshield like a meat torpedo. People were jostling, shoving, climbing all over each other, every man for himself, *the hell with the rest.* The sounds of screams and random gunfire echoed in the darkening corridor of office buildings, the sun ducking for cover beyond Jersey to the west. Mixed in with the usual filth in the gathered curbside snowdrifts was a new hue: deep red, and plenty of it, like big, bloody snow cones.

"Oh yeah, I can't wait to get down into all that," Abe said.

The stray who'd brought Larry limping in cowered, nearly catatonic, on the other end of the waiting room's lumpy sofa. She was a good-looking young Puerto Rican, maybe in her early to mid-twenties. Maybe Dominican. Abe couldn't tell. Young was young, old was old, Hispanic was Hispanic. Larry let out a chalky groan, farted loudly, and slumped forward, chin on chest, blood oozing from his nostrils.

"I think your friend is dead," the Latin girl murmured.

"He was dead when he came in," Abe replied. "You get to my age and death's one of the few things you can recognize easy."

Abe looked at the blood-soaked material around Larry's chewed up calf, the slacks shredded. He downed another shot of whisky and made for the door.

"Where you going?" asked the girl.

"I gotta pay Menachem Bender a visit."

"Who?"

Without explaining, Abe left the office of Cutie-Pie Infant Wear and hastened down the hall to Menachem Bender Men's Big & Tall to pay a visit. Abe tried the door. Locked.

"Bender, you in there?" He pounded a few times, rattling the pebbled glass with Bender's name and logo painted upon it. "Bender, c'mon! It's me, Abe Fogelhut! You in there?" No answer. Abe cased the hall, then elbowed the loose pane out of the frame, the glass crashing to the linoleum beneath. With care not to cut himself, he opened the door, experiencing the giddy thrill of breaking into his neighbor's business as well as a jolt of bowel tightening fear. "Bender!"

Nothing.

Abe gave the unlit room a quick once over, then stepped in, flicking on the overhead fluorescents, which buzzed in protest. A cursory look at Bender's books made clear Cutie Pie wasn't the only outfit in the garment trade to have a lousy last quarter. "Oy," Abe sighed. "My condolences." Abe stepped around the desk towards the storeroom, nearly tripping over Bender's body, a .38 clenched in his white-knuckled hand. Bits of skull and brain matter flecked the adjacent wall and floor. Abe raised a hand to his mouth and then lowered it, realizing he was going to neither scream nor throw up. He just shook his head and opened the stockroom, repeating his previous sympathies. Turning on the light he allowed himself to smile.

"Perfect," he said, eyeing stacks unsold winter wear for enormous outdoorsmen.

Moments later he returned to Cutie Pie to find Larry hunched over the Latina, violently munching on her entrails. The contents of Abe's stomach disgorged, searing his throat. Larry didn't even look away from his still-twitching repast as Abe, grateful he'd retrieved the revolver from Bender, emptied the cylinder into his undead partner. The fifth shot removed the top of Larry's skull and he collapsed onto the girl's remains. Abe spat bile onto the floor, took a gulp straight from the bottle of Cutty Sark, swished it around, then spat again.

"Okay," he said, affecting as much calm as possible. "Okay."

He wiped his mouth with his hankie, took a box cutter and sliced open one of the myriad boxes of his unsold stock of *Baby Sof' Suit®* infant winter onesies. "Okay," he said, "time to redeem yourselves."

Five-foot-five Abe, with his thirty-inch waist, stepped into a XXXL pair of *Bender's Breathable Sub-zero Shield® Sooper-System™ Weather Bibs,* a double-insulated hunting overall for fatties who like traipsing off into the winter wilderness to shoot innocent critters. Leaving the bib down, Abe began stuffing onesies down the pants, padding himself from the cinched ankles up. When he'd reached maximum density he pulled up the bib, heaved on the matching camouflage parka and stuffed in more onesies. With the hood pursed tight around his scarf and a pair of snow goggles, Abe resembled something between the Michelin man and the Kool-Aid guy.

"Okay," he said again, this time muffled, "let's go home."

July, *Now*

Flat on his back Dabney lay awake in the open, the stars obscured beyond a layer of gray-black haze. A sliver of moon peeked through, though, which he found reassuring. Beneath him the silver-painted tarpaper was lumpy and hot, still retaining the heat of the day. He felt the texture with his thick fingers, creased and peeling, much like his own skin, which was sunburnt from spending all his time up here on the roof. Let the others rot in their apartments, he figured.

Dabney touched his forehead and plucked a strip of his peel away and pressed it onto his tongue, tasting his own acrid saltiness on the paper-thin jerky substitute. He let the rind sit there for a while, building up sufficient saliva to swallow it. He knew this was disgusting behavior, but so what? He was doing a self-test of what senses he could stimulate. Taste; check. Touch; check. Sight; negative. Hearing? All was quiet above and below so Dabney forced an acidic burp. Check. Smell?

Smell.

Smell had taken a beating in recent months, not that smell had ever been his favorite. The nullification of smell was sort of a blessing, given the circumstances. So, three out of five, for the time being. Morning would come and sight would soon return to the roster.

Four out of five.

Not bad.

"Jesus, even a little air movement would be an improvement. Movement. Improvement. A *breeze* through the *trees* would *please* as it rolled over my *knees* like a *disease* or honey from *bees* and it would *ease* my … my … Fuck. Lost it."

With the rhyming game over, Karl rolled over on his side, the mattress where he'd been lying now damp with perspiration. Moisture he could ill afford to lose. Karl stared at the wall, or at least in the direction of the wall. It was so dark he couldn't see it, but it was there, a thin layer of protection between him and them. And he wasn't even thinking about the *big* them. The capital T *them.* He was just thinking about the them that constituted the others in the building. His neighbors.

All the windows of apartment 5B were open but you'd never know it, the air so still it felt like a vacuum. Karl inhaled deeply through his nose, some buildup within creating a high-pitched whistling. He breathed in, out, in, out, changing the tempo, attempting to mitigate his insomnia by nose-whistling some half-forgotten pop tune, the melody of which had come unbidden from the depths of his subconscious. What was that tune? Now he began to hum it, sans lyrics. But there were lyrics. He knew that much. This was killing him, now. The more he hummed, stretching out the notes, the less the words came into focus. This was killing him. Well, not really. But it wasn't helping.

Weighing like a hundred or so pounds was killing him.

Being dehydrated was killing him.

Not sleeping was killing him.

The earworm was merely aggravating.

With internal creaks and pops belying his actual age of twenty-eight, Karl swung his legs over the side of the bed and touched his toes to the bare wooden floorboards, which were as warm as everything else. Floors were supposed to be cool to the touch. Even in summer.

Before stepping from the bed, Karl groped at his night table for matches. Though he was loath to strike one and add to the heat even a little, he was more averse to stubbing his toes or tripping over something. After living in this apartment for the last few years you'd think he'd know the lay of the land, even blind. But he didn't. The book of matches found his sweaty palm and Karl snapped one into life, the brightness singeing his eyes for a moment as they adjusted to this pinprick of light in the absolute dark. The small dancing light found the blackened wick of one of the candles, which sputtered to life, creating a pool of comforting incandescence.

Karl had lots of candles, gifts from his mother, aunts, grandma, and past girlfriends. Even female coworkers—Secret Santa crap. What was it with women and candles? He'd gotten them as gifts, pretended he'd appreciated them, then thrown them all in a box in his closet. Now he was grateful for them—except the scented ones. It had only taken one Apples 'n' Spice candle to teach him his lesson. He'd lit the wick, basked for a moment in the delicious bouquet, and then retched from the crushing whiff of the ceaseless parade of rot outside.

So, unscented.

In the light Karl could make out the trappings of his bedroom. The posters on the wall—nu metal, old metal, some classic rockers—reassured him, though none of the bands displayed were responsible for the rogue tune assailing his brain at the moment. What was it? Familiar yet unfamiliar. It was sort of pretty in an annoying kind of way.

Karl's eyes roved past some MMA champions to his Wall of Beauty, an array of pinups, centerfolds, magazine clippings, and most personally gratifying (and now, in retrospect, most painfully sentimental), photos from the good old days when he was "getting some" and could occasionally convince his conquests to pose for him in the raw. When things had been different he'd been discreet and kept these pix salted away in a private place, but now? Now they were on permanent display.

Karl got up from the bed and shuffled over to the wall. The flickering candlelight almost made the images seem to writhe on paper. His prize was the glossy print of Dawn-Anne McCarthy, his junior high crush. He'd run into her years after they'd graduated, on line at a store here in the city. Her disdain for him in junior high had vanished and for a few dazzling weeks they'd fulfilled every last one of his adolescent fantasies about her, and several his pubescent mind had been too inexperienced to even conjure.

Until he'd blown it, of course.

"You were the best, baby," Karl said, touching the tip of his index finger to photo. He exhaled with conspicuous melancholy, not that there was anyone to notice or lend comfort. "You were my Everest."

Karl flushed with embarrassment at his floridity, then looked up at the ceiling and pondered going up to the roof. Maybe it was cooler up there. Maybe there was some air up there. Then he thought of Dabney and reconsidered, slunk back to bed, blew out the candle, and curled up on his side on the edge in an attempt to avoid the damp spot.

Which was warm.

"You asleep?"

Across the hall, in 5A, Ruth Fogelhut poked her husband of forty-six years in his xylophone ribs with her chicken claw of a hand, her hard, pointed fingers raking his translucent epidermis, leaving behind scarlet trails, not that either could see them in the dark.

"Who sleeps around here? Especially ..." Pause for a brief dry-throated coughing fit. " ... with you torturing me all through the night? Sleep? What is this thing you call sleep? I should be so lucky. Even a nightmare is preferable to your constant mutchering."

"You don't have to be so unpleasant, *Abraham*."

"Is that supposed to chasten me, '*Abraham*'? What, I'm a five-year-old and saying my whole name is a scold I'll abide? Abe, Abraham, call me whatever you like. Call me Ishmael, for all I care."

"I'll call you a shit, how's about that?"

In the blackness Abe smirked in triumph. In all her years Ruth was never one for cursing. It was beneath her, such vulgarity. Swearing was for the hoi polloi. But take away amenities like food, running water, electricity, hygiene, etc., and even Emily Post might call you a *shit.*

"I'm sorry, Abe. *Abe,* is that better?" Ruth's voice was croaky and plaintive. It sounded like it was coming from something not quite human, something rattle boned and cotton mouthed. Something mummified and meager. Oh wait, it was. Ruth, once a breathtaking, slightly Rubenesque ringer for a young Ruby Keeler, was now a crinkly sack of bones, nearly bald, with craters like eggcups holding her dulled, gummy gray eyes.

"Abe's fine," Abe mouthed, almost silently. Why raise one's voice? Gone were competing noise, like traffic and planes roaring across the sky. Gone were the cries of children, or mugging victims, or brawlers from the bar cater-cornered from their apartment. Gone were the ghetto cruisers with their booming systems, the bass so deep you could feel it in your colon. Gone were the nightly aural assaults from the garbage trucks, the thunderous growl of the crusher mechanism, the clash and clang of the emptied cans being slammed back to the pavement, the inarticulate badinage of the sanitation workers. Who'd think you'd miss that crap? "Abe's fine," Abe repeated, as much to reassure himself as Ruth. It felt better to talk about himself in third person; made him think of himself as not quite real. *Abe's not fine,* he thought. *Who the hell is fine nowadays?*

"I can't sleep."

"Really?" Abe said, the sarcasm edging out his miserable attempt at tenderness. "You could knock me over with a feather." The fact was you could knock either of them over with a feather, and not a particularly large feather at that. Two skeletons with a soupçon of withered meat held together by decrepit membrane lying side by side in a dilapidated lumpy sarcophagus.

One flight down, on the fourth landing, ear pressed against the door of neighboring 4B, Ellen Swenson clasped a hand over her mouth, suppressing the urge to call out to her husband, Mike, who dozed sporadically in their apartment behind their currently unlocked door. Ellen had left her left flip-flop wedged between the door and the jamb and tiptoed across the narrow hall to eavesdrop. Mike didn't buy her speculations about their neighbors, the jocks—the *former* jocks, at any rate. They were regular guys. Beer guzzlers. Hockey players. Bullies. Republicans. Wall Street bros. Mike's argument, by way of Freud, was that sometimes a cigar is just a cigar, but Ellen didn't buy it. With empty apartments still available, why'd they choose to live together when they arrived here from a few buildings north? She didn't just accept things at face value. *Is a cigar a cigar if no one's smoking it?*

She had her theory, she needed proof and this gave her something to do when insomnia hit, which was almost invariably, especially since nights became interminable. No light, no entertainment, no conventional diversions. So, Ellen made her own fun. As a girl she'd been a fan of Nancy Drew, Encyclopedia Brown and even Scooby Doo, so this meddling kid would tumble the jocks' game if it killed her. If it didn't, the boredom might.

The upside of a nearly silent world was that sound traveled. Sometimes that was a minus, but not right now. They must be in the living room, Ellen surmised. They sounded close. Really close. Like, right by the door. But sound had a way of tricking you in the absolute dark. All she wanted was to hear something incriminating. Something to lord over Mike, to prove she was right.

"I don't even know why I listen to you, Mallon," came Eddie Tommasi's voice. Eddie, Ellen figured, was the alpha dog. He barked louder and was the one Ellen feared. Pasty ginger Dave just kind of annoyed her. He was the wallflower. The beta. "You're wrong about *everything*."

"Dude, you need to take it easy on the water."

"*Vaffanculo*, dude. Don't mother hen me." Eddie slammed something to emphasize his dominance—*case closed.* "Fuckin' twerps across the hall," he spat. "Fuckin' Swensons!"

At the sound of her name, Ellen stiffened.

"We should just beat the shit out of Mike and take his woman. Make her our sex slave. Only two fuckin' women in here—"

"What about Gerri?"

"Gerri. *Please.* She's ... who knows what her deal is. Here. Here. In this dump. *Only two fuckin' women* and one's like ninety and the other's married and monogamous. Fuckin' monogamous! What kinda selfish outmoded shit is that, anyways? Don't the Jews share everything on those kibbutz things? This is like that now, yo. This here. I'm tellin' you, bro, *it ain't right*."

"Hey, chill out," Dave scolded in a hushed voice. "Sound carries, you know?"

"I don't give a shit," Eddie boomed. "Let her hear. Let 'em both hear. *Hey, Swenson, I'm gunnin' for your woman, bitch*!"

At that, Ellen's insides tightened. It wasn't funny anymore. Though neither Dave nor Eddie were the strapping behemoths they once were, both were still relatively formidable. Mike and she wouldn't stand a chance against them in a physical confrontation. *Sex slave.* As she began to tremble Eddie let out a burst of loud, bellicose laughter.

"I'm just fucking around, Dave. Chill."

Chill, indeed. Even in the stultifying heat, Ellen's skin erupted in goose pimples, sweat turning cool on her body. Like a silent movie blind man she extended her arms and groped back towards her apartment door, slipped in and triple-locked it in case Eddie wasn't "just fucking around."

In 3A, Alan Zotz massaged his temples, removing his glasses, which were streaked and stained with sweat and sebum. His "T-zone" was working overtime, his eyebrows smearing translucent patterns onto the lenses. Candles flickered, adding to the already oppressive temperature, but what was he supposed to do if he couldn't sleep, just lie there and stare into the void? He wasn't in the mood to draw, so reading was the only thing left to do since television and the Internet became extinct. All his batteries were dead, so music was becoming but a sweet memory, like everything else he'd taken for granted.

Alan kept rubbing, feeling his pulse throbbing away. He contemplated dipping into his dwindling supply of store-brand ibuprofen, acetaminophen or aspirin. His mother always warned him about ruining his eyes by reading in inadequate light. She also warned him about sitting too close to the TV, but that advice was now moot. He wanted to keep reading. This was a good book, a real page-turner. His father used to lecture him about wasting his mind on junk. He'd urged Alan to read the classics, to refine his mind. But Alan persisted in reading potboilers. He'd liked escapism when things were still good. Now escapism was his only luxury. His collection of sci-fi and crime paperbacks was worth its weight in gold. Scratch that; gold wasn't worth anything anymore. It was better than gold. *Sorry, Dad. Maybe Chaucer or Dickens or Goethe or Balzac or Sartre or whomever would have made me a more cultured person. But right now I'll take my fantasy, thank you very much.*

Horror, on the other hand, he left to molder on the shelf.

The pain in his temples encroached into the middle of his head, meeting at the bridge of his nose, the beat incessant, insistent, insufferable. He switched from massaging the sides of his head to working between the eyes. He was going to have to stop reading.

Alan walked to the front windows, which were all the way open. With barely any celestial light, the occupants of York Avenue were more abstract, their bobbing heads darkish blurry bumps, like moldy blueberries. At night they seemed to sway rather than dodder. *Do they sleep?* Alan closed the windows and flopped back onto his mattress. He licked his fingertips and pinched out the candles. His face itched, still unused to being so thickly bearded, he not having mastered the art of the dry shave. Alan depressed the button on his digital watch. The red LED display announced it was 3:27 in the morning. Sunrise was about two hours away. An eternity. From the vestibule echoed upward the rustling of zombies brushing against the corroding barrier just beyond the building's front entrance. The faint, almost subliminal, sounds in the silence a constant reminder of the things out there. The famished undead.

As Alan scratched and fussed he drifted off, the only person in the building actually asleep.

One flight down, situated above the boarded-up abandoned Phnom Penh Laundromat, apartments 2A and 2B were vacant. No one wanted to live that close to the street, and 2B housed bad memories.

2

As blackness ebbed the room began to take on a bruised, bluish-lavender tint, heralding the start of a new day. Ellen lay on her side, facing away from the twin windows alongside the bed, watching the wall change color. The purple drained away, replaced by jaundiced ochre, which as brightness increased lost pigmentation. Finally the normal drab off-white hue solidified, the glaringly bright sunlight accentuating every imperfection in the wall's surface, each crack, each patch of Spackle under the substandard paintjob. The wall was scarred beneath the paint, reminding Ellen of her former boss, a woman with an unfortunate complexion who'd applied way too much base in a sad effort to mask what imperfections lay beneath. Instead all she did was draw attention to each pit on her acne-ravaged face, a hopeless topography of dermatological strife. Too much makeup was the female equivalent of the shoddy toupee. Whenever Ellen had seen a man wearing an obvious rug—and most of them were pretty damned glaring—she always figured no one really liked or loved him, because no one would allow her husband or good friend go out in public looking that foolish.

The wall was pitted, a trifle buckled, somewhat bulgy in the middle. Their building was old, almost a hundred, but still settling. A couple years back she'd read that her block was right near a fault line. Maybe the earth would one day just start to shimmy and shake and swallow them all up. Better the earth than those *things.*

As hot as it was at night, it would be worse during the day, but at least she could see, not that seeing was much of a blessing. At night she could remember herself the way she was before. She could imagine some meat on her bones, some tone in her muscles. Hell, she could nostalgically remember some rolls of post-pregnancy fat that she'd wished would go away. *At night.* During the day she could really absorb how awful she and everyone else looked.

Ellen poked Mike in a furrow between his ribs until, with effort, his eyelids separated, revealing red-rimmed, mucilaginous eyeballs. His mouth, a thin, wide, arid trench while sleeping, clenched and unclenched, lines radiating in parched spokes from his dull lips, which back in the day were red and full and the most kissable in the world. His mouth, as it attempted to form his first words on the day, pursed like the shriveled sphincter it was, lost in curly beard growth. Ellen still kissed that puckered bunghole of a mouth, but now it was perfunctory, a sad nod to past romantic glory.

"What?" Mike's voice was Gobi hoarse.

"I think we need to bar the door better. Like, push some furniture up against it to make it impenetrable."

With considerable effort, Mike sat up and rubbed his eyes and nose.

"Why?" he croaked. "You think the shamblers are going to get up here? They haven't since that one time and I think it's pretty well—"

"Not them. Dave and Eddie. I heard them talking last night and—"

Mike gave her a sour look.

"Oh, *what?*" she said, folding her arms across her slatted chest, her breasts drooping like withered cutlets. Not the supple breasts of a successful thirty-two-year-old Upper East Side urban professional mom. They were more like ones seen in a magazine spread on depredation in Darfur or Somalia or some other godawful place—the kind that play landing field to legions of flies. These ruined teats had fed their child. They'd been large and full and life sustaining. They'd been ample and erotic. They'd been real ego boosters. Now they were depleted paps.

You're no longer a mom when your child is dead—your *former* child.

Everything was *former.*

"You're crazy," Mike managed. "If they heard you out there who knows what they would have done to you?"

Ellen had a pretty good idea, based on Eddie's brief but memorable rant. She didn't think they were above rape; if those jock assholes were slightly less malnourished she'd live in serious fear of them. Especially Eddie. Her assumption they'd adapted their appetites to amenably same-sex might not be as watertight as she'd thought, and losing the comfort she took from the notion they'd been focusing their brutish carnality on each other didn't improve her spirits.

"Anyway, promise me you'll never do anything stupid like that again."

"It wasn't *stupid,* Mike."

"Okay, not stupid. Uh, foolhardy. Ill-advised. Perilous."

"It's like you actually care."

"I ..." Mike began to sputter. "What the ... I ... Of course I ... What kind of way is this to start the day?"

Ellen shrugged and stepped off the bed, drifting toward the kitchen. "You want some water?" she asked Mike, whose face twitched with apoplexy. He blinked a few times, then nodded and she left the bedroom. Let him stew, she thought. She had no reason to torment him, but it killed the time. Besides, it would give her something to apologize for later. The hours had to be filled with something, so why not a little domestic turbulence? Sex took too much energy, and besides they were both so kindling-like it just wasn't fun anymore. Bones ricocheting off bones, bad smells. But it also passed some time and sometimes that was enough. They'd read all their books and magazines. Neither had any talent worth pursuing. Mike had been into photography, but that was no longer an option. She wrote bad poetry back in the day, but now why bother? What would she write about, the death of everything? Been done and done and done to death.

In the kitchen, Ellen poured half a glass from a bottle of Kirkland Signature Premium Water. But the water within was far from premium. It was rain water. Ellen couldn't remember how old the bottle was. They'd filled a whole case of them last rain. Ellen traipsed back into the bedroom where Mike now stood by the window staring straight across the alley at the neighboring building, not ten feet away. The windows there were stripped of any coverings and all were dark, bereft of life. There used to be noisy neighbors. Directly across from them there was this Latin couple who'd blast salsa music at all hours of the day and night. They'd openly do drugs by their windows, smoking pot, doing lines. Once, the man spotted Mike peeping at them and made a finger gun and mouthed, "Pop, pop, pop," then winked and flashed a gold-accented toothy grin.

Mike leaned out the window and peered down into the alley. Stragglers who'd broken off from the herd shuffled back and forth, having breached the gate that someone in a panic must have left unlocked. Mike cleared his throat and a couple looked up, their dulled eyes twitching in recognition of something delicious. One let out a faint, but audible gasp and began to limp in Mike's direction.

"Be careful," Ellen said as Mike leaned out further, bent at the midriff.

"It's like you actually care," Mike threw back at her, but when he did so, he smiled.

Ellen sidled up to her husband and put her hand on his back, feeling guilty about pushing his buttons, especially so early in the day. She could have at least waited until after their scant breakfast.

"I brought your water," Ellen said, holding up the small juice glass, an old jelly jar with Huckleberry Hound on it.

Mike lifted his hands off the window ledge and straightened at the waist, eager to drink, unmindful of the window frame. His head slammed into the sash and his feet lost purchase on the smooth floorboards, thrusting his upper portion forward. Ellen dropped the glass and grabbed for Mike, her hands moist with perspiration, muscles neutered by starvation. She made contact with his left bicep but it slipped away. He pitched forward, his bony naked ass slamming against the sash as his legs pinwheeled by her astonished face. An inarticulate screech was the only sound she could manage as her husband fell out the window.

Swallowing hard, she rushed to the other window, the one with the fire escape. It was possible he'd survived, that they could rescue him. She pushed the curtains aside to reveal the folding security gate and stared at the padlock like she'd never seen it before. The gate had been there from the previous tenant, a model not approved by the fire department. The combination. She couldn't remember it. Mike had it somewhere.

His laptop.

His dead, useless, worthless laptop.

Now the blood in her veins seemed to slow. She dragged her feet across the floor toward the open window Mike had fallen through. She didn't want to look, but desire was not a factor. She poked her head out, her posture exactly aping that of Mike's mere moments ago. In the alley below, Mike lay splayed on his back, his spindly arms and legs arranged almost comically about him. From her vantage point he looked like a human swastika, legs bent in a cartoonish running position. His face stared straight up and they made eye contact. He wasn't dead. Ellen's mouth opened and closed but no sounds came out. She wanted to shout something comforting; some final thought Mike could take with him. "I brought your water," seemed entirely deficient.

The zombies advanced on Mike. Ellen's teeth began to chatter and Mike's eyes implored her to say something. Anything. With effort she managed to mouth, "I love you," but mute. *Please let him die before they reach him. Please.*

A small pool of blood was forming beneath Mike's head, and Ellen noticed his neck was at an odd angle. A four-story fall. His neck was broken. He was paralyzed. *Please let him be numb all over. Please at least spare him the pain.* Mike's eyes began to swim and lose focus. *Let him lose consciousness.* The first of his defilers stooped over and dropped to its knees, baring its teeth. At least Ellen couldn't see its face, but she knew what it looked like. Cadaverous leathery skin, yellow as a dead plucked chicken, translucent enough to display dull plum-tinted veins, blackened gums receded all the way, teeth huge, eyes glazed—if it even had any.

A shriek echoed through the alley as they tore into Mike, picking the meager flesh off his bones with those horrible teeth, digging their jagged nails in, peeling him. Ellen was locked in position—sympathy paralysis. She wanted to close her eyes but was unable. She watched as they dismembered Mike. With ingenerate knack one scored perforations around Mike's left shoulder with its teeth then, with a few hard tugs, wrenched the arm off and began to devour it, ripping meat off the bones. Another disemboweled Mike, unintentionally inviting several others to mooch off the uncoiling spoils. Bestial growls accompanied the feeding frenzy, the things poking at each other, scrabbling, circling like hyenas. More stumbled into the alley from the side street, attracted by the noise, the scent of fresh blood. Soon all she could see were their backs hunched over the spot on which Mike lay. Her nails dug into the brick beneath the ledge, grinding them down, a rudimentary no-frills manicure. Tears blurred her vision.

"I brought your water," she said again, her voice thinner than she was.

"Ellen," a voice cried out from below. "Don't look at this! Pull your head inside!"

Was Mike trying to spare her? That was so Mike of him, always trying to protect her feelings, even now. She was sorry she couldn't oblige, though. *Sorry, Mike. Sorry about everything.*

By the time her temporary immobilization eased, all that was left of dear, sweet Mike was a dark crimson stain on the pavement and some picked clean bones. Not enough to reanimate. At least there was that. Ellen wrested her fingers from the mortar, contemplated jumping, reconsidered and slumped to the floor, hugging herself, taking no solace from her bony limbs and digits.

Former mother.

Now former wife.

Across the hall she heard Eddie bellow something unintelligible. But his tone, as always, was ugly and portended trouble.

And now she was alone.

"OPEN THE DOOR, Ellen!" Alan implored.

He'd raced up the stairs and now pounded on the door of 4A. This was excitement no one needed or wanted, least of all him, but he couldn't just sit in his apartment and pretend it hadn't happened. He'd heard the howl from the alley and had looked down in time to see Mike's head come off, a sight he hoped Ellen had been spared from her vantage point, but probably not. He'd looked up from the alley's floor and seen Ellen perched at her windowsill, eyes like saucers swimming in roomy sockets. Ellen didn't seem to hear him. He'd pled for her to look away. Instead she'd watched her husband transform from significant other to outdoor buffet. And it wasn't even eight in the morning.

"Ellen, come on!" Alan cried. "Open the door! Please, Ellen!"

Across the narrow hall the door to 4B opened and Eddie appeared, standing in his doorway in his boxers, which hung too low below his diminished waist. "What's the fuckin' ruckus?" he said, just oozing compassion.

"Mike ..." Alan began, then stopped himself. Eddie'd find out soon enough, but why tip the hand? If he was unaware of Mike's demise, why let him know? He'd just up the harassment ante on Ellen.

"What *about* Mike?" Eddie said, raising an eyebrow.

"Nothing. I just need to talk to Ellen."

"What for?"

"Jesus, Eddie, just mind your business. You're like a hausfrau looking for gossip."

"I've got no problem busting your fuckin' lip open, wiseass," Eddie growled, wagging a finger. "Just you remember that. For reals."

"Uh-huh. That's great," yawned Alan, indifferent.

"You just better hope I never bulk up again, prick."

And with that, Eddie slammed the door shut. Once upon a time Eddie had spooked Alan, but that was fifty or so pounds ago. Now they were both in the same weight class. Fact was Alan had a little *more* meat on him than Eddie because he'd been better at squirreling away; much better. Not that Eddie needed to be privy to that info. Alan tried the doorknob again, rattling it. Locked, of course. Who'd keep an unlocked door, especially with those goons across the hall? After several minutes the clack of multiple deadbolts unlocking came from the other side of the door and it opened a crack, revealing Ellen's gaunt shell-shocked face.

"I don't know what to say," Alan said, feeling stupid for having said it.

"Come in." Ellen opened the door wider and stepped aside, which seemed a formality considering she was too attenuated to block his entrance. She wore a pale pink tank top that accentuated her lankness, her neck cords so pronounced Alan fought the insane temptation to strum them.

"I saw what happened. When you didn't answer the door I was afraid you'd done something to yourself."

Ellen just stared at Alan, eyes glassy with trauma. She plopped herself down on a wooden dining chair and Alan could hear the bones in her ass knock against the hard surface. The sound made him wince, but she didn't notice. After a few hushed seconds passed, Alan pulled out a chair at the table and joined her, seating himself slowly, carefully, mindful of the hard-on-hard dynamic. No one had padding anymore.

Ellen's arms hung limp at her sides, the wrists grazing the lower rim of the seat of the chair. So many hard angles. Alan had lusted after Ellen when she and Mike moved in six years ago. That was before she'd been a mother—not that women who'd had kids weren't still sexy, but motherhood was a sacred institution. Wasn't it? Was anything scared anymore? Anyway, this wasn't a booty call. Ellen had no booty. Her ass had been so perfect, a flared ripe pear.

What am I thinking?

Now more than ever each life was precious. Mike had been precious to Ellen, even though they bickered. Alan heard them. Alan's thoughts were jumbled. He'd liked Mike well enough. Mike was a good neighbor. They'd even hung out together a few times back in the days before. Tossed a Frisbee. Talked current events. Nothing special. Hanging out after didn't count, because choice was no longer a factor. Alan slapped himself across the face, snapping himself out of this unproductive internal loop, the sound and action stirring Ellen from her torpor.

"What did you do that for?" she asked, somewhat horrified.

"Sorry, my mind was kind of malfunctioning. Nothing to be concerned about. I'm supposed to be here for you, Ellen. Sorry. Won't happen again. I don't even ..."

"No, it's okay. It was just kind of weird is all. But it kind of helped, in a way. Seeing you slap yourself was odd enough to wake me back up." She paused for a few long beats, then added, "Mike's dead, you know."

"Yeah, I know. I saw. I was calling up to you, trying to get you not to look. I don't know if you heard me."

"*Ohhhhh,*" Ellen said, a faint smile playing on her drained lips. "That was *you.* I thought it was Mike. I wasn't thinking too straight. That was really considerate of you. Thank you."

Ellen looked and sounded far away, which might be for the best. Though Alan knew they were dead, he'd been graciously spared having to witness any of his loved ones being devoured. Strangers, sure. By the dozens. But family? Mercifully no. As Ellen evinced the thousand-yard stare, Alan's eyes roved about the kitchen. Pretty bare, like everyone's. His eyes drifted over each surface, eventually finding their way back to his vacant hostess. He tried to envision her fleshy past self. He'd done her portrait a few times in pastel, pencil, even ink, so her face was pretty well ingrained in his psyche, but it was hard to superimpose on this diminished version. He'd wanted her to pose nude, but Ellen thought that would make Mike jealous, even if it was strictly business, no hanky-panky. *What the hell was the point of being an artist if you couldn't get beautiful women to pose in the buff?* Alan had wondered. *It wasn't "Me Too," it was time-honored tradition. The male gaze, such as it was now categorized, was woven into the history of art. The gray area between appreciation and objectification.* Alan had suggested that he document her pregnancy with some tasteful nudes, but again the answer was no, even though she'd thought it a good idea at the time. That was a real pity. Her breasts had gone from admirable to astounding during those months, and then stayed that way for quite a while. He'd never seen her nude back when that would have been a thrilling experience. Now he routinely saw her in various states of undress and it was tragic.

With the merciful exception of the Fogelhuts, most of the residents had adopted a slightly more "progressive" version of permanent Casual Friday. 1620 York Avenue was a "clothing optional" residence. Maybe it was hypocrisy or maybe it was modesty—which seemed so passé—but Alan kept his clothes on when dealing with his neighbors. It's not like he strutted around like a modern day Beau Brummell, but he kept his shorts and T-shirt on. *Let the others sashay around in the raw.*

"Can I get you anything?" he asked, attempting to stay grounded in the now.

"Huh? Oh, no, no. Just stay with me."

"Okay, as long as you need."

"No, I mean *stay* with me. Stay in the apartment. Move in with me."

Alan looked at her face, trying to glean how serious she was. *Serious as a heart attack,* as the old saying went. Once upon a time that would have been the answer to his prayers, but now?

"Move in?"

"Move in. I don't want to be alone, especially with those two Neanderthals. Listen, I loved Mike, Mike loved me, but these, I dunno … These are savage times. I can't think about what's prim and proper and what will the neighbors say? '*Look, that whore's shacking up with someone new already.*' Who would think that, except those creeps across the hall? Maybe that old biddy, Ruth. But can you imagine what my life will be like if they think I'm—Christ, I can't even *say* it. *Available*? Oh, Jesus. *Fuck that.* It's not like you have to move your shit up here, but stay with me. We don't have to even sleep in the same bed if you're not comfortable with that. There's a foldout couch in the living room, so …" She paused. "It would give me the luxury of grieving with some peace of mind."

Ellen rambled on, the stream of words blurring. Alan became aware that she was gripping his wrist, hard, her thin fingers clenched together like a vice. They went all the way around his wrist now. That was disturbing. Alan was very territorial about his drawing hand, Arty. Protective. Arty drew, Wipey wiped. Arty was top priority. Arty's neighbor, Wristy, was not happy right now. Alan had never before thought of his wrist having a name. Anthropomorphizing his hands originated with his ex, Tammy. Gentle mocking. Now it was a way to feel less alone. And not at all crazy. Which was what he was feeling now. That tenuous filament between peculiar and certifiable. Predicated on the invitation from freshly widowed Ellen Swenson.

Alan Zotz and Ellen Swenson, he mused.

Once upon a time he might have wanted to carve that on a tree, with a big "4E" under it. But what could he say? This was a cocktail of fresh grief and panic and adrenaline. When she calmed down she'd probably want him to move back out. This was temporary. Life was temporary. They'd all starve to death pretty soon, anyway.

Might as well go out one of the good guys.

KARL KNOCKED ON the door to the roof, not wanting to intrude—at least not without Dabney's plain approval. After a few more tentative taps, Dabney called out a brusque, "Whattaya want?"

"It's me, Karl. Permission to come above?"

Dabney half scowled and half chuckled at Karl's unfailing dorkiness. He appreciated the younger man's respect for his personal space, but this was the roof for Christ's sake. He didn't own it. If Karl wanted to come up—if *anyone* wanted to—who was Dabney to say no? Dabney had set up a lean-to of corrugated aluminum and loose brick. When it rained the buckshot-on-metal clatter to lulled him to sleep. It had been weeks since it rained last. Nonetheless, strewn about the roof were various containers for collecting water: garbage cans, buckets, plastic drawers and file boxes. And a few planters with failed attempts a vegetable farming, all dead before they yielded anything edible.

Karl stepped out onto the blindingly bright silvery tarpaper, the sun blazing full tilt to the east. He wished he'd brought sunglasses and sandals, but didn't want to go back down just to come back up. Instead he squinted and winced, scorching his eyes and toasting his feet. Karl nodded at Dabney, who returned the acknowledgment before resuming his post on the lip on the roof, belly down on a mottled canvas tarp, head hung over the edge. Beside him was a pile of chunks of loose brick culled from the neighboring buildings, the adjoined roofs separated by low walls which Dabney periodically demolished and raided for recreational target practice. The only constructive use the residents of 1620 had found for masonry—part of a renovation project that never got past the supply stage—was walling up the interior front entrance with cinder blocks, fortifying what the harried contingent of National Guard had hastily erected to bar entry to their building. Up and down the block, doorways both residential and commercial were boarded up with rusting slabs of corrugated sheet metal. FEMA had done a bang-up job of sealing everyone in and abandoning them. Now, many of the fortifications were shearing away, the elements having corroded the substandard no-bid bolts.

Karl walked over to where Dabney lay and squatted next to him, looking over the edge from a safe distance. Heights and Karl didn't cozy up. Besides, the view was torment. Directly across the avenue from them was the linchpin of their collective woe, a tantalizing siren that beckoned, but one they could never answer: the Food City Supermarket. Behind its boarded up facade, they imagined, lay a cornucopia of uneaten, unspoiled shelf-stable goods, bottled water, batteries that still had juice in them, you name it. Sure, the produce and meat had rotted away, but there was likely an embarrassment of provisions in there, all hopelessly out of reach. Sandwiched between the east and west sides of York Avenue, as far as the eye could see in both directions, north and south, was a sea of doddering bodies, all with but a single purpose: eat anyone stupid enough to venture from the safety of their home. Karl had witnessed it many a time.

Food City was situated in a big steel and glass apartment building, the only truly modern high-rise for blocks. Next door to the supermarket, its entrance raised and bordered by a small enclave of benches and shrubs, was a bank. Above the supermarket was a shallow inset area—maybe five feet deep, the full width of the market—that housed the air-conditioning units. Right above that were the windows of the first tier of apartments, permanently sealed, like modern hotels and office buildings.

All up and down the avenue, as the status quo grew worse and worse, either lots were drawn or people went nuts or whatever, but countless had made attempts to gain entrance to Food City. Karl had observed what in other circumstances might have been comical stabs at it all go awry—real life Wile E. Coyote-style maneuvers. Several folks driven mad with desperation tried the Tarzan thing, throwing a line out from a high window, lassoing a streetlamp, swinging, falling. Unlike Tarzan, though, they'd all ended up being torn to shreds, their final resting place the guts of those things down there.

Some had attempted a different approach, still from above, casting a line from their windows or roofs down to the streetlamp right in front of the market. They'd anchored the ropes like a clothesline, then shimmied across the street, only to find themselves stranded above the sidewalk, still with ten feet between them and the air-conditioning alcove. Even then, what would they have done? There was no way in from there unless you knew how to dismantle an industrial air-conditioning unit. These were regular citizens, not Special Ops personnel trained in breeching bulwarks. So they either shimmied back into their shelters, or dropped to the pavement and were devoured.

Some slapped together homemade armor. Egged on by hungry neighbors, they'd either lowered themselves to the sidewalk from windows or fire escapes, or even more imprudently emerged from within their blockaded front doors, which inevitably lead to an unstoppable tsunami of zombies surging into their dwellings, costing all within their lives. The ones with enough foresight to reseal the entranceways usually didn't make it ten feet from their homes before the horde picked them clean. One did get as far as the entrance to the supermarket, and even managed to detach the moldering sheet metal, but the doors had been automatic. No power; no way in. He'd pounded on them as much in exasperated fury and disbelief as in attempt to actually infiltrate the emporium. His makeshift armor just made the zombies work a little harder for their meal, but like a boiled lobster, the shell came off and they enjoyed the tender bounty within.

Now, because of one of Dabney's brick tosses, the supermarket doors gaped open, the pavement glittering with fragments of safety glass, taunting everyone.

And the avenue might as well be a thousand miles across.

"Watch this," Dabney said, selecting a chunk of brick from the pile. He hefted it once or twice in his palm, getting the feel for it, then lobbed it down into the crowd. It disappeared amid the shoulder-to-shoulder multitude.

"Shit," Dabney spat in annoyance. He picked another nugget from the stack and this time took aim. "That one," he said, not specifying which one, which would have been difficult to do anyway. Which one, the rotting one? The ugly one? The one with the bad skin? The one with its skin peeling off? With the exception of their clothing and hair, to Karl they all looked the same. It was a good thing there were no rules of political correctness regarding the undead. "They all look alike, huh?" Karl imagined someone saying, in that shrill, strident, bygone SJW tone. *Just what the world would need: zombie special interest groups: People for the Ethical Treatment of Zombies—PETZ.*

Karl sneered at the notion.

Dabney launched the missile and this time it slammed into the skull of a bald zombie. Even from the roof they could hear the crunch as it penetrated bone and what lay beneath. Brain? Only in name. The thing collapsed amidst its fellows, one less head bobbing aimlessly in the ocean of bodies. Dabney and Karl high-fived. This was one of those enjoyable rare male-bonding moments.

"Wanna have a go?" Dabney said, jerking a thumb at the brick pile.

"Yeah? Why not," Karl said. He chose a slab of jagged slate and stood up, Dabney maintaining his horizontal position on the tarpaulin.

"Flat ones don't throw as good," Dabney said, but Karl didn't intend to pitch it like a ball. He cocked his arm, pressed the slab against his chest, then swung out his arm, a light flick of the wrist sending the wedge spiraling like a discus into the crowd, where it sliced off the side of a female zombie's face with a satisfying thwack. She didn't hit the dust like the one Dabney clobbered, but she let out an edifying yowl and thrust both her hands up to the gaping wound.

"*Damn,*" Dabney said, awed. "I never would've thought to throw like that. I always go for the solids, but that was pretty sweet. Nice goin', little man."

Karl basked in the praise. As the runt of the building, he always felt nothing was expected of him but failure. This was a defining moment, scoring approbation from John Dabney, resident outsider. The others barely acknowledged his presence, but Karl found him fascinating. Dabney was … cool.

"It's only a matter of time, you know," Dabney said, eyes hooded.

"What?"

"This. This here's a waiting game. Look at those misbegotten things." He pointed down at the street-dwellers. "They're same as us, only different. Maybe they're reanimated flesh, I dunno, whatever it is. But they're not from Mars and they ain't made of plastic. Look at 'em. I mean really look."

"It's hard from up here."

Dabney shot Karl a scowl. "Don't be so damn literal. They're falling apart, same as us. They don't eat each other. How long can they keep on truckin' on empty? We know we're gonna die if we don't eat, but I figure so will they, eventually. I'd like to live to see it happen. I'd like to set my feet on pavement again, even if ain't exactly gonna be tiptoeing through tulips."

"Me too."

"It's a waiting game and nobody knows how it's gonna play out, but play out it will. It has to. Things rot. They're rotten as hell. Their hides might be tanned as shoe leather, but mark my words they'll fall. It's nature."

"You think that's natural?"

"You saying it's not?"

"It feels like punishment."

"You think this is some kind of divine retribution? Sodom and Gomorrah shit?"

"Could be."

Dabney sucked his teeth in rebuke.

"It could be," Karl repeated. "We don't know."

Dabney frowned.

"I can't do this kind of ruminating on an empty stomach. You want something to eat?" Dabney said. Karl's stomach growled in anticipation of food. He had stuff stashed in his crib, but an offer of food from Dabney augured something mysterious and tantalizing. What did Dabney keep in his private stash? "Yeah, you do," Dabney answered, lifting himself from the tarp. He strode across the roof to a sooty, bunged up metal and brick contraption fashioned from exhaust ducting salvaged from the laundromat. He bent down and opened a crudely hinged door he'd cut out of the cylinder. "It's a smoker," he said, by way of explanation.

"A smoker?" Karl repeated.

"Like a smokehouse. For smoking meat. Last I checked refrigeration went the way of the dodo, right? So, smoked meat."

"Meat?" Karl gasped.

"I got squirrel jerky and pigeon jerky. Doesn't sound so appealing when you know what it is, but it's not so bad."

Dabney reached into the box and pulled out a thin fluted strip of dusky matter and proffered it to Karl with a smile. Karl accepted the bark-like sliver and tentatively raised it to his nose, taking a sniff. Instantly his mouth began to water and with no further hesitation he took a bite. *Manna from heaven.* Karl almost began to cry but stopped himself. That would be unmanly and he didn't want to seem so in front of Dabney. Not today. Not after impressing him. The meat was salty and dense and tough, but the flavor sent him back to his abortive college days when he'd subsisted on mac 'n' sleaze and bags of teriyaki jerky from the 7-11.

"Enjoy that," Dabney said. "Won't be much more, I don't think."

Karl's heart almost broke at the thought. "What? Why? Why not?"

"Haven't seen any critters around in the last couple a few weeks or so. None airborne, none skulking around. No squirrels, no rats, no mice. Sure as hell no cats. Not even a waterbug. I think what I've got in there is the last of it. The bottomless empty is right around the corner. After that, we are all well and truly screwed."

Karl studied the older man's weathered face, peeling, dark brown, raw, not unlike the jerky he was consuming. If they started dying in the building would they mimic the behavior of those things on the street? Would this turn into some Manhattan version of the Donner Party? Karl flashed on the movie *Cannibal the Musical,* the comedy about the Alferd Packer, which didn't seem so funny anymore. He thought about Jeffrey Dahmer and Andrei Chikatilo and Ed Gein. *Oh fuck that,* Karl thought. *I'd rather die. I'd rather feed myself to those things than eat a human being. You have to hold onto who you are. Maybe those sons of bitches ate each other because there were still things to live for. Their circumstances had been way different. Packer and the Donners and those soccer players had a world ahead of them.*

Dabney eyeballed Karl's twitching face, sensing his thought process.

"Got some dark shit in there, little man?"

"When we really run out of food. Really. And we begin to …" He couldn't finish.

"You know what one of those Andes crash survivors had to say when they picked him up?" Dabney asked, his voice neutral. "It stuck because it was so fucked up. I was a kid into ghoulish shit, the way kids can be. The survivor was saying how they'd cooked their dead teammates. He described the meat as, 'softer than beef but with much the same taste.' Softer than beef." Dabney shook his head. "It's animal nature to survive. Man's an animal. To survive, animals adapt. Not saying we—"

Karl doubled over and puked. When he finished he remained bent over, hands gripping his knees to keep him from toppling over, thick ropes of bilious saliva drooping from his twitching lower lip.

"Last time I offer you any chow," Dabney said.

Eyes stinging, Karl glared at the lumpy puddle between his legs, his face broiling with shame. Whatever cred he'd established he'd just pissed down his leg. He'd reverted to Karl the Puss—no more, impossible to be less. He felt anger coursing through his wracked body. Anger at himself, anger at Dabney, anger at everything.

"If you had food this whole time," he bleated, revolted by his wheedling tone, "why didn't you share with us?"

Dabney sighed, not angry. Seemingly bored with the question. "Because I sing hard for my supper. No one ever stopped you from hunting and gathering. I don't own the roof. You want food, show some initiative. Don't come whining at me because you're a bunch of spoiled Upper East Side candy-asses. Grow some hair."

Karl straightened up and made to leave.

"Clean your mess up before you go, little man. I might not own the roof, but it's still my turf. Don't be leaving your mess here."

Karl opened and closed his mouth a couple of times, but he couldn't access any words that might redeem the moment. Dabney cocked his head and closed one eye in warning, shaking his head in silent rebuke. The gesture said, *DON'T SAY A WORD.* Karl looked around for a towel, saw none, then looked back at Dabney who offered nothing but the stern authoritarian glower of someone about to lose his temper.

"What do I clean it with?"

Dabney pulled a rag out of his back pocket and tossed it to Karl, the motion reminiscent of that old Coke commercial with Mean Joe Green tossing the kid his sweaty game jersey. Karl thought a joke might help, and when he caught it he said, "Thanks, Mean Joe," instantly regretting it. It wasn't because Dabney was the sole African-American in the building. It was a pop culture reference. It was …

Dabney turned away and resumed his vigil at the edge of the roof.

"Stupid, stupid, stupid," Karl chanted as he mopped up his puke.

"THAT ZOTZ BETTER watch his mouth is all I'm sayin'," Eddie said, stomping around the kitchen.

"Let it go, dude," Dave said. "It's no biggie."

"It *is* a biggie. It is. It's fuckin' *huge*. First he gets lippy like, what, he wants a piece of me? He thinks he can handle The Comet all of a sudden? Like suddenly he's a big man? He's a little pussy, that little bitch. I'd stuff his fuckin' crayons and paint brushes up his ass if I didn't think he'd fuckin' love it."

"Just chill, Eddie. Come on, seriously, you're gonna give yourself an embolism or something. Park it and chill."

Eddie paced a couple more times, then grudgingly heeded Dave's counsel, taking a seat on an ottoman. He clenched and unclenched his fists, kneading his thighs, swallowing his lower lip. He threw his head back, the veins bulging on the sides of his neck, his Adam's apple jutting out like a walnut. His nostrils flared like a horse's as he exhaled over and over. Dave watched Eddie attempting to decompress, to defuse. Ever since they'd met in high school they'd been inseparable buds, Dave the calm one, Eddie the hothead.

"The Comet" had been Eddie's hockey handle—hokey, but apt. He'd been an awesome center whose speed and ferocity earned him an athletic scholarship to Rutgers. Dave had been goalie but he'd often kept his eye more on Eddie than the puck. Eddie tossed bodies around like they were nothing, which to him they were. It was magnificent to behold. Unfortunately he spent as much time in the penalty box as on the ice. Too much high-sticking. Too much hooking. Too much fighting in general. Too much blood on the ice.

Dave came over and ran his fingers through Eddie's hair, petting him, trying to soothe him.

"Don't do that," Eddie snapped. "What're you doing? I don't need that shit, man." He stood up, vibrating with barely contained rage. "You can't do shit like that to me!"

Dave looked at his bro, incredulous.

"I'm a little confused, Ed," Dave said.

"What? What? What's to be confused about? I don't want you fuckin' touching me all girly like that."

"But we ..."

"That's not about ... fuck, what's the word?"

"Tenderness?"

"Exactly!" Eddie said, his face split in both triumph and disgust. "That's *exactly* it! *Tenderness.* Tenderness is for women and fags. We are not fags, Dave. We just have to let off some steam once in a while. Nothing wrong with that. Sex and tenderness have *nothing* to do with each other. You think all those guys in prison are homos? Hell, no, bro. They just do what they gotta do. Adaptation isn't conversion, okay? You think they trawl for dick once they get sprung? Bull-*shit*! They head straight for the punani! You need to remember that shit, bro."

Yeah, but we're not getting sprung, Dave thought. *This is all there is. And besides, some of us ...*

"Whatever," Dave said, and left the room.

"What's the matter, you on your period?" Eddie said. With that he erupted in laughter.

Dave paced a few times, then opened the front door and stepped into the unlit common hall. This was the world now. A staircase leading up from the barricaded street entrance, the larger landing of the second floor, the flights of stairs connecting each level, the narrow, strip-like landings, the roofs, period. The entire rest of the planet was off limits. *Why's Eddie have to be so nasty,* Dave wondered. *We're all under pressure. We're all in the same boat, not like he's the only one who's suffering, the only one who's hungry, the only one who's afraid.*

Dave trudged downstairs to the building's sealed-up foyer. In the pitch dark he pressed his back against the almost cool wall. Better to not dwell on Eddie and his foul moods and fouler humor. That kind of shit had been funny in the locker room before and after a game, but now it cut deeper; seemed uglier. In the dark Dave calmed down and collected himself. "Work it off," he said, then inhaled and exhaled deeply several times, centering himself. Midway through a half-assed stretch his elbow touched something clammy and fleshy and he let out a piercing screech.

"Work what off?" came the drab, croaky, response.

"Jesus," Dave said, "don't *do* that. Hey, who *is* that? Who the hell hangs out in the dark? You trying to give someone a frickin' heart attack?"

"Work what off?" The croaky voice was neither masculine nor feminine. It reminded Dave of the possessed girl's in *The Exorcist.* The question was posed without any urgency or even curiosity. It sounded mechanical. That's what made it so disturbing.

"Jesus Christ. *Gerri.*"

With his heart audibly thudding in his chest Dave began jogging up the stairs, taking each landing, then the next flight, and so on, up to the roof door. When he got there he hesitated for a moment, then gave it a loud rap with his knuckles and threw it open. Dabney was there, sitting in the shade of the stairwell, reading a battered paperback.

"Yo, John, mind if I do some laps?"

"Knock yourself out, kid," Dabney said, returning his attention to the book he'd borrowed from Alan. As Dave began to jog north, Dabney added, "But not literally. I don't wanna have to haul your carcass downstairs." Then he chuckled. Same joke, different day.

Goddamn Gerri Leibowitz, Dave thought. Eddie had dubbed their old neighbor from 3B The Wandering Jewess, a now bedraggled hag with a nimbus of ratty grayish brown hair radiating from her seemingly vacant head. Sometimes she was stark naked, sometimes she wore a thin housecoat, and always she toted around the withered carcass of her dead Yorkshire terrier, cradling it like a baby. She now had no fixed abode, sometimes sleeping in the neighboring building from whence they'd originated, sometimes in the halls, sometimes the roof—though not Dabney's. He didn't cotton to her at all. Gerri would occasionally spend a night or two in one of 1620's vacant apartments.

Though comprised of all the fleshly ingredients, in essence she was a ghost. Maybe she'd once been cute, in a kind of worried intellectual social worker/librarian kind of way. She was the kind of woman, back before, that Dave dreaded running into. Getting snared into a conversation laden with complaint and oversharing. Gerri's tremulous voice. Her worried face and fretful hands. But when she was younger? Bookish cute? Truth was, even so Dave wouldn't have been interested. The world was gone. So was the pretense. Eddie rebuffed the tender, now. But someday maybe. Someday he might feel different.

Dave and Eddie had come over from three buildings north, when that building was breeched. The zombies had flooded in and made short work of the residents on the lower floors. Dave and Eddie escaped, just barely. Since then, the rooftop door to the stairwell of that building was off limits. Nonetheless, no one could forecast in which building Gerri would materialize from day to day. Didn't much care, either, but she was a perpetually unnerving presence.

Dave built up enough speed to use the short walls dividing the roofs as hurdles. The sun broiled his bare back and sweat poured off him. This was stupid. He knew this was stupid. Who was he trying to keep in shape for? Himself? The end was nigh, as the Bible-thumpers put it. Why even attempt to stay fit? He was a rail, each muscle, each tendon, each ligament, each vein and artery stood out in sharp relief. He was a walking—or jogging, to be more precise—anatomical chart. This wasn't definition. This was depletion. Everyone in the building had a six-pack.

Six-pack.

Just the phrase made Dave want to bawl. How sweet would a six-pack be right about now? Some tasty ice-cold beer? As perspiration beaded and ran down his hairless chest, Dave imagined himself a glistening longneck, his sweat sexy commercial-style condensation on a bottle of his favorite brew. Exhausted, he sagged against a low brick wall and began to cry.

6

FEBRUARY, *THEN*

"THIS'LL PASS. YOU watch."

"I dunno," Dave said, then took a swig off his Stella Artois. Eddie and he sat side by side at the bar, eyes glued to the muted television mounted above the liquor shelves. Since both sets were tuned to FOX there was no need for sound, the text tickers scrawling across the screen covering the major points in bullet form. Dave's stomach was double-knotted and the beer wasn't helping. He drank it anyway.

"You dunno, Eddie scoffed. "Have a little faith. The government'll take care of it."

"That's funny, coming from you, Mr. Libertarian."

"Hey, I'm what you call a *social* libertarian. I just don't want no one tellin' me who I can and can't screw, what I can and can't drink, or if I wanna smoke a doob or do a bump I gotta go to jail for that shit. The government should keep its nose outta my private fuckin' business, know what I'm sayin'?"

"But they can bail us out when bad shit happens?"

"Catastrophic disaster shit? That's right. That's their fuckin' *jobs*, bro'. Our tax dollars at work. Send in the fuckin' Marines."

Dave was about to point out that they didn't have any Marines left to send in anymore, but bit his tongue and took another mouthful of beer. Most of our troops were still abroad and the National Guard was spread mighty thin as chaos was erupting everywhere. Footage of cities on fire filled the widescreen monitors. Dave was accustomed—indifferent, even—to seeing foreign cities ablaze, but *American* ones? It was bad enough when the towers came down, but this was epic. Presently, footage of St. Louis in flames was splashed across the screen, the visibly shaken anchorperson mouthing silently, worry creasing her copious makeup. The closed captioning was almost all near incomprehensible typos, which added to the sense of hopelessness. It had been the same all day: an epidemic of violence and cannibalism. Ridiculous sounding, but there it was.

"This is your WMDs," Eddie said. "Right there, in HD. This is some chemical shit the towel-heads cooked up in some fuckin' cave. Or maybe the North Koreans. Our guys'll come up with the antidote and then we'll get payback."

"Where'd you get that from?" Dave asked.

Eddie pointed at the ticker. Dave wasn't so sanguine about the source of this mayhem, nor about getting revenge. According to the news—and on this point there seemed to be no dissenting views—the state of affairs was global. What was happening here in New York was happening in Paris and Tehran and Madrid and Hong Kong and so forth. It wasn't a hoax. It wasn't fake news. Still, the cause was up for conjecture and debate and people needed to assign blame. What good was a crisis if you couldn't say, "It's so-and-so's fault"?

From outside the bar the assortment of unsettling noises grew louder. A concussion rocked the small building, spilling Eddie's beer in his lap.

"Fuck this shit."

"I think we should head home," Dave suggested, not wanting his mounting terror to show too much. Eddie looked at his emptied mug and wet lap and rose from his stool without a word.

The duo hesitated at the door. An SUV plowed down some pedestrians in a mad attempt to beat the light, sending bodies flying through the air, one thudding against the plate glass window, adding a red smear to the pink neon glow.

"Jesus!" Dave shrieked.

The bartender, an old school drink slinger with a permanent scowl, grabbed his keys and a sawed-off shotgun from under the bar.

"I let you out you're out for good," he said. "I ain't lettin' ya back in, no matter what I see happenin' out there. You're on your own."

"Uh-huh," Eddie said.

"I'm serious." He turned to face the others at the bar. "Anyone else wanna leave, now's the time. After these two, you stay until they says otherwise an' that's it. Lockdown time at Casey's."

A couple of other patrons polished off their drinks and plodded over to the door, reluctant to put the barkeep's edict to the test. The rest stayed put, watching the screens, shoveling in chicken wings. Eddie and Dave locked eyes and like they'd done before matches punched each other on the shoulders.

"You ready for this shit?" Eddie said, uncertainty tingeing his voice.

"No," Dave said, opting for honesty.

"You'll be all right," Eddie smiled. "You're with me."

"Awright," the bartender said. He undid the lock and pushed open the door a hair. "Get out, quick." As an afterthought he added, "An' good luck." Then pulled the door shut and locked it behind them. Eddie and Dave lived across the avenue and halfway up the block, but that short distance looked like an uphill battle, even though it was downhill. Dave looked south and saw black smoke rising from various unseen fires. The body that had hit the window lay dead a few feet away, its head collapsed from the double impact. A military troop transport rumbled up York Avenue with little regard for the foot traffic that surged around it in blind panic.

"See?" Eddie beamed, "Here comes the fuckin' cavalry!"

The vehicle roared by and Dave and Eddie saw bloodied bodies affixed to the sides, scratching at the armored plating. The bodies looked broken but agitated. A man clung to the side, his head facing away from the truck, twisted 180-degrees the wrong way. Drool and blood hung in long swaying loops from his shattered jaw. As the truck passed, Dave and Eddie gaped as they saw the troops inside being attacked and consumed by similar assailants. With another, "Fuck this shit," Eddie took off in the wake of the truck, the path behind it momentarily cleared. Dave followed, slipping once or twice on fresh blood that leaked from the vehicle. They were more like Custer's cavalry, with York Avenue as Little Bighorn and the infected as the Sioux and Cheyenne.

As Eddie fished for his keys at the front door to their building a freshly reanimated little girl, no more than five or six, sprang up and attempted to bite his forearm through his thick leather coat. Eddie knew this kid. Not by name, but he'd seen her and her mom in Carl Schurz Park. Her mom was a bona fide MILF and he'd always slowed his jog to get an eyeful of her cleavage. The kid had been cute, too, though more than once he'd seen her pitching a fit for ice cream or cookies. Now the kid's blood-streaked face was contorted into a parody of childish greed and human meat was all she craved. One eye bulged from its socket, the white showing all the way around the iris.

Without a moment's hesitation Eddie punched her square in the face, shattering the small skull within. She dropped to the pavement, disoriented but not motionless. Twitching, she rocked herself side to side, like an upside-down turtle.

"Fuckin' shit!" Eddie bellowed, examining the bite marks. Assured he was uninjured he raised his foot and stomped on her head, splattering bone and brain onto the sidewalk. Dave froze a few feet shy of the episode, raising his hands to his mouth. Eddie unlocked the vestibule door and with great impatience shouted, "In or out, Dave-o?"

Dave sidestepped the stain that used to be a little girl and, once safely inside the entrance hall, vomited. He then looked helplessly at Eddie, who was examining his bare forearm. A little discoloration from the bite was evident, but that was all.

"If that little bitch didn't still have her milk teeth," Eddie said, brow creased as he mulled this over. "Seriously. That was close."

"Yeah," Dave said, wiping his mouth.

Their neighbor, Gerri, stood at the top of the steps, looking bedazzled. As they stepped past her onto the second floor landing she pointed at the vomit.

"You can't leave that there. It's unsanitary."

"Yeah, yeah," Eddie grumbled.

Gerri's Yorkie, Cuppy, skittered down the stairs and began lapping up Dave's sick.

"Sorry," Dave murmured. "I'll get it later."

July, *Now*

"You really think Zotz is the man for the job if things start poppin' off in here?"

Eddie was doing his best simulation of concern, which made Ellen queasy.

"Meaning?" she said, not wanting to carry on this conversation but also not wanting to vex him. His arm was extended, acting as a barrier between her and her apartment. *That'll teach me to get some fresh air and vitamin D on the roof.*

"That barricade they threw together outside the building ain't gonna keep 'em out forever. You been down to the lobby lately?"

Ellen shook her head.

"Pinpricks of light shining through. That's shit's corroding. You think Uncle Sam shells out for the best materials? Remember Katrina?" Eddie paused to let out a knowing chuckle. "Fuck, remember when *that* seemed like a big disaster? The good old days, am I right? But anyways, all those low-bid and no-bid sweetheart deals? Dave an' I made bank off them, but the point is: shoddy work. So, shit's gettin' rusty and soon it's gonna come tumbling down."

"Your point?"

"You need a man in the house to protect you."

Ellen masked potentially wrath-incurring retching with a throat clearing, then said, "And chivalrous he-man you are, you volunteer?"

"That's right. Exactly."

"I'd hate to come between you and Dave."

Eddie's expression soured. *Fuck. You couldn't help it, could you?* Ellen self-chided. Her therapist had said she flirted with suicidal ideation. *There ya go.*

"Dave an' I are buds. *Buds.*"

"Besties."

"S'right."

"Well, thanks but no. I'm good."

Ellen ducked under the arm bridge and hustled down to her apartment door, hoping Alan was there and not a flight down, in his place. As she let herself in she stole a glance over her shoulder at Eddie, who hadn't moved an inch.

Creepy. So fucking creepy.

Alan looked up from napping on the sofa as Ellen did all the deadbolts.

"You're man enough," she said. *I hope.*

"Do something, you piles of pus."

Even before things got as bad as they'd gotten, Abe Fogelhut knew the drill. He was eighty-three years old, the TV and radio were shot, he'd never been much of a reader—except for the occasional newspaper, and even there it was strictly *The Post* or *The News,* never the bleeding-heart *Times*—so he did what old people do: he sat by the window and watched the world putrefy, counting off the minutes until the final letdown. If he had any balls he'd have hurried the process up. Why forestall the inevitable?

Because as lousy as this life was, this was all you got.

The final reward was finality, period. Except these days it wasn't, thus death had lost some of its appeal.

So Abe did what he did. Today, much like the day before, and the day before, and the day before that. He'd arranged his frail, emaciated body into a semblance of comfort in the threadbare upholstered chair, parted the dingy chintz curtains, opened the dusty Venetian blinds and took his position as eyewitness to nothing.

The throng milled about—same old, same old. Nothing ever changed. Even the ache in Abe's empty belly had quieted to a dull numbness. He'd actually welcome the sharpness of the hunger pangs, but you can get used to anything. And that was the problem. He was used to the way things were.

With some effort, Abe opened the window, leaned his head out a little, worked up some gluey saliva and spat into the mindless crowd directly beneath his fifth-floor dwelling. The pasty blob plopped onto one thing's noggin and the putz didn't even have the decency to notice, to become outraged or even annoyed. They never reacted. Abe sighed with resignation and eased back from the window, repositioning himself in his seat. "This is what it comes down to," he muttered. "This is what passes for entertainment in this hollow semblance of a world. *Feh.*" He mashed his head back into the cushion and clamped his eyes shut, grinding his already nubbin-like teeth, taking shallow breaths. "What's the point?" he moaned. "What's the goddamn point?"

"What's the point of what?"

"Exactly."

Ruth shuffled into the room, her slippers shushing against the worn carpeting. He kept his eyes shut. She was unbearable to look at. The skin under her sharp jaw was a loose curtain, the nasty business that lurked beneath barely hidden by nearly translucent skin. Abe could avoid looking at himself. He didn't bother with mirrors anymore, not since he'd stopped shaving. His whiskers had itched at first, but they concealed the sins of his lank flesh so they earned their keep. Plus, why waste water these days? Abe smelled like the old parchment he resembled, his skin like membranous cheap leather. He'd stopped changing clothes on a daily basis weeks ago. Why bother? He'd stopped bathing before that, except to wipe a damp sponge in a desultory manner under his pits, balls and ass.

But to see Ruth in the same situation was intolerable. She'd always taken such pride in her appearance. She had been quite vain, back when vanity wasn't so much a futile pursuit. Though her hair had long ago thinned, she'd taken to wearing a variety of expensive, very natural-looking wigs. She did it for her own self-esteem, but Abe appreciated the effort. Now she looked like a wizened mummy sheathed loosely in drab K-Mart dressing. If Abe had anything in his belly to vomit up upon seeing her, he would, as a eulogy to her former beauty.

"*What's the point of what?*" Ruth repeated.

"Of anything. Of everything. Of answering that question."

"Then what's the point of asking it every day?"

"Exactly. Exactly so. A salient and sagacious point."

"I hate talking to you when your eyes are closed," Ruth complained.

"I hate talking to you when my eyes are open."

Weeks ago that rejoinder might have brought tears to Ruth's eyes, but she knew what Abe meant and, besides, was dry as the Sahara. Abe listened to Ruth hobble back out of the living room and gradually opened his eyes again to stare out the window. Though Jewish in name, he'd always been an atheist, and nothing he'd ever seen or experienced dissuaded him from that. This was it. This was all you got. So, he'd live as long as possible, and when the time came that he keeled over in his chair from starvation and dehydration, at least he'd be able to say to himself that he'd ridden it out.

Whatever that's worth.

It wasn't like he didn't envy those that had faith. They were the lucky ones. They just assumed, even in light of the non-stop reality show outside, that when you died your soul departed for a better place, God willing. Those ambling piles of rot out there were just empty husks.

In the kitchen, Ruth foraged in the cupboard. They still had a few paltry provisions, most provided by the generosity of their neighbors, but those would soon be depleted. There was a box of Melba toast, some peanut butter, a can of lima beans, a can of Spaghetti-O's and an individual stick of Slim Jim beef whatever-it-is. There were also three plastic gallon jugs of water. The pipes were as arid as she was, so they no longer bothered to test the faucet. All it did was groan, and if she wanted to hear that she'd just listen to Abe.

Unlike her husband, Ruth's faith had come back to her, and that was before things had turned to Hell on Earth. Around the time of her mother's death, Ruth had renewed her bond to Judaism, which had caused much consternation in her husband who thought she was cured of that claptrap.

When Ruth turned sixty-six, her mother, Ida, at the time ninety-two and more vegetable than animal, finally gave up the ghost. At the time of her death, Ida's age and weight were the same; she was bedridden, had virtually no brain function and, if this was possible, looked worse than Ruth looked currently. Prior to her actual demise, bits of Ida had predeceased her in the form of amputated limbs gone sour from gangrene due to poor circulation.

At the time it had put Abe in the mind of an old WW2 joke about a captive American in a German POW camp who is on work duty fixing the roof in the rain. He slips while mending a hole and catches his leg on a rusty nail. He ends up losing the leg and requests that the guard send it back to the States to be buried. The guard is sympathetic and honors the request. The same POW is back on work detail and fixing another roof hole when the same thing happens. He loses the other leg and makes the same request, which is also honored. The POW, now legless, is on work detail in the lumber mill. He is feeding planks through a table saw and loses an arm. He makes the same request to have the limb sent back to the States for burial. This time the guard denies the appeal. "But why?" the POW asks. "Because," the guard says, "the commandant thinks you are attempting to escape, piece by piece."

That joke lost its appeal as old lady Ida escaped piece by piece from the Golden Acres Assisted Living Facility of Maspeth four times—plus she'd gone blind from diabetes, was incontinent, lost the power of speech, didn't know who the hell she was, where she was, if she was. And as one terrible thing after another befell her, Ruth began going to the local temple to make her peace with God. By the time Ida mercifully kicked the bucket—no mean feat considering she *had* no feet—Ruth was very active in the temple and Abe was very alienated from his wife. They lived together, but apart. It would have bothered him more if he was still sexually attracted to her, but that part of their relationship had "escaped" long ago. He'd watched Ida's nightmarish living putrefaction and thought to himself many times, *There is no God.* Ida had never been his favorite person, but no one should have had to go through what she did before snuffing it. He wouldn't wish that on Hitler.

Well, maybe Hitler.

And Stalin.

But that's about it.

From outside, a guttural yawp broke the silence and Abe heaved himself to the window in time to watch a spectacle blossom below. This was new: one of the pus-bags had sunk its teeth into another, much to its victim's dismay. As the aggressor tore out a chunk of the other's rotting flesh, both sputtered unutterably foul noises, setting off a wave of restlessness through the normally torpid crowd. The antagonist choked down the chunk of fetid flesh, quaked a little, then heaved it back up. A spastic skirmish ensued.

"You gotta see this!" Abe shouted. "Hey, honey …" *old habits die hard* " … these sons of bitches have finally started in on each other!" Abe clapped his hands in delight. "They're evolving! Soon the miserable bastards will be at each other's throats, just like regular people!" Abe began laughing and coughing simultaneously.

"What's so great about that?" Ruth said.

Abe caught his breath, sighed, and squinted at Ruth. "You really know how to suck the joy out of the moment."

"How is that joyful? What is joyful about those things attacking each other? It's horrible. They're horrible."

"Irony is lost on you, Ruth. You never could handle it. It's funny to me, see, because in spite of all the terrible things you could say about those sacks of waste out there, they always seem to get along. But now they're pushing and shoving. Even dead and reanimated we're hardwired for disharmony. Even those brain-dead heaps of flesh eventually manifest hostility towards each other. It's the human way, to be inhuman."

"And that's a good thing?"

"Just go away, Ruth. Let me enjoy this. Forget I said anything. Please."

Abe poked his head back out the window.

Things were back to normal. No pushing. No shoving. No tumult. Just the usual vegetable parade. He mashed his head into the upholstery and eyes shut pondered the quiet. Once upon a time he'd have cherished such silence but not now. He missed the sound of traffic. The buses that used to run along York; even their whining hydraulics.

Sitting there, eyes closed, a faint sound wafted past the discolored chintz and oozed into Abe's ears; one in addition to the brainless lowing of the shamblers. One that he couldn't place, dull and echoey. With effort Abe disengaged from the chair and craned his head out, looking north—*nada*—then south—*bingo*! Something was plowing uptown through the crowd, weaving past abandoned vehicles left at jagged angles. As it approached the sound amplified. Thumping. "The hell?" Abe said to himself. It was moving at a decent clip. A car. No, *taller.* One of those SUVs, only he couldn't hear the roar of an engine over the thud of rickety bodies jouncing off its hard surfaces. Maybe a hybrid; they ran silent.

Abe wanted to shout to its driver but there was no point; that machine wasn't stopping for anything. But unless those things had learned how to drive, at least there was evidence of life beyond this sapped bunch. As it neared the building Abe got a good, albeit fleeting, look at the vehicle. The front end was a dark mass of blood-drenched concavities. Though he was pretty certain those things didn't feel panic it was clear they weren't thrilled with becoming temporary hood ornaments as they were bounced up off the pavement and ground up below.

As the sport ute plowed northwards it hit a car obscured by the crowd. The savage impact echoed through the canyon of buildings. After a few agonizing beats, the SUV's passenger door creaked open. Maybe the airbag had deployed, maybe just the impact had rendered the driver insensate, but out staggered the occupant of the vehicle. Abe couldn't make out the gender, age, much of anything other than they were badly injured. Abe opened his mouth to entreat the driver to stay in the car but no sound would come. The driver teetered on uncertain feet. Abe winced, anticipating the crowd ripping them to shreds as the entrée du jour. But the mob didn't. An aperture opened in the swarm amassed before the now smoking wreck of the SUV. Like a drunk, the driver tottered to the car he'd—no, *she,* Abe was certain— plowed into and leaned on it, looking very much like she was about to lose consciousness. She.

"What the hell?" Abe croaked, confounded.

The zombies were spreading out, away from the area where the driver was leaning to steady herself. Abe could barely see her, she being out of range and shrouded by the multitude, but there was no doubt they weren't swarming her. Bestial moaning came from that direction, making the hairs on Abe's neck rise. "That's new," he gasped.

With reluctance, he tore himself away from the window as Ruth entered the room.

"What was that?" she cried.

"A crash," he said. "A car. It crashed. I gotta see if anyone else is seeing this."

"*Hey! Hey you!*" One of the neighbors was shouting. Alan? Dabney? Abe couldn't tell, the voice frantic, reedy and helpless. "Hey! Hey!"

As he left the apartment Ruth shuffled over to where he'd been for a look. In the hall there was a commotion of voices. In spite of his protesting legs Abe hied upstairs to the roof to get a better view. As he neared the top few steps an explosion rocked the building and he gripped the handrail to avoid tumbling back down.

"My heart," he sputtered.

When he stepped onto the tarpaper he saw black smoke churning up from below. Energy spent, he shuffle-jogged the rest of the way, joining some of the others at the edge of the roof.

"I didn't think hybrids blew like that," he panted.

"The car he hit did," Karl clarified. "Anyway, why do you think it was a hybrid?"

"I didn't hear the engine."

"Engine was makin' plenty of noise," Dabney said. "You're just a bit deaf, old timer."

Abe was about to protest, but Alan shouted, "Are you guys nuts? Who cares what kind of car that was? A person's dead!"

"Yeah, and they weren't eating him," Karl added.

"Maybe," Dabney said.

"I saw it, too," Abe confirmed. "And it was a lady. I'm sure of it. Pretty sure, anyway. If it was that makes it worse, somehow. Anyway, they were spreading out. Very weird."

"Maybe they smelled some leaky gasoline," Dabney countered. "Backed off 'cause they knew it was gonna blow."

"That's giving them an awful lot of credit," Karl said.

"Animals know when trouble's afoot," Dabney said. "Thunderstorms and earthquakes. We don't know shit about those things except they like eating us. They could have all kinds of animal cunning. Some heightened senses. They can smell blood."

Hearing that, Alan thought about Mike and turned to go downstairs to check on Ellen, who'd popped an Ambien or three earlier and was out like a light. Just as well. Two fresh kills in rapid succession would be too much. As he passed back into the building the others continued to debate what they'd just witnessed.

"Too much excitement for one day," he said to himself.

As he let himself back into Ellen's apartment, Eddie and Dave tore out of theirs heading upward and Alan was grateful, at least, to have avoided them.

ALAN STARED ACROSS the queen-size mattress at Ellen, who slept peacefully. He didn't know how to feel. When he'd come back in, through her Ambien haze she'd burbled something dreamily at him and before he knew it they'd been a tangle of naked limbs. Mike had died a scant few hours earlier. Died was the least of it. That made it seem peaceful—in their current predicament almost enviable. He'd been *devoured,* and here Alan lay, in Mike's bed, perhaps even on Mike's side—chances were that Ellen snoozed in her normal spot, so Alan was occupying a dead man's very personal real estate.

Ellen's body, even dissipated, still held attraction for Alan. Okay, it was a sort of hot emaciated supermodel Buchenwald kind of sexiness, but she still had that certain indefinable something. Alan grabbed a pencil and a scratch pad and began to sketch her.

Gone were the pleasing soft curves, but if he could get into an Egon Schiele state of mind he could do some good work. Some people found Schiele's nearly geometric nudes erotic. Alan didn't happen to be one of them, but one must adapt to the here and now. Ellen's areolas and nipples were dusky, almost burgundy, in sharp contrast to her pale skin. Her wasted breasts pooled on her chest, yet he'd sucked on them like they dispensed the antidote. Unlike the others, Ellen mostly steered clear of the roof and had gotten paler and paler in the weeks past. Against her ashy skin, the triangular mound of unruly black pubic hair stood out in sharp relief, thick and matted with sweat and the commingled fluids of their lovemaking.

It didn't feel like love. It had felt desperate, rapacious, panic stricken. At least for him. In the fog of Ambien, who knew what Ellen was thinking? Feeling. But it was consensual. That much Alan knew. Ellen had been quite vocal in her enthusiasm. Otherwise, it would've felt ... very wrong. Or more wrong.

Mike.

Still, even with their bones grinding together it was the fulfillment of an enduring fantasy. *Fee! Fie! Foe! Fum! I smell the blood of an Englishman. Be he 'live, or be he dead, I'll grind his bones to make my bread,* Alan remembered from childhood. *What the hell kind of fucked-up thing is that to teach a kid? Grind his* bones *to make my* bread? What kind of bread is that? And now the things out there wanted to do the same basic thing, only skip the carbs. We'll just eat you alive, thanks all the same.

Alan's drawing was not turning out the way he wanted. Ellen looked twisted and knotty, her contours convex where they oughtn't be, concave likewise. Her tangle of brunette curls a greasy amorphous blob, obscuring her face save for one closed eyelid tinted dark as a shiner. She looked as if she'd been elongated on the rack like some accused heretic during the Inquisition. His pencil said Ticonderoga but it might as well have read Torquemada by the way it rendered Alan's fluky new inamorata. The First Grand Inquisitor of Spain would have been proud to reduce a human being to Ellen's pitiful status. He looked at the crosshatching he'd done and noticed some on her actual flesh, on her upper, inner thighs. Maybe a trick of the light? He leaned forward for a closer look. Scarification. Faint, but visible. *Aw man,* he thought. *She was one of those cutter girls.* His artistic impulse waned, replaced by melancholy.

Ellen doesn't need to see this.

Alan crumpled the sketch and tossed it out the window, where it landed right on the blood-smeared spot Mike had met his fate. *What would Goya do?* Alan wondered. The phrase reminded Alan of those WWJD bracelets. *What Would Jesus Do*? Though Goya did plenty of pretty canvases, he didn't shy away from capturing ugliness. Alan thought of Goya's painting, "Saturn Devouring One of his

Children." In it, the mythological giant grips the partially dismembered naked body of one of his sons, the giant's eyes insane with paranoia and a perhaps tinge of grief as he gnaws off his progeny's head. Alan had plenty of firsthand experience seeing bodies being dismembered—and documenting them. In his apartment he had several walls covered top to bottom with drawings and paintings he'd done of the mob outside, both individual and group studies. He was the Audubon of the undead—keeper of the visual record of humanity's demise.

But for whom?

Who would look at these renderings? The likelihood of future generations was pretty much nil. Time travelers? Space aliens? No, this was art for art's sake. Like the need to breathe and eat, Alan had discovered he was predisposed to do art. He'd often wondered how pure his drive was. He'd mostly done work for print. Now there was no client, no audience. What a price to pay to confirm one's dedication. His apartment was a gallery devoted to but a single theme: *The End*. Pencil drawings, pastels, pen and ink, a few watercolors, which strictly speaking weren't done with water. He used urine, which worked out fine. The yellow pigment added authenticity to the subject matter. At least he could work in oils. Plus, the thinner got him a bit high.

So art still had its little dividends.

And he'd bagged the model of his dreams.

Who now stirred.

"*Mmmmm,*" she purred. "Hello."

Speaking of high, Ellen looked a trifle baked. He wondered how many Ambiens had she'd taken, then choked back the notion that she'd maybe tried to join Mike. Her eyes swam in their hollows, unfocused. As she blinked herself back to wakefulness she looked confused, rabbity.

"You're not Mike. What are *you* doing here?" Her query was accusatory. She shook her head, attempting to reengage her brain. "I'm sorry. I'm sorry. Mike's dead. Mike's dead now. Alan. I'm sorry." She attempted a smile, but her mouth made the wrong shape. "What a day, huh?" A failed attempt at mirth employing the frowsy cadence of a secretary at the water cooler.

"Yeah," Alan mumbled.

"What's that smell?" she said, wrinkling her nose.

"Uh, a fire outside. I'll tell you about it later."

"A fire?" she repeated, eyes still glassy.

"Yeah. It'll keep."

Ellen eased closer to Alan on the rumpled bedclothes and pressed her head against his bare chest. She draped her arms around him. "So," she whispered, "are you moving in or not?"

An entreaty.

An invitation.

A trap.

With the pretext of needing some things from his apartment, Alan disengaged from Ellen. With nimble assurances he edged out into the common hall and left her standing in her kitchen. At the cessation of the multiple clicks of her deadbolts engaging, the door across the hall swung open and there stood Eddie, looking wry and malevolent with a fishing rod in his hand. *Oh Christ.*

"You don't waste any time, do you?" he leered. "Y'know, I doff my lid to you, Zotz. You got right in there like a champ and snagged the booty. Respect."

"What are you ...?"

"Don't play dumb, champ." Waggling the fishing rod to make his point, Eddie held up Alan's smoothed out crumpled drawing of Ellen. "I did a little fishing in Lake Swenson." He turned the drawing over, the back flecked with bloodstains.

Alan stared at his handiwork in disbelief. "With everything going on outside you rescued that drawing from the alley? Are you fucking insane?"

"Car crashes are a dime a dozen," Eddie grinned, "but art is forever."

"*Car crashes are a dime a—*" Alan shook his head like a wet dog trying to make sense of that statement. "What? Name the last time you saw a car driving by."

"Been ages. But it didn't do us any good, did it? Anyways, other sounds were of more interest. Ellen never moaned like that with Mikey boy, I can tell you. Even back in the day."

Alan shoved Eddie into his apartment and closed the door behind them.

"Jesus Christ, Tommasi. She might hear you," Alan said, jabbing his finger into Eddie's ditch-like sternum.

"Everyone hears everyone, Casanova. Sound travels. Especially when you're bangin' a screamer. She was making so much noise I thought she was gettin' eaten alive. Maybe she was," Eddie smirked. "Munchin' puss is a little beta to my taste, but …" With a plastic magnetic banana he affixed the drawing to his refrigerator door, smoothing it. "Not like the old days, though, huh? Back in the day Ellen had some boasty titties. Well, make do with what you got, am I right?"

"Look, don't make a big thing of this, okay?" Alan said, hating the vaguely cajoling tone of his voice. "Ellen has enough on her plate …"

"None of us have enough on our plates," Eddie interrupted.

"Figuratively. Jesus. Anyway, this is just a temporary thing. I'm just trying to …"

"Get your dick wet. I understand. Dude, if there's *anyone* in the building who's on your wavelength it's this guy. That sensitive artist shit worked its magic. Some chicks dig alphas, some dig betas. I should've known Ellen was a beta-whore. Look no further than the late Mikey Swenson. What was his jam? Computers?"

Mike had been an IT guy at a hedge fund, so point to the observant jock.

"Look, just keep it on the DL, all right? Let the woman grieve in peace."

"Peace," Eddie sniggered. "On one condition."

Alan sagged. "Go ahead."

"Keep the nudie art comin'. I don't know why I didn't think to tap you sooner, what with all other resources being nonexistent. Not like I can log onto PornHub anymore."

"You want me to do porno art of Ellen for you?" Alan gaped.

"Not just Ellen. And not the way she looks now. I'll come up with some scenarios for you to do up for me. Custom whacking material. Okay? Okay. Now get the fuck outta my face."

Alan traipsed downstairs and fell onto his bed in a daze. Alan had always wondered if he could endure incarceration—especially long term. He figured his only survival skill would be doing pervy fantasy art for the other inmates. The rapists would want rape fantasies. The murderers would want murder fantasies. The hyphenates would want hybridized fantasies. And now a blackmailing ex-jock was leaning on Alan for post-apocalyptic pinups.

What would Vargas do?

APRIL, *THEN*

"SHE'S TURNING BLUE, Mike. She's turning fucking blue! You have to do something!"

"What am I supposed to do, Ellie? What? Go to the Duane Reade? Call a doctor?"

Ellen held Emily, barely a year old, and watched her tiny mouth open and close like a fish out of water. She'd wrung every drop of nutrition from her mother and the coffers were nearly bare. Ellen hated rationing, but what else was there to do? Mike was right, what could he do? Go out there? Sure, only to never return. Baby in tow, she tromped over to the front windows and radiated hatred at the undead things in the street below, milling about as ever, even in the freezing rain. She threw open the sash and leaned out, sleet stinging her face. She shielded Emily, pressing the small head against her depleted bosom.

"Fuck you all!" Ellen shrieked. "Fuck each and every one of you goddamned motherfuckers!"

Emily started to cry.

"What are you doing?" Mike bleated as he hastened to the window, grabbing his wife's arm. "You could drop her."

"And what, Mike? *What*? Maybe I'd be doing her a favor. Look at this fucking world we've got here. And look at this family. A *balls-less* dad and a *worthless* mom with *sand* in her tits. She's gonna fucking *starve*, Mike. *Starve.* So will we, ultimately, but Emily's got no reserves. She's wasting away. And *blue.*"

"'Balls-less'?" her husband peeped.

"*That's* your takeaway from that? Brilliant."

Over the prickly clatter of sleet the zombies heard the commotion above and stared up at the scene of domestic turmoil, hunger being the only urge left to animate their lifeless eyes. Ellen looked away from Mike back at the throng. She could win this bunch over in a second if she'd just fling herself and the petite hors d'oeuvre in the organic cotton sling down to them. The lunch crowd would go wild, then move on. She remembered how the world had gaped in stupefaction and revulsion as Michael Jackson dangled his infant son out a hotel window. The multitude below, with their caved-in faces and bleached skin, reminded her of Whacko Jacko, but *she* was the one dangling the baby.

She slumped against the wall beneath the window and joined Emily in tears. Mike closed the sash and crouched down to comfort his girls, but his touch and gentle tone brought none. They were disconsolate and he was, truth be told, *balls-less.* But who wouldn't be? Was it balls-less or just common sense to not leave the building? How could he? Ellen and Emily's wailing grew louder, amplified by Mike's sense of irrelevance. He rose and left the room to get some water for Ellen, but by the time he reached the kitchen forgot his reason for being there, opened the front door and stepped into the common hall, his own expression blank.

"Quite a racket they're raising," Abe said, gesturing into the door, which hung ajar.

"Huh?" Mike said; his thoughts muddled. He blinked and focused on his neighbors, Abe and Paolo, the good-looking South American from 2B. "Oh, yes. Rough day."

"Aren't they all?" Abe said, earning earnest nods from both younger men.

"Indeed," Paolo added. "These are dark days."

The hall light fixture flickered and buzzed. The three men looked up at it.

"Wonder how long we'll have power, still," Abe said.

Feeling the need to talk to people who presumably wouldn't scream at him, Mike joined in, though he wasn't feeling very conversational. "They're hungry, Ellen and the baby. Hungry and tired. And frustrated. Ellen wanted me to go out and get supplies, but that's not going to happen."

"And that, my friend, is the difference between your generation and mine," Abe scoffed. "If *I* had a starving child you can bet your last goddamn cent I'd be out the door trying to provide for her, damn the consequences."

"Easy for you to say—" Mike started, but Abe cut him off.

"Damn right it's easy for me to say. As I recall you were home when this all began. Me, I hadda schlep all the way from the Garment District to get home. I braved all kinds of madness to get home to my frightened little wifey. Granted, if I'd had some foresight I'd have stopped at the grocers, but hindsight's twenty-twenty."

"It was different then," Mike stammered. He'd really thought other men would commiserate with him over female troubles; bad to worse.

"Different! Feh. There were those lousy zombies all over then and they're all over now. What, you think they weren't chowing down on everyone in sight that day? Eighty-three years of age, *I* managed to get myself home intact. If any of you young *men*—" the word curdled in Abe's mouth "—had any *cojones* you'd go out and do what I did. Show the same resourcefulness and—"

Mike was tiring of having his gonads impugned and was about to protest—albeit weakly—when Paolo chimed in, his machismo also under attack.

"*I* have the *cojones*, Abraham," Paolo spat, indignation scoring his rugged features.

"Yeah, yeah."

"You challenge me? You saying I don't have the *cojones* of an old man?"

Abe chuckled. "I sure as hell hope you *don't* have a pair like mine."

Paolo's expression softened as Abe winked at him.

"These are dark days," Paolo repeated, a bitter smile sneaking past his anger onto his lips.

"Amen," Abe agreed. The sound of the crying, which hadn't abated, brought the three men back to the matter at hand. "Regardless—and I don't want to get into a shouting match—but the fact remains that there is a woman and a *child* who need sustenance and it's a *man's* job to provide."

Mike's face flushed. Sitting at computer consoles for the last decade hadn't exactly toughened him up or primed him for hunter/gatherer mode. Men of Abe's generation were built different. They were shaped and hardened by war. Abe was a veteran of some foreign conflict Mike couldn't recall. Mike's only combat experience was countless hours spent on *World of Warcraft* and *Call of Duty*. He nudged the door open an inch to look in on Ellie and Em. Though the volume had decreased, both were in a bad way. And Ellie had said Em was blue and meant it literally. The apartment could be warmer and even though they were all wearing layers, it was chilly and damp permeated the building. They still had power, but the boiler had run dry and space heaters only did so much.

"That baby needs to eat." Paolo said, voice steely.

"I know, I know," Mike replied, eyeing his shoes.

"If you are not enough a man to go, I will."

"Now wait a minute—"

"Abraham is right," Paolo said, in his formal, mild accent. "He is an old man and he made it here. He has told us many, many, *many* times of his perilous journey. We were lucky, you and I and some of the others, to be here already, but he and John came late. And they suffered."

Mike was about to assert that they'd all suffered, but point taken. Abe had walked the walk. As an old man was wont to do, he'd recounted his odyssey often—maybe even embellished a little—but scrawny old Abe Fogelhut had bested all the "young bucks."

"My gear is down in the locker," Abe said, but Paolo waved him off.

"I do not need hand-me-downs, *señor*."

Paolo about-faced and trundled down to his apartment.

"*What*? I insulted him?" Abe scoffed.

"You insulted both of us."

"Shaming isn't the same thing. A little shame is a good thing."

"If you say so."

From their respective windows the residents of 1620 watched Paolo make it halfway across the avenue before being overwhelmed and consumed in his insufficient version of Abe's improvised survival gear.

Abe retired his heroic saga.

A week later, Emily died.

Mike manned up enough to dispose of the petite corpse, sparing Ellen the details. He hoped the wrappings were sufficient to keep the creatures from eating her. But then again, they only seemed to go for live flesh.

Did that count as a blessing?

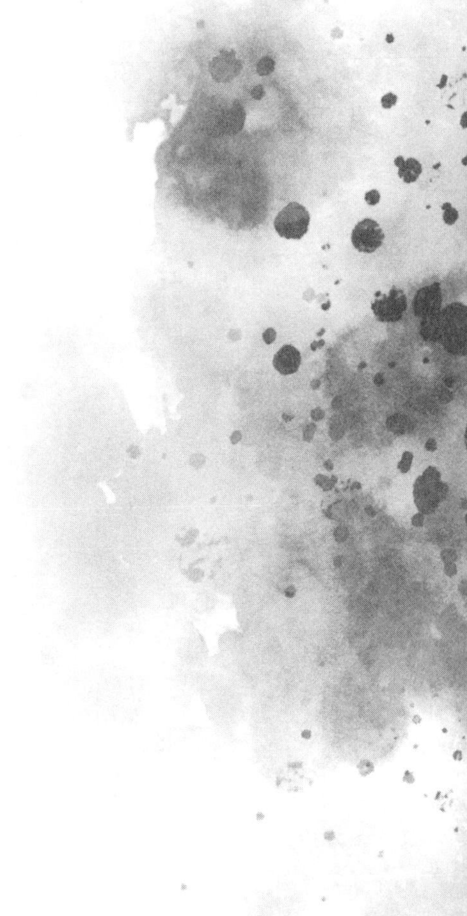

10

July, *Now*

Karl stood by his open window, looking out across York Avenue. Between the zombies and the abandoned cars—including today's freshly charred ones—the street was so packed you couldn't see to the bottom, but Karl knew it was sticky as a movie theater floor in the glory days of Times Square. The street below, however, was shellacked with incalculable quantities of blood. With the fire having burned itself out, the only noise was the faint hum of flies and the occasional grunt or moan.

Karl often wished he'd been old enough to enjoy the numerous adult entertainment palaces that had operated freely in the days before "America's Mayor," had Disneyfied the Deuce to entice tourists. New York had endured decades' of bad image, fostered by both fact and distortions of the media. America overall had a skewed conception of The Big Apple: graffiti-streaked, litter-strewn, oozing with degenerates of every ilk, ready to ply their vile talents on wholesome, unsuspecting visitors.

Karl had relocated to New York City from Ohio for the express purpose of being plied vilely, but it never happened. Seduced by candy-colored cinematic montages of neon and sleaze. Even if fleeting, those glorious hyper-saturated images beckoned. Like a nomad in the desert he'd followed a pipe dream of pendulous bosoms swaying to throbbing disco beats. By the time Karl got to

Fun City, however, Times Square no longer resembled the one captured by filmmakers like Martin Scorcese, Paul Morrissey and Frank Henenlotter. This Ohio boy had wanted *Taxi Driver, Forty Deuce,* and *Basket Case.*

Instead he got the *Lion King.*

Karl got a job, an apartment and an education in reality versus illusion. Not one for high culture, eschewing museums and so on, he'd settled into a different kind of drabness. Beige occupation, few meaningful connections, unfulfilling diversions. And after making peace with his lot it all went south. People started dying and coming back and eating each other and the rest was history. Who was to blame? No one knew, or at least no one was saying. And by the time maybe someone had figured it out media was gone.

"*Thanks, Mean Joe,*" Karl spat, tormenting himself. "*Thanks, Mean Joe. Thanks, Mean Joe.* Oh yeah, Dabney's really going to welcome me up there again. Beyond thinking that I'm the biggest dork in the world, now he probably thinks I'm a racist. *Thanks, Mean Joe.* What else is he going to think? Stupid dumb stupid-head! Of course some hick from the hinterlands is going to be a cracker redneck racist. I'm just fulfilling my genetic-slash-socioeconomic obligation."

Karl continued to glare at the graceless meat puppets stumbling around beneath his window, more vegetable than animal. Meat. Vegetables. Karl's stomach growled. He wished he had more of Dabney's vermin jerky. Rat. Pigeon. Squirrel. Whatever it was, it was good. The way they meandered down there, individual forms swallowed by the massiveness of the crowd, Karl could cross his eyes slightly and blur the overlapping double image. Meat. Vegetables. The surface pulsated like stew burbling in a boundless crock-pot. Meat. Vegetables. His life had been reduced to a sad homage to starving cartoon castaways on a desert island picturing each other as anthropomorphized hotdogs and steaks and hamburgers. Karl's stomach lurched and he cursed himself for having purged Dabney's vittles.

The shadows were beginning to deepen as the sun started to set. Soon the oppressive darkness would spread, drowning everything in pitch black and another seemingly endless night would begin. Another reason Karl had been lured by the city was that like heights, Karl wasn't a big fan of the dark, either. He loved the fact that the streetlights kept it bright all night long.

Now it was country dark.

Back in Rushsylvania, Ohio—a tiny blip in the already blip-like Logan County—it got so dark at night you couldn't see your hand in front of your face after a certain hour. There had been streetlamps, but they didn't saturate everything with that pervasive lambency that city lights did. For most of his childhood Karl slept with a nightlight, much to his father's chagrin. A nightlight was a crutch, and Manfred Gustav Stempler wasn't raising any cripples, emotional or otherwise. Manfred once got the bright idea to go camping in Hocking Hills State Park. Nine-year-old Karl had been dead set against it, preferring to stay home and watch late movies under his blanket on his eleven-inch black and white TV.

"Manfred Stempler is not raising a girly-boy," had been dear Papa's response.

So off they went. Did his father spring for one of the cottages in the park? No way. That wouldn't be "roughing it." A tent was pitched, a campfire was made and with as much detachment as a spooked nine-year-old could muster, Karl observed his older brother, Gunter, and their father enjoy themselves in the great outdoors. "Is this so bad?" his father kept asking, and though Karl's shaking head said, "No, no, no," his eyes held a different answer. When the last traces of daylight ebbed away, swallowed by the earth and foliage, the campfire's light seemed pitiful and inadequate. The woods made noises. Karl wasn't a superstitious kid, so he didn't believe in monsters—which in light of the current state of affairs was kind of funny—but there were things creeping about, rustling the leaves, crunching the soil, which unsettled him.

Small oases of light had dotted the periphery from nearby RVs, accompanied by the purr of generators and the occasional drunken whoop and half-heard tune, but it felt like the surface of Mars to Karl. Just because someone is born in the country doesn't mean he's not a city boy at heart. At home he'd secreted away a prized single from destructive Gunter and evangelical "all rock music is the devil" Manfred: David Lee Roth's "Yankee Rose." Roth was Manfred's worst nightmare: a sex-charged metropolitan hedonistic Jew in showbiz, put on this earth to lead impressionable youths—like his sonny boy—down the primrose path to perdition. Karl would listen in secret to Diamond Dave rhapsodize, "*Show me your bright lights, and your city lights, all right!*"

And Karl started planning his run from Logan from then on.

New York City was to be his Yankee Rose, resplendent in bright lights, city lights.

Even with its Lugosily ghoulish name, Rushsylvania—population just shy of six hundred—boasted a nearly one hundred percent white populace, all good Christian folk. Everyone was pink and fair-haired. His father—Big Manfred—was very active at Rushsylvania Church of Christ on East Mill, epicenter of nowhere. Every Sunday Manfred escorted Karl, Gunter, and their mom, Josephine, into the bland house of worship. White faces upraised praising their lilywhite version of Jesus, all soft mousy brown hair and blue eyes, very European, very not Middle Eastern—very, extremely, super *not* Semitic. The first time an electric guitar appeared during a worship service Karl perked up a little and Manny was at a loss. When Karl pointed excitedly at it that tipped the hand, and later Karl's enthusiasm was put in perspective.

For all the times his father whipped out the Bible—and occasionally whipped him *with* it—Karl couldn't remember a single time Big Manfred cracked it open. He wasn't even sure his father could read. But it had made a compelling prop, girthy and bound in chipped oxblood leather.

Karl remembered The Lord's Supper service on Sunday mornings, the bread representing the body of Christ, cups of juice representing the blood. Those that accepted Christ as their personal savior were invited to eat the bread and drink the juice. Though Karl didn't miss that old time religion, he could go for some of that body and blood right about now. He looked at the zombies on York. Mindless, conformist, primed to eat bodies and drink blood.

The sun was almost gone for the day. Five stories below the seething stew turned a deep burnt umber. Accompanied by a chorus of growls from his abdomen Karl stalked over to his bed and willed himself to sleep, intoning a sacred hymn.

"*She's a vision from coast to coast, sea to shining sea ...*"

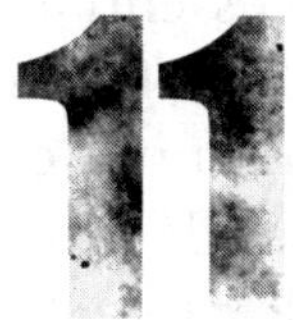

THE DEEPER ELLEN slept the harder she pressed herself into Alan's hollows, her spine folded against his sunken abdomen, the top of her head resting on the manubrium of his sternum. They were His and Hers anatomical dolls, spooned for easy storage. Or burial. Both were so skeletal they could easily fit together in a standard coffin, with room to spare. And yet her presence was comforting. Alan hadn't expected that. Now back in her apartment, he found the sound of her breathing, though a touch raspy, soothing. At night, beyond the depth of the darkness, it was chillingly quiet. Even the buzz of the flies abated. It was the kind of thought Alan only entertained at night, but he wondered if flies slept.

Somewhere out there, almost imperceptibly, a wind chime occasionally tinkled, a New Age death knell. It meant that somewhere there was a breeze, but that somewhere wasn't here. After a few moments the tinkling abated. To suffer insomnia, as Alan often did, was like a wakeful coma, sensory deprivation with no restorative benefits. At least summer nights were relatively short. If anyone were still alive once winter arrived—a very unlikely prospect—the nights would be unendurable.

Slick with her perspiration, Alan traced his fingertips along Ellen's chest, down along her lower abdomen, into her thicket of pubes. He let his hand rest there, cupping her bony mons veneris. Where there should be a rise of fatty flesh was just taut skin on bone. Alan had liked his women waxed or clean-shaven, but now pubic hair was a desirable trait. With no padding, anything to reduce potentially harmful friction was a good thing. He remembered those psychedelic posters of skeletons in various sexual positions, cheesy stoner *kama sutra* astrological home décor.

Back in Forest Hills, where Alan had grown up, he had a neighbor who was the quintessential Deadhead and Phish phan. This guy, Lazlo, a tad too young for the Dead, traveled all over to hear Phish warble the same tunes over and over. He had what seemed like thousands of bootleg concert recordings salted away in chronological order in file cabinets. He grew his own weed. He had a big Jew-fro and wispy teenage mustache. He made his own batik T-shirts. Alan wondered if Lazlo was still alive, and if so, what were his feelings on current affairs? Were the dead outside grateful?

That seemed like such a stoner musing.

Lazlo had the zodiacal humping skeletons poster. And R. Crumb's "Stoned Agin!" The rest were Dead and Phish posters by artists of varying quality.

It was strange not sleeping in his own bed. He was used to lying awake all night downstairs in his place. If he got out of bed he could navigate in the dark. Though the floorplan of Ellen's apartment was identical to his, the furniture placement was different. He couldn't get up and just instinctively move from point A to point B without lighting a candle, not that there was anyplace to go.

But what if he needed to relieve himself?

That did it. Just the thought made his urethra tingle. The more he thought about it the hotter Ellen's bony backside burned against his groin, trapping heat, preventing fleeting relief. The less he drank the more it stung to urinate, but it had to be done, even if it felt like passing acid. His insides rumbled with discomfort, the sensation of pins and needles inside his junk magnifying with each passing moment. He had to uncouple.

Easing away, Alan's crotch slowly broke free of Ellen's rear end with a moist *shluck*. She made some sleepy mouth noises, smacking her lips, then rolled onto her stomach. Free of contact Alan maneuvered off the bed, stumbling slightly as this mattress was further from the ground than his, then patted the air in front of him, blindly making for the nearest window, not lifting his feet off the ground, shuffle-walking.

Several muted toe-stubs later he reached the wall and felt along it. The moon was out and the faintest amount of bluish light outlined the window frame. As he edged to the right he remembered that this was the window Mike had fallen from. *Why tempt fate?* he thought, edging along to the window with the fire escape. As in most New York apartments, a sturdy window gate barricaded this portal, but beyond the gate the window was open and Alan positioned his penis between bars and let fly. The spattering ricocheted off the cast iron stairs, amplified by the all-consuming silence.

Ellen awoke, excited. "Is it raining? Mike? I mean, Alan?"

"No, no. Sorry I woke you. It's only … I was taking a leak. Sorry."

"Oh. Oh. It's okay. I just thought. Rain would be wonderful, though, wouldn't it? It's been so long. What, like a month, maybe?"

"Almost. It's been dry, that's for sure." Mundane chat about the weather. The more things change …

"Yeah. Remember how we used to have water shortages," Ellen continued, "and they'd tell you not to shower for more than five minutes. 'Don't wash your cars,' they'd say. Or, 'kids, don't run the fire hydrants! Not during a water shortage!' Those fuckers didn't know what a water shortage is." Though the words were sharp there was no bitterness in Ellen's tone. She sounded wistful. "You coming back to bed?"

"I can't sleep."

"Come back to bed and I'll suck your cock."

How could those words, cribbed from every hackneyed porno ever made, sound so melancholic and uninviting? Alan's junk, still scorched on the insides from the caustic urine, twitched in expectation. Even now it wanted what it wanted. No amount of *this is wrong* from the brain could dissuade the little head from wishing to be ministered to. The corpora cavernosa began to fill with blood. *Maybe it will help you sleep,* his penis coaxed. *Come on, we're all on the same team. You can't fool me with this self-righteous "do the right thing" hooey. Do this for me and we'll finally get some much-needed rest. Do it.*

"Come back to bed, Alan." And he did.

Ellen lay next to Alan, the aftertaste of ejaculate lingering in her dry mouth. It had been a while since she'd fellated Mike, so she couldn't compare offhand, but it had never been about taste or texture or any criteria she'd applied to other comestibles. Mike's was a bit acrid, like bleach and sprouts. Alan's was like nothing, really. And anyway, wasn't spooge a source of protein?

These are the thoughts of a lunatic, Ellen chided herself. *My husband is dead. The father of my dead child. Chunks of him are resting in the guts of walking corpses that still linger beneath my window. His bones are still in full view from the window. I did nothing. I could have gone up to the roof and dropped bricks on the heads of the guilty. I did nothing. My baby died. I did nothing. I'm not a wife. I'm not a mother. I have no career by which to define myself.*

"I *am* nothing," she said aloud.

Alan slept soundly. Good. Now it was Ellen's turn to leave the bed, only she knew the lay of the land and made a beeline for the front door, unlocking it. Ellen stepped onto the landing. She could hear Eddie berating Dave behind their front door, the dull roar of an underdeveloped mind. In the unbroken darkness she plotted her course upward without incident. It was only as she stepped onto the rooftop and felt a soft, wonderful breeze across her clammy skin that she remembered she was completely naked. Whatever. She closed her eyes and basked in the zephyr's gentle caress.

Though the sky was cloudy there was sufficient moonlight to see, the tarnished reflective paint creating an eerie network of geometric outlines to follow. The other roofs, topped in traditional black tarpaper, were invisible. It was like she was marooned on a trapezoidal island floating six stories above the ground. As an adolescent she'd had recurrent dreams like this, of being alone on a platform in a void, which a shrink had told her were feelings of isolation and alienation. This felt tranquil.

Ellen padded to the lip of the slight incline that led to the roof's west-facing edge. The pitch of the acclivity was maybe thirty degrees or less, wheelchair accessible should someone confined to such a chair wish to roll themselves off the roof to their doom. She was sure that was not the intent of the slope. And besides, the only way up to the roof was the stairs. There was no wall on the York-side border of the roof, just a faint rise of decorative cornice, then a straight drop.

No, she didn't want to join Mike.

Ellen lay on her back, staring up at the moon's pitted face, almost full but not quite. Gibbous. Somewhere nearby was John Dabney, either asleep or not. Made no difference. Modesty—or would that be propriety?—seemed a little outmoded. The air movement felt both invigorating and soothing. It was the middle of July and she wondered if any of them would live to see the fall. And those things on the street, how long would they continue to shamble around? How many survivors were there in Manhattan, or the outer boroughs? Were there other naked women lying on rooftops in the vicinity staring up at the moon? Or clothed ones? Or men? Or children? If so, was that a comforting thought? What was comforting? That Alan was sleeping in her bed? She wanted Alan there so she wouldn't have to be alone, yet here she was on the roof.

She used to define herself, like zillions of other people, by what she did for a living. Her career. Now her career was living to see the next day, for no discernable reason other than just to do it. Now she was defined by her sex. She and ancient Ruth were the only two females in the building—*maybe the world.* Gerri, almost spectral, barely qualified.

"Gettin' a moon tan?" came a deep voice from the dark. Dabney.

Whether modesty was démodé or not Ellen felt the flush of embarrassment. It wasn't like Dabney could see much, but her nudity made her feel vulnerable. *More* vulnerable. Ellen shook her head. Like *she* was anything to look at—a flimsy rack of bones, her slack abdominal skin lightly puckered by a petite frowning cesarean scar. What a fox. She didn't see much of John, not being a habitué of the roof, but he still seemed formidable. At least that was her mental picture, based on his frantic arrival.

"S'okay," Dabney said, his voice a baritone purr. "Moon rays don't do any harm. Sun'll just give you cancer, not that it much matters. Vitamin D versus the big C."

"I think I should be going," Ellen said.

"Not on my account, I hope. Only visitors I get up here are the fellas. Occasionally that ghostly lady, what's her name. But she doesn't say much. Nice to hear a feminine, if slightly husky, voice. That's a compliment."

"Oh." Ellen didn't know what else to say.

"How's your lesser half?" Dabney asked.

"Huh?"

"Your lesser half. I'm just joshing. Mike. How's Mike? He hasn't paid me a visit in a while."

"Mike's dead."

A faint breeze rustled dry leaves gathered in the corners of the roof.

"When did this happen?"

"This morning."

"I didn't know. No one told me." Dabney sounded baffled, embarrassed. "I'm so sorry. So sorry. With everything on the avenue, nobody said anything. How did it … I'm sorry. I don't mean to pry."

"Mike fell out the window. I think he broke his neck. He just lay there as they ate him. He was still alive. But not anymore. Just like my baby."

Hidden in shadow, Dabney leaned against the stairwell housing, where he'd been all along. Silence hung, answering the question is it possible to suck the air out of a room outdoors.

Yes.

12

"You're wasting candles," Ruth scolded.

"I want to read."

"In this light? You'll ruin your eyes. Besides, since when are you a reader all of a sudden?"

"Since there's nothing on the idiot box last I checked. Since I can't sleep and I'm tired of inspecting the insides of my eyelids. It's never too late to better yourself, right? So consider me bettering by the second."

"*Ucch.* All right, but do you really need four candles burning?"

"You want I should get eyestrain? Ugh, you've got me talking like a peasant."

"That's my fault?"

"You used to say I didn't read enough, that reading would better me. So here I am, reading, and now it's 'don't read, you'll ruin your eyes.' You're talking out both sides of your mouth, and with your teeth out it's particularly repulsive."

"Why are you so cruel?"

"It's all I have left. You need your beauty sleep, fine. I'll adjourn to the parlor, your majesty."

A clap of rainless thunder taunted them as Abe grabbed the platter on which the candles were arranged and left the room. *Tsuris* he did not need. He'd borrowed a couple of cockamamie science-fiction books from the kid in 3A. The writer, a clearly tormented fellow named Philip K. Dick, seemed bent on doling out as much torture as possible to his characters. Abe vicariously enjoyed others suffering even worse than he. At least Abe knew where the hell he was—he was situated in his misery. The poor schmuck in Dick's book didn't know whether he was coming or going; his reality kept shifting on him.

Another cannonade of rolling thunder followed Abe down the hall. "So rain already," he griped. "Enough with the foreplay."

Mixed in with the thunder were other sounds, the plaint of countless zombies.

"The natives are restless," Abe smirked. "It's a regular hootenanny out there."

In the bedroom Ruth stared into the void. Abe wasn't always easy to deal with, but at least he wasn't always such a bastard, either. She'd been spoiled, she realized, by all his years away at work. She'd kept a few jobs here and there in her younger days, but they were usually part-time and often for relatives. Sure it was nepotism, but for such lousy pay who'd make a fuss? She worked a little at a travel agency (Uncle Judah); a printing plant (cousin Sol); a catering hall (cousin Moshe); a small-time talent agency (cousin Tobias). When Abe came along she became a full-time housewife, then an over-time mother. Three children she'd raised, almost single-handedly.

That wasn't a job?

Abe made her feel like she was living the pampered life of a queen because she didn't have to schlep to an official place of work. Sure, Abe brought home the bacon—all right, not bacon; they kept kosher, give or take—but Ruth slaved, too. And for the meager allowance Abe doled out? It was indentured servitude. Even when they got along she'd prayed for liberation. Three children, and God only knows where they were or what their fates were. Was it too much to ask of God to at least know? Were Miriam, Hannah and David even among the living? In her head she thought it possible, but in her heart, and more persuasively in her gut, she doubted it. So that meant the grandchildren were gone, too.

When God doled out the punishment he really laid it on thick, but she *believed.*

Ruth believed because of the absoluteness of the fate of mankind. The scientists had their theories, back in the first few weeks, before the television and the radio were kaput, but the theories didn't hold much water. Biotoxins. Germ warfare. Terrorism. Advanced mutated Creutzfeldt-Jakob disease. Anthropoid spongiform encephalopathy. The rats had been Stage 1, aggressive, multitudinous. Swarming subway platforms, teeth bared and buried in human flesh. Like the classic plagues of yore. She'd seen the images.

Pizza rat was cute. Plague rat not so much.

No.

This was the work of a vengeful God. This was the work of a God who'd had enough, and who could blame Him? People had been doing terrible things ever since they arrived on the scene, but in just the span of her lifetime it went from not so good to bad to worse to unimaginable. Politicians got slimier and greedier and untrustworthier. Wars weren't waged for noble causes; they were pecuniary agendas. The younger generations kept getting stupider and more selfish and less humane. Popular culture was all in the toilet. Bad language was rampant. Pornographic imagery had proliferated regular television—Ruth didn't know from premium cable firsthand, but from what she'd heard it had been the telecast version of Sodom and Gomorrah. And the Internet. The super-spreader of bad ideas, bad impulses, bad, bad, bad.

Craziness.

Gone were any kind of values one could hold dear. The people of her generation were shunned by society. The only ones that cared at all about them were the politicians and that was only because the older generation still got out and voted. So, politicians and the pharmaceutical companies. Everyone else just was biding their time waiting for all the seniors to drop dead and vacate apartments like this one. Geriatrics and gentrification didn't often cozy up. The Tower of Babel had been built again, at least metaphorically, and this time God was playing for keeps.

God had had enough of his naughty children.

Death was near, Ruth felt. Abe would be in for a rude surprise when he found out his soul would continue to exist even after his mortal form didn't. In the next world—*Olam HaEmet*: "the World of Truth"—he'd have to answer for all his bile when they played back his life for him. Abe wasn't a bad person—mean, maybe, but not evil—but his lack of faith would surely not be looked on with favor. *Gehenom* awaited Abe. It wasn't hell, and he could move on, but he'd have to do some serious soul-searching—literally—to purify his untidy soul.

The depiction of the afterlife wasn't explicit in the Torah. That's where the goyim had it made. It was so black and white. They got scary fire and brimstone if they were bad or the Pearly Gates and Paradise if they were good. The Torah was more enigmatic. As a good Jew you were supposed to focus on your role in this, the material world. An eternal reward was a vague but effective motivator to stay on the correct path. All Ruth knew was that the soul went on for eternity and that was good enough for her. She just hoped that Abe would get his act together and make peace with God so they could link up in this nebulous afterlife.

And the children and grandkids.

And maybe Cary Grant.

Sure he was *trayf*, but *oof.*

Abe held the book close to the candle, straining to read the small print. Though he enjoyed Dick kicking the crap out of his poor deluded bozos in their subterranean Martian hovels, drugged to the gills with their little Perky Pat doll set ups, the pain in his eyeballs negated the pleasure. Besides, he was actually envious of these fictional characters. Sure they'd been forcibly evicted to live on Mars—which was a complete crud hole—but at least they could get bombed out of their gourds and have these collective fantasy trips courtesy of some kooky hallucinogenic drug called Can-D. Or was it Chew-Z? Whatever.

He put the book down and closed his eyes and rubbed them—hard. With spots and tiny patterns of organic hieroglyphs swimming on his orbits, Abe sat back in the chair by the window and enjoyed the phosphene fireworks. Abe rubbed some more, even though it was supposedly bad for you. When he pulled his hands away and opened his eyes again, flashes of light joined the spots and indecipherable microscopic pictographs. A distant clap of thunder echoed throughout the dead city, followed by a chorus of idiot groans from the undead. Abe blinked and pretended he was crocked on Dick's wonderdrugs.

"I'm on Mars," he whispered. "I'm in my hovel. Where's my dolly?"

As the spots and runes melted away Abe realized the lightshow wasn't self-induced. Lightning? No, this flash of light cut right across his ceiling. From below. *What the hell?* Abe manually uncrossed his sleeping legs, flung himself out of his chair and hobbled on unsteady limbs of pins and needles toward the window. Just as he hung his head out a swath of light was cutting across the tops of all the cabbage-heads, forging south—*a flashlight beam!*

"Jesus H. Christ! Jesus H. Christ!" Abe gasped. He ducked his head back in and shouted, "Ruth! Hey! Ruth!" Another small thunderclap swallowed his thin voice. "God damn it! *Ruuuuuth*!"

"What? What is it already?" Ruth screeched from the bedroom. "You'll wake everyone!"

"Good! Come in here! Quick!"

"What is it?"

"*Come in here*!"

Abe was trembling all over. He leaned back out the window and shouted at the departing beam of light. As it receded south down York the horde seemed to cringe away from it, creating a path.

"Hey, wait!" he shouted, his frail voice swallowed by another burst of thunder. In his excitement he launched into a convulsive coughing fit, his watery eyes following the light until it disappeared from sight. Now his coughing tears mixed with tears of despair.

"What's the commotion?" Ruth carped. Though she was shrouded in darkness Abe could picture her drawn, disbelieving face. "What're you dragging me out of bed for?"

"There was a light out there!" Abe said, gesturing at the street below, wiping his eyes.

"A light."

"A light, for Christ's sake. A light! A light!"

"Abe, it's thundering out there. Ever hear of a little thing called lightning?"

"It wasn't lightning. It came from down there! *Down* there! Not *up* there! *Down*!"

Ruth sighed the sigh of the long-suffering and returned to the bedroom, leaving Abe wondering if he'd dreamt the whole episode, his mind suggestible to the transcendental literary powers of Can-D.

Or Chew-Z.

"THEY'RE BEAUTIFUL IN a hideous kind of way," Ellen said, admiring Alan's ample studies of the undead. A week had passed since their ad hoc coupling and Alan had invited her to his shambolic studio to see his work. No one else in the building had been permitted into his sanctum sanctorum. "My God, there are so many of them."

"And no two alike," Alan said. "Just like snowflakes."

"Not quite," Ellen frowned.

"Fingerprints?"

"That's a bit closer. It's like you're cataloguing them."

"I guess I am. Passes the time. Cave paintings of the future."

Ellen's eyes roved over the dizzying array of renderings. Beyond their technical merit, Alan had captured something she hadn't stopped to consider about the things outside: their innate humanness. Those things weren't always *things.* They had been Homo sapiens. Alan's meticulous artwork, while unsentimental, betrayed an element of latent humanity in the subject matter. The tilt of a head, the softness of a brow, the turn of a mouth, all reminded her that these empty vessels once had inner lives. They'd been friends and neighbors.

"I'm amazed at how unbiased these are," Ellen marveled.

"They don't hate us. They didn't ask to be what they are. I mean, with the exception of the fact that they want to eat us, I think they're sort of an improvement on the old model."

"What?"

"The artist Brion Gysin once wrote, 'Man is a bad animal.' Those rotting things just stumble around, but at least they don't have any pretenses about anything. They're free of malice."

"I don't know ..."

"Who's superior, Eddie or those things?"

Ellen fingered the edge of a pastel of an armless male zombie with half its face missing. It had no pants and its penis was gone, but not its scrotum and testicles. She scanned the other images. Males, females, all dismembered in various ways. Not a single one was intact. How had she never noticed that before? She hastened to the window. Resting on the sill was a pair of binoculars, which she snatched up. Though they were packed together down there she confirmed what Alan's drawings portrayed; not a single one of them was complete. On some the damage was more evident than others—whole missing limbs were easy to spot—but all were mutilated beyond the general rot. It made sense. Most had been savaged when they were still people. They'd died and been resurrected.

Missing ears, noses, jaws, chunks of shoulder, gaping gashes, hollowed out cavities where their bellies should be. She noticed that several were nude, their clothes having either fallen off or been forcibly torn away. Some trailed lengths of dehydrated intestine, which others stepped on. Several had cutaways through which their withered internal organs could be seen, just like those "Visible Man" model kits her kid brother made, only less pristine. The legless pulled themselves along with their arms, almost lost in the crowd, trod on by the others, but they kept on. Ellen looked back at the wall of Alan's studies, trying to match ones there with the crowd below.

"It's like a Bosch painting out there," she said, sounding dazed.

"Bosch was a dilettante, comparatively speaking. The Black Death was a stroll in the park. Those pussies had it cushy." Alan smiled at Ellen.

"You sound like a more cultured version of Eddie."

"Oh Jesus, sorry. But seriously, the fine folks of the fourteenth century had it good compared to us. But what we've got going on is a logical extension. Rats and fleas spread the bubonic plague. See, rats infected with the disease were brought to Europe through trade with the east. At least that's the theory I remember. Fleas on the rats transmitted the disease to people. I mean those weren't exactly hygienic times. Open sewers, people shitting out their windows—excuse me, *relieving* themselves. Just like us, right? The plague spread like wildfire. And it's likely this whole mess started with fleas or rats. Who knows? I'm sorry, this isn't history class."

"Is the test gonna be essay or multiple choice?" she said, as Alan reached for a thick tome on his bookshelf. He stopped himself and patted the spine of the book.

"I'm sorry, I'll spare you the lecture on pandemics and wars and all that. But this? Out there. I just don't see humanity making a comeback from this."

Ellen just stared out the window. "No, I don't suppose so. But maybe."

Alan smiled and suppressed a patronizing shake of his head. That there was even the slightest room for optimism boggled his mind. He felt a small pang of envy. And then a larger pang of hunger. He stepped out of the room and into the kitchen, his departure unnoticed by Ellen, who seemed in a sort of trance. He opened a cabinet and took down a can of pork and beans and fished the can opener out of his cutlery drawer. After licking every atom of sustenance off the lid he scooped out two equal portions onto plates, then used the can opener again to remove the bottom, which he also licked clean. He then used metal clippers to cut the can from top to bottom and carefully parted the cylinder, making sure not to cut himself, and tongued the exposed insides of the can, leaving them gleaming.

When he returned to the living room, which he used as his studio, Ellen was lying on the art materials-strewn floor, eyes closed. At first Alan thought all that death talk finished her off, but he saw her ribcage rise with each soundless breath. Had she fainted?

"Ellen?"

"*Mmmm?*"

"Want something to eat?"

Ellen propped herself up and nodded, looking dreamy. Spaced out. She remained seated on the floor as she accepted the dish of beans and they ate in silence, slowly. No one but the zombies wolfed down food anymore. When they'd finished cleaning their plates, Alan took them back into the kitchen. He wiped the plates with a grubby kitchen towel. That was as good as cleanliness got.

When he returned, Ellen was on his couch with her back to him, nude, her body arranged in an undernourished homage to the classic Ingres canvas, "Grande Odalisque." She'd even wrapped a towel around her head and held a flyswatter where Ingres's model held a feathered fan.

"Want to immortalize something alive? 'I want you to draw me like one of your French girls.'" she said. "A really malnourished one, but …"

"Maybe I'm into the whole Dachau chic thing."

"I suppose *you* can make that joke."

"I'm an atheist," Alan said.

"You're a Jew. I don't know why you'd deny it. I partly moved here because I like the whole Jewy New York intellectual vibe. It's a compliment."

"If you say so."

"So, you gonna immortalize me before I perish, or what?"

"You'd make a good Jew, too. You're very pushy."

"I'd prefer to think I'm assertive."

"I thought Jewy was a compliment."

"*I* meant it as one. *You*, not so much. So, you game?"

Alan thought about the drawing of her he'd inadequately disposed of and his unsavory arrangement with Eddie. If only he'd burned it. This wasn't about the drawing, anyway. It was about protecting Ellen from Eddie's malign appetites. And was Ellen ready to see a truthful depiction of herself? That was the bigger issue. Alan had tossed away that drawing because he thought it would hurt her. How should he proceed? Whenever he'd done portraits of *aesthetically challenged* people he knew, he always flattered where possible while maintaining sufficient fealty to the model. He'd hand over the art and the subject always seemed pleased. But Ellen would likely see through such a chivalrous ruse. Better just to portray what was.

Alan opened his paint box, a sturdy wooden one that had belonged to his grandfather. He kept his brushes bristle up in a mason jar nearby and selected a hog bristle filbert and a hog bristle round to lay in the basic structure in thinned burnt sienna. He already had a primed canvas stapled to a lapboard. Proper stretchers were a sweet memory. The canvas, with its dry bluish gray layer of wash, was on the smallish side but would have to do, like everything else in short supply. Alan never wanted to be a miniaturist, but so be it.

As Alan sketched Ellen's basic form in small but confident strokes he really studied her body. It was about ten-thirty in the morning, the light in the room was somewhat diffuse as the sun was still at the east end of the apartment. By the time the sun hung over York casting direct light into the room he had the basic form blocked in. The light would be strong for a couple of hours. As the illumination grew stronger, so did the highlights on Ellen's body, sweat glinting on each raised vertebra, each dorsal rib, her raised hipbone. Though emaciated, the essence of her former loveliness was still evident. Lighting made such a difference. Maybe this painting could be both flattering and honest. There were still traces of suppleness. He could work with that.

"Can I have a glass of water?" Ellen asked, breaking what Alan realized had been several hours of total silence.

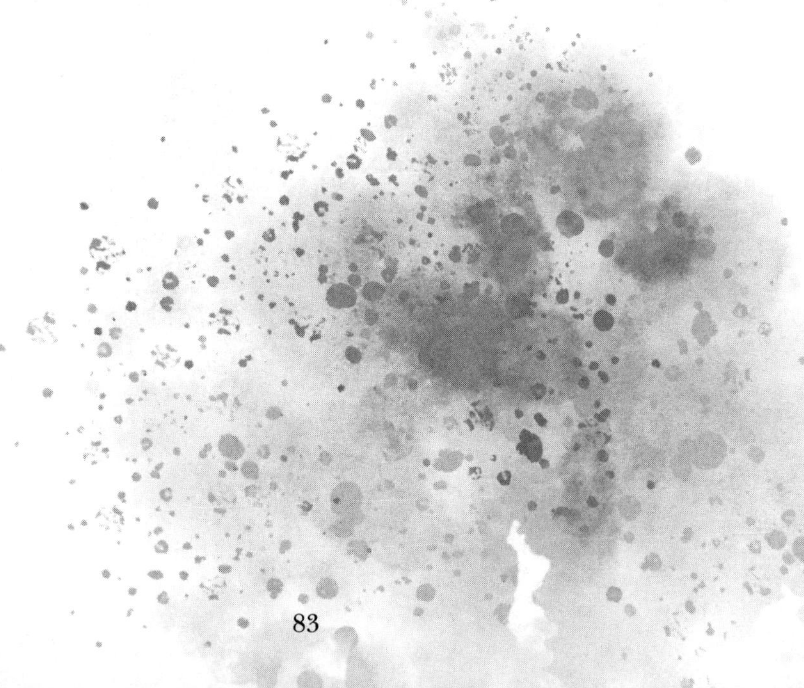

"*Ooh! Ooh!* THERE, across the street. Something's happening over there at the Food City! I saw somebody go into the market. Someone's stealing our food. Well, not *our* food, but you know what I mean!"

"It was bound to happen," Ruth said.

"What? A food thief? You bet your sweet bippy! I keep vigil, nothing gets past me!"

"No, no, *no,* not the alleged food thief."

"Alleged? Then what? What? What was bound to happen?" Abe turned away from his post at the window and glared at his wife.

"Losing your marbles. Senility. Dementia. Whatever you want to call it. You spend all day staring out the window and you're bound to start seeing things."

"I'm not seeing things," Abe sputtered.

"Exactly. You're *not* seeing things because there's *nothing* to see. Like the lights in the sky the other night."

"Not the sky, the ground."

"Uh-huh."

"There was some kind of fracas."

"Fracas," Ruth repeated.

"A brouhaha."

Ruth just stared, her mouth pursed. Abe dabbed his forehead, wiping a trickle of stinging saltiness from the corner of his eye. He blinked a few times and looked back out the window. Nothing was any different than usual. The congregation of rotting cabbages was muddling en masse in perfect, unbroken harmony.

"I just thought I saw … Ah, nuts."

Abe looked again, his eye drifting to Food City.

"Aha!" he shouted. "Aha! There!" He pointed at the doors, the glass to one of which was broken. "There! The door's busted. I heard that. I heard a noise. So there!"

"The colored on the roof broke that ages ago, remember?" Ruth said, unmoved.

"Oh," Abe said. "Oh yeah. Shit."

"You should come away from the window. You're seeing things," Ruth said.

"I don't think so," Abe said.

But didn't know if he believed it.

"Much as I hate guns, I wish I had a rifle," Dabney said as he lobbed a half brick from his perch. "And bullets," he added. "Lots of bullets. And a scope for aiming. This brick throwing shit's all well and good if you're a fucking caveman, but …"

Karl, after having started an apology for last time, which Dabney waved off with a "no harm, no foul," sat nearby handing chunks to Dabney, like an old-time cannoneer supplying his gunner. He'd mind his p's and q's today. No repetitions of the "Mean Joe Green" incident as he'd come to think of it.

"Another nice thing about having a scope would be I could really see the damage I inflicted," Dabney continued. "I wanna see the chunks spatter up, the bits of bone and brain. I wanna know that I've put 'em down for good. Sometimes I think I see 'em get up again and there's no way I can hit the same ones twice. I don't have that kind of aim, least not freehand. But with a rifle? Heads would be popping, little man."

"Yeah, that'd be cool."

"You humoring me?"

"No. I think it would be totally cool."

Karl didn't think it was *that* cool, but why make waves? Rifles and scopes reminded him too much of Big Manfred, who'd been as devout a hunter and gun enthusiast as he'd been a Christian. "Hey, Bambi, have a little of this," had been his oft-repeated catchphrase when "thinning the herd." "Hunting whitetail" sounded like one of the triple-X titles Karl had yearned to see on the marquees of The Deuce, but he'd kept that to himself. Big Manfred wouldn't have seen the humor. The same went for "Buck Fever," which sounded like gay porn. Big Manfred definitely wouldn't have found that the least bit amusing. Guns. Bullets. A scope. The truth is, Karl thought if you're going to make a wish, why not just wish none of this had ever happened in the first place?

Dabney lofted another hunk into the crowd and it dropped between bodies. He clucked in disapproval, then turned away from the cornice, massaging his bicep, sweat spilling off him. Above the sky was clear and bright and in other circumstances would be lovely to behold. Dabney lay on his back on the tarp and closed his eyes, shielding them with a large hand. Karl studied the older—but not old—man. He was still, in relative terms, beefy. When Dabney had shown up he'd weighed in at close to three hundred pounds so even now he looked formidable.

Karl's attention drifted over to Dabney's smokehouse. Was there still meat inside? Karl wondered if he should ask. Didn't he deserve a second chance? Could he risk sneaking up when Dabney was asleep? No, that would be a bad idea. Lined up along the low wall on the southern side of the roof were Ruth's flowerboxes. With seeds she'd collected from the last fresh vegetables—cucumbers, green peppers, peas and tomatoes—she'd attempted to grow food for the building; a noble effort that never made it. Small spindly tendrils had poked out of the soil, but the lack of rain and the oppressive heat baked them before they'd blossomed.

Dabney rolled back onto his belly, then hoisted himself onto his knees, crawled to the edge of the roof and looked straight down.

"You know how frustrating it is looking down there every day and seeing the top of my truck taunting me?" Dabney said. "Every day. Least those motherfuckers could do is turn it over, but they got no strength it seems. Just numbers. Turn it all the way over, onto its back like a turtle. Then I wouldn't see it any more."

Jutting out into the street at a forty-five degree angle languished the van Dabney had plowed into the building all those months earlier. Painted on the pale blue roof in black was the legend,

DABNEY LOCKSMITH & ALARM, then smaller, SERVING ALL FIVE BOROUGHS SINCE 1989, followed by his phone number in really big purple numerals. The front end was crumpled, the small hood popped open, revealing a blackened engine block. The back doors hung open, jostled every few moments by figures that passed by. No doubt sun-shy zombies squatted within.

"It mocks me. Reminds me I didn't make it home."

"Home is where the heart is," Karl ventured.

"You say some stupid-ass nonsense, little man," Dabney said, but he was smiling.

"I know."

"My van and that goddamn supermarket. Ain't that a bitch?"

"Yup."

Eddie and Dave, back when they'd been brawny, had hoisted Dabney from the roof of his van as the zombies groped for him. It was the first and last altruistic act either of them had committed, and even there Eddie had needed lots of persuasion. "That black bastard'll just eat all our food," he'd complained. "I mean look at him. He's a fuckin' house. He'll probably rape all the women, even the old bitch." The old "project your sin onto others" dodge. Ever since the rescue, Dabney was merely "that spook on the roof," as far as Eddie was concerned, though he'd never have the nerve to utter those words within earshot of Dabney, lest he end up pitched down to the mob as a tasty morsel. Not that Karl would object. Eddie was every jock asshole that had terrorized Karl over the years all rolled into one.

He reminded Karl of his dear old papa.

Big Manfred was a sportsman.

Big Manfred was a bigot.

Big Manfred hated almost everything Karl held dear.

"I miss my music," Karl squawked.

Dabney turned from his perch and looked at the slight young man. Karl was shivering with agitation, eyes popped wide and despairing. The right corner of his mouth was twitching.

"What kind of life is this? What are we doing with ourselves? We're biding our time until we just shrivel up and die!" Karl's voice was stretched almost as thin as his small body, but there was vitality is his anguish. He sprang up and fists clenched at his sides glared up at the sky. "What is this? What the fuck *is* this?" He waved his arms around, gesticulating at nothing and everything. "What? What? What is this? What is the point? What is the fucking point?"

He began to hyperventilate.

Dabney rose and stepped toward him, unsure of what to do. Talk to him? Tackle him? Give him a hug? Karl's face was pulled taut, like his skull was trying to escape its fragile prison of skin and muscle. Dabney reached out and Karl slapped away his hand, then sidestepped Dabney and walked in measured, deliberate steps up the rise toward the ledge. Karl stood right on the lip of the drop and stared straight ahead.

"Are you happy?" he asked the air in front of him. If the question was meant for Dabney it didn't sound that way. "Are you? *Are you?* I'm not."

"No one's happy, son. Listen, Karl, step away from there. I mean towards me. Back away from there. Not forward. Don't jump."

"Don't jump."

"Right. Don't jump."

"You ever see that old cop show, *Dragnet*? Or any old cop show, for that matter? Episodes where some kid would try LSD, or sometimes just pot, and he'd be up on the roof of the local high school or church or wherever. He'd be some square from Central Casting's notion of a hippie or beatnik or punker. Bad wig. K-mart version of counter culture. Or sometimes he or she would be the good kid who's fallen in with the bad crowd. And there's this twenty-five-year-old high school student, saying shit like, 'I can fly, man. I can fly. I just know I can,' and Joe Friday or some other stiff in a porkpie hat and skinny tie is trying to talk the kid down. 'Don't do it, son, you're having a bad trip.' Yeah.

"I don't want to jump. I don't want to fall. My balance is fine. I used to play games like this as a kid. I'd pretend that I was way up high; only I'd be down on the sidewalk, walking along the thin edge of the curb. If a breeze came and unsettled my balance, if my footing got away from me and I dropped to the asphalt, in my mind I'd fallen into a bottomless chasm. Or lava. Or quicksand. There's no breeze. I'm challenging God to knock me off this roof. Bring a wind. Sweep me away. I'm not worried. My dad always said 'God is in the details,' and I believe that. Because look at this world of ours. Seems like God's missing the big picture, don't you think?"

"I thought it was 'The Devil is in the details.'"

"No. That's wrong. What's funny is that we're not quite sure who to attribute the quote to. The consensus goes with Flaubert, but some say Michelangelo. Others go with the architect Ludwig Mies van der Rohe, or Aby Warburg."

"How come you know this shit?"

"It's called retaining trivia. Maybe someone would be kind and call it knowledge, but it's not. It's trivia. It's why I kicked ass at Trivial Pursuit. It's why I came home with pub quiz winnings. My sad version of being the champ. I can be little Mister Facty Facterson and lob stats and quotes and all kinds of shit at you. But it's all meaningless."

"It's not meaningless."

"Yeah, it is," Karl pooh-poohed, with a dismissive flourish of his wrist. "Every Sunday my dad dragged us all to church, but you know what? In spite of that I *still* believe in God. What I want to know is are we being punished or did God just get bored and come up with a way to wipe us all out and have some fun watching the carnage in the bargain?" He caught his breath and refocused on Dabney, who looked perturbed.

"I'm rambling," Karl said, almost apologetic in tone.

He stepped back from the ledge and headed for the stairwell. As he opened the door he turned to Dabney.

"Sorry." His voice robotic.

The door closed behind him and Dabney just stood and looked into the empty space Karl had just occupied at the ledge. He felt tired all over. Two roofs away he saw Gerri staring off into space like one of the things.

Maybe it all was meaningless.

"Is that what I look like to you or is this what I actually look like?"

Ellen stood at the easel taking in Alan's immortalization of her in oils. With tiny orangey highlights on her back from the interior candles and her extremities rim lit from the lightspill from outdoors, she actually looked radiant. All but she was softly de-emphasized, warmly enveloped in rich shadow. The pose was Ingres but the painting was pure Rembrandt, its understanding of chiaroscuro complete and accomplished.

"Alan, it's remarkable."

Ellen recalled ads in her mother's supermarket magazines for art prints, "limited edition" plates, you name it, adorned with art by a syrupy hack named Thomas Kinkade, so-called "*Painter of Light*™," that self-appointed appellation rendered in precious curlicues. Kinkade's work embodied American kitsch at its most cloying and banal. Alan was a genuine painter of light—and dark. Though the figure on the small canvas was gaunt it radiated eroticism. The sweaty pinpricks of light drew attention to the sharp contours, but somehow didn't detract from the innate femininity of the subject. The subject. Ellen. Herself.

In all her years she'd never been captured so vividly. There were probably thousands of photographs of her, maybe even some good ones, but they all fell short. They were surpassingly two-dimensional. This representation didn't just lie there, and even though it was a portrait of her present condition it had life.

"May I have this?"

Ellen could see Alan was debating inside his head. For the first time in months she felt like she wanted something that wasn't just a staple. But maybe this *was* a staple; one she'd forgotten a woman needs. This fed her sense of self. This fed her vanity. How long had it been since she'd applied makeup or thought about her body as anything other than a rundown withering collection of deprived tissue? Alan had painted a twiggy but desirable woman, and that woman was her. Twiggy. Ellen's mind raced back to the waifish 60s icon. Small breasts perched on a rack of bone—Keane-eyed and shaggable.

"Yeah, of course," Alan said after what seemed like an eternity of deliberation.

"I'll cherish this," Ellen said. "I didn't think I was capable of cherishing anymore. Or coveting. But I couldn't bear to not have this painting. And besides, you'll get to be with it every remaining day we have. *Mi casa es su casa,* remember?"

"Uh-huh."

As Ellen reached for the artwork Alan stepped between her and the canvas.

"Wait a little while. Oils take forever to dry. I can't just pluck it off the board without wrecking it."

"I'll take the board."

"I need the board to paint on."

"Are you reneging?" Ellen's face split in puzzlement with a hint of dander.

"No, not at all. Just let it dry a while longer. I'll bring it up later. Or tomorrow."

"You're sure you're not reneging, because ..." There was an edge to her voice.

"No, no. I swear," Alan said. "I don't want to mess it up or tear it. Later. Scout's honor."

As Ellen went up the stairs, touching the wall to guide her, she felt a curious combo of long dormant emotions. She felt flattered, acquisitive, manipulative, feminine. She'd already manipulated Alan into cohabitating with her. Isn't that what she'd done? Fresh on the heels of Mike's demise she'd played on Alan's empathy and guided him into her tender, needy trap. And it felt good. At first she'd felt she'd been pathetic, but now, in light of Alan's painting, she retroactively amended that take. She'd used her feminine wiles. She beamed. She still *had* feminine wiles. She'd *seduced* him. Maybe it was with shock, grief, and tears, but he'd taken the bait.

She still had *it.*

"Here," Alan said, handing Eddie a dashed off, slightly altered pastel copy of the painting. In it Ellen was more robust, her buttocks rounder, her spine less protruding.

"*Pfff,*" Eddie sniffed, his disdain slap-in-the-face obvious.

"What's wrong with it?" Alan sighed.

"It's too nice."

"Nice?"

"What's the word? *Tasteful.* How's The Comet supposed to get his jerk on with something like this? Maybe if her ass cheeks were spread or—"

"No. Nuh-uh. No can do."

"Why not?"

"Because it's totally disgusting. Listen, this is too high school for me, okay? *Junior* high, actually. I used to con my way out of schoolyard beatings by drawing naked ladies for jagoffs like you, but forget it. What're you gonna do, take my lunch money?"

"I'll beat the shit …"

Alan arched an eyebrow.

"I'll spread the word that that whore is spreading for you like Velveeta. You think she wants to hear that shit, the widow lady in her hour of grief?"

As Eddie smirked in triumph Alan's indignance slackened to indifference.

"You know what?" Alan said. "Whatever. Do whatever you want. I did you a nice piece of work and you didn't like it. I used to get paid good money for art like that. The one aspect of the apocalypse I kind of dig is assuming all those unappreciative art directors are dead. I'd hand in a beautiful piece and they'd either grunt approval or pick it apart. I don't need bad reviews from a whittled down gorilla. You know what else? You can tell whoever you want that Ellen guzzles my dong morning, noon and night. Tell them whatever you want. Make up any kind of deranged shit your feeble mind can come up with. Who cares? Be a gossipy little bitch. Everyone knows your 'secret,' so why should I protect Ellen's? She's a big girl. It's the *end of the world*, Eddie. No one cares who's diddling who. No one even cares that you fuck Dave, or vice versa or whatever."

"That's a fuckin' lie!" Eddie growled. "The Comet don't play that!"

Sniggering, Alan yanked the drawing from Eddie's table and strode out the door.

"The Comet. What a moron."

"*Oy*, my sciatica," Abe muttered, rubbing his thighs at the top of the stairs to the roof. He unlatched and pushed open the door and stepped onto the puckered surface. The bubbles in the tarpaper reminded him of pizza, with its enticing puffed up reddish orange surface, peaks and valleys of sauce and cheese. Up the block from his office in the Shtemlo Building was a hole-in-the-wall pizzeria that made the best sauce—not too sweet, not too bitter. Perfect. The Punchinellos who worked there were torn straight from the pages of an Italian joke book, stereotypes all—bushy eyebrows and mustaches, arms hairy as apes', speaking in *Dese'a, dems'a* and *dose'a* spumoni-Inglese. For twenty-two years Abe had gotten pizza there and never knew their names. That was New York in a nutshell. Intimate anonymity. You could see the same people day in, day out and never know a damned thing about them.

"You know the latch was closed."

"Yeah," Dabney said. "I forget who was up here last, but sometimes I get locked out. S'alright. Not like I come down anyway. Knees bugging you?"

"Knees, back, everything. Bursitis, arthritis, a little bronchitis, you name it. I'm an old Jew. Everything hurts. What doesn't hurt doesn't work."

Dabney laughed. "Don't have to be Jewish for that shit."

"Oh yeah? So what hurts you, Mr. Non-Jew?"

"No, I don't want to have that conversation. I'd rather keep this as upbeat as possible, if it's all the same. Whyn'tchoo come on over and park your narrow behind?"

"Suits me." Abe, clutching Alan's Phil Dick paperback, stepped over to the shady spot where Dabney sat, his back against a low wall. With some difficulty Abe took a seat on that wall, the top of which was capped with curved ridge tile. "I can't sit on the ground like that. I'd never get up again." He propped open the book and slipped on his smudgy reading glasses. Dabney took the cue and fished out his own and was about to read when Abe slapped the paperback closed and said, "How can it never rain and be so goddamned humid? It's getting maybe a little gray on the horizon, do you think? Or am I crazy?"

"No, there's some gray. Could just be haze."

"Haze. But from what? No cars, no industry. No nothing. The sky should be virginal blue, again. Ah, what do I know?" He trailed off. "What are you reading?"

Dabney held up a copy of *Time Out of Joint*, by Philip K. Dick. Abe showed Dabney his borrowed copy of *The Three Stigmata of Palmer Eldritch*. They both smirked.

"Courtesy of that Zotz kid, am I right?" asked Abe.

"You are correct."

"I think maybe that's all that kid has is Dick."

"No, that would be the meatheads in 4B," Dabney said.

"I don't think they even … *ohhhhhh*."

The two men laughed.

"I don't know who those schmucks think they're fooling. You can hear their *mishegoss* whenever they get up to it. When I was in the service we had some fellas like them: straight-laced and hard as nails on the outside. Guys with the pinups of femmes fatale. But they didn't fool anyone. Once they were safely away from home, they were off to the races. You know that's why New York and Frisco are, um, *were* knee deep in *faygelehs*, right? All these fellas come home and they've got a choice: go home to Podunk and step back in the closet, or stay in the port town and make a new life. They chose wisely, I think."

"So you think it's okay to be homosexual?"

"I don't care one way or the other. Never did, so long as their attentions weren't on me. I had a few make goo-goo eyes at me; *that* I didn't care for. But live and let live, I say. And now, what difference does any of it make? People are going to expend energy on carnality come what may, and use the available outlets. So to speak. I'll tell you, the best thing about getting old was that my libido, which dominated me all my post-pubescent life, finally died. Too bad it came pretty much right along with all this mess. I never got to enjoy my belated Age of Reason. And the hell with Viagra. Viagra's only good if you've got a young honey waiting in your bed. No pill in the world could make me want to *shtup* the pill I'm married to." Dabney snickered. "Yeah, you laugh. That woman is no picnic. Neither am I." After a reflective pause, Abe looked up and rubbing his knees said, "I need to take my constitutional. Care to join me?"

Dabney helped Abe up off the wall and the two men strolled the roof. After two circuits of their building, Abe suggested they walk to the end of the row, assuring his companion he could make it over the walls. Dabney was in no mood to carry Abe back home. When they reached the north end of the adjoined roofs, Abe needed to sit again. There was a rusty folding chair near two oxidized bicycles permanently bonded to a metal guardrail. With their tires rotted away and everything glazed in a multihued orange patina, they looked more like modern art than defunct transportation. Abe was huffing and puffing like he'd run the marathon. Twice.

Dabney looked at Abe, who sat there panting, hands gripping his quaking knees. Though the geezer's face looked all right—partly because it was enshrouded in beard—his hands were cadaverous, the skin like yellowed tracing paper mottled with liver spots. His fingertips came to disturbing points, the skin so close to the bone it barely masked it. A drop hit Dabney's nose and he wiped it away with annoyance.

A drop?

A drop!

Annoyance transformed rapture, his eyes shooting up from the old man to the sky above, which was thick with dark gray clouds. Another drop plopped right in his eye and Dabney's grin was so broad he feared his face might halve itself. More drops began to pelt the two men. Abe stopped rubbing and looked up in disbelief. "I don't believe it," he exhaled. "I don't believe it. The haze makes good." Within the minute a downpour was dousing the two men, linked arms and began a low-impact Zorba-like Hasapiko. After a few laugh-filled passes, Abe uncoupled shoulders and began to unbutton his shirt. "Modesty be damned," he cried.

"Under normal circumstances I'd protest that no one needs to see that, but damn straight," said Dabney.

Both men peeled off their clinging duds and basked in the refreshing deluge.

"*Jesus*," Abe said, looking at Dabney's groin. "Good for you. Ooh! We have to tell the others!"

"You're talking about the weather, right?" Dabney winked.

"Don't flatter yourself *that* much."

"I'll do it. I can get to our building faster than you, old timer."

Dabney hustled across the rooftops doing the low hurdles in record time, the water streaming down his naked body. When he reached the stairwell he threw open the door only to be greeted by a scream. He stepped back and there stood Ellen and Alan, both clutching various containers to collect water.

"I'm sorry," Ellen said. "I didn't mean to scream. You just surprised me. I'm not used to having a naked man greet me on the roof."

"S'alright," Dabney said, stepping out of the way. "Come, come!"

They quickly arranged the assortment of bins, pots and other vessels, which joined the garbage cans, buckets, plastic drawers and file boxes already there, then stripped nude and joined Dabney in the aqueous bacchanal. Alan handed Dabney a bar of soap.

"You don't miss a trick," he said, accepting it gladly.

Dave appeared at the door, followed by Karl, who escorted Ruth upstairs. Straightaway everyone was naked, except Ruth, who looked away in embarrassment.

"Where's Abe?" she moaned.

"Oh shit," Dabney snorted, mid-lather. "I'll go get him." Trailing suds, Dabney tore ass across the roofs. When he got there, Abe was sitting in a concavity full of water, like a shallow tub, kicking his feet like a toddler in a wading pool. Dabney tossed the soap into the basin and soon Abe was lathering up, his eyes closed in euphoria.

"You forget the simplest of pleasures when you're denied everything," Abe said. "Bathing. Being wet. It's marvelous."

"Ruth was wondering where you were. She's up on our roof."

"Is she naked?" Abe gasped, his beatitude shaken.

"No."

"Oh thank God. No one needs to see that, least of all me."

Dabney looked at Abe. "No comment." Abe chuckled.

Four rooftops over the tempest revels continued. For the first time in months laughter was the dominant sound—that and the roar of torrential rainfall. Karl and Dave had erections, though neither thought of sex. They were just pleasure-boners from the sheer joy of being wet. The cloudburst was luscious. Karl and Dave were splashing each other with bucketsful of water. Their bodies, virtually hairless except for rain-matted pubes and armpit patches, glistened in the diffuse light. Ellen looked at Alan's hairy body, his thin chest carpeted in wet black fur. Even dissipated, his was a man's body. The others were boys', not that that was a bad thing. Even Dave looked enticing. Eddie was the one who really frightened and offended her.

She was delighted he wasn't present, but his absence was peculiar. Still, her answer for now: who cares? His loss.

Safely on the other side of the stairwell housing, Ruth tilted her head up and let the cataract wash over her cataracts. She'd been scheduled to have phacoemulsification the week after martial law was declared. Now she was stuck with cloudy vision of a cloudy sky. She pulled some matted strands of hair way from her eyes, her fingers straying up her forehead, which seemed to go all the way to back of her head. Maybe it was better she couldn't see that well. In her mind she could still picture herself as she was. Abc, too.

"Hey," Abe said, making Ruth flinch.

"Oh, you scared me." Even with muzzy vision she could see he was starkers. She retained her thin housecoat, which clung to her. "*Ucch*, Abraham. Even you?"

"Even me what?"

"With the nakedness. Isn't it bad enough those youngsters are doing it? And the colored? From them I expect it, but you?"

"Even in the rain you manage to rain on a parade. Uncanny."

Abe joined the others as they clasped hands and gamboled around.

"This feels so … *pagan*," Karl cried with glee.

The others agreed and Karl basked in the moment. Big Manfred would vomit if he ever saw his son cavorting like this, naked, turgid, wanton. After a while the rain subsided to a light drizzle and various moans of disappointment rose from the group. The air actually smelled fresh. Dabney trotted over to his customary perch, lay on his belly in a deep puddle and peered down. The legion hemming in his wrecked van was soggier than usual, but otherwise unaffected by the rain. They stumbled and jostled same as ever. Seeing his van always made his stomach ache. Dabney looked away, not wanting to dampen his spirits. A rainbow spread over the buildings to the west.

It was so corny he couldn't believe it.

FEBRUARY, *THEN*

"Come on, man, move that shit!"

Dabney leaned on his horn again, knowing full well it was an act of futility. Traffic was snarled in every direction. He'd decided to take the FDR, but what a mistake that had been. After a few hours he managed to exit onto York Avenue. Awaiting his return to their home, a two-bedroom apartment on the twelfth floor of the Martin Luther King, Jr. Houses on 110th Street and Lenox Avenue, was his terrified wife, Bernice. Already, within hours of the crisis's advent, looting and street violence were rampant. Road rage was devolving into something worse, every face of every driver and passenger in every other vehicle transformed by primordial fear.

Pedestrian traffic wasn't any better. Dabney looked out the side windows and saw donnybrooks everywhere. Store windows were being smashed both accidentally and on purpose. Some just gave when too many bodies pressed up against them causing explosions of cubed glass, like geysers of diamonds. Mixed in with the hysterical humans were these new bloodthirsty monstrosities. Across the hood of a car jutting diagonally half-in and half-out of its space a woman was being disemboweled and devoured by a trio of dead-eyed freaks, her fluids splashing onto the asphalt. Dabney fought the urge to open his door and try to help. Help what? She was dead. All up and down the avenue similar scenes were happening.

And no one stopped to help.

The few cops that remained were looking out for their own welfare, and Dabney couldn't blame them. Pop-pops erupted from all over, some of the bullets downing the cannibals, others ricocheting off hard surfaces. A slug pinged off a lamppost and put a dime-sized crater into Dabney's windshield, small fissures radiating from its pinprick center. Dabney pressed a finger to the spot, feeling cool air passing through a tiny hole. He hoped the integrity would maintain. Just long enough. He had to get home. He hit autodial on his phone again, but nothing doing. All circuits were tied up. *Please try again.* There was nothing to do but keep pushing northwest.

Something heavy slammed onto his roof and Dabney felt as if his blood stopped circulating for a moment and a vacuum formed in his lungs. A body rolled down his windshield and under all the noise of chaos he heard that twinkly crackle of the glass straining under the body's weight. If the windshield broke those crazies would get in and get him. With mere inches between his and the next vehicle, Dabney accelerated, then reversed, bumping both cars to his front and rear. The body rolled off his hood, its smashed face casting a dead glare as it dropped out of sight under the van. The door of the car to his front flew open and the incensed driver starting walking back towards Dabney, slapping a 5-cell Maglite flashlight against his open palm. Dabney couldn't believe it. In the eye of the shitstorm this moron was going to give him grief about a tiny bumper-thump.

"What the fuck, dude?" the guy said, glaring at Dabney. No one was in his right mind. No one. Dabney checked his door locks.

As the guy neared another blood-drenched cannibal scrambled over a motionless car and sank his teeth into Maglite guy's throat. Dabney's mind raced even as all around him remained stationary. His thoughts came rapid fire: *Okay, now that asshole's definitely not moving. His car is stuck in my way. Can't reverse. Can't move forward. He was gonna kill me. In all this, he was gonna start a ruckus. Maybe kill me. I gotta get home. Bernice. Look at this shit. On the sidewalk it's more spread out. I'm near a hydrant. There's a gap. I'm near a hydrant. That guy was gonna kill me. But now he's dead. I gotta get home. Bernice!*

Dabney clamped his jaw tight, then yanked the steering wheel hard to the right and bulled his van past the hydrant onto the sidewalk. *Fuck it,* he thought. *Everyone out here is gonna die, anyway.* Even as he rationalized his decision to mount the sidewalk and plow through the pedestrian pandemonium he couldn't help but vacillate between *I'm committing vehicular manslaughter big time,* and *I'm performing euthanasia on an epic scale.* There really was a fine line between mercy killing and mass murder. And did it count as murder if they came back to life? Dabney could lose sleep over that ethical dilemma later, if he lived that long.

Bumps, thumps, screams and percussive squelchy crunching sounds were the soundtrack to his trek north, his shallow hood being battered and spattered. His bowels convulsed in terror and even with everything going on he prayed not to come home having fouled himself. As his windshield wipers strained against the profusion of blood and viscera, a stream began to leak through the small aperture. Bodies bounced off the front grille. After fifteen infinite minutes he ran out of wiper fluid and the blood began to congeal, even as it was slicked back and forth. Visibility was nearly nil.

"God dammit," Dabney said, his voice a low growl. "God *dammit.*"

Tears flowed down his round cheeks and collected in his mustache. This was wrong. Everything about this was wrong and fucked up. What was he thinking? He'd left the house to install locks and window gates. Panic was good for sales and of late sales had been slow. He needed the business. He shook his head. How had he let this happen? All kinds of folks—mostly white and willing to pay extra for rapid emergency service—had phoned. He smelled cash. But for what? Greed was a sin, sure, but seven was hardly enough for the deadliest. Stupidity should be the eighth deadly sin, because it was going to get him killed.

Bernice. Fuck.

He saw an opening on York and veered off the sidewalk, which was too obstructed, and pressed ahead. Darting across York, dodging carnage, a scared little mouse of a man was attempting to get somewhere. Something desperate behind his aviator glasses caught Dabney's eye. This was a human, A fellow human. The people on the sidewalk had been, too. Some of them, anyway. It was hard to tell. But this one. Their eye contact hung and something in Dabney's must have beckoned because the dude started darting toward his van. Before Dabney could protest the man was slapping his open palms against the passenger side window.

More blood-drenched maniacs flowed toward him. More eye contact.

Fuck. Human. This little mouse of a man.

Dabney popped the passenger door lock and the guy slid in so fast it barely registered. One second, empty shotgun seat; next, scared little young white dude. The guy hit the lock as his pursuers grasped and grappled with the door handle. Dabney once again pressed down on the accelerator. Inching forward. The clearing had clotted with writhing bodies. Visibility was poor. Air blew in through the pinhole, only now accompanied by the reek of an abattoir.

"I live nearby," the young guy said. "I live nearby."

Dabney stole a quick glance at him. Hair was plastered down on his forehead, glasses fogged. "Thank you. Thank you." Dabney wasn't sure if he acknowledged the gratitude, his mind only on getting out of this mess. Getting home. Bernice would be pissed. She'd warned him. She'd known better. It was all popping off and he had to go and try to make hay while Rome burned. Or something.

"A block up."

"I'm not stopping, little man," Dabney snapped, shutting that shit right down. "I got someplace to be. I got people waiting on me."

"I don't," the young man said, voice reedy. "This youth pastor … he was looking for walk-ins. I was just walking by and he …" The mousy guy stopped talking.

"You can't …" Dabney was going to tell the guy he couldn't come home with him like some stray, but he'd let him in. Was there a code of conduct for this kind of thing? He decided there was. He'd mowed some down, he'd picked one up. This one. It was almost funny. Dabney stole another quick glimpse. Like a little Jeffrey Dahmer Milhouse-looking nerd.

Bringing home a stray.

Bernice would love that, too.

Dabney hit autodial again.

This time it rang and his heart nearly stopped. Right before the second ring Bernice's voice. Cracked. Strained. Relieved. "John!" His mouth went dry with gratitude. "John?"

"Yes," he managed. "Yes. Baby. Yes."

"Where are you? They're tearing things up! The news ..."

As she spoke, her voice loud over the van's speakers, he whipped his head side to side to isolate an opening to get him home through all this pandemonium. Her voice a welcome siren song, even if it was drenched in panic and fear. On autopilot he mouthed reassuring words, or at least he hoped they were. His mind was focused only on getting to her. *Plow through this. Plow through them. Plow through anything. Everything. No obstacles. Get there. Get home. Do it.*

He hit the accelerator and surged forward for a few glorious, optimistic seconds and then *WHAM!* A westbound Volvo sprang forth from the side street and spun Dabney's van. His blood-caked windshield imploded, covering him and his passenger in wet fragments of laminated tempered glass. Unseeing and startled, his foot slammed down on the gas and his van plowed into something more unyielding than another vehicle. The engine sputtered then fell silent.

"I live here! Mister!"

Young Dahmer was shaking Dabney, who was dazed by the impact, the driver's side airbag streaked with viscera, mercifully not his own. With both ears ringing and feeling like he'd been punched in the face, Dabney wiped the blood, sweat and tears from his eyes and saw a mob of cannibals rushing toward his vehicle. The accident had smeared several all over the pavement, but there were so many. More than he'd seen anywhere else. These weren't cannibals. These things weren't human. They looked human, but they weren't. Not anymore. Some had been gutted and dismembered but here they came, nonetheless, dripping gore and spilled innards. People didn't do that. The news was right.

These things were dead but still moving around.

And hungry.

"*Mister! I live here!*"

"Okay for you," Dabney shouted. His head was swimming. "Great!"

He tried starting the engine again. No use. He looked at his crumpled hood, steam billowing out. He had moments before the ravenous mass outside reached the van. His passenger, smaller, sprightlier, was already on the hood and reaching in to help Dabney out. Dizzy, he forced his bulk onto the hood and climbed onto his roof. The horizon wouldn't stay still. Concussion? A distant explosion. Concussive. The van bounced. The young man threw arms around Dabney to steady him. He'd saved the kid. The kid was saving him. *Now we're even.*

Over the high-pitched roar in his ears he heard voices. Though the front of the building he'd crashed into was barricaded with flimsy, hastily erected, FEMA-branded fortifications, there were people calling out from the open windows above the hidden storefront.

"Karl!" they shouted. "Karl!"

Hands reached down.

A rope.

He was saved.

And getting home was no longer an option.

16

July, *Now*

"Hey, where's Eddie?" Dave asked.

Ellen was flabbergasted. "*You* don't know where he is?"

"No. I haven't seen him today. I can't believe he missed the rain.""That is odd," Alan said, glad the mook hadn't been there to ruin it.

"I'm worried," Dave said, looking it. "I knocked on his bedroom door on the way up. I just assumed he'd follow and once I got up here I got all jazzed and forgot about him."

Dave's face creased with anxiety, the practiced subterfuge constructed around his and Eddie's circumspect bromance momentarily abandoned. Without dressing, he went back into the building and ran down to their door. In the cool, dark hallway his bare, wet skin goose-bumped. He stepped into their apartment and called out a couple of times, going from room to room, leaving footprint-shaped wet spots. Eddie wasn't there. He stepped back into the hall. On each landing he pounded doors and called Eddie's name to no avail.

"He's not in the building," Dave said as he stepped back onto the roof. The others were all there, except Ruth who'd hobbled back to her apartment in disgust. Abe still sat naked on a low wall, basking in the waning precipitation. After being distracted for a moment by how long and low the old man's testicles hung, Dave stalked off in search of his comrade, unsurprised that no one offered to help.

Working his way north, the first building Dave tried was the one directly next door. Dave gave the stairwell door a few yanks but it remained locked tight, the norm since they'd thrown together this tattered commune. The next building the stairwell door was unlocked, and blackness waited within. Dave poked his head in, reticent to venture into the strange building. Maybe it wasn't as secure as theirs. Who knew? It all depended on how well the slapdash exterior fortifications had held up and if the former occupants of the building had bolstered them from within. No, if the zombies had gotten in they'd have made their way to the roof by now. In the back of his mind Dave remembered the front door was secure, but that gloom yawned like a hungry mouth. Maybe just Gerri lurked down in the dark. The Wandering Jewess's absence at the rain party didn't disturb Dave at all. She was a ghost; what did ghosts need with rain?

"Hello?" Dave called. "Eddie? You there?"

No answer.

"Eddie?" Dave shouted. The sound reverberated off the walls. Dave was in no mood to go spelunking in an unfamiliar building. Not naked. He wondered if he should go back for his clothes. It had stopped raining and like the moisture on his body, his jollity had evoporated. Any dampness now was fresh perspiration. After a few more tries, Dave gave up and moved on to the next building, which was the one he and Eddie had resided in previously. Maybe Eddie had gotten homesick or something. Maybe he needed something they'd left behind. Eddie did periodically make trips over there to loot their old digs for abandoned keepsakes. The rooftop stairwell door was blocked, as ever, but he pounded on it a few times anyway, to no avail.

Dave stepped onto the fire escape and with added care walked down to the top floor. Both windows were closed and locked, gated inside. According to Eddie, gates were for pussies. "I'm not paying to live in a cage," he'd declared. "Cowards wanna live like zoo animals, that's *their* problem." On the next landing the right window was gated, but the left—theirs—slid open, vulnerable as ever. About a year earlier he and Eddie had crouched in silence out here stifling giggles as Eddie videoed the couple next door doing it. It wasn't that they were that great looking, but it was still exciting. Eddie would play that recording often and had even made a few animated GIFs from it to email to buddies; he'd called it his "nature film." Dave stepped into the dark apartment. The sky had turned colorless but was bright, so his eyes adjusted quickly.

"Eddie?" Dave called again.

"Don't come in here," a husky voice responded.

"Eddie?" Dave ignored the admonition and bounded into the apartment, tripping over a pile on the floor. His knees hit the bare floorboards hard and he yelped in pain, then rolled onto his side to massage the injured joints. Both were abraded and wet with blood. He clenched his eyes shut as he rubbed them, stars swimming inside his closed lids. "Ouch, Jesus."

"I told you not to come in here." It was Eddie's voice, but he sounded different.

When Dave opened his eyes he looked directly into another pair, only these were glassy. He blinked a few times, then jerked bolt upright and scooted backwards away from the unblinking visage.

"Gerri!" he gasped.

Though dim, there was sufficient light to see that Gerri was dead, yet still with one hand she clutched the husk of her late Yorkie.

"What happened to Gerri?" Dave whispered.

"I did."

"Whattaya mean, Eddie? What happened here?" Dave stood up and looked down at Gerri's body. It was folded in half at the waist and pearly gelatinous spume speckled her rangy bare buttocks. One of her flap-like teats spilled out of the V-neckline of her tattered slip, her signature robe heaped nearby. Her neck was twisted at an unnatural angle and fluid leaked from both nostrils and the corner of her mouth. Purpling hand-shapes marked her shoulders. Dave looked up from the cadaver at Eddie, who from the waist down was bare.

"Why don't you have your pants on, Eddie?"

"You're one to talk." Eddie said.

"What did you do, Eddie?" Dave asked. It was a formality. It was obvious what he'd done.

"I was wandering around, y'know, burnin' off some energy. I decided to visit the old crib, grab some copies of *Sports Illustrated*—like that one with the chick with the seashells on her boobs—and anyhow, who's sittin' on our couch but the Wandering Jewess. Some rat was bitin' on her ankle and she's just sittin' there, so I stomped the little fucker. See?" He pointed at its furry remains. "So I ask her if she's okay, right? I tried a little, what's your *special* word? *Tenderness.* Anyway, one thing led to another and in the dark she didn't look half bad. Darkness forgives a lot. Zotz is bonin' the merry widow, D. Doesn't leave much for the rest of us swingin' dicks."

"Was it consensual?"

"Guy does one year pre-law and he thinks he's Alan Dershowitz."

"Jesus Christ, Eddie."

"Hey, least she died with a smile on her face."

On Gerri's dead face was a rictus grin nobody in his or her right mind would describe as a smile.

"Oh, *Eddie.*"

"Hey, hey, hey. Don't take that tone with me. The Comet needed to get his freak on with some genuine *la fica*, okay? You jealous? That what this is? You know, fuck this third degree, all right? I put it to her good and she didn't make a peep. No struggle, no fuss, nothing. So, yeah, I guess it *was* consensual. She didn't complain a bit. Least she could've done was moan or something. Shown some appreciation. Like anyone ever paid her any mind. She should be fuckin' flattered The Comet made sweet, sweet love to her." Eddie chuckled, well pleased with himself.

Dave was about to say something when Gerri sat up and let out a noise that shrank his balls—something between a hiss, a growl, and the toilet backing up. Her head jerked on its shattered neck, the jaw opening and closing, tongue lolling. A small amount of blood and bile spurted out and she was up on her feet.

"What the fuck!" Eddie shouted. "Gerri, you're alive? I mean, *see: she's alive!*"

Whatever she was, alive it wasn't. Her body twitched and spasmed, the movements marionette with its puppeteer having a seizure. She made guttural gulping noises, the air bubbles struggling up through her wrecked windpipe.

"She's not alive, Edward."

"Oh fuck man, *fuck*!"

Nude or not, Dave knew something had to be done before she got her bearings—fresh ones moved *fast.* He grabbed an antique elephant's foot umbrella stand near the front door and smashed Gerri in the face, snapping her head backwards. The sickening sound of her top vertebrae shattering lurched the meager contents of Dave's stomach into his mouth, but he swallowed it back and continued to bludgeon her. Even with her head upside down and resting against her upper back, she kept uttering bestial grunts, blood thickened saliva oozing down into her flaring nostrils. With her head on the wrong way Gerri groped blindly and Dave pummeled her with the stand, which spilled umbrellas with each blow. How many umbrellas were in the damned thing? Big ones and small ones fell to the floor, which was also now drenched in Gerri's various leaking fluids.

Finally he drew back the elephant foot and rammed her in the chest, sending her toppling back toward the rear windows. Steering her spastic body wasn't easy, but after several more strategically aimed blows she crashed through the window and plummeted to the ground in the alley that had claimed Mike Swenson. Dave looked out the window and saw Gerri twitch a few times, then stand and merge with the others shuffling around down there. Dave dropped the battering ram and slumped to the floor.

"Wish you'd been that hardcore on the ice, bro," Eddie said. "Respect."

"Thanks for the assist and fuck you very much."

"Hey, The Comet's impressed, buddy. I'm giving you props. That was awesome.'"

"Yeah. Just leave me alone, okay?"

"Fine. What*ever.* Just tryin' to give a compliment is all, bro. No need to get all menstrual and shit. The Comet's outta here."

Eddie pulled on his shorts and left through the front door as Dave dry heaved and collected his wits. A hug might've helped. Some of that reviled tenderness. No such luck. Not from Eddie.

The Comet.

The Rapist.

The Murderer.

17

"GOD-*DAMMIT*, STOP bitin' on me."

Two days after the rain the mosquitoes came, spawned in pools of shallow water. The tenacity of some life forms was incredible. Dabney refused to leave his spot, but the bites were a stiff price to pay for the hour or so of jubilation. He sat in his lean-to and swatted at the pesky bloodsuckers, swearing under his breath. After a while he couldn't bear to sit still anymore and got up and walked to his perch. Though the sun hadn't fully set—and when it did the skeeters would really get to their deviltry—it was too dark to see whether the undead were being fed upon, too. The thought made Dabney's mind race. If fleas and such could spread plague, if bugs bit on the zombies, then bit on a human, could that spread the contagion or whatever it was? Dabney thought about the West Nile virus and how the city had trucks drive around spraying poison through areas beset with skeeters. The only result he could recall was lowered birth weights in the areas the insecticide had been deployed.

West Nile was another so-called medical emergency that the local media had blown all out of proportion. Fear was always a powerful ally to keep people tuned in. *Look out, West Nile will get you,* like it was some kind of microscopic boogieman. A few old folks got ushered into the afterlife minutes before their time by West Nile, but that was about all. Still, it panicked the city and suburbs several seasons in a row.

Malaria.

That was another story. Dabney had done some time working freighters in his youth and had traveled through some places rife with malaria—Haiti, Panama, and bits of Southeast Asia. He'd seen locals, but more frighteningly shipmates come down with it. One by one the crew of his last ship were afflicted. Fever, the shakes, head and muscle aches, tiredness. Nausea, vomiting, and diarrhea. In the most extreme cases kidney failure, seizures, confusion, coma, and death.

Maybe, unlike yellow fever and malaria, zombification wasn't transmitted through mosquito saliva. Studies had disproved that AIDS could be spread through mosquitoes, so that was of some comfort. It was bad enough to get turned into one of those shambling sacks of meat from getting attacked by one, but to have it happen through a bug bite seemed so wrong. *Here's to hoping zombie fever is more like AIDS*, Dabney thought.

"Jesus God," he sighed. "This is what passes for optimism these days."

Dabney stepped over to his smoker and retrieved a small sliver of jerky. There wasn't much left. Dabney hadn't eaten anything but his homemade charqui and the occasional canned vegetables. It was funny how the white folks in the building had donated their okra and black-eyed peas to him—well intentioned, but borderline racist all the same. Why'd they have this stuff in the first place? Someone on the cooking channel must've inspired them to buy these "exotic" ingredients, but then they chickened out when it came to actually eating them. *Give 'em to the black fella; those people eat anything.* Dabney smirked. He recalled holiday trips to rural Tennessee, eating his Aunt Zena's chitlins and bear liver loaf. That was some crazy shit. Or chitlins with hog maws. Shit, anything with chitlins was pretty fierce, especially drowned in hot sauce. Neckbones, backbones. Black folks had to be resourceful in their cooking; recipes formulated by dirt-poor and disenfranchised people making do with what the white folks considered garbage.

And now, at the end of the road for humanity, Dabney was chewing on vermin jerky.

The more things change ...

18

Ellen stared at the painting, now freed from the lapboard and perched on the mantlepiece above the decommissioned fireplace. She couldn't take her eyes off it. It was her. That assemblage of angles, shadows and highlights. Complex forms. Complex lady. Lady with a complex. Lady with a complexion. Ravaged, maybe, but her skin remained unblemished. Her eyes on the small canvas, her fingers traced her cheekbone, the skin under her eyes. She ran two fingertips down her chin, her throat, resting them in her clavicle.

Her lips began to tremble. No. She steeled herself. *No.*

All her life she'd flirted with depression, but denied it. Compartmentalized it. *Not me. Sure, I'm moody, maybe even given to negativity. But actually depressed? No.* Her mother was a clinical depressive, as was her mother's mother. Fact was, Grandma spent even some time in a mental health facility. "You're lucky it skipped a generation," Mom had told Ellen time and time again. How much of what informed her unhappiness was nature or nurture? New York was not a nurturing place, yet she'd chosen to move there of her own volition. "That's a tough town, missy," her mother had cautioned. "Might eat you up."

So had suburbia, for different reasons. It was the suffocating banality of Conformity Acres—not its real name—that hastened her escape. Beige houses, white privilege. Homeowners' association Nazis patrolling to make sure no contraband plantings had occurred. Hydrangea? Approved. Hibiscus? *Verboten.* Aluminum siding masquerading as wood. Exclusionary selling policies masquerading as "quality of life." And in the privacy of her bedroom, she etched her inner thighs with an X-acto, creating a latticework of otherwise unexpressed desolation.

But across the river, New York City.

And it in spite of its many sterling qualities, its culture and nightlife, it exacted its toll. Cramped spaces, teeming population, high-stress occupation, high-cost living, infectious anxiety. She looked out at York. Even with everyone dead there was no room to breathe. To exist. A rat race to nowhere. She laughed, the sound disrupting the pervasive silence.

"What?" Alan asked from the other room.

"Nothing," Ellen replied. "Nothing at all."

"I don't even know why the fuck you're worried. Who's gonna care? And if they did, what would they do, call the cops? Stop sweatin' it, bro."

Dave had been freaking ever since the Wandering Jewess met her fate and it was getting on The Comet's nerves, big time. Granted, her lickety-split resurrection was a tad harrowing, but shit happens, you deal. That was Eddie's personal philosophy. If muff wasn't available, you made do, hence he and Dave Mallon's "arrangement." But if the genuine article presented itself, detours were made to be taken, even if they were skanky and gross.

"Seriously, bro, you're wearing me out. Relax."

"I can't. You killed her, dude. Then I *re*-killed her. How fucked up is that?"

"First, I don't think I did. I think it was just her time, is all. So, no, no, no. But also, that was fuckin' *awesome.* You were just like, *bam-bam-bam,* workin' her over with that fuckin' elephant hoof." Eddie laughed as he conjured the image. "That was *awesome*!"

"It wasn't awesome, it was fuckin' horrific."

"Dude, *whatever.* You wanna be a wet blanket, go ahead, but don't harsh my mellow. For the umpty-umpth time, bro: *no one cares.* No one even knows she's missing. She was a ghost even before she got ghosted. Just a creepy shadow lurking in the dark. And in the dark—the very *dark* dark—she was looking kinda nice. All nipply in her negligee." Firmly, with pronounced finality, Eddie added, "*I paid her a compliment.*"

Dave stopped pacing and considered Eddie's words.

"Listen," Eddie continued, slapping away a mosquito, "I don't want you to waste any more time on this. Think of it this way, she died in the service of makin' your bro feel better, like a washed-out Laura Nightingale."

"Florence Nightingale."

"Whatever. She saved a life. *Two* lives."

"How do you figure?"

"I was ready to kill Zotz, so she saved his life, not that that's that good of a thing, but fuck it, man, she helped me get the crazy out and fuck it, it was on accident, anyway. It's not like I *meant* to perish her scrawny ass. She just kinda broke is all. Dem bones, dem bones, dem *dry* bones ..."

"I'm made of tougher stuff," Dave said.

Eddie smiled and slapped Dave on the back. "That's the boy. It was a '*tragic*' mishap," Eddie smirked, framing his face in air-quotes. "Simple as that. Like a veteran, I thank her for her service."

"Well, that's the last of it," Karl said, staring into his empty cupboard. Not a morsel of food was left. In the last week he'd nursed each scrap in his coffers; now all he had to chew on was air. He looked at his shoes and remembered how much he hated Chaplin. His stomach growled and he punched it hard. "Shut up," he growled back. The kitchenette blurred as his eyes teared up. His knees felt rubbery but he willed himself to stay on his feet for fear if he hit the linoleum he'd never rise again. "This is so weak," he moaned. Was there anyone he could hit up for nourishment? Even the experts at rationing were down to fumes. The end was closing in, all righty.

He stepped out into the hall and at the top of his lungs shouted, "*Tenants meeting! Tenants meeting! All convene in the hall, please! Tenants meeting!*"

What could it hurt?

The first to answer the call was Eddie Tommasi, with a curt, "The fuck do you want, runt?" Dave followed Eddie, hopping as he cinched up a pair of sweatpants. It made Karl think of couples he'd known who'd pick up the phone during sex, then sound annoyed. Why'd they pick up in the first place?

Ruth Fogelhut stepped onto the landing across the hall and glowered at Karl. Though he stood only five foot five-and-a-half, he still towered over Mrs. Fogelhut, the only one in the building significantly smaller than he. It was her only endearing quality. "What's the commotion?" she asked in her grating way.

Joining Eddie and Dave on the fourth-floor landing were Alan and Ellen, both of whom emerged from her apartment. Eddie had mentioned she'd shacked up with the artist. Karl's mouth drew into a jealous slit. *Artists always get the chicks,* he thought bitterly. Then he mentally kicked himself for such a trifling thought.

"What's going on?" Ellen asked, looking up at Karl, who clung to the banister for balance. He felt woozy from nerves and hunger, but though he wasn't a fan of public speaking he was even less an admirer of starvation. "Yeah, what's up, Karl?" Alan added. The range of expressions varied from concern (Ellen), to puzzlement (Alan), to annoyance (Eddie), to indifference (Dave), and finally incomprehension (Ruth). Abe and Dabney weren't present, but Karl felt satisfied with the brisk turnout. At least he still had his pipes. He hadn't planned out his spiel, but he knew he should choose his words carefully. Eloquence might be the only armament in his arsenal. Feeling all the eyes burning into his fragile form he looked down, took a deep breath and cleared his throat.

"Get the fuck on with it," Eddie snarled.

"I'm hungry," Karl peeped.

"Oh for Christ's sake," Eddie spat. "Like you're the only one jonesing for chow. Don't be pullin' that shit," he said wagging a threatening finger at Karl. "Next time you call a meeting make it your funeral, you whiny little bitch."

"Except for the miserable mosquitoes, we're *all* hungry, Mr. Stempler," Ruth echoed, stepping back into her apartment.

Karl hung his head, braced for the final rejections.

"You all out?" Alan said, his face evincing the pained look of a man about to do the decent thing even though he didn't want to. Karl nodded, shame coloring his bleached-out features. Like an ashen Johnny Olson, Alan waved the little guy over with a halfhearted, "Come on down."

"Not much left," Alan said, gesturing at Ellen and his combined provisions. "But what's ours is yours, right?" Ellen nodded. Karl's shoulders began to heave up and down as he tried, but failed, to stifle tears. He began to wail like a baby, collapsing to the hard kitchen floor with a rickety kerplop. Once a mother, always a mother, Ellen's maternal instinct kicked in and soon she was cradling Karl's head in her lap, absorbing his plentiful tears with her thin cotton summer dress. Though the touch of another human being, especially a female one, was of some comfort, Karl tasted every flavor of shame a person could as he sobbed into Ellen's flat stomach. Ellen joined Karl, and soon both were sobbing. Alan stood there not knowing what to do, flapping his arms at his sides.

"I, uh," he said. "Yeah."

As the two entwined figures on the floor filled the air with grief, Alan arranged three small plates of Melba toast, turkey jerky and dried fruit of undetermined classification. All that remained was some uncooked pasta, a few cans of chicken broth, tomato paste, and artichoke hearts, a half jar of olives with pimentos, and some stale zwieback from when Ellen's baby had begun to teethe. That and the water jugs was all there was. Maybe they could stretch it for a week or two, but after that, hello starvation. August was just a couple of days away. Alan wasn't about to blub like his two companions, but one tear escaped as the absolute hopelessness of their situation sank in. Autumn was his favorite season. Too bad he'd miss it.

ABE FINISHED YET another Dick book, *Time Out of Joint*, and stuffed it between his scrawny thigh and the armrest of his chair. This one was less tripped-out than *Three Stigmata*, but still pretty wacky. In it, the main character discovers things aren't quite as they seem. A soft drink stand replaced by a slip of paper that reads: SOFT DRINK STAND. The mundane tilted on its ear. Things spiral off in a Dickian direction from that moment on. Illusion or whatever, Abe could use a soft drink right about now. Although it was the second day of September and a faltering breeze actually paid intermittent visits, it was still hot as hell and a frosty grape Nehi would sure hit the spot. Did they even make Nehi anymore? The quick answer was no one made anything anymore, but recently. Did they make it as of days, weeks, or months before Armageddon arrived? Just the thought of that carbonated purple nectar put a nostalgic smile on his face. Grabbing a ballpoint pen he scrawled "Soft drink stand" on a notepad. *Bubkes*. A while back he'd read some article about some kooks believing this was all a simulation. Virtual reality or some such crock of shit. If this was all fake, Christ what a use for technology.

Abe inched his chair a bit closer to the open window and leaned out, aiming the TV remote at the gathered throng below.

"I'm sick of this show," he grumbled, pressing the Channel button. "Don't they ever show anything but reruns?" *Click-click-click*. "How's about another NASCAR smash-up? Do something new, you cabbage-heads! Anything!"

As Abe's shouting grew louder some of the undead listlessly raised their heads and looked up. A noseless one moaned as it and Abe made eye contact, but there was no further reaction. Abe snatched the paperback from where it was nestled and hurled it out the window, beaning the one missing its schnoz.

"How ya like them apples?" Abe bellowed, then winced as he realized he'd pitched Zotz's book. "Ah, shit." End times or not, Abe figured it was a crappy thing to not return something he'd borrowed. He also noted he chose Zotz's book rather than the clicker, feeling extra-selfish at that. "Ah, fuggit," Abe mumbled, standing up and unzipping his fly. A deep amber stream scorched its way out as Abe grimaced and pivoted his creaky hips side to side, drizzling on as many of those undead piles of pus as possible. "Fug all you fugging sons of bitches!" As the last droplet leaked out, Abe's eyes went wide, and not just from his scorched urethra. Something very odd was unfolding below, and this time it wasn't some murky nighttime phantasm. This was happening in broad daylight.

From the south a tiny figure forged north through the multitude, parting it as Moses had the Red Sea. As the lone figure moved forward the undead closed ranks behind it, sealing the temporary divide. Was this some machete-wielding maniac on a death trip? If so, how'd he last this long? Body armor? What? Abe squinted and fished his smudgy glasses out of his breast pocket. The figure was a block south, still too small to make out, but even from here it was obvious that no violence was occurring. This individual brandished no weapon. He just seemed to be strolling through the crowd, unmolested. Maybe this *was* some mirage. It was broiling hot, as per. Abe took off his glasses and wiped them as clean as possible.

The figure made slow progress, but this was happening. This was no delusion.

"Hey! Hey! Hey!" Abe shouted. "Hey, up here!"

No reaction.

Abe kept shouting, loud as he could. Still the figure advanced, but never looked up. With all his shouting, where was Ruth? Ignoring him, most likely, convinced he was the old man who cried wolf. *Fug her.* Abe tried hollering a few more times without luck. He tried to move but was petrified by the sheer anomalousness of what was happening. The figure was now half a block south and Abe still couldn't make out its gender or age. The zombies pulled back from it, some letting out foul noises of displeasure. The figure seemed completely unperturbed, walking placid as a Zen monk.

"Hey! Hey! Hey!" Abe shouted again. "Hey, up here! Please!"

As the figure neared their building, Abe could see it was a woman. No. Not a woman, a *girl*, maybe in her teens. From the fifth floor it was hard to tell, but she was young, that much he could see, and dressed in black even in this heat—a black long-sleeve top, at any rate. He could only see her from the waist up, the cabbage-heads blocking his view somewhat. He had to tell the others but as she came fully into focus, Abe's mouth dried up and stopped working. With Herculean effort, Abe uprooted himself to leave the room. He staggered into the kitchen and took a swig from the water bottle. Mouth lubricated, he ventured into the hall and after a few inaudible croaks managed to yell, "*Help! Help! Help!* Everyone come *quick! Help*!"

Once again Eddie was the first to answer to call. Since he'd not been interrupted in-flagrante-delicto, he was only slightly hostile. "The fuck's all the noise, old man?"

"There's a person outside!"

"Another maniac pullin' a Dale Earnhardt? I woulda heard that."

"You missed it *last* time. Anyway, no! A *girl*. Just a person! No car!"

"Yeah, right."

Karl stepped onto the landing as Abe repeated his last thought. "What?" Karl stammered. "What person? What're you talking about?"

Ellen and Alan joined the others, as did Dave. Ruth was a no-show.

"For the love of Mike—" Abe stopped and looked at Ellen. "Oh! Sorry, *sorry*. Figure of speech. Look, come to my apartment, quick! She's out there! *Quick*!"

"It's a woman?" Karl asked, dazed.

"This is bullshit," Eddie sneered. "Grampa Munster's popped his cork."

"Listen, I *saw* what I *saw* and if you don't believe me, fine! Go fug yourself! But everyone else please, please, *please* come see!"

"If you weren't so old …" Eddie began, but all ignored his half uttered half threat and followed Abe into his apartment. When they crowded around the two front windows all was normal, just the usual Undead Sea. Abe poked his head out and looked up and down the avenue. Nothing. Ruth shuffled in and groaned in exasperation.

"It's bad enough you drag me into your lunacy," she lamented, "but the others? Leave them alone, Abraham."

"Did I imagine that car? Was that just some phantom hallucination? No, it wasn't, was it?" Abe twitched with emotion. He'd seen her! She was there moments ago. "You were all too slow," he grumbled. "She was there, I swear it! *She was there.* She must've gone inside someplace."

The others stayed by the windows for a few more minutes, then began to file out of the Fogelhut's apartment. Alan gave Abe's shoulder a squeeze and said, "It's okay, Abe. No harm, no foul."

"Fuck you, 'no harm, no foul.' Don't patronize me. I saw what I saw and if you had any brains you'd help me draw her attention. Maybe she was deaf, because I raised a fuss and she didn't even notice. She was cutting through that crowd down there like a shark. It was like a zipper opening and closing, the way they got out of her way then closed ranks after she passed. I'm telling you, *it happened.*"

"Okay, I believe you." Alan turned to Ellen, who hovered by the door near a mortified Ruth, and said, "I'll be down in a few. I just want to give Abe the benefit of the doubt."

"Again with the patronizing," Abe groused. "Fine, whatever. Let those *putzes* do as they will. Show some sense and give your *benefit of the doubt.*" The last sentiment came out curdled, but Alan didn't mind. Each manned a window and watched the street. Ruth shuffled back into the bedroom and closed the door, fed up with Abe's figments. After about fifteen minutes Abe himself began to doubt what he'd seen. He mopped his sweaty brow with a heinously discolored hankie, his features compressing in sorrow and embarrassment.

"Maybe I am losing my marbles," he said in a hushed tone.

"Who isn't?" Alan allowed, hoping it didn't sound condescending.

Alan stepped away from the window and as if on cue the girl emerged from Food City, a shopping bag in each hand, which she placed on the ground to adjust something in her ears. Headphones! She was wearing headphones!

"There! There!" Abe shrieked, spinning Alan around. Alan's jaw nearly hit the floor. As the girl stood before the supermarket the undead backed away, moaning and hissing. They gave a wide berth and she stepped into the street, aimed south. Abe sputtered, "She can't hear 'cause she's got one of those Walkman thingies!"

Alan tore out of the apartment and into the hall. He ran down and pounded each door, all the while shouting, "Abe's right! Get down to the second floor, Abe's right!"

Others rapidly joined Alan in vacant 2A, Abe kvetching, "Sure, *him* they believe."

Everyone crowded by the windows screaming at the tops of their lungs as the figure, now patently obviously a young woman, began to head south.

"We can't let her get away," Ellen squeaked.

Redoubling their efforts they shrieked raw-throated over and over, "*Help us! Help us! Help us!*"

With her back turned away from 1620, the girl stopped to readjust some items in her bags. Seizing the moment, they upped their clamor, shrieking, "*We're here! We're here! We're here!*" like a nightmare version of the wee folk in *Horton Hears a Who.* Nothing. No response. The girl lifted her bags, shrugged her backpack into position, and started moseying south. Collective horror washed over all gathered at the windows. *No, no, no.* Panic and desperation fueled their entreaties. She seemed in no hurry but their voices weren't cutting it.

As she neared the corner a large dark object whizzed down past the windows and exploded against the roof of Dabney's van, the sound shocking, metallic and very, very, loud.

"The fuck," Karl gasped. He poked his head out and in a new crater on the van's roof saw the ruins of the obliterated makeshift meat smoker. "Dabney, you fucking genius."

The girl stopped and plucked an earbud out, head cocked like a dog hearing an unfamiliar noise. She looked this way and that, but didn't turn around. As she was about to replace the earbud they screamed at the tops of their lungs. It wasn't even words, just a sound of pure distress. She turned and saw them. *She saw them!* With their hearts almost escaping their chests, everyone let out a collective gasp, then began waving their arms in a frenzy. As the girl walked toward the building the zombies recoiled from her, their noises of reproof stomach turning. The girl moved leisurely, like she didn't have a care in the world. Now that they'd gotten her attention, in silent awe they watched her approach. Without a doubt this was the most extraordinary thing any of them had ever witnessed. Ever.

When she was right below them, the zombies spread out around her, she the pupil, the exposed street the sclera of the eye she'd opened in the crowd. She looked straight at them and plucked both buds out of her ears. Even through the low din of zombie protestations they could hear the tinny ratta-tat-tat of loud percussive music piping from the tiny speakers.

"Sup?" she asked in the tone of someone just running into an old acquaintance. Her nonchalance turned every person by the windows into one big goose-bump, hairs rising on necks and arms, Adam's apples bobbing in quandary. Maybe Abe's derangement had affected them all, because no one in this world or the next had ever displayed such placidity, least of all in a circumstance like this.

Not even Buddha.

"We need your help," Ellen managed, forcing out each word like a fist-sized chunk.

"Uh-huh." Big pause. The girl stuck a finger in her ear and jiggled it. "Whattaya want?"

"For starters, we're starving."

"Uh-huh."

And with that she put down her full shopping bags, turned around and headed back into Food City, the zombies after a few beats closing the zipper. Everyone stood by the windows, immobilized and mute. On York the scene coalesced into its usual monotonous norm, no breaks in the rotting mob, no sign anything different had ever occurred. Ellen blinked herself out of her stupor and whispered a faint, "Did we just see what we just saw?"

Part Two

As they hoisted the fifth load of shelf-stable goods into the windows of 2A, the girl looked up at them from the roof of the van, indifferent as when she'd arrived, casually edging bits of smoker debris off with the edge of her boot. Everyone was sweatier than usual, but there was a feeling of giddiness and camaraderie that hadn't been evident in the group since ever. One bag toppled over in the excitement and several mouths involuntarily began to drool at the site of such delicacies as Hormel Chili, Broadcast Corned Beef Hash, Dinty Moore Beef Stew, Del Monte Lite Fruit Cocktail, and more. Even good old SPAM. Several eyes were also leaking, but for a change with anticipated pleasure.

"Okay, then," the girl said, her voice wholly monotone. With that she lowered herself off the roof, picked up her own shopping bags, turned around and began to head south in no particular hurry. On her back was a bulging button- and badge-festooned Hello Kitty backpack, its beady black eyes as blank as hers.

"Wait! Wait!" Ellen screeched, hating the desperation in her voice.

The girl stopped and looked back. "What?"

What?

"Can't you stay?" Ellen shouted, regaining composure.

"Why?"

Why? Was this chick for real? Was she so shattered by the world she couldn't even be horrified by it anymore? It was possible. It was certainly possible. Around her, for the first time in months, the zombies' barely functioning brains were engaged, and they didn't like it. The bounty in the building above tantalized them, out of reach. For a moment Ellen wondered if the zombies were as hungry as she was. The girl was clearly abhorrent to them. Inarticulate confusion and chagrin reigned, displayed in a chorus of guttural grunts and thick, phlegmy hissing. In direct contrast, the girl stood there, calm as a mink at a PETA rally.

"Why?" Ellen repeated, dumbfounded. "Because we *need* you to stay. Won't you *please* stay and help us?"

The others all nodded encouragement at Ellen, mutely acknowledging their acceptance of her as their advocate. As they fought the urge to tear into the groceries they watched the back and forth between the two females, their heads looking up, then down in unison, like spectators at a lopsided tennis match.

"Stay. Here," the girl said, sounding it out for her own benefit.

"Yes. Yes, please. Please stay. Please. We'd be so grateful if you did."

Ellen was trembling, trying to keep it together. The girl stood there and looked at her feet, which were encased in scuffed black Doc Martens boots. She wore longish black cargo shorts, low on her hips, exposing a hint of her very healthy-looking belly. Even under her long-sleeve black concert tee it was clear she had no boobs to speak of, but possessed wide, womanly hips. Her hair, also black, was short, choppy and boyish. She wound and unwound the cord of her earbuds around her hand, pondering, occasionally fanning away a pesky fly. Epochal seconds passed.

"Yeah, okay," she finally responded, voice flat as the world before Columbus.

Ellen and Alan set up her expandable dining table on the roof, and Dabney fired up the slightly rusty hibachi he'd found two roofs over, preparing to share their first communal meal since they'd been forced into these straits. Paper and plastic plates and utensils were distributed, freshly liberated from Food City along with all the comestibles. Everyone greedily eyed the various cans and boxes as they were freed from plastic shopping bags, their colorful labels beacons of the feast to come.

"Fuckin' awesome," Eddie declared, holding aloft a bag of Doritos.

At first the meal had been hard to enjoy, everyone's reawakened sense of smell welcome as the scent of grilling meats and veggies seduced them, then not so welcome as they got a whiff of the stench of their rotting neighbors on the avenue. But good smells triumphed over rotten, and soon dishes brimming with steaming hot meat products and vegetables were devoured with relish. Real relish. Jars of it. Condiments had reverted to accent status, to enhance but not *be* the main course.

The mood was high and the behavior almost courtly, each course consumed amidst choruses of "please" and "thank you." Even Eddie was caught up in the graciousness. His mama would've been proud. The SPAM family of products—Hot & Spicy, Lite, Oven Roasted Turkey, Smoke Flavored, and Classic, of course—had never tasted so good.

"This is like filet mignon," Abe said, savoring a chunk of the briny potted meat.

"Better," Karl said, shoveling a heap of baked beans onto his plate. "Oh my God, I can't believe how great this is." Karl looked heavenward and, closing his eyes, added, "Heavenly Father, it is with sincere hearts that we thank You for Who You are and all You have given to us, by Your grace. Thank You not just for this food, but for your Son, whom Scripture calls the Bread of Life. Uh … I can't remember the rest. Thank you, anyway. Amen." Karl looked at the others and saw none looking prayerful. But they did look grateful, so he chased away any fleeting self-consciousness.

When everyone was too stuffed to budge, Abe, being the resident old man of Jewish persuasion, uttered the customary cornball joke that follows big meals: "Waiter, check please." But rather than the groans of embarrassment he'd gotten in the past from his family, laughter erupted, even from Ruth. Abe blinked in astonishment and said, "No one ever laughs at that line. We should starve to death more often."

"*Ucch,* Abraham. Quit while you're ahead." Even Ruth got a laugh.

It had been a long while since anyone's stomach ached from overeating, but that was the case, and the pain was delectable. A symphony of gastric juices breaking down adult-sized portions serenaded the residents of 1620 as they rubbed full bellies and had seconds and thirds. When no one could cram down any more, Alan and Karl brought the soiled disposable dishes and so forth to the edge of the roof and rained the debris down on the zombies below. Ellen's smile faded as it hit her the girl was not among them. She hadn't even partaken of the feast.

"What kind of ingrates and assholes are we?" she gasped.

"Huh?" Alan said, turning to face her.

"The girl. *The girl!* Our Good Samaritan! We didn't even invite her to join us. Are we insane?"

"Crazed by hunger, yeah," Eddie said.

"It was an oversight," Abe said. "No disrespect intended."

"No disrespect? We're idiots," Ellen said.

"Don't ruin the mo—"

Ellen raced downstairs and into 2A, formerly the super's apartment, where the girl sat by the window, feet up on the sill, nodding her head to the rapid beats assailing her ears. Ellen comported herself, then stepped over to the girl and gently tapped her shoulder. The girl plucked out an earbud. "Sup?" she asked. She didn't look directly at Ellen, her hooded eyes focused somewhere middle distant.

"I, uh. We just ate, and I feel like a total shit that we got so caught up in our celebration and all that we, uh … Christ, this is mortifying, that we, uh, forgot to invite you. It's unconscionable and …"

"I ate earlier." She was about to replace the earbud, but Ellen grasped the girl's wrist and prevented it, then withdrew her hand, horrified by her own aggressiveness. The girl wasn't miffed at all. She was indifference incarnate. Her sangfroid ruffled Ellen.

"Still," Ellen said, "it was wrong of us and I'm really so, so, so very sorry."

"No big." Again the girl made to replace her headphone.

"I, uh," Ellen half laughed and managed a fretful smile. "I, that is, we don't even know your name. We should have been having this dinner to celebrate your arrival. The food just made us forget the whole raison d'être for our party, which is pretty unconscionable."

The girl shrugged. "Can I?" She gestured with the rappity-tapping earbud.

"Your name. Could you at least tell me your name?" Ellen hoped she didn't sound hysterical, but this girl's demeanor was rattling her, big time.

"Mona."

"Mona, hi. I'm Ellen," she said, offering her right hand, which Mona shook. Her handshake was unexpectedly firm, though it might just seem so to Ellen, her hand being so frangible.

"Okay then." And with that Mona slipped the earbud back in and resumed nodding her head, eyes closed. Conversation, such as it was, over.

Ellen stood there, uncertain what to do. Though there was no belligerence from Mona whatsoever, she felt dismissed, which was irrational. Maybe Mona was just getting her bearings, a stranger in new surroundings. Up close and personal, Ellen admired Mona's complexion, which was smooth and perfect, the bridge of her nose and cheeks lightly freckled. Her lips were bee-stung, and pointed up slightly in the corners, as if caught in a permanent smirk. Ellen's eyes traveled down Mona's neck, which was solid and round, not a course of concavities and sinew like her own. Maybe now that food was back on the menu Ellen could look forward to being curvy again. What a thought.

Mona's shoulders flared out in a strong V, and while covered in long sleeves, were clearly solid, like the rest of her. Ellen cast her eyes toward Mona's legs, which rested on the sill, one ankle cocked atop the other, the toe of the boot tapping out the tattoo of her private tunes. Tattoos. Ellen wondered if beneath the black long-sleeved tee lurked sleeves of elaborate ink. Mona looked the type to have embellished flesh. Very metal. Or Goth. Something. Ellen, not being conversant in that culture, felt like an old. The ends of the sleeve were frayed like they'd been chewed on, evidence betraying a nervous habit the girl kept under control around others. The girl's calves looked formidable. She did a lot of walking. Maybe in no hurry, but she'd been out there on foot, somehow surviving. *How?*

"Okay then," Ellen echoed, certain Mona wasn't listening, and turned and walked back towards the door. As she reached for the doorknob Mona said, "Hey," causing Ellen's chest to seize.

"Yes?" Ellen answered, heart thudding.

"This mine or I hafta share?"

"N-no. This is yours, if you want it. This used to be the super's apartment. The apartment across the hall is vacant, too, if you'd like that one better. It's more furnished. The guy in there, Paolo, was gay and he had really great taste. Not to stereotype, but ..." Ellen's face felt hot. "Or there's one on the third floor if you ..."

"This is fine."

Ellen was about to say something more, but Mona poked the buds back in and that was that, which was probably for the best. Ellen stepped into the common hall, closed the door to 2A, and stood there, still feeling that sense of unreality. Her heart was pounding hard and her chest felt like it was on fire, though that might have been heartburn from the meal. She could hear sounds of reverie from the roof, the jubilant mood persisting. Ellen felt none of it now, but didn't want to be a killjoy. Let the others luxuriate in the moment. *Eat, drink and be merry*, she thought, *for tomorrow we suss out our benefactress.*

"Maybe she's just antisocial," Alan said, wanting to fall asleep while still enjoying the sensation of fullness. How long had it been since anyone in the building had gone to bed not hungry?

"It's more than that," Ellen said, her tone firm. "It's like she's not quite there."

"That's kind of a snap judgment, isn't it? How long has she been here, five hours? She's been out there on her own for who knows how long, probably lost everyone she ever knew. Yeah, she seems a little out of it, from what little I saw, but she'll come around. We're like a bunch of needy kids she's been saddled with out of nowhere. Give her a little time to adjust. You should be grateful she showed up."

"I am. *Jesus.* Don't put words in my mouth, or thoughts in my head, or whatever. I'm deliriously happy she's here. Hopefully we can get her to stay and go out and get more. If she's immune to those things, hell yes I'm grateful. I didn't hear any of the rest of you getting her to help, so cut me some fucking slack, Alan."

"Jeez, relax. Just get some sleep, please. Tomorrow's another day." And with that he rolled over and blew out the candle, illustrating that the conversation was over. Dismissed twice in one day. From Mona it was okay, but Alan.

No, don't get angry. This was a good day. A great *day.*

Ellen lay on her back absent-mindedly rubbing her full stomach. *Her full stomach.* What the hell was she so worked up about? This girl was a godsend, simple as that. Was she jealous? Oh Jesus, if that was it she needed help. A young nubile girl arrives and what, she's afraid she'll lose her man? Oh that's insane. But maybe that was what was troubling her. Mona was a pretty young thing with a pretty young body. On the one hand maybe Alan would cast an impure eye her way, but on the other, so might the apes across the hall. That would take some pressure off.

No. Not them. Eddie. This girl had shown up like a fucking miracle and Eddie had better keep his filthy mitts off her. That girl, Mona, had survived the undead out there, repelled them somehow, but Ellen doubted her mojo would keep Eddie away. *Maybe,* Ellen thought. *Maybe I protect her? Quid pro quo, or something.* Would Eddie's animal needs be so unmanageable that he could jeopardize everything just to get laid? It was certainly plausible.

Ellen lay there staring up at the unseeable ceiling, the blackness total. She massaged her rumbling stomach, which felt firmer. If Mona stuck around, Ellen could maybe fill out her skin again, put the curves back. Her breasts had once been sustainers of life, the tiny mouth of her infant daughter nursing there. Mike had grown jealous, even resentful of the baby. "That's my turf," he'd said, insisting it was a joke, but Ellen knew full well that more truths were said in jest. "She gets one year grazing privileges, tops," Mike had said, "then all rights revert to yours truly." They'd laughed, but Mike would watch the baby nursing, raise an eyebrow and tap the crystal of his watch. "One year," he'd repeat. "Not a day longer."

Ellen's hand drifted up from her belly and felt the diminished lobes of flesh.

Her baby.

Her dead baby.

She almost had to struggle to remember her name.

Fully hydrated for the first time in ages, Ellen lay there and shed nary a tear. She was all cried out. The world was a dead place full of dead things too stupid and stubborn to realize it. She remembered the boys in her old neighborhood tearing around playing cops and robbers or cowboys and Indians. They'd finger guns at each other shouting, "Pow! Pow!" Then the recipient of imaginary lead was supposed to fall down. "You're dead!" the boys would shout. "Fall down!" If the victim defied them with an impudent, "Uh-uh, you missed," or "Make me," arguments ensued and sometimes fists would fly.

Those things outside were poor sports that refused to fall down.

She could feel them, still restless from their encounter with Mona. There was *some* cognizance there. Maybe it was rudimentary, but those things knew something was up. Some groaned in their clabbered subhuman manner, sounds thick and ugly. *Think happy thoughts*, Ellen commanded herself. *You will be beautiful again. You will be desirable again. Alan already desires you. You will be vital again.*

Mona is a blessing, not a threat.

But she is a mystery. Why weren't the undead all over her?

As her emotional upset subsided that was the real question.

Why?

Dabney lay on his tarp, staring up at the cosmos. The haze had cleared and for the first time in weeks the sky was pinpricked with countless stars. He ran his tongue around the inside of his mouth, sucking small deposits of food from between his teeth. His belly churned happily. There were leftovers on the table, which remained on the roof. Leftovers. How decadent. The only thing lacking in this equation was a cigarette. *Oh sweet Lord above, a cigarette would be glorious.* The thought sent a shiver through his body. Dabney eased up off the ground and trod over to the table and scooped out the remnants of a can of peas, then drank the pea water, swishing it around like a funky mouthwash. He thought about dental hygiene. Maybe that girl could get some toothpaste and Scope and whatnot. Listerine, but not the nasty medicinal kind. That minty stuff.

And cigarettes. Definitely cigarettes.

He was sorry he hadn't spotted her. All his time up here playing lookout when there was nothing to see and the one time something was brewing he'd been napping on the job. Abe got that glory.

"Thank you," he said aloud, just in case he seemed unappreciative.

With his lantern burning, Dabney polished off every morsel that remained.

"I wouldn't mind breaking off a piece of that," Eddie said, the only one in the building rubbing south of his belly. "I didn't get that good of a look, but she looked fuckin' young and doable. A little light in the tit-tay department, but I don't care."

"Sure, whatever," Dave replied.

"Whatever? *Pfff.* Okay, bro, fine. More for me."

Dave let out a theatrical sigh and shook his head.

"What? What, dude, *what*? You're actin' like her showin' up isn't the greatest thing since … *ever*."

"Of course it is, but jeez, Eddie, you're already thinking about nailing her and she just got here. Plus which, unless rape is your new thing, maybe you oughta test those waters before you go assuming she'll have anything to do with you. She looked a little butch, to be honest. Kinda dykey."

"Y'know, I never noticed what a downer you are. And you better stow that shit about rape. One, it wasn't. And two, that's *our* business and no one else's, *capisce*? I get wind of you spreadin' that around and …"

"And what? Oh that's right. Murder's on your résumé, too."

Eddie got up off the futon and stomped over to Dave, who sat on the carpet, back to the wall. Eddie stood with his legs spread wide, a posture of unquestionable dominance. He kept making and unmaking fists as he stared down at Dave, who looked up with defiance.

"What? You gonna hit me?" he asked. "You gonna *kill* me?"

Eddie glared at Dave, looked away, looked around the room. After a minute his posture relaxed, the expression on his face uncertain. "Why you gotta push my buttons, Mallon?" he asked, his voice a soft whine. "This was a good night and you had to go bringing up that old business."

"*Old business*?" Dave whisper-shouted. "It was what, a *week* or so ago? If that?"

"You know what I mean. Look, whatever, okay? The Wandering Jewess was a mistake. I told you I didn't mean to … The Comet just got a little out of … Anyway, truce. Okay, bro? I don't wanna end the day on a note like this."

Dave fumed for a few more moments, looking away from Eddie, who stood his ground, but now contrite. Or contrite as he got. Dave looked up into those big brown eyes and fought the urge to say something romantic. Tender. Instead, he said, "How about a note like this?" and tugged Eddie's shorts down.

"So who's the boy who cried wolf now, huh, Mrs. Bigshot? Who's the *gontser macher* around here?"

"It isn't nice to gloat, Abe," Ruth said, but she smiled in spite of herself. Abe had done well. Very well. She curled around him and in the dark allowed herself to imagine Abe as he'd been when they met. To her complete surprise, Abe put his arm around her shoulders instead of shrugging her away. "Okay, maybe you can gloat a little. Our hero." She kissed his cheek and restrained herself from smacking her lips to ease the tickle from his beard. Let the goyim have visions of sugarplums dancing in their heads. As Ruth drifted off she dreamt of shaving cream and fresh razors for Abe.

And soap and paper towels and deodorant.

She seldom cleaned the house anymore—just the occasional cursory run with the broom—but now a radiant vision of Lysol and Comet and Soft Scrub and refills for her Swiffer, both wet and dry, floated through her brain. Suddenly she was young again, dancing like Fred Astaire—to heck with Ginger; Ruth wanted to lead! Her partner was a mop and the setting a palatial kitchen. As she danced every surface she passed gleamed, shaming every commercial for every domestic cleaning product ever made. White surfaces shone bright as a thousand suns. Was that a speck of grease on the stovetop? With the grace of a dozen Baryshnikovs, Ruth leapt through the air and obliterated the offending stain with a balletic stroke of her sponge. And not some off-brand sponge, but a good one! An O-Cel-O!

Joined by a spectacular rainbow, sunbeams flooded the immense chamber. Disney-esque forest animals capered about—small cartoon birds chirping, tiny white bunnies hoppity-hopping, deer sweet and charming as Bambi—and Ruth shooed them all away with her magical mop. "No animals in my spotless kitchen," she scolded in tones dulcet as Snow White's.

As the last critter fled the kitchen began to shake and shimmy, cabinets opening, dishes spilling to the floor, smashing to bits, creating fissures in the immaculate ceramic tile. Shards of shattered glass and china littered her utopia and her ears were assailed by the cacophony of an avalanche of utensils. The sun faded and the sky turned an ominous gray. The booming stentorian voice of God rang out.

"Get off of me. Ruth, *please.* Get off."

"What did I do?" Ruth said, voice quaking.

"You're crushing my arm. My arm's gone numb."

Ruth awoke to Abe jostling her in an attempt to free his sleeping arm.

"Oh for heaven's sake," Ruth jeered. "For this you wake me?"

"I got pins and needles. You want me to get gangrene like your mother?"

"You have to bring my mother into this, may her soul rest in peace? *Ucch,* Abraham."

Ruth turned away from Abe as he rubbed his arm. *Please God,* she thought. *I don't ask much. Just send me back to my happy kitchen. And while you're at it, send Abe some more pins and needles.*

Karl pressed his lips to the boudoir photo of Dawn-Anne McCarthy, then with a gentle flick of his wrist sent it spiraling down into the crowd below. "*Au revoir, mon amour,*" he whispered. He'd spent the last fifteen minutes plucking all the pinups and centerfolds from his wall, balling them up, tossing the crumpled wads of paper out the window, watching them bounce off the empty noggins of the horde. The repetitive motion reminded him of feeding the animals at the Cleveland Metroparks Zoo in Cuyahoga, one of the few enjoyable memories he could conjure from his childhood that involved the presence of his old man—and equally rare for its involving animals *not* being slaughtered by Big Manny. Each wadded up piece of smut stood in for a bygone peanut or piece of bread, and for a change thinking of those edibles didn't make his empty stomach lurch because it wasn't empty. Praise be.

"It's raining porn. Hallelujah."

The cleansing had nothing to do with faith, though. Not faith in the Almighty, at any rate—faith in maybe making time with the miraculous new arrival. So maybe there was some faith and gratitude. But at the moment faith was secondary to earthier notions. Though he'd only glimpsed her as he'd hoisted up bag after bag of groceries, she looked incredible. And the way she was all dressed in black with that funky knapsack? She'd probably be into the same tunes. She looked very metal. Maybe Goth, which wasn't really Karl's thing, but he could fake it. He knew The Cure and Bauhaus. Maybe Gothic metal? How cool. He had some Cradle of Filth and Type O Negative. Wasn't that enough? If she was Emo he'd improvise.

This cleansing was an act of optimism, his first since even before everything hit the shitter. Her arrival was miraculous. It really was. But if he thought about God he'd inevitably think about Big Manfred. Why ruin the moment? He was still young enough to pursue a girl like that without feeling like a dirty old man. She looked to be "of age," not that a thing like that matters when all the lawmakers and law upholders are dead, dead, dead. *What's the age of consent in New York?* Occasionally Facty Facterson still had to fight the urge to reach for his phone to Google something.

Karl would have to be shrewd and charming. As sure as he was that he wanted her was his certainty that Eddie would make a play for her, too. Not that a groovy NüMetalEmoGoth hipster like her would ever fall for a knuckle-dragging throwback like him. Dave, on the other hand, seemed perfectly content in his "secret" love for Eddie. He reminded Karl of all those so-called conservative politicians and pastors that had preached intolerance while pursuing clandestine same-sex relations of their own. In public toilets. With male prostitutes. With underage senate pages. Real paragons of virtue, they were. Big Manny had supported them all, the hypocrites. Oh irony. And all it had taken to nudge Dave out of the closet—mostly—was the apocalypse. *Good for him,* Karl thought. *But Eddie …*

Karl plucked the final vintage Playmate off the wall, a sloe-eyed Hawaiian hottie, Miss June 1982. This was tough. He'd "gone steady" with this gatefold since finding her in a thrift shop back in Akron that didn't care how old you were as long as you had cash. He'd secreted her into his childhood bedroom and made sweet imaginary love to her countless times, his eyes tracing every velvet inch of her soft tan body. He'd overlooked her taste in music—The Rolling Stones, Bette Midler, The Cars, Bob Seger, Jimmy Buffett, The Eagles—in light of her overwhelming beauty. Bette Midler? *Jimmy Buffett?* Well, she *was* from Hawaii.

Was she dead, too? Most likely.

She was probably one of those shambling piles of flesh-hungry rot. Maybe she'd been torn apart. The thought was too awful to contemplate. He held her in his quaking hands, unable to cast her into the abyss.

"There's such a thing as too much optimism," he said, folding her up with care and stowing her in a drawer. "Always have a back-up plan," he added, patting the closed dresser.

Just in case.

21

DABNEY WAS IN his usual spot, selecting a suitable chunk to lob. When he found one that felt right, conformed to the hollow of his palm, he inched closer to the edge and scoped out the scene below, looking for a target. In his day he'd been a fair hand at amateur pitching and darts, so even though nine times out of ten he'd pick a target and miss, he at least liked to make the effort. He spotted a likely candidate, a slightly rotund one seemingly stuck in one spot. From Dabney's vantage point he couldn't see why, but the corpulent corpse's spilt entrails had tethered it to the base of a nearby streetlamp, further anchored by the feet of its companions. Whatever the reason, it stood perfectly still, even as its cohorts shambled aimlessly around it.

Dabney rotated his wrist a couple of times to loosen up, then chucked the brick, admiring its graceful arc as it plummeted across the avenue, then delighting in the unexpected as it collapsed the skull of its intended target. The fat zombie disappeared as it sank into the crowd. Dabney chuckled as he opened a can of Mandarin orange slices and took a swig of the tangy syrup, the small, soft wedges of citrus brushing against his lips. He swished the liquid around in his mouth, savoring the sweetness. He remembered when, as a boy, he'd been laid low with chicken pox and then later mumps, and how his mother had given him dishes of Mandarin orange slices as a treat. They'd perked him up then just as they perked him up now, but thinking of his momma added a touch of grief and he put down the can and let out a mournful noise. "Oh, Momma," he sighed, then took in a big mouthful of preserved fruit.

"Why'd you do that?"

Dabney nearly did a spit-take, unaware he had company. He spun around and saw the girl. He was the only one in the building who hadn't met her yet.

"You startled me," he said, smoothing his features.

"Sorry." She didn't sound or look sorry, but she didn't seem sarcastic either. She wasn't looking at Dabney, but rather the space beyond the edge of the roof. She repeated, "Why'd you do that?"

"Do what?"

"Throw the brick."

"The brick? Oh, it's something to do. Gives 'em something to chew on besides us."

The girl contemplated his answer, then stepped over to the ledge and peered down, the toes of her boots resting right on the lip. Dabney began to sweat. "You ain't planning on doing anything rash, are you, miss?" he asked. "Uh, miss? What's your name, again?" He said *again*, but he didn't know in the first place. For the first time since he'd arrived he felt out of the loop and rude, to boot. He should have come down and introduced himself. Thanked her. These tasty citrus slivers had come courtesy of this spooky little white girl and he hadn't the manners to let her know he felt much obliged. He was too taken with his self-appointed role as The Roof-Man, like some powerless superhero, or enigmatic loner, or plain old antisocial oddball.

"Mona," she replied.

"Mona," he repeated. "Well, Mona, you're not thinking of doing anything foolish are you?"

"Like what?" she asked.

The feeling of déjà vu struck Dabney, this scene less heightened than Karl's would-be jumper scenario, but weirder. Karl had been in an agitated snit. This girl was quiescent as a newborn at her momma's teat.

Stop thinking about Momma, Dabney thought.

"Your standing right on the edge has me a little nervous is all," he said. "Maybe you oughta come away from there and let's get introduced. My name's John Dabney. Most visitors to my roof just address me as Dabney, but either will do. And I guess technically it's not *my* roof, per se, but I sort of think of it that way." He felt foolish running his mouth but didn't stop. "I guess I owe you an apology, Mona." He paused, hoping he'd engaged her, waiting for the stock response that didn't come. The buzzing of flies filled the pause with white noise. *Why was it called* white *noise?* Dabney wondered. White neighbors. White noise. He blinked back to the moment, looking at the girl who hadn't moved an inch. She was stolid as a figurehead on the prow of a ship, expression blank, skin unblemished. "I owe you an apology," he repeated, trying to anchor himself in the present.

Thoughts of his seafaring days assailed him. That fat zombie sank like a ship in the ocean of ambulatory corpses. Thoughts of his momma ricocheted around his upper story, too. Maybe those orange slices were spoiled. No. They tasted just fine. Delicious. He'd smoked hashish many moons ago, while in Tangiers. He'd sampled peyote and psilocybin mushrooms while out west. This was the way of the mind and Dabney didn't pretend to know what he was all about, least of all on a neuron-by-neuron basis. It was the girl, maybe. Dabney was used to dilapidated specimens like Ellen and Ruth, even though they barely ever visited his domain. To see a healthy female so spectral was putting the whim-whams on him. She turned to face him and sat down, crossing her ankles, still not making eye contact. Relief flooded Dabney. Even if it weren't his fault, had the girl tumbled off he'd have felt responsible—at least partially. Worse yet, the others might tar him with a grief-stricken guilty brush. The only thing worse than having no luck was to get some then lose it just like that.

"What for?" she asked.

"Huh?"

"The apology." Stated with unblinking eyes. She was looking in his direction, but several inches below his head. It made Dabney think that he'd spilled on his shirt. As if that mattered. He looked down at his chest and felt foolish for doing so. Her stare seemed to be not at his chest, but through it. He snapped out of his momentary trance.

"Oh, *oh.* Oh, for not introducing myself earlier. For not showing my appreciation for the wonderful food you brought us. I should have come down and said thank you. I would have. I don't wish to make excuses, it's just ..." Dabney trailed off and considered his next words with care. He was aware his tone had taken on an affected formality. He wondered whether this was psychological or whether this girl was, indeed, uncanny. He felt weird in her presence. He looked at her and though dressed in black and solidly built it was she that seemed transcendental. Only not. *The fuck?* "I hope you don't take this the wrong way, 'cause I mean no disrespect, but, uh, how come those things don't attack you like everyone else?"

At the directness of his question, she squirmed almost imperceptibly. Almost. Her eyes were downcast, open yet occluded. Unreadable. She inhaled slowly through her nose, exhaled likewise.

"Guess they don't like me."

Dabney looked at her, waiting for the rest, but that's all there was. No further elaboration. The statement lay there like roadkill. As he waited for something more, she got up and with no adieu drifted back into the stairwell, the door hushing shut behind her.

Dabney stared into the half empty can of orange slices.

Or was it half full?

"We need to send Mona out for more supplies," Alan said. "Specifically *toilet paper.* I don't mean to be disgusting or anything, but just as with great power comes great responsibility, so too does food come with an unfortunate byproduct. Not that responsibility is unfortunate but ... All I'm saying is ..." Alan moaned from behind the closed door, tossing the crap-smeared wad of newsprint out the bedroom window—there was no window in the bathroom. Only a couple of broadsheets remained of his last copy of *The New York Times.* "Who'd ever think you could be sentimental about something like toilet paper? Or moist butt-wipes? Yeah, those!"

"Agreed," Ellen replied. She knew just how he felt. Unlike the rabbit pellets she was used to producing, all those victuals had gotten her innards producing again, and it wasn't pretty.

"I mean, it's bad enough hanging your ass out the window, but to then sandpaper yourself is the icing on the cake," Alan continued with an audible wince. "So to speak. It's all so medieval."

"Enough already," Ellen said, hurrying away from the closed portal. "We need to have a building meeting and compile a list of necessities, provided of course that Mona's zombie repelling wasn't some fluke and that she's even willing to go out there and do it again. So, I'll get some paper, and top of the list will be sanitary wipes."

"*Huzzah,*" Alan shouted. "Thank you!"

Alan vacated the window and looked around for anything else to tidy with. Maybe Mona would come through with the goods, but until then he needed to do something. As depressing as the *Times* was to read, it was twice as bad to wipe with.

A year or two ago Alan had undergone a minor surgical procedure and had been given an overnight basket by the hospital staff, mostly dull items like a cheapo toothbrush, travel-size toothpaste, a packet of generic facial tissues. But the highlight was a pump-spray bottle of *Personal Cleanser.* Friends would come by and he'd amuse them with its label, which bluntly proclaimed it to be "No-rinse, one-step cleansing for the perineum or body" containing "Gentle surfactants [to] aid in the removal of urine and feces." He'd brought it home as a goof, but it had made his life far more bearable over the last several weeks. When he'd moved in with Ellen, he gallantly shared the last few spritzes with her, and now he almost wished he hadn't.

Oh, for those gentle surfactants.

Alan felt distinctly unclean. He felt like some tormented Bible character, which was already easy to do given the state of the world. But this was more personal. He rummaged through a nearby drawer and filched a pinkish baby-T and completed his hygiene ritual. The soft cotton-poly blend did a better job and was much kinder. Satisfied he'd done the best he could, he lobbed it out the window to join the *Times* in the alley. Hopefully Ellen wouldn't mind or even notice that he'd used a garment of hers.

Then it hit him.

Oh fuck me.

Oh double fuck me twice.

Not hers. This wasn't some hipster baby-T, it was an *actual* T-shirt that had belonged to her baby, no doubt imbued with all manner of sentimental value. Perspiration began to pour off his forehead.

Oh goddammit.

As a child, Alan and his mother had been invited by a coworker of hers to spend a weekend at the workmate's cabin in Upstate New York. The work chum was a charming man, but wee Alan disliked him, assuming this weekend getaway was a pretext to put the moves on Alan's divorcee mother. Little had unworldly seven-year-old Alan realized the guy was gay. After dinner, his tiny innards riled up by emotion, Alan excused himself, then raced into the guest bathroom. After several fitful and productive minutes he found himself confronted with an absence of toilet paper. Panicked, sweaty, sore-bottomed from the torrential outburst and too humiliated to cry out for toilet paper, he searched the tiny rustic chamber in vain for anything to wipe with. He ended up using a flowery lavender hand towel, which he balled up and tossed out the window. In a private after-dinner moment Alan fled outside and buried the evidence of his shame in the adjacent woods, further spooked by woodland critters creeping about nearby. Weeks later the coworker asked his mother if she had accidentally packed the towel with her things.

Hopefully Ellen wouldn't notice.

"I want batteries," Karl said, clutching his lifeless boombox. "Lots of batteries."

"Maybe some of those emergency lights, like for when there's a blackout. It would be awesome to have light after dark again. To read without eyestrain? That would be amazing," Alan chimed in, Ellen playing secretary and jotting down all the suggestions. All but Mona had gathered in Ellen's sweltering apartment.

"Hey, what about one of those camping generators?" Dave said.

"Good one," Eddie said, slapping Dave's back.

"I'd like some fresh razors. Oh, since we're talking batteries, how's about some of those electric shavers?" Abe suggested, earning him appreciative *oohs* and *ahhs* from the hairy-faced men in the room.

"And a hair clipper," Dave said, ruffling his scraggy hair. "And please oh please oh please, some fuckin' *beer*. 'Scuse the language," he added, looking at Ruth's reproachful expression.

"Eventually, and I know it's not a necessity, but maybe some art supplies," Alan said.

"Yeah, like you said, '*not a necessity*,'" Eddie sneered. "So chill on that shit, Picasso." Since Alan stopped furnishing him with custom whacking matter Eddie had ceased to be an art lover.

"Slow down," Ellen said. The list was getting pretty long. The basic necessities were more non-perishable foodstuffs, fresh water, moist butt-wipes as well as traditional toilet paper, soap, toothpaste, dental floss and dental rinses, more candles and flashlights, and deodorant. "I don't know how many trips Mona is going to want to make."

"Hey, if she's immune to those things, what else has she got on her schedule?" Eddie snapped. "We makin' her miss her soaps? *Pfff.*"

"Yes, the exercise will do her good," agreed Ruth, earning her a rare smirk of approbation from Eddie.

Ellen's pen ground to a halt.

"What the fucking fuck. Are we all fucking kidding, here?" All eyes locked on Ellen. Ruth's mouth hung open, about to protest, which Ellen waved away with an admonishing flourish. "And who says she wants to be our little errand girl at our beck and call?" Ellen countered. "Who's to say she won't look at this, go '*the hell with these a-holes*' and hightail it out of here, list in hand, gone, gone, gone?"

"You're the one suggested we have this confab and make a list," Eddie said, each syllable thick with resentment.

"Why so negative?" Alan asked.

"Yeah, control your woman, Zotz," Eddie added, earning a sharp glare from both.

"Moving on," Ellen said, "I just don't want to overwhelm the girl by being too greedy. We have a very good thing with Mona and I don't want us to turn into a bunch of jackals who drive her off with our yard-long shopping list."

"Girlies love to shop," Eddie said.

Ellen ignored him and reviewed the list. "Okay, in terms of needs versus wants, this is a semi-reasonable list. But how's she supposed to carry all this?"

"She could take my shopping cart," Ruth suggested.

"Old ladies and their shopping carts," Eddie scoffed.

"I don't see you making any useful contributions to this discussion," Ruth bristled.

"Maybe she could boost a car," Eddie said. "I could tell her how." No one was surprised that Eddie possessed this know-how.

"You think if she knew how to drive she'd be hoofing it?" Karl said. "Besides, all the wrecks and abandoned vehicles down there would make it tough going."

"Kenny Irwin Jr. was doing alright until he pancaked himself. Or did we forget his smash 'em up guest shot?" Eddie flicked a Dorito into his mouth and crunched for emphasis.

"Maybe she could just take the shopping cart from the market. It's not like anyone will mind," Alan threw in. Nods all around.

"One more thing," Eddie ventured. "*Guns.*"

"*Ooh,* I don't know," said Ellen, with a slight wince.

"What don't you know? Guns'd come in mighty useful on those fuckers out there."

"How? You can't shoot them all. We'd still be stuck here."

"We should have guns," Eddie reiterated.

"I wouldn't hate a rifle," Dabney agreed.

"It would be sport shooting, nothing more," Ellen added.

"So?" Eddie said.

"So what's the point? I don't like the thought of guns in the building."

Typical patronizing Upper East Side Jewy liberal, Eddie thought. What Ellen thought was, *I don't like the thought of* you *having guns, Eddie Tommasi. Too dangerous for the rest of us chickens.*

"Just ask her, okay?" Eddie said, smoothing his features. "Let her be the judge. She brings 'em back, great. She doesn't, so be it."

"Fine," Ellen said as she tilted the pad and pantomimed writing it down.

Having omitted Eddie's request for firearms, Ellen handed over the list and asked, "Is that too much, Mona?" She'd decided to always address the girl by name when speaking to her. Her theory was that maybe she'd had her sense of identity eroded by walking amongst the undead for however long she'd been out there on her own.

"It's okay," Mona mumbled, folding the slip of paper and tucking it in her pocket.

"And you're cool with going back out there, Mona? We don't want to pressure you. You know how much we appreciate this, right? It's like a miracle."

"No big."

And with that she wedged the earbuds in—her signature gesture—and rappelled out the window via the ratty rope they'd used to haul her in. When she touched down on the roof of Dabney's ruined van she looked up at Ellen and the others, all of whom wore the expectant look of latchkey kids afraid mommy would never return.

"Getting new rope, too," she said, dangling the frayed end.

The others nodded and Mona climbed off the vehicle, the zombies spreading out with a sibilant chorus of reproach. As she headed north towards Eighty-sixth, her vapid Hello Kitty knapsack looking back at them with its beady black eyes, the throng opened and closed, a long wide mouth that couldn't devour this one small girl. When she turned the corner everyone but Abe, the self-appointed lookout, exited 2B. Abe sat in one of the tasteful mid-century modern chairs and watched as the zombies settled down, some still hissing and spitting like rabid bipedal cats. He pawed his scruffy chin, images of cranky and crotchety cowboy sidekicks floating in his mind. All he needed was to be stirring a pot o' beans on an open fire to complete the picture, and now, with this Mona girl, the pot o' beans was attainable.

That's who I look like, Abe mused. *A Jewish Gabby Hayes. Well, not after I shave off this soup-strainer. Oh, I can't wait.* He leaned on the windowsill and his smile faded, his stomach soured. From this same vantage point he'd watched this apartment's previous tenant, Paolo, get devoured down below.

Abe hoped Mona could remove that stigma from this empty dwelling.

22

THE SUN WAS setting and although there was plenty of food in the building, Ellen couldn't stop herself from looking out the window every few minutes. This wasn't about food, anyway. If anything, at this moment having a full stomach just stoked her agita.

"You're gonna wear a groove into the floor," Alan said, in a poor attempt to break the tension.

"I'm just worried, okay? Am I allowed to be worried? She left hours ago and it's almost dark. Maybe something happened to her. Maybe she isn't immune and it was some fluke and we sent her out there and now she's dead. And if that's the case then it's all our fault and we're responsible for sending a young girl to her death."

Alan opened his mouth to say something and then shut it. He'd already paid lip service to Ellen's anxiety and it had done no good. It was troubling that Mona had been gone for the better part of the day. He'd posited several plausible scenarios. It was possible that several items on the list had proven more difficult to procure than others and that Mona was traipsing all around town in an attempt to accommodate every request. It was also possible that she had forgotten her way back, even though she had neatly printed the address of the building in big block letters. Maybe she lost the list. It was imaginable that she had gotten to one of her destinations and gotten jammed up by the zombies—*but that she was all right.* She was just temporarily waylaid and would be back soon. For Ellen's sake he had to keep the propositions upbeat.

But it was also quite reasonable to assume that Mona had been devoured.

He also couldn't help but wonder if there were other survivors out there, ones not as desperate and pathetic as the ones here. What might such folks do if they encountered a, let's face it, very trusting unicorn like Mona?

Ellen's eyes darted back and forth from the street below to the sky above, each growing darker and more ominous. She wound her hair around her fingers and chewed the ends. Alan again attempted levity by suggesting she'd get split ends doing that but Ellen just looked at him like he was an idiot. Alan sat there internally reciting the names of hair products and quoting lines from TV commercials. *'If you don't look good, we don't look good.' Vidal Sassoon. Pantene Pro-V. Paul Mitchell. L'Oreal. What the hell was the one with those stupid commercials where girls would rub it into their scalps in public and semi-public places? And for all intents and purposes they'd be having noisy orgasms? Then they'd emerge, from like the restroom on an airplane, tousling their shimmering manes and everyone would look at them with lust and envy? What was that stuff? Some herbal something? Maybe Mona should pick up some of that. Ellen could do with some shiny locks. What kind of thinking is this? Yesterday there's no food. All that matters is potable water and food that will sustain the organism for another twenty-four hours. Now it's 'Ellen could use a nice shampoo.' I must be out of my friggin' gourd.*

"Seriously, Ellen, I'm sure she's fine."

"Oh really? You can say that authoritatively? You know that for a fact do you? How interesting. Because, see, the way I see it, none of us knows a damned thing right now and for all we know chunks of her are being digested—if those things even digest. I mean, do they? Do they shit? Do they breathe? What do they do besides stumble around and eat us when they can? They sure made short work of Mike. They gobbled him down like no tomorrow. But are there piles of zombie scat out there composed of my husband? Are there? We don't know. I don't know. None of us knows anything!"

Should I get up and hug her? Alan wondered. When he'd gotten into fights in the past with women—various girlfriends and one ex-wife—after all the sour words and recriminations and accusations and *you did this* and *you did that* it always came down to something like she just needed a hug and a kiss. Reductive, sure. But often the right move. Then it would calm down and laughter would come, then maybe, in the best of times, they'd get naked. Was this one of those occasions where a hug was the answer? Alan got up and gently placed his arms around Ellen's shoulders.

"What? *What?* You want sex now? What the hell is *wrong* with you?"

"I don't. I don't want sex," Alan stammered. "I just thought maybe a hug would ..." Why bother finishing the thought? He withdrew his arms and turned to resume his place on the couch.

"Where are you going? I didn't say I didn't want to be hugged. I just ... I'm just freaking out." She shot another glance out the window. "Maybe you *should* fuck me."

"What?"

"Did I stutter? Maybe you should fuck me. Now."

"But this wasn't about sex, honest. I swear. I wasn't being ..." Was she toying with him?

"*Just fuck me.* I need to be penetrated. I need to have something tearing my mind from Mona. But don't think about Mona while we're doing it. I know she's healthy and young and I'm not. Well, I'm young, but you know what I mean. Her body versus mine. Don't fantasize about her. Or don't think about her being torn limb from limb like chicken. You won't get an erection from a thought like that. Maybe Eddie would, but Christ, I don't want to think about what gets Eddie off."

Ellen stomped into the kitchen, shucked off her baggy shorts and cotton undies, grabbed the counter and pushed her ass out. "Do it," she commanded. Normally a take-charge woman was a turn-on, but this was a lot of pressure combined with deeply troubling extenuating circumstances. Alan dropped his pants and massaged into being a serviceable if slightly spongy erection. "Don't be gentle. Don't be slow," Ellen ordered. Such hard words. Such hard angles. Though he didn't want to think about Mona he did think about the food. Food would soon inflate everything back to normal.

Alan followed Ellen's edicts and pounded away. She gritted her teeth and bucked against his pelvis, meeting each thrust with equal force. Alan thought about stacking china. He thought about building model kits as a boy, then dropping rocks on them or blowing them up with firecrackers. He hoped their bones were up to this punishment. It had been a while since he'd run out of vitamins. How was his calcium? How was Ellen's? They should have added a good multivitamin to the list. And Jesus, lots of items from the pharmacy. What were they thinking? Just food and batteries? They'd been discussing keeping it to necessities. What could be more necessary than vitamins and headache remedies? Some pink bismuth. And not store-brand. Pepto Bismol. Or Pepcid AC! Some anti-diarrheal. Oh yeah, that's hot stuff. That's the stuff of a *Penthouse* letter. Why not just start contemplating osteoporosis? Or scoliosis? Or any other bone-wrecking -osis?

This was very odd. This wasn't a hate fuck. Alan had only experienced that phenomenon once or twice in his past, especially with his ex-wife. This wasn't like that exactly, but it was certainly angsty. And very aggressive. Ellen snapped her head back and her hair whipped across his face.

"Clairol," he said, slapping his forehead. "Clairol Herbal Essence!"

"What?"

"Nothing," he said, feeling lava pump into his face. He smacked her ass and pumped harder to throw off the scent of his wandering mind. After several more minutes of violent hammering he climaxed. His knees and thighs immediately turned to jelly and he sank to the floor. Ellen slumped beside him. She pressed her head against his chest and murmured, "Hold me."

So, yeah, a hug.

And as he ran his fingers through her oily hair he silently mouthed, *Clairol Herbal Essence.*

February, *Then*

It had been two weeks earlier that Ellen had teased Alan as he trudged up the stairs, Bataan Death March-style, with case after case of bottle water. Nothing had really happened yet—certainly not on the level into which it would blossom—but Alan's girlfriend, Tammy, had convinced him that preparedness wasn't anything to scoff at. So there he'd been, doing the lion's share of lugging, wishing for an elevator.

"All you need are some camouflage fatigues and a headband," Ellen smirked as he approached her on the landing, her infant daughter Emily suckling a full, barely veiled breast. Though Alan found nothing sexy about nursing—lactation was not a kink he found appealing—he was enamored of Ellen Swenson's boobs, and any peek was welcome. Tammy, tart-tongued and efficient, was all nipple and no tit, her chest a smooth plain of milky white skin dotted with two pencil eraser-sized pink protrusions. Though not in love with Tammy, Alan was fond of her, but he craved suppleness and Ellen had it. He blinked away his lewd thoughts and refocused on Ellen's eyes.

"Huh?" Despite the temperature outside, his face was awash in perspiration.

"You and the gal-pal are really kicking into prepper mode."

Alan eased the cases to the ground with a thud and panted, "Better safe than sorry. That's Tammy's philosophy."

"It's just some infected rats," Ellen countered. "They'll be dead in no time. You've seen all the open manholes everywhere."

"Yeah, I know. Between the rats and the noxious fumes, driving back with the supplies was a bitch."

"You keep a car in the city?" With all that was going on, *that* was what Ellen marveled at. It made Alan smile. These were the real concerns of New Yorkers. Not swarms of rats biting and infecting commuters down in the subway and pedestrians on the street. Not crews in hazmat suits probing the city's subterranean infrastructure for the last two weeks, pumping who knows what kind of toxic gas down there in hopes of obliterating the ferocious rodents. Not people either stumbling around hacking in each other's faces looking like death warmed over or sporting N95 respirators. Where you parked: *that* was a thing at which to marvel.

"Tammy keeps it in Brooklyn. It's her car."

"Ah," Ellen said. "*Brooklyn.* Remember when Manhattan was the place to be? Now it's Brooklyn."

"Now it's Brooklyn," Alan agreed.

That exchange had been two weeks ago. Now, Alan was side by side with Mike, Ellen's husband, hammering nails into planks of plywood to further buttress the closed-off entranceway to their building. Over the clatter of their work Mike shouted, "This doesn't bode well!"

"What?" Alan stopped hammering, as did Mike.

"This. This doesn't bode well. Us sealing ourselves in, FEMA barricading the only exit; this doesn't look like it's gonna be resolved anytime soon."

"Soon?" Alan replied, taking a breath.

"Yeah, soon. I've got faith. This'll blow over. Everything does. A monsoon hits, people die. Still, life goes on, normalcy resumes. Tsunamis. Collapsed levees. Earthquakes. This'll blow over. New York's a tough town. But soon? Maybe not."

Alan nodded at Mike's hopeful platitudes but wasn't buying. And anyway, according to the news, New York wasn't alone in this predicament. This was global.

"I tried to load up on reserves," Mike continued, "but it was pretty picked over at D'ag's and Gristedes. I don't get why Food City closed up so soon. What's that all about?"

"Maybe 'cause it's not a chain," Alan posited. "The owners probably just took what they needed and booked."

"Maybe," Mike allowed. "Should've taken it more serious when all the toilet paper disappeared. Still, I think we're pretty well stocked. I think if we pushed it we could go a month, but *that's* not gonna happen." Mike smiled without conviction and looked to Alan for reassurance. Alan smiled, but his thoughts were of his closet heaving with toilet paper and canned goods. "We'll be fine. London during the Blitz and so on. We'll be okay," Mike nattered.

Alan closed his eyes and drifted inward, Tammy's face imprinted in the darkness behind his eyelids. Phone service had been spotty at best and it wounded him that she and he had parted badly. Right after the Costco trip they'd had a nasty public fight and after he'd finished hiking his half of the supplies up to his apartment she'd screeched, "Don't thank me all at once you fuckin' prick. *Aw,* your arms hurt, your poor, delicate, artist's arms. *Aw,* you got a fuckin' callous on your precious digits?" She'd grabbed his wrist and waggled his drawing hand, which she'd named Arty. The other was Wipey. "*Arty* will be fine, *princess.* And you'll be fuckin' glad I'm 'an alarmist', asshole! Mark my fuckin' words! You and your fuckin' mom! Because I really wanted to drive all the way out to fuckin' Queens today to deliver more fuckin' emergency goods! Fuck. You." She'd slammed into her Honda CR-V and sped off and though they'd since made up via texts, that was their last in-person contact. Phone lines were tied up or nonoperational. Cell service? Spotty. And now the Internet was iffy, too. Overtaxed.

Even though Tammy had stocked up equally, Alan wished she'd stayed, not because of that but because she was on the ground floor of a private house in Bay Ridge. He thought of the Three Little Pigs, he residing in the brick house, she in the wood. At least it wasn't straw. He suspected he'd never hear her voice again. He also thought, tempestuous or not, it would be nice to quarantine with someone, especially someone female.

Tammy's face rippled away, replaced by Ellen's. Alan wasn't sure why but he always went for tart women (as opposed to women who were tarts). Ellen, whose serial hallway flirtatiousness—*especially* since she'd had the baby—always seemed seasoned with a smidgen of sarcasm, was close to Alan's ideal, at least physically. At the moment, convinced he'd never know the touch of a woman again, Alan resented Mike. He resumed hammering, then stopped, sighed, and gave Mike's arm a gentle squeeze.

"I'm taking you into my confidence, Mike. I'm serious, no fucking around."

"Okay."

"Seriously, Mike. This is life or death stuff here."

"I know, I know. This is super serious."

"No. This isn't just fortification, Mike. We're sealing ourselves into our crypt. The cavalry isn't coming for us."

"Sure they are."

Alan looked deep into Mike's worried, wearied, eyes. People with kids had to think positive. "No, Mike, they're *not.* This is it."

"You artistic types are so gloom and doom," Mike said without judgment. "I don't roll like that. It's a disaster, granted, but people rally. Maybe we batten down the hatches and wait, but—"

"Fine, cling to your illusion, but," and here Alan lowered the volume to a barely audible whisper, "I've got plenty of supplies. Tammy and I bought a buttload."

"Yeah, Ellen mentioned you were stocked up."

"Not so loud," Alan hissed. "I'm offering—*so long as we keep it on the QT*—you and Ellen some of my stuff. Water, canned goods, whatever. You've got a kid to feed. But it's between us. I don't want the others to know. I can't feed everyone."

Conspiratorial, Mike nodded and then threw his arms around Alan, his voice cracking. "We're fucked, aren't we?" He began to sob and Alan, ensnared by the other man's limbs, mourned the death of Mike's optimism. He thought about his last exchange with his mother—and it was a *last* exchange, with her Luddite tendencies and shunning computers and the Internet even when Alan had offered both so she could be more connected. She of the landline and kitchen wall phone. There's one sound no child ever wants to hear and that's the sound of a parent frightened. His mother's final words to him, choked and perforated by little intakes of air, trying so hard not to cry, to be strong for her boy, were, "I'm afraid."

I'm afraid.

Those two words made it all real for Alan. Not the news. Not the panic on the street. *I'm afraid.* He wanted to comfort her but it was impossible. Now he couldn't get to her. A lifelong Mama's Boy and he was trapped, travel between boroughs prohibited. In that moment his insides turned to liquid.

"Mom," he'd begun.

The line went wild, wailed electronically, died.

He'd held his phone like it was imbued with the essence of his mother. It had held her voice, a voice he'd probably never hear again. Why hadn't he stayed with her at the onset? Or brought her here? Because he'd been dumb enough to think this would pass, too. Just like the media had encouraged him to think. Downplayed. Minimized. He just held his phone and stared at it.

The thought of his mom, alone and terrified.

His mom, the rock. The tough lady.

Yeah, Alan thought now, eyes stinging and wet, *we are so fucked.*

August, *Now*

Karl and Dabney lay on the tarp, the brick pile untouched. Both were eyeballing the crowd below, awaiting the return of Mona, both psyched to see her Moses schtick again. Between them were a couple of empty cans, one cling peach slices in light syrup, and the other string beans. Both men were happy and felt a sort of father and son companionability. Dabney rolled onto his side and belched, the gassy reflux sweetened by the aftertaste of peaches. In direct response, Karl let out a melodious fart and both men laughed. Their spirits were fine and low comedy wasn't beneath them.

"Did you like *Blazing Saddles*?" Karl asked.

"Why, 'cause it had a black sheriff?"

"No, because it had farting. That scene by the campfire, all those cowboys eating beans and letting off."

"Oh, yeah. That." Dabney chuckled, feeling foolish for having thought this was some well-intentioned attempt at ebony and ivory bonding. It just had to do with passing gas, something everyone could enjoy. Why was he feeling stuck on race? The only races that mattered now were humans versus zombies. Skin color was passé.

But still he was abundantly aware, at least since the Latin guy met his brutal end, that he was the lone person of color here.

And plagued with regret that his van never made it home.

He'd lived in public housing, a honeycomb of ten fourteen-story buildings. When he and Bernice first moved in, all manner of mayhem went down up there. Project rats—the human kind, not the rodent kind—whose idea of fun was setting small fires in the elevators and stairwells. Graffiti. Litter. Noise on top of noise. Every time his wife went out after hours he was nervous that she might not come home or would get molested or what have you—no matter how many times she assured him that other men didn't lust for her the way he did. Bernice. Over time things improved. The climate changed for the better. *Then* …

"Yorkville's about as white a neighborhood as you can get. Not saying I haven't been made to feel welcome—except for Tommasi; he's made his feelings plain. But do I belong here? I do not. Yet here I am. And anyway, who knows what's out there for me. Probably nothing."

"You don't know that."

"I suppose I don't. Which makes it worse."

If you hadn't picked me up maybe you would have …" Karl couldn't finish.

Dabney reached over a ruffled the younger man's hair.

"What'd you do that for?" Karl asked, trading guilt for confusion.

"Never ruffled a white boy's hair before."

"You're not getting all funny on me now, are you, Dabney?"

Dabney chuckled. "Not if you and I were the last two folks on earth, son. I'm just missing my own boys and they didn't exactly have the kind of hair you could ruffle."

"You had sons?"

"Two, plus a girl. Both boys grown, left home. I like to think maybe Johnny, my eldest, might be alive—he left the city. Days before I ended up stranded here I spoke to my youngest, my girl, on my cell phone, but she couldn't make it back to town. And I don't even have a picture of any of them to torment me. Had a ton on my phone but that's dead, like everything else." Silence hung between the two men, neither articulating the thought that Dabney's offspring were likely dead, too. Dabney looked down at the roof of his van. "No one ever calls the locksmith when they're having a good day. Or seldom, anyway. Sometimes it's 'cause they got a new apartment, but mostly it's they've been robbed. So you're another intrusion. Another violation of their space."

"You're not violating anyone's space."

"Maybe. Least not while I stay up here."

"That's your choice."

"Yeah, well. At any rate, I hope that Mona comes back soon."

"Me too."

"Is she back yet?"

At Ruth's grating query Abe shuddered to wakefulness, slapping a fly off his nose. He'd dozed off, the constant ache of hunger no longer there to keep him vigilant. Just like the good old days, after a thick pastrami and tongue sandwich from Second Avenue Deli, he'd grown slumberous on a full belly.

"You were sleeping?" Ruth's voice rose, her tone accusatory. "*Ucch*, Abraham, you're given one simple task, to keep an eye out for our fairy goddaughter, and you botched it."

"It's not like I fell asleep on purpose!" He lifted himself off the chair, numbness blossoming to painful prickling in his quaking legs, and hobbled off to pee in the bucket in defiance of his prostate. "If she came back she'd have said something. I would have heard. What, I'm the only one around here who can keep a lookout? If she came back she'd call up, wouldn't she? Hah?"

"Who knows? She's an odd girl. Quiet. I tried to talk to her and it was very uncomfortable. I think maybe she's a little mental or something. And anyway, don't go blaming everyone else. You volunteered to keep an eye out for her."

"Yeah, yeah, yeah." Abe shook off the last few burning droplets and zipped up, wishing he'd asked Mona to pick up some Flomax for his prostate; maybe next time, if there was one. He maintained his ornery posture but he knew he'd screwed up. He'd admit it to almost anyone but Ruth; she took too much pleasure in seeing him fail. How long had she been watching him slumber? It would be just like her to watch him rather than the street below, just to needle him for having blown his responsibility.

"No, not 'whatever.' You had an important task. Maybe a *younger person* should do it. I thought you were at *least* capable of doing a job that involved basically *sitting around* doing *almost nothing*, but apparently *nothing* is the only part of that you're actually *qualified* for anymore." Her pointy voice lanced through his ears.

Abe exited the bathroom with the sloshing bucket and fought the urge to empty its contents on his fishwife's head. With all the dignity he could muster he padded by across the moth-eaten Oriental rug and tossed his amber-colored discharge out the front window. The last vestiges of light faded, darkness returned, Mona didn't.

"This is not good," Abe muttered as he lit a candle. "This is not good at all."

"So where is she?" Ruth said, her voice small.

"Like I know. Like suddenly I'm the Amazing Kreskin." Abe looked at Ruth's face. Even in the shadows it was obvious she was more than upset. She wasn't hollering and screeching and fussing and nagging. She was silent. Abe shuffled over to her and held her, pressing her balding pate against him. It would be too cruel if Mona didn't come back, but life was nothing if not immeasurably cruel. He patted his wife's back gently and tried to make his assurances sound heartfelt. Even if Mona didn't come back, the coffers were well-stocked. They'd last a few more weeks. He kept petting Ruth, hoping the tears leaking out of his eyes wouldn't drip on her. Then the jig would be up.

"I can't believe that little bitch ditched," Eddie muttered to himself.

That's what he said, but he could *totally* believe it. Why the fuck would *anyone* voluntarily stay with a bunch of losers like the ones in this building? Eddie yearned to be someplace else. There had to be other survivors, somewhere. Pockets of tough motherfuckers holed up, giving the zombies what for—*real* men with guns and weapons. That totally sucked about this bunch. No weapons. Sure, some kitchen knives, even a couple of professional grade meat cleavers, but no guns. If Eddie'd stayed in Bensonhurst he'd have access to plenty of fuckin' guns, but here on the Upper East Side? Please.

What had he been thinking moving up here?

Okay, so he'd enjoyed the bar scene on York Avenue. He'd nailed a lot of slim high-maintenance Jewesses on his innumerable pub-crawls and contrary to stereotype, those women sure knew how to put out. Eddie had thought Italian chicks like the ones in his old neighborhood were proficient, but they were rank amateurs compared to the JAPs he'd scored with 'round these parts.

In Brooklyn, as a Catholic stalling act to keep the cherry intact until wedding day, pretty much everything else was up for negotiation. What a joke. In cars, attics and basements, in stairwells and on rooftops, in all the clandestine locales available to him in his youth he'd done everything *but* get in the front bottom. He'd lost his own cherry, so to speak, at fifteen to a sixteen-year-old she-devil named Roxanne who perched in her bedroom window and smoked menthols and taunted and teased all the neighborhood boys. Eddie thought she'd singled him out for her affections, but it turned out she'd done every kid on the block, and some from not on the block, and some from Borough Park, and some from Bath Beach, and some from as far as Bay Ridge. And some who weren't even so young, like her uncles and cousins.

And so Eddie formed the opinion that maybe the fairer sex were nothing but whores, like his pops implied in a not so subtle fashion when addressing Eddie's mother as such. Eddie's mother was such a flirt it was easy to see why his pops drank and on occasion showed her the back of his hand. She didn't fight back much, maybe a little harsh language, but she knew she was guilty of whatever and besides, why screw up a good thing? She had a nice house and a nice car. Eddie's sister Patty, though. She was a tramp, no doubt.

So anyway, here he was, in a limp-dick neighborhood, bereft of quim, settling for blowjobs from his former Ice Knights teammate. *Go Rutgers.* Dave had gone full-homo and there was nothing to do about it. The facts were the facts. Look no further than Dave's complete lack of interest in the spooky little shorty who'd shown up and brought home the bacon. And Dave harshing on him for wanting to tap that ass? Whatever. The little chick was probably never coming back anyway, so Eddie would make do.

He stepped away from the widow. Any port in a storm.

"Yo, Dave ..."

23

THREE IN THE morning, give or take. Moans of brain-dead protest accompanied by regular knifelike squeaks of a wheel in need of a spritz of WD-40. The squeaks increasing in pitch and loudness, and then silenced. The inhuman groaning continues, growing in fervor. The strike of a match, the smell of sulfur followed by paraffin, and then barely audible bare-footfalls creeping across bare floorboards.

Alan slid the front window open the whole way and looked down at York. Standing in the center of the aperture of the crowd of spread-out zombies stood Mona, looking up at the building, nodding her head in time with whatever tune she was mainlining. Alan just looked down at her for a moment, waiting for her to call out and announce her return. But she didn't. She just stood there leaning her forearms on the push bar of the extra-large shopping cart she'd liberated from wherever, the cart overstuffed.

The crowd was well illuminated, Mona having affixed a high intensity dual-beam LED flashlight to the front of her cart. In the shockingly bright cool white light, the faces of the undead looked especially ghastly. Every deformity, every laceration, every cluster of rot underscored by deep dramatic shadows, like the ultimate campfire ghost-storyteller. During the day the zombies kind of blended into an undifferentiated earthen-toned mass, but now, lit up in the dark, deep black shadows separating them like bold outlines in a woodcut, each one boasted a uniquely disturbing visage.

Alan fought the urge to grab a pencil and begin sketching, but he studied these specimens, making mental notes. One in particular caught his eye, a female with its head dangling backwards from some hideous past injury. Its deadened eyes stared up at him—or at least in his general direction—and Alan found himself craning his head upside down to make out the face.

Gerri!

"Holy shit," Alan gasped. He'd wondered where she'd gotten off to and here was his answer. *When did this happen?* Before he could get dizzy he righted the angle of his head and looked again at Mona. Finally she glanced up and saw him in the window and gave a minimal wave. Alan gestured for her to stay put, then scampered into the bedroom and roused Ellen with an urgent whisper-hissed, "Mona's back!"

Ellen lay there for a second or two, then sprang up like a Jack-in-the-box.

"*What?*"

"Mona. She's downstairs. We gotta help her unload the cart and get her back inside."

Ellen bolted off the bed, stark naked, and headed for the door.

"Uh, Ellen?" Alan said, gesturing at his own unclothed body. Within seconds both had thrown on shorts and shirts and bolted down to 2B. When they reached the front windows Mona had changed position. She now sat in the lotus position on the roof of Dabney's van, another flashlight in her lap, the beam fanning across SERVING ALL FIVE BOROUGHS SINCE 1989. She also held a brand-new length of Day-Glo pink mountaineering rope, which she tossed up to Alan who, after a few embarrassing misses, caught it and secured it to the nearby standpipe.

Later Mona, Ellen and Alan were sharing a round of warm Pepsi around the dining table, Mona sitting on the edge of her chair, her Hello Kitty backpack mashed against the backrest.

"This used to be Paolo's apartment," Alan said as a conversational gambit.

Mona nodded.

"He was a good guy. He was the last one in the building to make an attempt to get some groceries. It didn't work out so well."

Mona compressed her lips like, *I get it,* without saying so.

"Unlike you. You're just crushing it," Alan said, instantly feeling stupid. He looked at the new rope and then at the old ratty one, which lay on the floor. "The new rope was also brilliant. That old one was on its last legs. If ropes had legs." Alan was sweating. "That rope was from the old super, Mr. Spiteri. Why he had it is anyone's guess. I mean, I—"

"Shouldn't we tell the others that Mona's back, safe and sound?" Ellen asked, cutting him off. His gushing was embarrassing to witness, not that Mona showed any reaction one way or the other.

"If no one came to help, guessing they're all asleep. Let 'em rest," Alan said. "They can enjoy a nice start to the day tomorrow." Alan surveyed the piles of stuff Mona had brought back. "You really did an amazing job out there. So great. Thank you."

She shrugged again, looking down at her lap.

"We were getting pretty worried, I don't mind telling you, since you were gone so long," Alan added. He wanted to stop talking but he couldn't. This unnerving girl's unnerving silence was just plain … *unnerving.* "Not that I mean to imply that we thought you should have been quicker," he added. "Far from. We just were concerned."

"Yes, Mona. Thank you. Thank you *so* much." Ellen gently placed a hand atop Mona's and gave the lightest squeeze to emphasize her gratitude, hoping Alan would take in the less-is-more approach.

"Uh-huh," Mona said, making no eye contact. Gently easing her hand out from under Ellen's. Passively delineating boundaries.

Is it just me? Ellen wondered. She looked at Mona's blank, pretty face and tried not to stare, not that Mona would notice anyway, she having closed her eyes and turned up the volume. From the tiny speakers Mona's music always sounded fast and metallic, like angry insects devouring her brains via the ear canals. Maybe that was it. Maybe all the conservative pundits had been right. Maybe heavy metal, or whatever Mona was listening to, *did* cause brain damage. Maybe Mona had numbed herself with aggressive music as a way to cope with the harsh reality of the world. Maybe, maybe, maybe. But she was among friends now. Needy friends, admittedly, but friends nonetheless. Maybe she could wean Mona off the tunes—no cold turkey, no need for anything that dramatic, but some nice music to set the tone. *Oh my God,* Ellen thought. *I'm turning into my mother. What, some nice Barry Manilow? Some Michael Bolton? Get a grip.*

"Check this out!" Alan cried as he held up a cardboard box. In the murk Ellen couldn't make it out, so he read off the box. "'Solar Hand Crank Emergency Lantern'. It's a camping lamp. You crank it and voila. How cool is that? She brought back ..." he quick counted, "*six* of the suckers."

Clutching the box, Alan hastened back to the table and planted a kiss on top of Mona's head. Mona sort of half smiled and Ellen felt a pang. *What the fuck?* she admonished herself. Taking his seat, Alan fished a lamp out of the box and squinted as he read the instructions by candlelight. Ellen could see tears well up in his eyes. *Jesus,* she thought. "It also works as a charger for small electronics," he said, his tone awestruck. "USB ..." His voice hitched. "And ... Micro USB." He began to gently weep. "I can read at night. I can work at night! How awesome is that?"

"What makes you think they're for you?" Ellen asked.

"Wha' ... Well, I, uh ..."

"I'm just teasing, Al. Relax."

Ellen threw Alan a smile that was supposed to be reassuring but came off kind of askew. She was she suddenly feeling a little mean. *Please tell me this isn't jealousy,* she thought. *Please. I can't be* that *stupid. That insecure. That stereotypically womany. Because that would really piss me off.*

Alan was about to lavish more thanks on Mona, but he could see her eyes were closed and she was nodding in time to the music. He looked over at Ellen whose own expression was ambiguous at best. Before he blurted something he'd end up regretting he sized up the situation as best he could. Two females, one hale and hearty, the other weak and wan but on the road back to wellness. Ellen's eyes were adrift and she was agitating her fingers, fidgeting, picking at the cuticles.

"Ellen?" Alan whispered. She looked over at him, her head turning in slow-mo. "You okay? What's up? Aren't you happy Mona's back? And the haul? She rocked out. I mean, solar-powered lanterns? We didn't even *think* of that. And check this out: walkie-talkies." Alan tapped his temple with an index finger. "Smart cookie," he said, bulging his eyes for comic effect. Mona opened her eyes and looked at Alan as he was making the gesture. She eased out an earbud. He felt his cheeks flush as he stammered out, "I was just remarking how savvy you were to get those solar lamps. Very cool, indeed. And I saw some freeze-dried grub, too. Outstanding."

"Had 'em same place as the rope."

Eyes heavy-lidded, glassy with disinterest and aimed at that woolly middle distance, Mona popped the bud back in and turned up the volume. She then closed her eyes and resumed gently rocking to the ungentle music.

"Wow," Alan said with a smirk, "I thought she'd never shut up."

24

EDDIE LIKED WHAT he saw as he stood before the full-length mirror on the bedroom closet door. He liked it a lot. Nude, he turned to his left and assumed a bodybuilder's pose, flexing his muscles, which were oiled with sweat, then turned to the right and did likewise. He'd taken the liberty of shaving his chest and stomach and he'd tweezed any stray hairs on his shoulders. He'd even shaved his pits and pubes. The sad excuses for men in the building had shaved their faces and Alan had gone so far as to have his woman give him a haircut, but none of them had physiques worthy of a full-body depilatory. Eddie knew he wasn't quite there yet, but soon. In the last few weeks the surfeit of food the spooky chick had furnished filled him in nicely. He'd resumed a workout regimen and Zotz had resumed a respectful distance, his smart remarks all but disappeared. Sweet.

"Oh yeah," Eddie grinned, rippling his abs. "Look at those pecs. Look at those delts." He did a half pirouette and clenched and unclenched his buttocks. "And for the piece de resistance, look at those glutes. *Marone,* what a sight to behold." He gave them an appreciative slap and then, with great reluctance, closed the closet door and stepped away.

His hair, deep black and long enough to wear in a ponytail, he now wore loose about his shoulders, Tarzan-like. He slipped on a pair of tight black Calvin Klein boxer-briefs and espadrilles, and then stepped into the common hall. Sunlight directly overhead shown down through the skylight in the stairwell housing and he gleamed. He liked the others to see his return as resident Adonis, even though he didn't know who the fuck Adonis was—just that he was buff and handsome as fuck. Well-fed and in fine fettle, the only thing lacking was *una bella fica.* Ellen was beginning to look doable again, but she was glued to that *sfigato,* Zotz. It was real fuckin' adorable the way she latched onto that pencil-pushin' pencil-neck. Made him wonder if maybe she and Zotz had been boning while she was still married to good ol' whatshisname.

Wouldn't that be fuckin' perfect?

Oh, it *totally* made sense, too. Artsy-fartsy Alan worked at home, made his own hours. Who better to have a fling with? She was on maternity leave—what a con. Have a baby, get paid to stay home, watch soaps, canoodle the neighbor. What a racket. Then, when it gets boring, snag a nanny and back to the grind. You get to be a professional woman and an amateur mom. Fuckin' women. Eddie's mom, *puttana* though she was, knew her place was in the home. Maybe she took some extra deliveries of protein paste from the odd mailman or FedEx guy, but she was a housewife. That's what a woman should do once she decides to drop a litter. Tell that to these Upper East Side chicks. *Well, now they're all fuckin' dead, so fuck 'em.*

Oh, how Eddie wished he could.

The new shorty with the mojo made him uncomfortable, though. He'd tried to engage her in some friendly chitchat, but she seemed bored. Never looked him in his big browns. How rude was that? With those earbuds stuck in her jug ears. And yeah, her ears *stuck out,* too. Like Alfalfa or Alfred E. Whatshisface. Only hot.

Eddie was beyond frustrated. That spooky little chick was always either nodding her head in tune with godawful noise, or out on errands. She was accommodating, he had to give her that. Any request and *voom,* off she went in search of. He'd asked for one of those travel DVD players and she'd brought back enough for everyone, which maybe made it seem a little less special to him, but so be it. *How fuckin' fun must that be?* he wondered. *Going into any store and boosting any shit you want?* With the combo lamp charger thingie he now had a reason to return to his old digs to retrieve his impressive cache of porn. If he couldn't have the real thing he'd make do with some spicy viddies.

He wanted to tap that ass, but you don't shit where you eat.

Or fuck where you eat.

Something like that. The time would come. She was a weirdo but she wasn't blind. Eddie remembered a TV special about this special kind of chimps called bonobos and how they had a pecking order. The top males had priority mating rights. The bonobos preferred fucking to fighting, but the males spent a lot of time intimidating their rivals for female affection. Eddie was an alpha all the way. She'd see that. Females always came around to the alpha. Soon enough he'd have the spooky chick *and* Ellen Swenson. He just had to play it smart.

As he mounted the steps, the old bitch in 5A stepped into the hall and let out a gasp as she took in his buffness. Though it creeped him out a little, he liked the thought that she'd have his physique scorched into her psyche. Imagine the horror she'd feel looking at herself by comparison. Or her shriveled, impotent husband. Hilarious.

"Can't you have the decency to put on some clothes?" she scolded.

As he passed by he stooped over, jutting his noggin like he was going to give the old bag a head-butt. She flinched in terror and he sniggered. "Just messin' with ya, *ma'am*," he said. "Chill. Why do I gotta put clothes on, anyway? It's hot as hell and so am I."

She clucked and retreated into her dwelling, locking the door behind her. It was so unfair that the females in this building were all so lame. Old and wrinkled. Braindead and spooky. Kinda hot but taken. *Taken.* Now that Ellen was looking kind of nice again it just ate away at Eddie that a little weasel like Zotz was keeping all that lovin' to himself. Wasn't it just like a Jew to hoard the precious? Zotz. That was Jewish, right? Of course it was. And in the meantime, here was Eddie, fitter than them all, plodding upstairs to cut across the roofs to get his porn. No justice.

Eddie pounded open the door to the roof with the flats of his palms, earning a startled yelp from Dabney. Good. Eddie liked spooking the *mulignan*. Reminded him of past glories. Eddie remembered one night in particular that gave him pleasure but also chafed his sac. Pleasure was the fact that he and some buddies had beaten the holy hell out of a couple of wayward black dudes that had strayed into Bensonhurst and were trying to make time with a couple of the local girls—nice *Italian* girls. Well, not *nice*, exactly, but Italian. Annoyance was because it never made the news. At least he'd gotten away clean. Going to jail would have sucked, big time.

"The hell is wrong with you, son?" Dabney hollered. "Slamming up here like that. You wanna give me a heart attack?"

As a matter of fact, Eddie thought as he stalked by, ignoring Dabney's upbraiding.

Eddie reached his old building, stepped past the pyramid of cinder blocks from some long-forsaken reno project, and headed down the fire escape to his window, still open like Dave had left it. Eddie hadn't returned since the Wandering Jewess incident. That was intense. Eddie thought about the way Dave had handled her and he felt pride swell in his chest. Dave was a *finocchio*, but still a man. The way he knocked her block off—or almost off. With an elephant's foot? Just thinking about it made him chuckle. Reminded him of *Rock 'Em Sock 'Em Robots*. Two robots pounding the bolts out of each other, one red, one blue. Eddie was always blue because his dad said red was a commie color. But then states that voted the ways Pops did became red and libtard ones blue. It got a little confusing. Anyway, it was still a cool toy.

Eddie recalled his time with Gerri. Sure she was nearly a vegetable—at least until she became the meat course—and nothing to look at, but he'd almost forgotten how nice vagina felt.

"Gotta get the porn," Eddie said. "Stay on point. Focus."

He vaulted through the apartment to his old room and threw open the door. At the foot of his bed, under a pile of clothes, was his dad's old army footlocker. He might've spurned gates, but some things needed stowing away securely, just in case. He knelt down and undid the combination lock, which opened with a sturdy pop. Inside was his treasure trove. He'd forgotten to bring a something to carry home the boodle, but nearby was his old gym bag, still overstuffed with dirty laundry. He unzipped it and dumped its contents on the floor.

"So *that's* where these were. Duh," he said, shaking his head as he put his Nike cross trainers back in the bag. He then started loading DVDs into the sack. "Physical fuckin' media," he said, like he'd been gifted the wisdom of Solomon.

As he struggled with the zipper, the bag now stuffed to bursting, he heard a sound from the living room. He ceased his activities and froze. There it was again, a soft shuffling. The Wandering Jewess had been evicted so what was this shit? With care Eddie placed the overstuffed bag on the bed and tiptoed into the hall. He held his breath and eyeballed the exit window. He was curious, but how curious? Wasn't the cat killed by curiosity? Eddie hated cats, with their rough tongues, bad breath and haughty attitude. The sound happened again. There was somebody in the other room. That spooky chick? Nah. Why would she come here? Cursing himself for pursuing it, Eddie stepped into the hall and slunk toward the living room.

A plastic cup from 7-11 rolled towards him, settling at his right foot.

"Hey," Eddie said, voice steely. "Who the fuck is there?"

Eddie poked his head into the room and several zombies stood there, the front door wide open. As he turned to flee two more stumbled from the bathroom, which was between here and the exit window.

"Fuck me," Eddie growled, cursing himself for the *stunod* that he was.

From the living room, one loped towards him, then tripped and fell as its legs became entangled in its own leathery intestines, which dangled from a gaping cavity in its lower abdomen. Its jaw hit the linoleum floor and came loose, leaving it cocked to one side and toothless. Eddie would have enjoyed the zombie's clumsiness were there not several others that shuffled his way, their paths free of stray innards. Eddie cursed the narrowness of the hall, a mere four feet wide, but long. *Goddamn railroad apartments.* The ones emerging from the john effectively blocked his exit, so he'd have to bull through. Hockey penalty time. Still, he wished he were less exposed. *Maybe the Tarzan wardrobe wasn't the best idea.*

Eddie gulped a few deep breaths, then ran forward. He caught a female zombie in the face with his fist, sending her careening backwards, ass over tit. Her head hit the doorsill and split open, spilling coagulated gunk, dark and thick as molasses. Her bathroom buddy, a rangy male with graveyard halitosis, lunged for him and from behind, slung his gangly arms around Eddie's waist. Eddie couldn't turn around, so he did a backwards head-butt ramming the back of his skull into the zombie's face, praying all the while that the zombie wouldn't bite him. *Fuck that shit.* The zombie's grasp loosened and Eddie shrugged him off, spinning on his heel. Even though he knew he should flee, he was now pissed. He blundered back into his bedroom and slid open his closet door, the action so violent the door came off its tracks and fell against the inside wall. Eddie grappled with the door and flung it off to the side, groping for his hockey stick.

"*High-sticking*, huh? The Comet'll show you motherfuckers some high-fuckin'-sticking!"

Like some po-mo Spartan warrior, Eddie turned back into the hall, stick in hand, helmet his only other garment besides his briefs and jute-soled summer shoes. With a vicious upward slash he took the head off the one that bear hugged him in the hall. From his bedroom in the middle, Eddie still needed to get to fire escape at the rear of the apartment. The headless body convulsed as Eddie stepped over it and a palsied rotten hand shot up and grabbed the back of his briefs, tearing them.

"The fuck?" Eddie cried. "Oh, you wanna play fuckin' games?"

He stomped on the thing's solar plexus, its withered organs emitting muffled popping noises. The arm went limp but the rigor mortis grip on Eddie's Calvins intensified, pulling them down like a macabre pastiche of the Coppertone pooch yanking down that little pigtailed girl's bathing suit. Eddie tore free, now wearing just the waistband and pouch in the front, like some poorly constructed jockstrap.

Only one adversary left, an eyeless one-armed creep of indeterminate gender, face composed—or decomposed—solely of strands of muscle tissue barely masked by shredded papery epidermis. Eddie jerked back the stick, then rammed it as hard as he could through the thing's chest, impaling it. He raked the stick back and forth, the zombie clawing at it, trying to free itself. Eddie jerked it upwards, lifting his foe off the ground. The ribcage split open like a zipper, bits of bone and sinew raining down as Eddie worked the stick up and down until the thing split in half.

As it twitched pitiably on the floor, Eddie swung down the stick and shattered its skull.

He grabbed the gym bag and stepped onto the fire escape, slamming the window shut after him, hoping against hope that those zombie *gavones* were the only ones to breach the building. Still, he wouldn't be coming back to the old roost. On the roof he slumped back against the warty black tarpaper and caught his breath, quaking. So, they got in. That meant the half-assed fortification the Guardsmen had installed was compromised. Great. He gulped air and punched his chest. Now that he was safe the fear sluiced over him. Though it had to be ninety degrees he was shivering. *Calm the fuck down,* he admonished himself. *Don't be a fuckin' woman. Calm the fuck down.*

He'd be damned if he shared what happened with the others, even if he came out awesome in the end. Nevertheless, the stairwell door needed to be secured. Scattered like relics of the Analog Age along the periphery of the roof jutted a few rusty TV antennas. Eddie snatched up the cables and yanked them free, then looped them multiple times around the door handle and then looked for something to tie the other ends to. On the other side of the housing stood a cylindrical smokestack. *Perfect.* Eddie tried to remember the fancy knots his Uncle Sal had shown him at the Bay Shore Marina but nothing came back to him. He'd never paid much attention, preferring time on the boat to mooring it.

A few minutes later Eddie admired his sloppy attempt at a buntline hitch.

After a few tugs on the door to check his handiwork he smiled, now calm.

"Good enough," he said, and headed back to the crib.

25

"I'D FORGOTTEN HOW comforting banality can be," Alan said as he shut off the little the DVD in his laptop. He'd been watching back-to-back episodes of *Three's Company.* "What a stupid show. Why did you have this in your library?"

"It was Mike's. He loved John Ritter."

Alan sat back, feeling a little bad about maligning the show. It *was* bad, though. Seriously bad. Maybe it had been nostalgic for Mike.

Alan looked over at Ellen. She was doing a crossword puzzle. The scene seemed oddly peaceful. Comforting. It was hard to reconcile this image of domestic tranquility with the sea of undead shamblers outside. Ellen had filled in a bit and looked more like her old self, which was to say she looked very attractive. But to what end? Mona's arrival on the scene was a stay of execution, not a repeal. Okay, there were creature comforts. They had food again, and light at night. Alan was clean-shaven and his personal hygiene had gone up several rungs, so when the time came he'd now leave a moderately good-looking corpse, or at least make an attractive main course. Moments ago he'd felt comforted by a moronic sitcom and now he felt like everything was utterly pointless. Seeing the predictable pandemonium that was the bygone world of Jack Tripper, Chrissy Snow and Janet Wood just amplified the horror of reality. Alan pressed the eject button and replaced the disk in its case, vowing not to revisit their sunny vale of canned mirth.

Enervated, he plodded to the window to soak up a solid dose of reality.

"That show was kind of funny," Ellen said, looking up from the puzzle book.

"It was horrendous," Alan said.

"I thought you just said it was comforting."

"Yeah, well I misspoke. Sue me."

"It's funny." When Alan didn't ask what was, Ellen continued, "There's a clue in this puzzle, 'ThighMaster mistress from *Three's Company*'. Isn't that a funny coincidence?"

"Hilarious."

"Bad moods can be very contagious, especially in close quarters."

"You saying you want me to leave?"

"No. Don't put words in my mouth. I'm saying is there anything I can do to alleviate your funk?" Ellen rose from the table and began to undo her blouse, but Alan turned away.

"Not everything can be solved with sex," he muttered.

"It really is a different world. Used to be sex solved almost everything."

"There are a lot of *used-to-be*'s. Used to be Manhattan wasn't a massive graveyard full of corpses too stupid to stay still. Used to be we could go outside and walk around and not worry about being eaten. Used to be ..."

"Okay, fine. I get the picture," Ellen snapped, refastening her buttons. "Look, I *really* don't want to get into a *thing*, okay? Why don't you go to your apartment and do some drawing or something? Maybe take a walk." Alan raised an eyebrow, but before he could say something snide Ellen added, "*On the roof.* Or the hall. Just go out for a while."

"I thought *this* was my apartment now."

"It doesn't have to be," Ellen said, and instantly Alan regretted his snippiness.

"I'm sorry," he said, but Ellen fanned him off, gesturing toward the front door. "Really, I didn't mean it. I'm sorry. I know how good we've got it. Relatively. I'm grateful. Really. I just ... I mean ..." He trailed off as Ellen about-faced and resumed the puzzle, her nonverbals communicating loud and clear: *this conversation is over.*

On the landing Alan stared at the outside of the closed door. *A domestic squabble*, he thought. *How banal. But not in the least bit comforting.* Could Jack maintain his pretense as a preening homosexual, keeping the Mr. Roper ever at bay? Could Chrissy wear a top that was even lower-cut, but not so low-cut the network censors wouldn't let it air? Could Janet utter some pithy platitude that neatly wrapped up their dilemma with a trite little bow? Could he and Ellen pretend to be a happy couple while all else was unimaginably bleak?

Stay tuned.

Karl sat on his bed in his bare-walled apartment.

Along with all the pinups, gone were the posters of MMA champions and heavy metal demigods. *Thou shalt have no other gods before me.* Since the arrival of Mona he'd reevaluated his secular values and desires and felt nothing but shame. That he'd intended to attempt to bed her was something he'd have to live with in private. He'd sinned in his heart. Thank God he hadn't articulated his impure desires to anyone, least of all her. In the passing weeks he'd borne witness to her selflessness. And the way she moved unscathed by the ravenous masses outside.

Karl didn't believe in the Rapture, but he didn't *not* believe in it, either. The husks shuffling around outside weren't "left behind." At least that wasn't how it was supposed to go. But maybe they were. The Bible and Bible prophecy were so open to interpretation. He thought if you didn't get sucked up to Heaven you were to remain on the hellscape that was Earth and live out the remainder of your days, biding time until you went to hell. Where did those things outside fit into God's plan? Karl remembered some lines from Corinthians. "Death has been swallowed up in victory." And "Where, O death, is your victory? Where, O death, is your sting?" Death's sting and victory were pretty evident to Karl's eyes.

If Karl remembered right, at the Battle of Armageddon everyone who wasn't a believer would be slaughtered. Were those the zombies? That's a whole lot of unbelievers. Maybe those things outside were the husks of the righteous that had ascended to Heaven, sort of the ultimate in recycling. Their earthly bodies no longer needed, they now were used to punish the remaining infidels—like him and his neighbors. Supposedly, after the Battle of Armageddon, Satan would be defeated and Jesus would set up the Millennial Kingdom in Jerusalem. Karl's posture slumped. It sounded so gaga, but then again, look out the window. People eating people—or at least things that used to be people eating people.

People used to whine about their bad luck or what a cruddy day they'd had. Sometimes people would try to equate a lousy day at work with the calamities of Job. A mean boss was hardly comparable. Your job sucked, but *being* Job sucked worse, *yet he still loved God.* So maybe this was the Tribulation. In which case, Karl hadn't seen the light until it was too late. He wondered if it was too late. It definitely was for those brainless pods outside, but Karl could still refill his heart with love for God. God was supposed to be merciful, though the physical evidence seemed contradictory.

Karl's feelings about Big Manfred had altered, too.

Honor thy father and thy mother. Though Manfred Gustav Stempler had been a stern and brutish presence, perhaps Karl hadn't understood that he'd been so to fashion his sons into better adults. Karl wished he had a Bible, but didn't and was too embarrassed to ask around. Besides, the others were likely heathens. Alan kept only escapist fiction and was an avowed atheist. Ellen, who could tell? Probably agnostic at best. The Fogelhuts, Jews, which was perfectly all right. Jews, Big Manfred had said, were merely unperfected Christians. Eddie and Dave? Sodomites. Maybe Dabney was different, though Karl cautioned himself not to assume African-American equated churchy. He'd strayed into unintended casual racism already. Perhaps he could ask Mona to obtain a Bible for him on one of her sojourns among the unclean. If it wouldn't be too much of an imposition.

Karl was mighty confused. Mona could walk among the undead. Wasn't that a

Bible-style miracle? Was she an emissary of God? Her perpetual serenity seemed to denote some sublime characteristic. Was she imbued with the Holy Spirit? Karl heard her tunes, though. While he couldn't make them out, they sounded far from saintly. Sure, there were some metal Christian bands, but the nearly unreadable band logos and graphics on her ever-present long-sleeved black tees seemed tacitly unchristian. He was pretty sure they were Scandinavian and in all probability Satanic. Still, she was humble, no doubt. She never made eye contact, which at first he thought rude, but now seemed modest.

"Are you there, God? It's me, Karl." He made a face. Was it blasphemous to paraphrase Judy Blume in a time of spiritual crisis? "Anyway, forgive me for this inferior supplication, but I'm a little out of practice. Scratch that. I'm a *lot* out of practice. I'm so confused and everything. I've never stopped believing in You, but there's so much I don't understand, nor do I think I'll ever understand it. Forsooth. I'm sorry. I'm trying to be fancy. That's false. But my entreaty is for real. Sorry, I won't try to talk all grandiose and whatnot. Ugh, this isn't coming out right at all. Listen, I know I've thought many impure thoughts, but I cleansed my chambers, okay?" His mind flashed to Miss June 1982 stashed in his dresser drawer. "I don't want to cast out Lourdes Ann. Please. There has to be some beauty in my existence. I haven't masturbated in ages. Doesn't chastity count for something? I don't mean to grovel. You wouldn't have created perfection such as Lourdes Ann if it wasn't meant to be admired, right?"

Karl stared up at his ceiling, noting a long crack that ran diagonally from one corner to the other, bisecting the expanse of whitewashed plaster. The crack had widened; deepened. Old buildings settle, but this seemed symbolic. He stared into that gap. *I'm too dumb,* Karl thought. *I wish I could interpret the signs. Not the big ones. Not the undead. The little ones. I'm sure there's a Message.* One reason Karl had turned his back on the church was that its loudest and most passionate proponents all seemed so corrupt, hypocritical, bullying and insane. The clergy, the televangelists, the propagandists; few seemed all that holy.

Karl fingered his one tangible souvenir from Big Manfred, the one his old man had insisted he take before heading off to New Sodom: a .44 Magnum Smith & Wesson Model 29 revolver. Karl had left it tucked away in its case since he'd arrived in New York, unclear whether its license was valid across state lines. Probably not and he never registered it since moving here. But now he held it in his hands. It felt alien, but it was the one thing he owned that his father had touched. Not a cross, a gun. Ellen was right. It would be pointless against those things outside. Karl ran his finger around the muzzle, sighed, then replaced the gun in its foam-lined case. Guns were not his bag.

If Eddie ever found out I had this … Karl let that thought die.

He got off the bed and returned the carry case to his underwear drawer, then stepped into the hall just as Mona was walking down the stairs from the roof, head bobbing and expression impassive as ever. Sunlight poured down the stairs through the open door and skylight, enshrouding her in a blinding white glow. He flushed and cast his head down as she edged past him.

"Mona?" His thin voice didn't penetrate the din in her headphones, so with reluctance he reached out and tapped her passing shoulder, then retracted his hand as if he'd touched something molten. She stopped and popped out an earbud, but said nothing, canting an ear in his direction without looking at him.

"I'm kinda embarrassed, but could you pick up something for me?"

"'Rhoid cream?"

"Huh?"

"Roof dude wants 'rhoid cream."

Karl forced a laugh. "No, no. Ha. Boy, um, TMI? Am I right?" No reply. "No, no. I want a Bible. Either the *King James* or the *New Revised Standard Bible.* The simpler the writing, the better. But anything, really, as long as it's officially a Bible. I don't want to put you out." Mona jotted it down in her notepad but showed no reaction. "I want to brush up a little and see if I can make any sense of what's going on out there."

"Uh-huh."

"I mean, maybe these are the End Times?" Karl inflected the statement as a question, hoping to engage Mona. "You know, like in the Bible? Like in the Book of Revelation?"

"Mm-hmm."

"Okay then," Karl said, wincing and smiling. "I guess that's all for now."

As Mona retreated down the steps Karl tried to make out Mona's thumping music of the moment.

"Uh, Mona?" he shouted, to be heard over her tunes. She stopped at the foot of the stairs and looked up, removing the earpiece again. "Uh, Mona, I was just wondering what you're listening to?"

"Ministry."

"Oh. Uh, what song?"

"'Jesus Built My Hotrod.'"

"Oh. Okay, thanks."

She nodded and headed downstairs.

Karl was so confused.

"Are you still sulking?" Ruth asked, incredulity marring any attempt on her part at a sympathetic tone. "My God, Abe, get over it."

"'Get over it,' she says. Unbelievable. She accuses me of being derelict in my duty. She accuses me of being obsolete. *Get over it.* Maybe a younger man should take the crow's nest. Maybe I'm not the one to watch for the lights in the tower window."

"What tower window?"

"'One, if by land, and two, if by sea; And I on the opposite shore will be ...'" Abe recited, rote grade school memorization still etched into his gray matter.

"Sarcasm I do not need."

I wasn't being ..."

Ruth shuffled out of the room, back to the bedroom. *Good,* Abe thought. *Like I need a stoop-shouldered harridan eroding the last vestiges of my manhood.* He sat by his post, a cup of coffee—neither hot nor iced, but room temperature—in his hand, staring out the window, awaiting Mona's return, walkie-talkie nestled in his lap. He'd be damned if he'd allow Ruth the satisfaction of catching him slacking off twice.

"'Beneath, in the churchyard, lay the dead," Abe continued, in schoolboy cadence, "In their night-encampment on the hill, Wrapped in silence so deep and still, That he could hear, like a sentinel's tread, The watchful night-wind, as it went, Creeping along from tent to tent, And seeming to whisper, 'All is well!' Yeah, right. *All is well,* my ass. *Gottenyu,* what the hell kind of poetry would Longfellow have wrought from this *paskudne* situation?" Abe settled back and wondered if anyone anywhere was writing poetry about the current condition. If they were it was probably awful, like everything else in the last quarter century.

Beneath, in the churchyard, lay the dead.

Abe leaned forward and looked at the dead, or rather the *un*dead. How long could they keep going? They ate when they could, but that was infrequent at best—happily. Were their reserves of energy infinite? That seemed so unlikely. Those things kept going and going, like that stupid battery bunny, none keeling over from depletion. *You'd think,* Abe thought, *that eventually they'd just all collapse and the worst would be over. Sure, there'd be a lot to clean up, but what a small price to pay.* Then again, as Abe often mused, you'd think a lot of things in this life. You'd think death was the worst that could happen. You'd think the dead would stay dead. You'd think getting terribly ill or the cessation of your Social Security checks would be the worst that could happen in your dotage. You'd be wrong. But being wrong was the biggest part of life. Wrong choices and regrets; Abe was up to his neck in both.

"You cabbage-heads have got it good, you know that?" Abe hollered out the window at the crowd below. "Not a care in the world, eh? You think anything anymore? Probably not! How lucky is that, you lucky sons of bitches? You don't even need TV anymore! No phones! No social media! No causes! It just hit me! This is the end of the evolutionary ladder, the perfect twenty-first century man! Not a thought in its head! Not a care in the world! Idle yet active, going no place, doing nothing, taking his sweet time, and vicious as hell if given the opportunity! Hey, Darwin, you bastard, congratulations!" Abe laughed, pounding his fist against the splintering slate windowsill, doing his old bones no favors at all.

At the other end of the apartment Ruth eased the bedroom door shut, muffling the splenetic ravings of her husband.

26

"You actually want to keep debating the merits of old TV shows? Are you fucking kidding me?" Ellen scootched away from Alan's side, unable to believe her ears. Alan clicked off the little player.

"I just think if you prefer SNL to—"

"*Stop!* Stop it. Now. It's a matter of taste, not sanity, for God's sake," Ellen countered. This was stupid. How could Alan get so frothed up over a TV show? A long-gone obscure sketch comedy show, at that.

"Or the *lack* thereof. Everyone says they like *SNL* better, but trust me, it wasn't."

"I never even *heard* of this other thing before. It's nice you find solace in it. *Good for you.* Great. But I, *me*, I can't tune out the world, so pardon me if I'm not busting a fucking gut. I don't even get most of who they're supposed to be or what the fuck they're spoofing or anything. This is like trying to laugh at a fucking cave painting. Plus, *nothing* is funny anymore."

"It is if you look at it the right way."

"So, not laughing at an old show—a show that was fucking old *before you were even fucking alive*, might I add—makes me see it the wrong way? Why do you even know about it? Was it your parents' favorite or what? Some comedy nerd uncle? It's pop culture. Who fucking cares? Why do *you* fucking care? It's fucking stupid."

"You curse a lot."

Ellen's eyes flashed and she let her mouth hang open, debating how to respond. *You curse a lot?* Is this what a little comfort yields? Full stomachs and access to distraction? Mike had been one to belittle Ellen for her "pedestrian" taste. That she liked things marketed to her. That she was a receptive audience for middle-of-the-road mainstream fare. And now, with all this, Alan was sitting on *her* couch in *her* apartment taking up the mantle of *the guy with more sophisticated taste.*

How much protection did Alan's presence here really provide?

Ellen's mouth compressed to a thin line. Eddie. Alan. Mike. All these fucking men. She felt crampy but refused to believe this was hormonal. How many times had that been lobbed at her? Hormonal impulses because she'd had the temerity to voice an opinion contrary to Mike's? Or to some male coworker's? *Are you on your period?*

"I just can't see how an intelligent woman such as yourself—"

"This is the point where you think *real hard* about the next words to come out of your mouth, then think the better of them and shut the fuck up."

Ellen composed her features, her eyes cautioning but not fiery. She was not going to allow herself to be painted irrational, emotional or worst yet, hysterical. Alan's met hers and silently acquiesced. She accepted the small triumph with grace and said, "Thank you."

"I'm sorry. You're totally right. I'm just … Nothing. You're right."

They met in the middle of the room and gave each other a perfunctory hug, then retreated to their safe spaces, he to watch another episode, she to do another *Times* crossword. Ellen looked up from her themeless Friday and watched as Alan plucked another disk from the case. Perhaps a little theatrically she cleared her throat.

"*What?*" he asked, the single word failing to not be defensive.

"You haven't painted lately. Or done any drawing."

"I'm taking a breather, okay? Maybe I haven't been touched by the muse. Maybe I just want to chill and medicate with a little video. *Am I allowed?*"

"Of course you're allowed," Ellen said, her own tone faux neutral. "It's just you were such a dynamo before you got that gadget." She stopped, now disappointed in herself for protracting this. Arguing over old comedy was stupid. Needling Alan over taking a breather was stupid. It all felt stupid, even continuing this wafer-thin pastiche of life. "Never mind. Sorry. Watch your show. Enjoy."

"*Thank you.*"

Ellen watched Alan slip on headphones, the gesture eerily evocative of Mona. As he lapsed into a state of televisual torpor, Ellen felt a powerful wave of grief. Alan's posture mimicked Mike's, the way he slouched, legs up on the ottoman, ankles crossed. Alan's face relaxed as the vintage comedy soothed him, but Ellen's expression hardened. Arguing over comedy felt like an unearned luxury. The grief turned into nausea and Ellen bolted to the bedroom window in time to release a torrent of partially digested food onto the zombies below, none of whom seemed to mind.

Ellen retched up a few more dollops, then slumped down and let her head drop between her knees. For a few long unhappy months in high school she'd wrestled with bulimia. It was during those years she'd taken to cutting, both classes and herself. And medicating with booze and MDMA, when she could get it. Alan reliving happier times in the living room; Ellen reliving unhappier times in the bedroom. Her puke lay like a sloppily placed wreath of boluses and bile where Mike had been slaughtered by those filthy, despicable, unnatural things.

Mike.

Her husband.

Former.

Father of her child.

Former.

Former husband. Former child.

Former everything.

Could I have done more? Could I have saved her? Could I have saved him? The answer to both was a resounding *NO*, but that didn't mitigate the guilt that consumed her. Helplessness didn't feel like a reason, it felt like an excuse. A rationalization. Even if it was true. She'd been the resourceful one. The problem-solver. Her father-in-law had patronizingly called her "a very capable woman" on many occasions. And yet this. Incapable. Her sobs drowned out by Alan's headphones, Ellen's body drew in on itself, convulsed in sorrow and helplessness. *It burns. It fucking burns.*

Dave sat on the couch and thumbed through an old issue of *Time*, the cover story of which was rampant obesity in America. Ah, for the good old days. But he wasn't really reading, though. He feigned indifference to Eddie's incessant onanism since he'd retrieved his precious stash of porn from their old crib, but inside Dave seethed. And hurt. How Eddie could prefer to service himself to having actual sex with an actual human being was beyond Dave. It was like what they'd developed together was an accident, a phase. It's not like Eddie hadn't, on multiple occasions, made clear their sex life was a stopgap measure until he could get his hands on a lady. His mind flashed on the Gerri incident for a second, but he banished it just as quickly. But Dave could see in Eddie's eyes something more. Something he wasn't willing to own up to. Or at least Dave thought he saw that. Maybe it was just wishful thinking. Now that Eddie had scored his whacking material, Dave was out of the loop.

He got off the couch and hovered near Eddie's open bedroom door.

"How many times can you watch the same scene?" Dave asked.

"You know what you sound like? You sound like a fuckin' woman," Eddie said with a scowl. "Anyone ever tell you that?"

"Just you."

"So maybe you should let it penetrate that thick Mick skull of yours."

Dave chose not to take the bait and left the apartment, garnering nary a peep of protest. Fine. Let Eddie indulge in his pathetic backslide. Then he'd come crawling back and maybe, just maybe, Dave would have him back. Who was he kidding? Of course he would.

Out in the hall Dave pressed his face against the cool stucco and sighed. When had his life devolved into a same-sex soap opera? Were all the girls he'd banged throughout high school and college just a smokescreen? His attraction to them had felt real at the time, but then again he never bonded emotionally with any of them. Real bonds had only been forged with male companions, especially

Eddie. He let out a soul-deep sigh and walked up the stairs to the roof. Dabney would be up there. Could he fake conviviality? It didn't matter. Dabney wasn't the type to chitchat on unless you invited it. Let him sit with his pile of bricks and play "stone the zombie." Dave took another deep breath and pushed open the door.

Though the sun was masked by gauzy white haze, the light was intense, especially since Dave had been indoors for so long. He shielded his eyes and fished his Rangers baseball cap out of his back pocket. Instead of lying belly down on his tarp, Dabney was seated at an aluminum folding card table doing something Dave couldn't quite discern. A conversational gambit presented itself—something to distract from his relationship woes—so Dave, attempting to affect insouciance, strolled over and took it.

"Whatcha doing?" he asked as he approached. Dabney was hunched over and wearing thick magnifying glasses, something Dave had never witnessed before on the older man. He neared the table and saw many small parts, some loose, some still connected to plastic sprues. Dabney was building a model kit. *How adorable.* Wait a minute. Did Dave really think that? Was he being ironic or facetious or patronizing? No, it *was* adorable, this middle-aged man using a pair of eyebrow tweezers to delicately assemble parts from this, what was it, model airplane?

"Makin' a North American P-51D Mustang. Good way to pass time, plus the glue gets you a little high." Dabney looked up and smiled. "Just kidding. Takes more than a little glue for me. Speaking of which, you want a beer? You look like you could use one."

Dabney handed him a bottle of Heineken and Dave held back the urge to weep with gratitude, not just for the brew but the kindness. Dabney continued, "All these little parts and pieces. Been a while since I put one of these together. My boys used to be wild for these things. They liked doing the hotrods and whatnot, but I prefer planes." Dabney looked up at the sky, scanning for nothing. "I used to complain about the roar of jumbo jets, 'specially during TV shows. Used to have to turn the volume up to compete with them. Now I'd give my left nut for a plane to go zipping by up there. Even if it wasn't meant for me, least it would be a sign of something going on out there. Some sign that maybe there were others. Before Mona showed, last sign we had of life was that crash and that was snuffed out before it even made an impression. I asked Mona if she's encountered any others and she said no. And that's all she said before scurrying away. There's gotta be others. Just maybe not around here."

"How does she do it, is what I wonder."

"Yeah, well that's the million dollar question, ain't it? How come those godless motherfuckers don't eat her up like the rest of us mere mortals? Yeah."

"I tried talking to her about it and she got all squirrely."

"Yeah. Yeah, that's a thing." Dabney took a sip and placed the bottle on the table. "I had a dog, back when. A rescue. Who knows what happened before I got him? A good boy. Mixed breed. Buster. Wouldn't make eye contact. You looked at him and he'd look away. 'Who's a good boy,' you're saying and he looks away. Couldn't ask him what happened before. 'You're safe, now, Buster. It's okay.' Didn't matter. And whatever happened happened and who knows?"

"But Buster was a dog."

"Dog with a backstory."

"Mona's not a dog," Dave said, then wished he'd phrased it differently.

"No, she is not. But almost as talkative. But there's a story. Just like Buster had one. When she was up here, I caught a glimpse of her itching her arm. Couldn't see too well, but she had marks under her sleeve."

"Tats?"

"Maybe scars."

"Maybe she got bit by one of those things and built up a ..." Dave trailed off, not buying his own hypothesis.

"I dunno. Maybe. Like I said, I only caught a glimpse. Could've been eczema or psoriasis. Or mosquitoes. We all got bit up pretty bad after it rained. What do I know? She's not much for talking and I'm not about to ask. If she's got a story to tell she'll tell it in her own time. Or won't."

Dabney finished off his beer, then tossed it over the edge of the roof, not even watching its trajectory. Dabney snapped a tiny piece off the sprue and smoothed it with a small wedge of fine sandpaper, his eyes on the instructions, held in place by a small boombox that warbled a well-worn tape of Ben Webster. "I'd like to see several squadrons of these strafing the bejeezus out of those assholes down there," he said, holding the box art up for Dave to admire. "Imagine that? A bunch of these babies blasting the holy living hell out of those bastards? That'd be sweet."

Dave nodded, sipping his beer. It was warm, so Dave pretended he was in Europe. He'd read somewhere that Europeans drank their beer warm. Sounded weird, if given the choice, but he'd never know firsthand. Dave looked out at the horizon to the north and wished he'd traveled, seen the world, broadened his vistas. Too late now. He then looked south and gasped.

"Look over there," he said, pointing.

In the distance a thick black cloud churned skyward from below, its origin blocked by buildings. But somewhere, looked like maybe in the east forties, a fire blazed. Was that a sign of life elsewhere? Or maybe a gas line blew all by itself, entropy taking its course.

"Hold on a sec," Dabney said, reaching to click over to radio on the boombox. He stopped, mid-gesture, and let out a derisive snort. "Idiot. I was going to turn on the news. Pavlovian response, I suppose. You'd think after months of this shit I'd be reprogrammed. Then again, I got some sweet notes serenading. I'm building a model kit. I'm drinking a beer. It feels almost normal, 'cept for me living up on a roof of an Upper East Side building full of white folks. No offense. But even that feels kind of normal. Amazing how the definition of what passes for normal is always changing. If normal means what's most common, those zombies are normal and we're not."

Dave nodded, taking another swig. Normal didn't used to entail a physical relationship with Eddie—or at least not a sexual one. It had always been pretty physical, between horseplay and hockey. The only time in their past that had been sexual was when they'd fucked a couple of co-eds in their dorm room. Dave shook his head, trying to dislodge the memory. He didn't want to think about Eddie now.

Both men's attention remained southwards as a loud thud, dulled by distance, was heard, followed by a ball of fire which shot into the sky, only to be absorbed by the black smoke. A succession of muffled explosions followed. Easterly winds bent the plumes of smoke into choky question marks in the sky.

"What do you suppose it is?" Dave asked.

"I dunno. Could be the old Con Ed steam plant, near the U.N. Or did they tear that down? I can't remember now. Could be a lot of things, though. And unless we send our girl Friday down there to check it out, we'll never know. And frankly I don't think that would be a very good use of her time."

"No, I suppose not. Jesus, you think it will get up to us?"

"I wouldn't want to be in that vicinity, but we got us a few miles between here and there. Don't sweat it. And think on the bright side, maybe it's frying up a mess of ghouls. Wouldn't that be something?" Dabney held up the half-finished Mustang and mimed a few swoops, adding appropriate *pew-pew-pew* sound effects. "Not quite as cathartic as a good strafing, but it'll have to do."

Whatever was going on downtown it was dramatic. Volleys of muted concussions recurred and a significant portion of the southern sky was smudged, the undersides of the dark clouds tinged orange from the blaze that raged out of sight below. The cloud of smoke and soot blew north and soon the sky directly above began to sicken. The charcoal gray began to leech pigment away, turning the already anemic sky greenish gray. The air smelled bad, a combination of charred solid matter and burning petrol. Unwelcome flashbacks of the months following the attacks of September 11th, 2001 pushed into Dave's mind. He and Eddie had worked in lower Manhattan, mere blocks from Ground Zero. Horripilation broke out across the back of his neck and arms in sense memory. He and Eddie had evacuated their building along with thousands of others. Confusion reigned as the sky snowed whitish ash. He'd thought at the time that was the worst that could ever happen. Never challenge the cosmos, he'd learned.

"Something always gotta come along and rain on your parade," Dabney muttered. A heavy drop fell on his nose and he frowned, adding, "Literally," as he restored the remaining parts of his model kit to the box. As more drops began to pelt the roof Dave bid Dabney a quick adieu, and then reentered the building.

With the door between him and Dabney closed and the sudden downpour mixed with far off thuds, Dave felt safe in the darkened stairwell housing to let tears run free.

Karl had forgotten how reader unfriendly the Bible was, no matter which version—although he vaguely remembered the *Good News Bible* being dumbed down quite a bit. Karl rested the fresh copy in his lap and closed his eyes. Clearly it was the message and not the messenger. No wonder his mind had often wandered during church and Manfred's sermonizing. The language was nearly impenetrable. After browsing through the earlier sections, he skipped to Revelation, figuring it the most germane.

Karl had forgotten—or maybe blocked—the particulars, but the imagery came flooding back: God and His four demon monsters covered with eyes sitting by His throne, the monsters incessantly chanting, "*Holy, holy, holy, holy, holy, holy, holy, holy, holy* is the Lord God, the Almighty, who was and who is and who is to come!" The first creature like a lion, the second like a calf, the third with a face like a man, and the fourth like an eagle—four creatures, each of them having six wings and loads of watchful eyes. Surrounding God's throne were twenty-four other thrones, occupied by twenty-four elders dressed in white garments, with crowns of gold on their heads. God's throne emitted constant lightning and thunder, much like the current real-life soundtrack. The ultimate booming system.

It sounded more like a rave than Heaven.

And God, evidently, had the appearance of jasper and sardius, a forgotten detail that sent Karl scurrying to his dictionary, which explained that jasper was, "an opaque form of quartz; red or yellow or brown or dark green in color; used for ornamentation or as a gemstone," and that sardius was, "a deep orange-red variety of chalcedony," which he also needed to look up, only to discover that chalcedony was, "a translucent to transparent milky or grayish quartz with distinctive microscopic crystals arranged in slender fibers in parallel bands," which frankly didn't help at all. It wasn't very comforting to picture The Almighty made of stone, perched on His throne, with catchphrase-spewing monster lapdogs for company. Though irreverent, it made it easier on Karl to picture them all as Muppets.

Some of Revelation rang true, or at least true-ish. The things outside *had* been raised from the dead. But Karl couldn't recall witnessing any procession before a large, white throne, nor did he see those not written in the book of life being cast down into a flaming lake of sulfur. And while the zombies were horrible—indeed *biblical* in their horror—Revelation was so specific about the plagues to befall mankind that omitting them didn't jibe.

Angels with giant sickles killing thousands.

Marks on everyone's foreheads, some put there by an angel, others put there by the beast. The infamous 666 drummed into his eyes in comic book tracts Big Manfred had given him as a boy. Comics to both scare and indoctrinate him.

Locusts flying out of hell, each with a human face and wearing a miniature crown and breastplate, bearing the hair of women, the teeth of lions, and the stingers of scorpions.

Millions of angels riding horses with the heads of lions.

Hailstones and plagues.

Okay, so maybe there'd been a plague.

Reading this stuff was giving Karl the sweats. He felt like he'd submitted himself to regression therapy to recall repressed memories. When he got the part about dogs not being allowed into Heaven he remembered Chessie, their retriever, and frowned that she wouldn't be there. Dogs got lumped in with sorcerers, the sexually immoral, murderers, idolaters, and everyone "who loves and practices falsehood." Karl didn't like that.

Karl did like that the Devil's new army was called Gog and Magog. That was kind of cool, but a bit beside the point—although Karl considered referring to the things outside as Gog and Magog from now on, to spruce up conversation. It seemed better than "those effing zombies." In Karl's opinion, the apostle John, who'd penned this book, might not have been the most reliable narrator. He might, in fact, have been an unmedicated raving lunatic. This was just one man's account, which by current standards seemed like fairly sloppy reportage. How about corroboration? How about three sources? But then again, who knew? What was supposed to be metaphor and what was literal? What was parable and what was prophecy? Was the whole thing allegorical? Was it about destruction or renewal? Everyone in the building was pretty secular, if not outright areligious and irreligious, so between that and the Internet gone, Karl had no one with whom to consult. His head throbbed. As he popped a couple of Tylenols he heard faint concussions in the distance.

Karl's apartment was in the rear of the building so he didn't bother looking out the window—his "view" solely that of the building across the alley. He hurried upstairs to find Dabney on the roof, nude in the rain, the sky above a miserable hue. Dabney didn't seem to notice Karl's presence; his head thrown back, his eyes clenched shut. Was he humming or just mumbling to himself? Another dull thud erupted and Karl looked south, divining the direction of the noise. The sky there was blackened, flame licking up from below. As if in a trance, Karl made his way to the southernmost of the adjoined neighboring buildings. On the corner he stood on its fascia and stared at the distant conflagration, his stomach churning. He steadied himself, gripping a metal pipe.

"Oh my God," he said in a hushed tone, remembering a passage from Chapter Nine:

The fifth angel sounded, and I saw a star from the sky which had fallen to the earth. The key to the pit of the abyss was given to him. He opened the pit of the abyss, and smoke went up out of the pit, like the smoke from a burning furnace. The sun and the air were darkened because of the smoke from the pit.

Maybe mutant locusts would be coming after all.

27

This is unusual, Alan thought, paintbrush in hand, mid-stroke on the full-size canvas. Across the room reclined Mona—fully dressed—on a vintage velvet chaise; yet here he was painting while being tormented by a very insistent erection.

Mona's pose wasn't particularly sexy and her expression was inscrutable and mildly sullen as usual, her eyes lightly closed. In her lap was the Hello Kitty backpack, which she held like a real kitty, its face aimed out and imperturbable as hers. Mona remained perfectly still, which was a great plus for a model, except for her head, which almost undetectably nodded in time with her assaultive tunes.

So why was he hard?

She wore her usual longish black cargo shorts, long-sleeve black tee, Doc Martens boots. Nothing racy. Mona's right leg dangled off the edge and the left was bent at the knee, the foot resting on the cushion. And there it was: betwixt her feet and the hem of her shorts. It was her calves. What a bizarre time to pick up a fetish, but there they were, round and firm and strong. Calves. Alan had noticed calves in the past, but usually in conjunction with high heels, but other than that they'd held no fascination for him. Breasts, yes. Ass, definitely. But calves? And Mona wasn't wearing pumps. But now that he'd noticed them—especially the left one, which bulged from the bend of her knee and the pressure from her foot resting on the cushion—he couldn't take his eyes off them.

Alan took a swig from a can of lukewarm Fresca, stifled a burp, and got back to work. He'd blocked in the figure and was tightening up the areas of flesh, the clothing indicated as black negative space. He considered whether or not to add detail like the creases and folds in the material and the abstruse band logo, but opted to keep the treatment more graphic. He focused on her face, drawing his eyes away from that fetching drumstick. Instead he studied her lips, always pursed in a slight moue. Highlights of early afternoon sunlight coruscated on them and periodically her tongue would poke out to keep them moist. *Focus on the work.* Alan swirled his brush against the palette, mixing a pink subtle and sensuous enough for those lips.

As he daubed on small touches of roseate-hued pigment he felt a light touch on his shoulder and flinched, causing the brush to skate across the surface of the canvas, marring the work he'd done.

"Christ!" he barked, spinning on his heel to see who'd caused this accident.

Ellen was there, her expression conciliatory—until she noticed the protrusion. Then her expression hardened almost as much as the business within Alan's drawers.

"You asshole."

"What?" he asked. "What? *I'm* the one who should be mad. You just made me ..." Once again his words trailed off as Ellen looked up and locked eyes with him. He feebly gestured at the canvas, a Francis Bacon-like diagonal streak across the painted Mona's face. "I mean," he sputtered, and then his face assumed Ellen's previous expression of guilty conciliation. "Is it that obvious?"

"I should have known," Ellen said, voice flat.

"I'm just painting her portrait," Alan said, defensive.

"Yeah, with a hard-on."

"You know," Alan stammered, "sometimes they come unbidden, involuntary, like breathing and the beat of one's heart. Autonomic. I wasn't even *thinking* about sex. It just happened, honest."

Mona, eyes shut and oblivious to this exchange, kept time with her tunes.

"It just happened when a pretty young thing came to model for you."

"With all her clothes on," Alan added.

"Yeah, for now. This time."

"Don't be absurd. I would never ask her to disrobe."

"Disrobe," Ellen said, now a cruel smile playing on her lips. "The model was *undraped. Dishabille.* You artistes and your Victorian euphemisms."

"I seem to recall you posing undraped for me. Unprompted, I'll add. I'm just painting."

"You get wood when you paint the zombies outside? If you do, then all is forgiven. Go on, tell me that."

"I can't. I don't think I have, but ..." His plea fizzled out as Ellen raised an eyebrow. Alan's face reddened, like the hue he'd started blending with his brush. "I don't. But that's different."

"Well, that's fine. This is fine. Go ahead and *schtup* that little girl on the couch. Maybe then there can be another preggo in the house. See if *I* care."

"*You're* the one that wanted me to paint again," Alan whisper-whined, his words chasing her out the door. "*What,* I'm only supposed to paint zombies and *you*?" Ellen, gliding out on the high ground, shut the door behind her. Mona's eyes opened. "What?" she asked, looking at Alan, whose unwelcome tumescence had abated.

"Nothing."

Mona closed her eyes and Alan began to correct the pink streak.

Wait a minute.

Another preggo in the house?

"It just bugs me is all," Eddie said. "She gets to go out and we're cooped up in this dump forever. And I'm sick of her evasiveness. Bitches with secrets are the story of my fucking life. No, she's onto something and she's too selfish to share the secret with us. This is some kinda bullshit head games power trip."

"That's crazy," Dave said. "What could possibly motivate something like that? She doesn't seem the type. That's too, I dunno, devious."

"Bitches are all devious, bro. *All of 'em.* I don't buy the whole brain-damaged thing she's putting over on us. Little Miss Lookaway. Little Miss Saynothing. The whole shtick. She knows what she's doing and *I don't like it.* Everyone in this lame building should be tag teaming her for how the fuck she does it. Instead, it's kid gloves. Like she's gonna fuckin' break. She ain't the fragile one, for fuck's sakes."

"She's our savior, dude," Dave said.

"Yeah, yeah. She's our *savior,* dude. We're her fuckin' *pets.* She goes out and walks around and what? She's touched by an angel or something? Nah. She's a *person,* same as us. She's got some kinda secret and I wanna know what the fuck it is and I aim to find out, even if she's withholding. *Especially* if."

"And how do you propose doing that, pray tell?"

"You know, sometimes you talk all fancy and I just wanna flatten you, Mallon. You pull that lawyery shit on me one more time—*one more fuckin' time*—and I'll lay you out. Count on it."

"Jesus Christ, Eddie. What's gotten up your ass?"

"Look, just get the fuck outta here, okay? I wanna be alone for a while and sort some shit out."

"*Fine.*"

"Fine."

"And thus endeth the nagging," Abe said, sitting on the edge of the bed, holding Ruth's wrist. No pulse. No breath. Dead. Abe sighed and moved his grip from wrist to hand, his fingers meshing with hers, his posture defeated. He didn't look at her face, the mouth hanging slightly open, but just stared ahead at the floor between his feet, nudging ruts into the pile of the carpet with the toe of his slippers, then smoothing them with the flats of his soles. At least her eyes were closed. He sighed again, stretching it out. He tightened his grip on her hand. It had been years since he last held her hand, just held it. They used to walk hand in hand all the time. They even had correct and incorrect sides. It never felt right when he held her left hand; something seemed unbalanced. With his free hand he stroked his freshly shaven chin, a small scrap of toilet paper stuck there by a dot of blood. He plucked it free and neatly placed it on the bedside table.

"Ruthie," he said, then sighed again. In place of tears was a lot of sighing, Abe not being given to such displays, even when there was no audience. No living audience, at any rate. With reluctance he turned to look at her visage. Her skin already was draining of color. With the pneuma gone, it was distressing how fast she no longer looked look like herself. Waxen. Hollower than even moments earlier. He didn't believe in the soul, but that animating force, once departed, transformed its vessel. She didn't look restful. She looked … He hesitated, but it was true: she looked like an object.

He pulled the sheet over her, debating what to do next. Tell the others? He supposed he'd have to. It seemed unlikely that Ruth would be springing back to life—or *unlife*, take your pick. She died the old-fashioned way, free of zombie molestation. She was clean. Well, sort of. Abe wrinkled his nose. Ruth had, as it was euphemized, "voided herself," filling the air with yet another bad smell and the sheets with something worse. How very un-Ruth-like. "Oy, Ruthie, Ruthie, Ruthie."

So much for the family plot, he mused. Ruth had made such a to-do over her desire to be buried alongside her parents and sister. She also figured he'd predecease her—so much for woman's intuition, too. What was he supposed to do now? She'd want a eulogy, a service of some kind. She'd expect the Mourner's Kaddish, in Hebrew, no less, and since his Bar Mitzvah he'd forgotten pretty much everything. Did she have a prayer book tucked away somewhere? Probably. He seemed to recall her filching one from her sister's funeral. Hopefully it was phonetic. He'd look later. But if he was to respect her wishes, which seemed the right thing to do, silly though it may be—pointless, even—so be it. She wouldn't be getting the whole *megillah,* but he'd do his best to accommodate her as best he could. He stared across the room at his reflection in the mirror of Ruthie's dressing table.

"*Avel,* vhat can you do?" Abe said in comic Yinglish inflection. In Judaism the mourner was called an *avel.* It was a self-admittedly bad pun. It brought him no comfort. "There goes that second Social Security check." Again the joke didn't help. He was bombing to an audience of none. Miriam, Hannah and David had never laughed at his jokes, nor did their kids. Ruth had seldom laughed at them. It had been ages since he'd even attempted mirth, except for the hackneyed waiter joke at the celebratory dinner on the roof. Everyone else in the building was listening to music again, and watching videos. Those little screens hurt his eyes. Most of Abe's music was on vinyl or, God help him, reel-to-reel. And what he wouldn't do to be able to listen to some of his comedy records right now. The best medicine there is.

On shaky legs, Abe trudged into the living room and dropped into his threadbare upholstered chair, parted the dingy chintz curtains, opened the dusty Venetian blinds. Déjà vu on top of déjà vu on top of feeling beaten down and laden with wearied grief.

More déjà vu.

A little Bob Newhart would be nice.

The door to 2B remained open at all times, that dwelling being Mona's point of entrance and egress from the building. Since taking up residence in 2A, she'd taken to keeping the door locked, especially when she was out on errands. Everyone agreed she was entitled to her privacy and security, after all everyone else kept their doors locked, so why shouldn't she?

Karl's knuckles barely grazed the surface of Mona's door, his rapping so feeble even he could barely hear it. His chin mashed into the pit of his collarbone, his lower lip twitched in self-disgust. He was having such a hard time getting up the nerve to approach her. *Well, duh, you think maybe it's because you see her as some kind of heavenly force? Like some kind of earthly angel or at the very least some kind of saint or whatnot?* It was absurd. Not that Mona was possibly imbued with some holy powers, but that he was petrified. She was mellow, Karl told himself. Fact was Mona was mellowness incarnate. Almost nothing seemed to bother her. Not even the things outside.

Karl's hair stood up all over.

Not even the things outside.

There was an angle he'd never considered. Maybe the things outside stepped out of her way not because she was imbued with the Holy Spirit, but rather was an emissary of Lucifer and her minions knew better than to obstruct her path, let alone devour her. *It made sense.* Everyone in the building was on death's door, starving, dehydrated, vulnerable, then along comes this pristine, beautiful young girl—temptation made flesh—offering every secular comfort. Maybe in their final moments the denizens of 1620 would have found their way back to God, and here was this serpentine interloper, sent to obscure their potential moment of spiritual clarity.

She dressed in black.

She listened mainly to metal. *Oh Jesus*, he thought. *Oh Jesus Christ*. How could he have missed this? Everyone was so blinded by her gifts that they couldn't see her for what and who she was: Lilith! Or if not capital L Lilith, then lower case lilith, which was still not good. Even her last name was suspect: Luft. Luft was German for "air," a tricky name. Mona's personality seemed lighter than air. Air was a sustainer of life. She was keeping them all here, alive physically, but spiritually dead.

He was at last seeing through her deception. He'd seen The Light!

And now it was his job to let the others know.

Then they could vote whether to let her stay or drive her from the fold.

28

Ruth's naked body lay on their bed wrapped in a clean white sheet, as dictated by Jewish tradition—it was the least he could muster since she'd have to forgo the plain pine box. In the back of Abe's mind he seemed to recall something about no coffin and the body being laid to rest, face up, and then concrete blocks being put on it, but the memory was sketchy. Sweltering in his mourning suit, tie cinched tight at his collar, Abe petted Ruth's "earthly remains" and chewed the insides of his cheeks.

He'd disposed of the sheets and mattress pad she'd soiled and tidied as best he could, masking any residual odor with copious amounts of Glade air freshener. It was not a pleasant task and his estimation of those in the funeral trade became more sympathetic as he'd toiled to prepare the body. It wasn't Ruth anymore. Odd how once the life force had departed the body it ceased to resemble its former occupant. Sure, the face was the same, but the slackness removed the humanity. Abe didn't believe in the soul, but Ruth's death had transformed her, in spite of the homely details. It was the peacefulness. The body had relinquished her driving, vital force. In repose she didn't look like the pinched yenta she'd become over the years. It was simple as that.

He'd told the others. Ellen and Alan said they'd attend the service, as did Dabney and Karl. It came as no surprise that the guinea bastard had shown nary a jot of sympathy or respect. At least his boyfriend had paid his respects, even if it was just lip service. What did come as a surprise was the first to arrive was Mona, who'd made no show of condolence when Abe had mentioned news of his wife's passing. On this occasion her customary black wardrobe seemed apt, as did the unheard-of absence of headphones.

"Mona," Abe said, ushering her into his parlor. "Thank you for coming."

"Uh-huh," she said, but it didn't sound unsympathetic. It was just her way.

"Can I, um, do you want a drink of something? Water? Juice? Seltzer?" Abe felt funny offering her provisions she'd furnished, but what else could he do?

"No thanks." Mona scratched an ear, no doubt feeling naked without her earphones. A few moments of silence passed, Abe standing there at a double loss, Mona looking at her feet.

"You know," Abe said, "I was the only one in the building who had fight his way home through the first—what would you call it—outbreak of the zombies? The events of Feb Five. It's true. The rest were home or nearby—except Dabney, who's got his own horror story—but I was at work when it really began to hit the fan. I managed to get home, all the way from the Garment District to here. That's three miles, give or take. On these old pins." Abe smiled and patted his upper thighs for emphasis. "I couldn't leave Ruthie to deal with this alone. Oy, did she sound scared. Well, of course she did. Why wouldn't she be? She wasn't an easy woman, but I loved her. Maybe I didn't show it enough, especially lately, but I did. In my way, which maybe wasn't so good. I tried. I did my best."

Mona sniffed loudly, and for a moment Abe thought this moment of human-scale tragedy had reached her; that she was moved. But no. It was just plain old congestion. She removed her backpack and opened a side pocket. "Can I get that water?"

"Certainly, dear." *Dear?* Abe shook his head as he walked into the kitchen to pour her a glass of water. *Dear?* Though she looked nothing like his daughters, save for the color of her hair, Mona put him in mind of them. Miriam and Hannah, his brunette beauties, they having gotten his coloring, not Ruth's. Abe returned to the parlor and handed Mona the glass, which she accepted with a simple nod and another sniff.

"Allergies?" Abe prompted.

"Maybe."

Abe had never been one for small talk. At social gatherings it was Ruthie that carried the conversation, he happy to let her do the heavy lifting. He stole a look at her shrunken remains, then looked back at his youthful guest. The contrast was harrowing.

"So, you really never encountered anyone else out there in your travels? No one. No other survivors. No enclaves like ours. Nothing."

"No."

"Have you walked far? Covered a lot of ground? Sometimes I look at the sky and see all the stars and think how arrogant to think we're alone in the universe. The one planet special enough to host intelligent life, such as it was. Or any life. When I'm on the roof, looking this way and that, I feel the same. But nothing, huh? Not a soul."

"No."

Her monosyllabic response hung in the air like a vague but disquieting smell until it was dispersed by the arrival of Ellen, Alan and Karl, then Dabney and shockingly the Irish *faygeleh.* Conventional sympathies were expressed, handshakes exchanged as well as a couple of hugs and a peck on the cheek from Ellen. Considering he knew Ruth wasn't exactly well loved—or even liked—it was an excellent turnout. She'd have been pleased. After pleasantries and so forth they adjourned to the bedroom and Abe fished out the little prayer pamphlet. Looking a trifle embarrassed, Abe put on his reading glasses and cleared his throat. He'd never liked orating before a group.

"Okay. Thank you all for coming. I know I said that already, but thank you again, anyway. It would have meant a lot to Ruth. Okay." He cleared his throat again. "Okay, so I'm going to read this little prayer, even though I don't go in for all this nonsense. Okay. I should skip the editorializing. Sorry. And to Ruthie I say sorry, too. I can't do it in Hebrew. I don't remember how." Abe smoothed the codex and again cleared his throat. Sweat was pouring off him, his suit darkening further in the pits and back—like it mattered. "Okay …"

Karl piped up, "If you're too overwhelmed, I could say a few words." Abe noticed the shiny new Bible Karl clutched and tamped down his impulse to scoff. That's all Ruthie would need, the resident poster boy goy to preside at her funeral service. Abe forced a smile and politely declined Karl's well-intentioned offer. Abe patted his forehead with a cleanish hankie and began.

"May His great name grow exalted and sanctified in the world that He created as He willed. May He give reign to His kingship and cause His salvation to sprout, and bring near His Messiah in your lifetimes and in your days, and in the lifetimes of the entire family of Israel, swiftly and soon. Amen.

"May His great name be blessed forever and ever. Blessed, praised, glorified, exalted, extolled, mighty, upraised, and lauded be the name of the holy one, Blessed is He beyond any blessing and song, praise and consolation that are uttered in the world. Amen."

What a load of horseshit, Abe thought amid a chorus of hushed amens. *So be it.*

"Listen, there's all kinds of nonsense you're supposed to do for Jewish funerals, but let's face it, we're not equipped and I've done what I can. None of that *chazzerai* means anything anymore anyway. I'd rather eulogize Ruth in my head than aloud. It's too tough. You people never got to know Ruthie at her best. Quite the opposite, to be frank. But trust me, Ruthie was a sweet lady, way back when. She was a beauty, too, and a good mother. Maybe a little overbearing, but good. Anyway, there's supposed to be a procession and all that rigmarole, but forget it. I don't even remember which is supposed to come first. The tent of prayer. The rending ritual. Without a cemetery to orient me I'm at a loss."

"So what do you want us to do, Abe?" Dabney asked. Maybe because he was the second oldest in the room he had some sense of the absurdity, as well as solemnity, of the occasion.

"I just want Ruthie's body removed from the premises. I know burial's out. Same for cremation. So, all I ask is dispose of it in as dignified a manner as you can. But I don't want to see. I'd rather lie to myself that she got what she deserved."

"Okay, Abe. You got it."

Abe sat on the upholstered bench before Ruth's vanity and watched as Dabney and Alan lifted the enshrouded corpse of his wife of forty-eight years. Hunched over Ruth's vanity Abe held his head in his hands, the grief beginning to hit him and take hold. All her powders and liniments, her tinctures and paraphernalia neatly arranged on the low table reminded him of the great pains she'd taken to look attractive for him before it all went south. His nose ran but his eyes remained dry. He sniffled and kneaded his scalp. Wife, children, grandkids—all gone. He snorted back the snot and clenched his eyes shut.

"Allergies?" came a soft, female voice.

Abe started, nearly toppling from the bench. He thought he was alone, but there stood Mona in the doorway, clutching her childish bag.

"What?" Abe said.

"Your nose."

"No, not allergies. Just plain old anguish," Abe said, adding with a touch of sarcasm, "You got anything for *that*?"

Rather than look insulted or display any recognizable emotion, Mona opened her bag and rummaged through it. "Valium. Prozac. Paxil. Zoloft. Wellbutrin. Parnate. Nardil. Effexor." Not five words in a row from this girl in the last month and now this checklist of multisyllabic antidepressants. "I did a quick run. Because …" She gestured at Abe. Tears did come, now. A true gesture of kindness in this fallen world.

Abe wiped his nose and stared at Mona as she crouched by the door, still foraging in her cartoon backpack. The backpack reminded Abe of the baby snowsuits. The more he looked at her the more she reminded Abe of his granddaughter. Danielle hadn't been as phlegmatic, but she took her job as a teenager seriously and was as sullen and uncommunicative as possible. Abe missed her.

"My God, I am touched. Genuinely touched. What a gesture."

"S'okay."

"I've never really partaken. I guess I'll try some of that Zoloft."

"Takes awhile."

"How long?"

"Couple weeks. More longterm."

"And the others?"

"Valium's quick."

"Okay, I'll go with that."

Two tabs later Abe slipped off into narcotized slumber, his body in the exact spot Ruth's had been. He slept the untroubled sleep of a babe. And four rooftops away, like a perished sailor at sea, Dabney and Alan cast her from the northernmost building. That roof dropped to another roof, rather than the street, so her body would remain unmolested, to decompose in peace.

29

"YOU CAN'T BE thinking of keeping it," Alan said, straining to sound as reasonable and nonjudgmental as possible.

"And why not?"

"Why not?" He tapped the home pregnancy tester on his knee. "I really want to phrase this right. I don't want to be patronizing or insulting or anything like that ..."

"You're *already* being patronizing. If you're going to hammer me with a whole laundry list of how shitty it is out there, spare me. Duh. I'm not fucking blind, I'm not fucking stupid. I think I'm pretty well caught up, thank you very much."

"Then how can you justify such a selfish act?" *So much for diplomacy.* "How could you even remotely think having a baby is a good idea? I'm sorry, but there is no good rationale for it. Is it some innate female desire to procreate? I couldn't know that firsthand. You need something that will love you unconditionally?"

"Who said anything about that? Don't go putting words in my mouth!"

"Then explain it. I'm sorry. Maybe I'm totally wrong. Please. *Enlighten me.*"

Ellen's eyes flared and she gripped her knee to suppress the urge to smack Alan. "You said something about *not* being patronizing?"

"I don't mean to be," Alan said. He inhaled for effect, then modulated his voice. "This is a very emotional moment. Let's calm down."

Ellen was all too familiar with this playbook: Reasonable Male vs. Irrational Female. *Nope.*

"Is this your first rodeo?"

"Excuse me?" Alan looked confused.

"You were married once, right? Wanna fan the fire? Affect that artificial mansplaining 'reasonable' tone. See how that works out for you."

Alan fidgeted. "You're right. I'm just …"

"You're out of your depth. And this isn't about you or what you think or want or feel, okay? I'm talking to you like we're partners, but is that what we are? *Not really.*"

"You wanted me to …" He hesitated. "I think we are. Or could be. I'd *like* that."

Ellen eyed Alan with growing disenchantment. Her fear that some of this was hormonal was pissing her off. But not irrationally. Not unprovoked. Overall, she'd been pretty pleased with her response to the world turning to shit. To permanent house arrest. To loss and privation and everything. A laundry list of pros and cons unspooled behind her eyes. She had asked Alan to couple with her, true. But did she need it? Eddie was growing more robust. But was Alan a deterrent if push came to rape? Probably not.

She looked over at Alan. His expression acknowledged crossing lines, fucking up, wanting to make amends. She could see the recalibration going on behind his eyes. The course correcting. It was all apologies, which annoyed her.

"I'm not going to be the villain, here," Ellen said.

"No, of course. I was out of line. *Way* out of line. The *worst.*"

It wasn't her first rodeo, either. With bouts of interpersonal discord or with bouts of morning, noon and night sickness. With Em she'd felt NVP— nausea and vomiting of pregnancy—at about week six or seven. Mike hadn't been gone for even a month, so this was definitely his. Not that Señor Puppydog flashing his big browns at her knew that. He hadn't seemed to object to boning her without the benefit of a condom. What, did he assume *she* was taking precautions? Didn't most men put the burden of responsibility on the woman? Alan had seemed so atypical at first, but now? Since the reintroduction to creature comforts like video he'd been a lot less attentive.

"You just don't know what it's like," Ellen said.

"You're right, I don't."

"I lost a child. Do you have any idea what that's like?"

"I had pregnancy scares, but …"

"I'm guessing you and your significant others put the kibosh on those."

He nodded.

"Consensually, or did you pressurize those with 'reasonable' words?"

"Hey, look …" He stopped himself before digging in. "We agreed. We were too young, the time wasn't right, et cetera."

"Yeah, et cetera. So in other words, you don't have a clue. And I don't really have the bandwidth to explain it. Losing a child. It's not the same as …"

"All the other losses. I get it."

Ellen looked at him and allowed that maybe he did. Or at least was trying to, which counted for something. Even Mike hadn't been as psychically wounded by Em's death as Ellen had. He'd cried. A lot. And it didn't seem performative. But maybe men just couldn't feel that connection. With men the whole procreation equation came down to: *Spurt! My work is done.*

"Does the human race just call it quits?" Ellen said, her voice flat. "Like Peggy Lee said, *is that all there is*? I can't believe that. Those things out there can't run on empty forever. Someday they'll start dropping and then it will be time to rebuild and repopulate. That's the function of every organism, Alan. To perpetuate its kind. Is that so bad? I'm not trying to bait you. I'm asking, legit."

"It's not that it's bad, but what kind of risk are you willing to take? You see those things out there as being transitory? Maybe you're right. I hope you're right. But since their arrival I don't see any signs of them going away. Maybe I could see what you're doing as a positive if they were keeling over out there, but they're not."

"Maybe this makes it worse for you. Maybe not. But this is Mike's, which makes this also my last piece of my husband."

"I know it's his. And I'd say maybe wait, but I had a vasectomy, so …"

Ellen looked at Alan and laughed, shaking her head. "And there's new information. Jesus." She then rubbed her stomach.

"I'd rather think of *this* as Mike's legacy than that stain in the alley. So ..."

Alan leaned over and gave her knee a tender squeeze, mute capitulation, as if he had a vote, anyway. In silence Alan rose from the sofa and exited the room. Ellen sat back and softly began to sing, "*Is that all there is, is that all there is ...*"

"They can't last forever," Abe said, his manner chemically muted.

Alan paced Abe's floor, periodically looking out the window at the mob.

"Tell *them* that," the younger man said, agitated by his exchange with Ellen. "They don't seem to have gotten that memo."

"Eventually they'll run out of steam. Maybe not in my lifetime, but—"

"I'll repeat myself: *tell them that.* They don't seem to be going anywhere. And who's to say we outlast them? They've been running on empty for months. With the exception of Mike, none of us fed the flock, so what, they just do us a kindness and drop?"

"I've seen some of them do just that," Abe said. "Drop. They can't keep going on and on and on, eternally. And if we can outlast them, that'll mean we can get out of this building and move on. Or at least you youngsters can."

"To where?"

"Anywhere. That's immaterial at this point. But you've gotta cling to some kind of hope. You have to be optimistic," Abe said.

Alan looked at the old man with befuddlement. Though he wasn't about to spill the beans about Ellen's natal bombshell, Alan had come up here to commiserate with the resident curmudgeon, to buttress his negative worldview. Instead he was having a chat with Pollyanna. Abe sat in his armchair, shirt open and little round belly pooched out over his undone slacks. His face pharmaceutically beatified, he resembled a scrawny Jewish Buddha.

"You're going to make me laugh," Alan marveled, "and I'm not sure I'm up for that."

"Why? Why laugh? Hope is the most vital asset we have. It's all we as a species ever really ever had. Hope is the only reason to get up in the morning."

"Hope is toxic."

Now Abe chuckled. "Hope is essential."

"Who *are* you?"

"You've gotta have hope," replied the old man.

"If you start to sing, I'm gonna scream."

"The stuff I'm taking, I wouldn't care."

"Stuff?"

"Mona's a heckuva pharmacist." Abe closed his eyes, chuckling to himself. "A heckuva pharmacist." The old man closed his eyes and began to hum "High Hopes" and Alan left, irritated that he'd been "played out" twice in a row with classic oldies.

"So I sent her out for more of that rope and some other stuff," Eddie said, his smile devious.

"Why?" Dave asked.

"I got me an idea for some leisure activities, but mainly I wanted her out of the way for a while. I wanna check out her digs, snoop around and see if I can figure out what her secret is."

"You still on about that?" Dave said with derision as he pondered the vagueness of Eddie's unspecified "leisure activities."

"Fuck yeah, I'm still on about it. *She gets to go out,* Einstein. She gets to leave the compound. She's holding out, bro. I *know* it. I can feel it in my bones. What'd they call me, back in the day? What?"

"Mr. Intuitive."

"Boom. Mr. Intuitive. That's right. Commodities, derivatives, *intuitive.* Yes. These fucks think I'm stupid, especially Zotz. But we know better. *I* know better. *Me.*"

Dave didn't feel like arguing. Instead he slurped another wedge of syrupy peach out of the can, letting it roll against his tongue and lips, hoping the suggestive visuals would derail whatever scheme Eddie was hatching. Instead, Eddie just snapped at him for eating like a pig, and then left the apartment. Dave gulped down the rest of the sweet liquid and followed Eddie into the hall, then downstairs. Two flights down Eddie placed a small flashlight between his lips and aiming the focused beam on Mona's top cylinder began to pick the lock with some small, spidery tools.

"Where'd you get those?" Dave asked.

"Among my treasures rescued from the old crib," Eddie said, his hushed voice slightly slurred by the flashlight. "Keep your voice down. I don't want to get caught in the act." And with that the top lock opened. "Fuckin' Yale," Eddie whispered with a smirk, removing the drippy flashlight from his mouth. "Never would've gotten it open if it was a Medeco."

He opened the door and in they slipped. The apartment was almost identical to when Mona had taken occupancy, the only difference being she'd moved Paolo's mid-century recliner next to the left front window.

"So what are we looking for?" Dave asked, nerves straining his voice.

"Hey, *you* don't have to be here," Eddie snapped. "I'm happy to do this on my own. You wanna help, great. But if you're gonna honk like a woman, beat it. 'Cause I don't need that shit."

After a cursory couple of circuits around the apartment, Eddie began to rummage in earnest, opening drawers and riffling through them, closing them in disgust when nothing extraordinary was unearthed. Though he'd never been here before he had the sneaking suspicion all was as it had been in the Latino fruit's time. Drawer after drawer revealed nothing.

"C'mon, Eddie, Mona will be back soon."

"How about you settle down? Sometimes she don't come back for hours or till the next day. She left less than an hour ago. For real. Be useful or piss off."

Eddie opened one of the hall closets, cursing softly as a small avalanche of shoeboxes pummeled his scalp. "Your mother's ass!" he shouted, clapping a hand over his mouth and cursing himself for making noise. Lid after lid revealed nothing. "These shoeboxes got nothin' but shoes in 'em," he griped, filing them back on the upper shelf. Board games, a scuffed soccer ball, garment bags filled with nice suits no one would ever need again, two garbage bags labeled "For Goodwill"—it was all shit. And clearly not one bit of it was Mona's.

Eddie stepped into the bedroom and switched on the solar camping lantern within. The bed was immaculately made, with taut hospital corners. Either Mona was quite the skilled domestic—which seemed unlikely—or she didn't sleep in the bed. Who knows, maybe the spooky little freak didn't sleep at all. With diminished enthusiasm Eddie opened dresser drawers and foraged, turning up nothing but the former occupant's unmentionables and workaday clothes. There was a box of condoms well past their fuck-by date, but Eddie palmed them anyway. What a waste of—

"*Hey, Eddie,*" came Dave's voice in a whisper-hiss. "*Check this out.*"

Eddie stepped into the kitchenette and found Dave standing on the kitchen counter holding a bumpy sheet of something shiny—a blister pack of pills. "Whuzzat?" Eddie said, snatching it from Dave.

"*It's drugs,*" Dave said, sotto voce. "But check *this* out." He opened the top cabinet. Inside were mounds of identical pristine blister packs, as well as prescription bottles of various sizes, all full. Eddie looked at the stockpile of pharmaceuticals and felt both vindication and annoyance that he hadn't discovered the goods.

"See what I told you?" he said. "You *see*?"

"I see a lot of drugs, Eddie. But what does it tell us about Mona? That she's a drug addict? That would explain her zonked out personality, but …"

"*But, but, but.* You sound like a fuckin' Vespa. Maybe it's her whole *everything*, bro. It could …"

Both trespassers froze at the squawk of the homebase walkie-talkie, which announced Mona's return.

"That was fast," Eddie seethed, stuffing a blister pack into his pants.

"Shouldn't we put that back?"

"Fuck that. I wanna know what this shit is. Like she's gonna miss one sheet of it, whatever it is."

"But …"

"But me no buts. We gotta lay low while they help her in."

Dave pressed his ear to the door and when the pounding of footfalls subsided he looked through the peephole. He turned to face Eddie and gave the thumbs up. Like an old-timey silent comedy burglar, Dave opened the door a crack. Everyone seemed to be in the neighboring apartment—they could hear Alan calling out to Mona. Dave and Eddie stepped into the hall.

"What're you guys doing in Mona's place?" Karl asked, standing on the landing out of the fisheyed peephole's range, clutching his Bible. "If you're investigating, I have a theory." Eddie suppressed the urge to just swat the smaller man aside and instead loomed over Karl, allowing the full impact of their disparity in height and brawn to sink in. He smirked and thug-purred, “And what theory might that be?”

“That she’s an emissary of Satan?”

Eddie’s face relaxed into smirking disdain. “Lemme ask you something: are you a fuckin’ moron? Don’t even, okay? And also, *we were never here, capisce?*” Karl nodded. “*Bene,*” Eddie said as he and his compatriot ascended the steps. “*Molto bene.*”

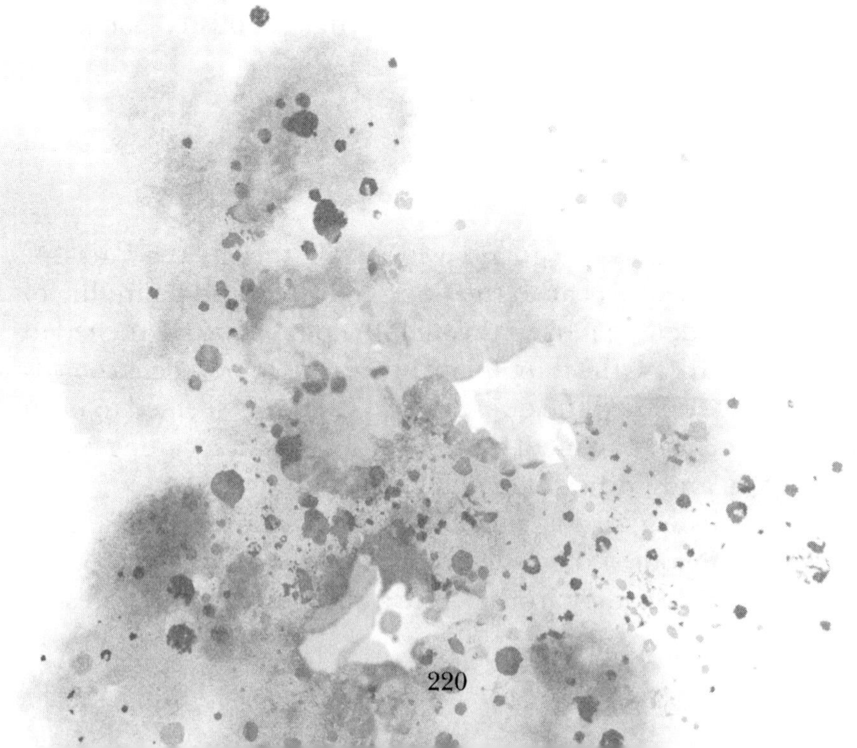

30

ALAN DIDN'T SHARE Ellen's hopefulness, if that's what you could call it.

If anything, Alan took some comfort from the hypothesis that he and the others were the last of their kind. The reign of man—*nature's biggest mistake,* as his dad had characterized it—was nearly at its end. What an honor, to be cognizant of the end of your own species, to be members of The Last Generation. The dinosaurs didn't know that their number was up. It was a shame that all of humanity's finer contributions—art, literature, music, architecture, *some* science—would in time completely disintegrate, but the notion that the earth would be free of man's influence, that the planet could heal itself and be cleansed, was heartening. Still, if he wanted to stay—or more to the point *get back*—in Ellen's good favor—and he did—he'd have to quash that kind of thinking.

Or at least dilute it.

He swirled his brush in some linseed oil and studied his subject. Mona sat on a stool between the front windows, one leg perched on the footrest, the other dangling limply a few inches above the floor. Though fully dressed—Alan didn't wish to invite further scorn from Ellen—Mona was barefoot and once again Alan was attempting to not be aroused by Mona's sumptuous calves and now, of all things, her well-turned feet. Most feet he'd encountered, male or female, were functional but unattractive collections of jutting tendons, knots and joints, often rough and calloused. Mona's were just the opposite, their tops smooth and doll-like, almost like an adult baby. How could a girl who did so much walking have such pampered-looking feet?

As a precaution, to mask any unwanted flare-ups should they occur, he wore a paint-smeared oversized smock-like shirt. But there was something innate to Mona. Something intangible. Maybe the same thing that repelled the undead attracted him. What a thought. Was it a pheromone? Made more sense than something paranormal.

He refocused on technique and execution, his strokes deft and provocative—but not *too* provocative. What a waste that no one of note would ever see these works. He'd always been modest about his art, having been raised to believe humility a virtue. All diffidence had ever gotten him was a whole lot of nothing. He'd barely gotten any public accolades and never would. Not that doing art had anything to do with that, but, well, yeah, *yeah it did.* Ellen thought he was a genius, even if that was an audience of one. That counted for something, even if she was pissed at him. And rightly so.

Alan looked away from the canvas to the most cluttered wall. Amid myriad zombie studies hung four portraits of Mona. Unconsciously he'd spread the zombies away from the paintings of Mona, manifesting the old precept of art imitating life. Zombies. Mona. Sure, she was alive, but in spite of her pleasing appearance she lacked vitality, her eyes communicating no more than those of the undead outside. Maybe less, actually. In the eyes of the undead he'd catch glimmers of who they once were. Some looked sad. Tormented. Confused. Her eyes, when she'd spare you a rare and fleeting direct glance, were glassy. He thought about the concept of the uncanny valley. That something closely resembling a human, but a bit off, a bit shy of the mark, induced a feeling of aversion. Mona was human, but elicited that eerie sensation. Her manner. Her reticence to make eye contact. Her smoothness. Her almost complete lack of verbal communication. And of course, the elephant in the room: *her meticulously undiscussed gift.*

An erection. Just like that. Unreal.

It was like a second adolescence. The smock masked it but he was sure he was reddening with embarrassment. Pathetic. A shame spiral took him back to rebukes in middle school. Girls he'd crushed on crushing his soul with cutting remarks. "Stop staring at me." *Was I staring? I was. Fuck.* And now *this.* And he wasn't even attracted to Mona. Not really. Was he? *It's the end of the world as we know it and I feel …*

Like an idiot.

Like all things, this too would pass. Artists were notoriously oversexed, but was that really true or was it just innately male? Did artists just try to justify it? Give themselves a pass? He pointed his brush and resumed detail on her lower extremities, perfecting the hues, his mind in an abstracted place of nearly rote application. *Paint a robot, be a robot.* It almost made him smile.

The unwanted protrusion ebbed.

That did make him smile.

"*Why not?*" Eddie said, trying not to sound like a whiny little bitch. Mona stood before him, implacable. More infuriating than her unwillingness to comply with his simple, reasonable request was her refusal—or was it inability?—to elaborate. She'd gotten them every little goddamn thing, but now this sudden veto? It made no sense. Eddie mopped his forehead and stared in disbelief at this petite yet immovable object. He grimaced as a stinging trickle of perspiration leaked into his eye.

"No guns," she repeated.

"But come on, it's a good idea. You *know* it."

"It's a bad idea."

"But we could start takin' 'em out. We could cut a path for you ahead of time."

"No need."

"Maybe *we* could even go out. You ever think about that?"

"No guns."

"*Fine,* we'll discuss this later. Maybe hold a vote. You believe in democracy or are you some kind of …" he stopped himself. What was he going to call her? A commie? That seemed a little out-of-date. "Maybe the others can convince you."

"No."

"*Fine.*"

"Fine." Uninflected. It wasn't even snotty. He hated that.

"You know, you got your whole thing happening here. Your hoodoo. The rest of us are trapped in this fuckin' cage and that ain't right. But you …" He gestured her hourglass outline in the air around her. "*You.*" That she didn't react pissed him off. That she didn't look at him pissed him off. Karl flinched, like a good boy. This one, all five-foot-nothing of her, *niente.* "You're holding out." The most reaction he'd gotten was she lightly tugged the chewed-on hem of the slightly too-long sleeve of her shirt. Eddie turned his back on her and stomped upstairs, pausing for a second to throw open his apartment door and bark, "Dave-o, grab your gear, we're goin' fishin'!"

On the roof, Dabney snored as he napped under his rickety lean-to. Eddie scowled as he waited for Dave. Fuckin' Mallon might've gone homo, but at least he still knew how to be a man, have fun like a man, whatever. The whole gun thing had put Eddie in a foul mood. Why that stupid little cooze couldn't see the advantage to scoring some firepower was beyond him. What, she was afraid of guns? Guns could do some serious damage to those rotten skinbags down on the street. That's not a plus? *Please.* Eddie thought about his little zombie encounter in his old digs. A piece would've been sweet. *Pow!* From ravenous ghoul to dark wet stain.

"What's up?" Dave said as he barged onto the tarpaper.

"*Shhh,* I don't wanna rouse the coconut," Eddie whispered. "You brought the gear bag?"

"Yeah, but what's it for?"

"The Comet wants to go sport fishing, bro."

"Huh?"

Eddie beckoned Dave to follow him across several rooftops until they reached the one furthest north. Eddie opened the bag and pulled out the two heavy-duty Penn reels. "You can haul in a fuckin' three-hundred-pound marlin with these babies," Eddie grinned.

"So?"

"So, we're going hump-angling, Davy. Gonna catch me a zombie, bro."

Dave stood back and watched as Eddie put together the rod and reel assembly. For a change it wasn't that hot, but sweat poured off Eddie's brow like a mini-Niagara. His eyes were wild. His bare chest shimmered. "This'll be just like angling for sailfish or shark or any of those big motherfuckers. You remember that Costa Rica vacay, bro? Same such as that, only better." He patted a toolbelt slung around his waist for emphasis.

"Eddie, dude. I dunno, man, this is a little weird, don'tcha think? I mean, what if you actually catch one? And what are you gonna use for bait?"

"You mean *you* don't wanna get on the hook? I'm just fuckin' with you. Okay. Okay, I don't need to use a lure, okay? I can make a noose. Oh, dude, that is perfect. What a combo: fishin' and lynchin'. Call it *flynchin'*! Oh, dude, that's genius. *Genius*!"

"Scary is what it is," Dave said. "You seem a little zippy, bruh. But not zippy like *zip-a-dee-doo-da*. Zippy like that time you did three bumps of blow at the company holiday party. Tweaked."

"This is supposed to be a bonding moment. Tryin' to reconnect with my bud."

"Eddie, have you been taking those pills you kiped?"

"Keep your voice down." Eddie nodded toward Dabney.

"You have been, haven't you? You even know what they are?"

"They're her fuckin' secret," Eddie whispered, teeth clenched. "Why else does she got so many of them, huh? Dude, it's so perfectly clear. *I* figured it out. Mr. Intuitive."

Eddie stood up, rod and reel ready for action, and cast the line into the crowd below. Within seconds the line jerked, the tip of the rod dipping. Eddie positioned himself behind a sturdy steam pipe, bending at the knees for more leverage. "Grab my waist," he commanded as he laughed in triumph. "This bitch ain't gettin' away!" Dave wrapped his arms around Eddie's midriff and dug his heels in. Eddie dipped forward. The thing on the end of his line was putting up a struggle. His bronzed biceps bulging with each crank of the reel, Eddie looked like a well-oiled part of the apparatus. "Help me reel this fucker in!" Eddie roared, no longer caring about Dabney.

Dave added muscle and soon a rotted head appeared at the edge of the roof, monofilament cutting into its wrist, which was caught between the noose and its neck. Eddie yanked the rod vertical, cackling at the sight of the zombie's stricken visage. For something brain-dead it looked plenty scared and more than a little riled. Thick darkened blood oozed from where the line was scoring the epidermis and it groaned piteously. Eddie jerked the rod again, attempting to heave his quarry over the edge. Instead the line cut straight through the purulent flesh and dismembered the wretched thing. With the zombie's weight no longer balancing them, the sportsmen toppled backwards, Eddie's coccyx crunching against Dave's groin, eliciting a doglike yelp. Dave rolled out from under his laughing companion and cradled his injured batch.

"Almost got 'im," Eddie guffawed. "The little fish that got away!"

"Who fuckin' cares?"

"What's your problem?"

"Never mind." Dave lay there moaning, cupping his area.

"Wanna give it another go?"

"Do I look like I wanna?"

"*Pfff.* What a killjoy. S'matter with your nads, bro?"

"Forget it, okay? Just forget it."

Eddie sauntered over to the roof wall and looked down, his prize absorbed by the crowd, no sign of it below.

"That sucks," he said.

"Well, what would you have done with it, anyway? Hung it over the mantelpiece?"

Eddie slipped a hammer out of a slot in the belt. "I wanted to smash all its teeth out and then basically torture it for a while. Cut on it and take it apart and shit."

"Oh. Sorry that didn't work out for you."

Eddie smiled and said, "Thanks," not noticing the sarcasm. Eddie clapped his bud on the shoulder and said, "We can try another time, right, amigo?" Dave nodded. "I'm goin' back down, you coming?" Dave shook his head. "A'right, catch you later, bro."

Eddie trotted across the rooftops, then disappeared into the stairwell.

As Dave stepped onto their roof, Dabney sat up and said, "Your homeboy is a goddamn lunatic, you know that, don't you?" Dave nodded again. He was temporarily at a loss for words. Words just didn't seem to cut it right about now. Even "inadequate" seemed inadequate.

From his bed, Karl lobbed The Good Book across the room. What was so good about it? It was riddled with riddles, chock-a-block with baffling parables. No wonder people spent their whole lives reading the same tome over and over and over again. No one could make sense of this, at least not in a practical, how-to-apply-this-to-my-daily-grind kind of way. Karl had always noted people reading the Bible in public, especially on the subway, their brows always creased in intense concentration, and highlighter pens poised to accentuate key passages for future rumination. Karl had gone to college and couldn't fathom half what he read and re-read. He'd ask Mona for a highlighter pen of his own.

Karl knew there was a God, but His guidebook was the work of human beings, and humans could seldom be trusted. It was a book created by committee, too. Karl had a rule of thumb: any movie with more than three screenwriters was likely going to be a mess. The stories in The Bible had been circulated plenty before they were set down on parchment. It was like the telephone game.

Big Manfred had an LP called, "Satan is Real," by these gospelers, the Louvin Brothers. Big Manny had found nothing funny about it, however, especially not its title. Satan *was* real to the Old Man, and there was nothing even remotely amusing about that. Sure, the record cover displayed a hokey image—the lily-white brothers dressed in snappy white suits in the flaming pits of hell, a ridiculous cardboard-looking red devil on the horizon—but the album's message was clear: don't sin; obey The Bible; be a good Christian. Simple as that. The weirdest part was the Brothers looked mighty cheery as they simultaneously preached and roasted.

Karl rolled over onto his stomach to ease the knot there, a combination of hunger and anxiety. He hadn't eaten in three days in protest of the foodstuffs procured by Mona, but what if he was wrong? Maybe she wasn't in league with Lucifer, in which case this boycott was in vain. Plus, if she were an emissary of The Lord, wouldn't his hunger strike be blasphemous? It wasn't like he could just ask her, either. If she were a hellish minion, surely she would lie and say otherwise. But if she was sent by God, she'd likely lie or evade the question, too. It was not for him, a mere mortal, to question the divine. And as sure as he was that God existed, he wasn't as certain about Beelzebub. Karl always figured the devil was the invention of man, kind of a scapegoat for rotten behavior. Why be burdened with personal accountability when you could blame Satan?

"This is unbearable," Karl moaned into his pillow. He dropped off the bed and assumed a posture of supplication, interlacing his fingers and tilting his head heavenward. "Am I being tested? I mean, wasn't I being tested *before* Mona arrived? Isn't this whole stinking mess a test? If I starve myself, isn't that protracted suicide, which is a mortal sin? So, I guess what I'm saying is, I should eat, right? If Mona is here on Satan's behalf, I'll need my strength to outwit her, right? Or if she's one of Yours, I should …"

What was the point? He gave up. No answer was forthcoming, ever. Maybe on Judgment Day. Karl wondered if the line into Heaven was like the ones at Six Flags. Each depiction he'd ever seen rendered of the line to the Pearly Gates was evocative of the ones at every theme park he'd ever attended. Did technology in the afterlife move forward as it did in life? Had Saint Peter upgraded from *The Book of Life* to a computerized database? Maybe he just had a smartphone.

Karl punched his thighs and attempted to center himself. He was out of practice in the hunger racket. He'd become accustomed to eating regularly again, and now, three days empty, he was going mental.

He stood up and did some jumping jacks and toe-touches; grade school calisthenics. He looked in the mirror. Five-and-a-half-feet of solid dork. He trotted into the kitchenette and tore open a Slim Jim, devouring it in three barely chewed bites. Then another. And another. He attempted to eradicate the pungent aftertaste with two cans of Mountain Dew, then felt buzzy as the double shot of caffeine coursed through his system, accompanied by a volley of violent vurps.

An image of Mona popped into his forebrain, tan and bare-bellied, radiant as Botticelli's "The Birth of Venus." Karl snatched the Bible off the floor and contemplated swatting himself to subdue any impure thoughts. Sinners of yore were often self-flagellants. Did medieval times call for medieval measures of self-purification? The caffeine, the caffeine, the caffeine. And whatever dastardly additives there were in those Slim Jims. *Oh mercy.*

"Jesus H. Christ!" he groaned as he swatted himself in the 'nads.

"So what's your story?" Ellen asked as Mona sat across from her. They were seated in Mona's apartment, one by each window, Ellen gently swaying in a rocker-based Eames armchair, Mona motionless in her usual recliner, feet propped on the windowsill. Paolo really had exquisite taste and Ellen kind of wished she'd claimed this apartment after he'd been … *Shut up!* She scolded herself. *My god.*

"Story?"

"Sorry. Does that sound confrontational? I don't want it to. Or intrusive. I'm sorry. But yes, your story. Where are you from? Who were your parents, your background? Who are you, basically? We've all really been trying to bite our tongues and respect your space. But how do you survive? How come the things don't attack you?"

"They just don't."

Ellen frowned at Mona's ambiguous response. "No, I mean really. Okay, look, I don't want you to feel like you're on the spot. This isn't an interrogation. Just two girls having a chinwag, okay? Or a girl and a slightly older girl. There's a good start. I'm thirty-two. How old are you?"

"Eighteen."

"Eighteen. Wow. So young. And where are you from?"

Mona shifted in her seat. Though her face remained implacable, Ellen recognized that as a tell. Though of what remained to be determined.

"Here."

"Here, where?"

"Around here."

"Yorkville."

"Uh-huh."

"What street?" *It's like pulling teeth.*

"Seventy-seventh. And Second." Mona stared straight ahead out the window. Though Ellen could see Mona's eyes they remained, as ever, hooded and avoidant.

"Okay, now we're getting somewhere. I grew up in Teaneck, New Jersey. You know where that is? It's a township in Bergen County. I went to the very imaginatively named Teaneck High School." Ellen smiled and tried not to stare at Mona. Her bland stab at humor got no reaction, of course. "Where did *you* go to high school?"

"Didn't finish."

"I see. That's cool, no shame in that." *Don't editorialize, idiot. Let her speak.* "But before you didn't finish, where did you go?"

"Talent Unlimited."

At that Ellen lightly balked and a whisper of incredulity colored her response. "*Really?*" *Fuck. Keep it neutral.* "That's a performing arts school, isn't it?"

"Yeah."

"Okay," Ellen said, stretching out the second vowel, and when that produced no elaboration, added, "And what did you take? What was *your* talent?" *Was it stonewalling?* This girl was unbelievable. She was the most unforthcoming individual Ellen had ever met and it was really trying her patience. *Emily died before she was even verbal. This is teen practice. This is good. The world resumes. This life growing in me happens. It adores me, then turns on me, then comes back to me. This is good.*

"Singing."

"Really? And yet you're so quiet." Ellen hoped her tone wasn't sarcastic. She couldn't tell, but apparently neither could Mona, who sat there, unruffled as ever.

"Uh-huh."

"What kind of singing? Jazz? Gospel? Pop?" *Pop*? Ellen again felt like an old.

"Opera. Mezzo soprano."

Unbelievable. Unbe-fucking-lievable. Ellen took a few beats to absorb this startling tidbit. Whether Mona had been any good or not—or for that matter was still any good—was immaterial. It was almost unimaginable that this shut down introverted girl sang opera. And what about the din always pummeling her eardrums? That wasn't opera. Had Mona dreamt of segueing from opera to metal? Hadn't Pat Benatar done something along those lines? Who could remember? Was it a lie? Was Mona fucking with her? Why would she?

She wouldn't.

"Isn't this nice? Getting to know each other?" Ellen smiled hopefully. Mona, her eyes downcast, looked in Ellen's direction, at her middle, then back out the window. *Nearly impenetrable.* What if the embryo taking form in her uterus turned out to be like Mona? Was it something in the air? Maybe Mona had been a vital, zesty, free spirit before all this—an opera-crooning voluptuary. Maybe the same contaminant that spawned the living dead had stunted her personality. Maybe this was some kind of autism. Certain mold could cause that in developing babies. Maybe she was just displaying the symptoms before the rest of them, a result of her youth. That was a possibility. Maybe she was the first, but in time they'd all follow. Nature was all about adaptation. Mona had forged invisible armor. The zombies didn't attack her, but maybe the cost of survival was death of the self.

It makes sense. To survive one must adapt.

But what kind of life is that?

Though it was way too early for the agglomeration of cells in her uterus to do anything independent, Ellen felt a kick in the guts nonetheless.

"So why don't they attack you? Why? What is it about you?" Ellen's voice was weak, wheedling and womany and she hated it.

Mona stared out the window. She was so still she almost seemed inanimate. Her breathing was soft, barely audible, which made Ellen lean in. As she did, Mona inhaled more audibly and her brow ever-so-slightly furrowed.

"I'm not supposed ..." Another breath. Ellen froze, gripping the armrests, willing the chair not to creak and break the moment. There was a major struggle going behind Mona's deadpan eyes and its subtlety was mesmerizing. "I have ... a theory."

And that was all.

The words hung in the ether, each weighing a ton. But that was it. And as teasingly cryptic as those four words were, Ellen couldn't help but feel triumph. *It's a start. It's a motherfucking start.*

"Jerking off to paintings of the woman I love—or at least *think* I love—because I've driven a wedge between us. Wow, I'm so fucking rad I can't stand it." On the paint-speckled floor of his atelier Alan knelt pantless, his shamed attention wavering between his flagging erection and his second, more well-nourished, homage to Ingres's "Grande Odalisque." On the canvas, Ellen's back was sturdier, less a contour map of privation; her posterior rounder, more beguiling. He'd had to use that previous painting for reference and embellish from memory. They hadn't been intimate since she'd announced her pregnancy. And since he'd buried himself in a pit of his own making. "And to think I had issues about doing whacking material for Eddie. *Path-et-ic.*" Alan stood and tossed the sodden wad of tissue out the window.

He stepped away from the window in just a sweat-sodden t-shirt. "Look at me: Porky Pig, over here." Not since junior high school had he masturbated to his own art, and it didn't feel good. This was not how he'd envisioned forty. But then again, none of the current climate fit his vision of the future of his past. By forty he was supposed to have had at least one solo show in Soho, Paris and London. By forty he was supposed to have at least one hardbound monograph of his works. By forty he was supposed to have found true, everlasting love. By forty a lot of things were supposed to have happened.

Alan sat down across from his most recent canvas, a half-finished portrait of the enigmatic Ms. Luft. The painting was perched on the easel. Behind it was the wall of Mona portraits surrounded by the halo of zombie studies. Across the room were the Ellen canvases and drawings. He placed the new painting among them and felt the heaviness of remorse, shame, guilt, stupidity. And hunger.

"I gotta eat something. I gotta eat some peaches. I need a sugar fix. That's what I'm gonna do. And I'm gonna announce it first and then do it. I'm going to speak in declarative statements announcing my imminent actions and then do them. I am going to get some canned peaches, open the can, eat the contents and then fling myself out the window. Wait, *what?* No. No I won't."

But why not?

"Mona's right. We shouldn't have guns. Because right about now, a nine-millimeter lead sandwich sounds very appetizing."

Alan chugged the peaches, sputtering as he choked on the last couple of slices, a small, stinging upsurge of syrup leaking out his left nostril. His mother used to caution him about wolfing his food—another indication of his regression. Alan wiped the syrup off his nose and chin and then licked it off his hand, which he hadn't washed off since he'd masturbated. *Wonderful.* Washed off. Bathed. There was a quaint custom gone dodo. Mona had at least scored cases of hand sanitizer, so Alan traipsed over and pumped a couple of squirts into his palm and cleaned up. He stroked some onto his flaccid penis, too, which stung as the alcohol penetrated the sensitive skin. A little pain seemed appropriate. Like redress for transgress and regress. A friend had once asked Alan how a guy raised with no religion could be so prone to guilt and shame. Alan had no answer then, nor now. Something inborn; that *Jewiness* Ellen found so enchanting.

Or did.

"Cucumber Melon," he mused aloud, looking at the label.

As Alan took a few whiffs from the bottle it hit him that the stench of the undead didn't bother him anymore, even when his sense of smell was rekindled by a pleasant odor. The renewed appreciation for scent made him hungrier, and he ate a can of peas. Then a can of baked beans, including the disgusting wad of pork. Staring at his work in progress, he sat down on his couch and noticed he'd only given Mona four toes on each foot, like some cartoon character.

"That's stupid," he muttered as he slipped into dreamless slumber.

Eddie stared at the screen of his laptop. Two girls making like a lollipop on some *ragazzo fortunato*, but within his hand his dong lay in repose like a fish out of water. The hell? He watched the action but nothing doing. His junk wasn't in a very cooperative mood. For that matter, he wasn't much engaged by the raunchy tableau on his fifteen-inch HiDPI display. And this was one of his favorites. He clicked over to the menu and scrolled through the titles of dozens of MP4s but nothing leapt out at him. He looked at the DVDs and they seemed too old-fashioned.

"Just not in the mood, I guess."

He shut the laptop and placed it with care on his bedside table.

"Whatever. It's a beauty of a day. Why waste it inside?" That's what his pops always used to say whenever young Eddie'd been jamming on the PlayStation. It's a beauty of a day. Why waste it inside? *Okay, Pops, fair enough.*

With purpose, Eddie slipped on his cutoffs and barged into the living room.

"Dave-o, let's hit tar beach!"

"We should get a generator," Eddie said as he toyed with the fishing reel, sweat streaming off him like a race horse. "It's not gonna be summer forever. Nobody took my car-boosting idea serious, but if Mona can drive, she should take a car, you know, a pickup or van and snag us some gennies. I could teach her how to siphon gas. Maybe seeing that would plant some thoughts in her head." He grinned smuttily, arching his eyebrows in case Dave didn't pick up the innuendo. Dave frowned. "Anyway," Eddie continued, "It'd be sweet to get some power going. Maybe some AC, for a change."

Dave nodded. "Yeah, that'd be cool. But you couldn't keep the whole building chilled."

"So we get everyone in one apartment and crank it. A sleepover."

"A sleepover. Because I know how much you *love* hanging with the others in here," Dave scowled. "But, yeah, I see where you're coming from."

"For real, right? The people in this dump, they got no vision. These pampered Upper East Side scrubs would just shrivel up an' die if Mona hadn't come along."

"So would you and me," Dave interjected.

"Yeah, but not without a fight. They'd of gone out like babies, all curled up in a fetal position. If I knew for sure my number was up I'd of gone outside and taken a few of those fuckers out, *mano à mano*." For emphasis Eddie threw some jabs and ducked and countered phantom opponents. After a little fancy footwork, he stopped and spoke in a sedate tone. "If Mona don't drive, I could teach 'er. Maybe she could use a laptop and do one of them driving simulators."

"I dunno if that's a thing."

"That's stupid. Five zillion driving games, but none that teach actual driving?"

"None that I heard of."

"Wow, that makes no sense. I think you're wrong."

"Would you have played one?" Dave asked.

"Fuck no. I only like shooters." Eddie dropped the fishing rig on the floor and got up. "I'm gonna go talk to Little Miss Spooky." On his way to the door he picked up the blister pack and popped a neon pink pill.

"You really shouldn't do that," Dave said.

"Fuck you, Mom. And anyway, these pills don't do shit."

"Maybe they're placebos."

"Maybe they're female shit and I'm gonna sprout some titties. Time will tell, bro, but in the meantime I plan on testing the waters a bit longer."

"Yeah, well when you start menstruating, drop the regimen."

"*That's* the Mallon I'm talkin' about! Zing."

Eddie laughed as he sailed out the door, letting it slam as he galumphed downstairs. When he arrived at Mona's door he affected a more relaxed demeanor and then knocked. After a few gentle raps he pounded the side of his fist on the door. Fuckin' skank was probably listening to her usual noise. He tried the doorknob to no avail, rattling it in frustration. *Oh come on,* he thought. After several more thuds the door opened a crack, held that way by the chain, and Mona greeted him without even having the courtesy of looking up at him, her earbuds draped around her shoulders. *If this chick had tits,* Eddie started thinking, then stifled the notion. Even with knockers she'd be kinda *schifosa,* and anyway he was here on a different kind of business.

"Sup?" he said, flashing his winningest smile.

"Nothing," she replied.

"Can I talk to you about something?"

"Uh-huh." To his amazement, Spooky undid the chain and opened the door the whole way, ushering him in. As he stepped past her he took in their disparity in size, he standing at least a foot taller than she.

"What are you," he began, "like maybe five one or something?"

"Just five."

"Wow. Nailed it. It's so fuckin' weird a tiny little shorty like you—no offense—can just truck around town with all those zombies and a big guy like me who could take care of himself can't. I can't figure it out."

"Uh-huh."

I'll "uh-huh" you, you fuckin' ... No, no. Stow that shit. Make nice. "So, okay, what I was thinking was this: you're always going on these errands, right? And the most you can carry is what you can pile in a shopping cart. So that limits what you can score. So maybe, I dunno if you can drive, but maybe you could make the most of your trips out there in the world, if you drove a truck or Hummer or something. Even a Mini Cooper. *Anything*."

"Can't."

"I could teach you."

"They have to sense me."

"Huh?"

Mona took a breath, looked even more fixedly at her Docs, and with hushed deliberation said, "In a car they can't sense me so they don't disperse."

Eddie was doubly stunned. Not only had she answered his question but also it was a complete sentence and it made sense. Sense. The senses. Eddie didn't even think about that before. The zombies still had senses, even if they were a bunch of rotting braindead skinbags.

"Sense," he repeated. "Like maybe you give off a stink—no offense—that those pusbags can't abide. Wicked. Like because maybe you ..." Eddie cut himself off before he tipped his hand. He didn't want her to know he'd filched those pills. But this was the lynchpin. This was *it.* He felt sure. The pills. The quantity. She'd been mega-dosing those pills and it made her immune to attack. *Oh, this sly bitch.* And she didn't want to share. He'd tell the others and they'd flip. All those smarty-pants. Should he tell them?

Yeah, because then they could decide what to do. He didn't want to flat out accuse her, but if they were all on the same page, like a committee, then they could move as a unit. That was *strategy*. He felt like he did when he was playing hockey. Strategy was never his strong suit, at least not formulating it, but he had some dope—literally and figuratively—that the others didn't. He'd present his findings and they'd take it from there.

"I tried once. They tipped the car over." Her dull face actually betrayed a trace of anxiety. She didn't like the memory.

"That's really interesting," Eddie said with unaccustomed sincerity. She was a waste-case, all right, but she was human. "Listen, I didn't mean to freak you out. I just thought maybe it was a good idea about the car and all. Sorry. I'll leave you alone, a'right?" She nodded and Eddie let himself out, grinning as he turned his back on her. It was cool knowing something no one else did. And *he* got it out of her. *He* did.

Suck on that, you mutts.

Part Three

"IT WOULD BE a total betrayal," Ellen said, rubbing her abdomen, phantom kicks pummeling her innards. "We shouldn't, and you had no right to do what you did. For fuck's sake, if she discovered what you did it could mean the end of everything we've got."

"Yeah, maybe," Eddie sulked.

"Or the beginning of a brave new era," Karl added. "Really. If she isn't sharing knowledge of how to walk among the unclean then she's done nothing to engender our loyalty."

"*Unclean? Engender?*" Alan echoed.

"What? Country boy's not entitled to be articulate?"

"Um, of course you are, it just sounds a little unnatural, you know? You never spoke in such a *grandiloquent* manner before."

"Oh, and so what's 'grandiloquent,' then?" Karl bristled.

"It's mockery." Alan pushed back his chair and smirked.

"It's not helpful, either. Shut up, both of you," Ellen snapped. "This is serious. Eddie's proposed betraying Mona's trust, and moreover turned it into a conspiracy of *us* against *her*, which, frankly, is pretty fucked."

"Hey, I didn't put it like that," Eddie said.

"You didn't have to. And listen, I wasn't ready to share this little tidbit yet, but I'm pregnant and I'm not about to risk poisoning my baby in some experiment with mystery drugs." Ellen looked at her watch to confirm how long Mona had been away on her current errand. She felt tired and irritable, some of which was hormonal, but mostly it was disgust. The others offered no comment on her condition. Whether that was in deference or indifference was anyone's guess.

"Well, I'm in," Karl said. "I need to know whether she's graced with the divine or just a druggie with a heckuva side effect."

"I guess I'm in, too," Dave said, winning a clap on the back from Eddie.

"Include me out," Abe said, softly. "That little girl has been good to us and I don't plan on returning the favor with treachery."

"Yeah, me neither," said Alan.

"Same here," said Dabney. "Unless we keep it honest and talk to her about it, I don't want any part of it."

Outside heavy rain pelted the windows, but no one was rushing upstairs to frolic and strip. The sky was an oppressive, ever darkening gray and the climate inside wasn't conducive to abrupt shifts in mood. Even though this meeting was taking place in Ellen's dining area, four floors above pavement, a bunker mentality prevailed. Ellen wondered if this was how Hitler's staff felt as they plotted his demise. Was that an apt comparison? She hoped not. How about Kennedy's people plotting his? Ellen believed the conspiracy theories. Not all of them, but some.

She got up from the table and stretched, then stepped over to the front windows. Below, the horde shambled, aimless, ugly as ever, pockets of unrest visible from this elevation. Some pushed and shoved, others stumbled, fell from view, trampled underfoot. It always looked like the least festive New Year's Eve gathering ever down there; Times Square, apocalypse-style.

Behind her the others continued to dicker about whether or not to raid Mona's pharmaceutical stash. Abe had no interest. Since Ruth's death Mona had gotten him hooked on Valium and he almost matched his supplier in newfound equanimity. He was like the pod people version of his former self. It didn't seem possible that a chemical cocktail was what kept Mona safe out there, though pounding drugs certainly went a long way toward explaining her personality, or lack of one.

"Pregnant, huh?" Dabney sidled up to Ellen and took a spot beside her at the open window, rain spatter stippling them both with dark spots. Lightning flashed, followed by voluminous thunder. Ellen just nodded.

"Is this a joyous kind of thing or an unexpected problem?" Dabney continued. "I don't mean to pry, but it's a big development."

"Yeah, I know."

Ellen caught Dabney stealing a glance at Alan.

"It's Mike's."

"I wouldn't presume to ask." Dabney smiled with apology

"It's okay." She then gestured at the conspirators. "*That* isn't."

Ellen smelled alcohol on Dabney's breath. It wasn't beer breath, either. It was whiskey breath, complemented by cigarettes. His eyes were red-rimmed and hooded. It seemed to Ellen that almost everyone was in a mad rush to be medicated. Or anesthetized. Dabney gave her bicep a soft, paternal squeeze and left the apartment. *He'd rather be up there getting soused. I don't blame him.*

From the table, Eddie pounded his fist like a gavel and declared the meeting adjourned. He and his confederates would break into Mona's apartment and steal drugs. Ellen took a deep breath, the air wet and redolent of death and ozone. Sheet lightning whitewashed the sky, leeching the remaining pigment from an already colorless vista. If the world weren't already in such dire shape, she'd find this a lot more portentous.

Psychosomatic or not, her insides churned, and she wondered if taking this baby to term was a good idea. The zombies weren't going anywhere. It had been over five months since they'd supplanted mankind. For all Ellen knew, the occupants of 1620 were the only ones left, at least in New York. What hope did her baby have? Alan was probably right.

To hell with him and his rationality.

To hell with 'em all.

As the last of her "guests" filed out, she slumped against the wall, wanting nothing more than to cry, but no tears came. She just sat there, hunched over and desolate. A baby. New life for a dead planet. Was that hopeful and wise, or just selfish and stupid? One of the last public events Ellen had attended was a Pro Choice rally in Union Square, with Emily in her baby sling. Some anti-choicers had shared a few choice words with her, calling her a hypocrite. Because the concept of choice was apparently too complex for them to handle. She'd made hers; let others make theirs. And now here she was. Perhaps later, in keeping with the narcotic theme of the day, she'd ask Mona to venture out and fill a prescription of her own: mifepristone and misoprostol, aka "the abortion pills."

It made her heart hurt, but better safe than sorry.

Abe lay on the bed on the spot Ruth had succumbed. Alan and Karl had flipped the mattress for Abe, since her seepage had done a number on the other side, even with the mattress pad in place. The air in the bedroom was stale but Abe didn't mind. He was comfortably numb. Where had he heard that phrase before? Maybe he just made it up. The room was dark and Abe stared at the ceiling. After a short while he wasn't sure if his eyes were even open. It made no difference. The Valium made Abe aggressively apathetic, which he supposed was oxymoronic, but who cared?

For a man as formerly opinionated as he, indifference was unnatural, and drug induced or not, becalmed or not, he felt the unnaturalness deeply. It wasn't Abraham Fogelhut's role in the universe to be its calm center. It conflicted with his essential Abe-ness. Was this what the hippies and yippies experienced, he wondered? When they were all dosing themselves to the gills back in the sixties, when all that nonstop navel-gazing was happening, when everything was *a happening*, when *happening* became a *noun*, was this that? If so, Abe, in soft focus, needed to revise his opinion of the sixties drug subculture: it was even dumber and more self-centered than he'd suspected.

Happening as a noun.

Party as a verb.

Vacation as a verb.

Summer as a verb.

Summer as a *verb*?

Jesus H. Christ.

If the plague hadn't come along when it did, given the trajectory on which English was headed—at least as spoken by Americans—pretty soon the younger generation would be reduced to tribal clicking languages. Or not speak altogether, their necks forever goosenecked to fiddle with their devices. Was Mona's aversion to eye contact cultivated by the mobile phone culture? If so, maybe the zombies did everyone a favor.

This wasn't relaxing.

It was too soon to have developed a tolerance for the drug, wasn't it?

When was the last time he took a pill?

Take a pill, take a pill, take a pill. *Ugh*, that was what weaklings did. *Take a pill.* The world is shit. *Take a pill.* Your wife is dead. *Take a pill.* The kids are dead. *Take a pill.* Take two pills. Take a whole bottle of pills and be done with it. As an old person all he did was take pills, for what hurt, for what didn't flow right, for his heart. Fuggit. Forget it. Man was made to suffer. Didn't some poet say that? Somebody said it. Maybe it was a song. *Okay, I'm making a deal with myself,* he thought. *In the remaining weeks I read. I read everything Mona can get her hands on. The classics. I read some, but not enough. I need to make a list. Let the others do what they will, chase their tails, fritter it away, but I'm going out enriched in the brains department.*

Abe got off the bed, grabbed a bar of Ivory soap and walked up to the roof, shedding garb as he made the ascent. Modesty? Antiquated notion. The downpour drummed against the pebbled-glass skylight, its rhythm beckoning Abe forward. Let the others stew in their hidey-holes. Or whatever they were up to. From the sounds of it as he passed the Italian ape's digs, some vigorous sodomy. To each his own. Abe dropped the last of his attire as he stepped onto the tarpaper, which shimmered with wetness, reflecting each flash of lightning. His body, even well fed, was lank and colorless. Had his balls always hung this low? Who could remember? The sky looked like a backdrop from an expressionist German film of the silent era, thick black clouds set asymmetrically against deposits of leaden gray. With the recurrent lightning the buildings all became, at least in flashes, monoliths of pure black and white.

Absolute.

As a youngster Abe had been instructed in absolutes. There was good and there was evil, period. Good folks and bad. As a youth there was little to contradict that. The Nazis were unadulterated evil, easy to hate. Their atrocities left no room for debate and he'd wished often he was old enough to go fight them. Then came the march of Communism, so when he was old enough Abe joined up and deployed to Korea. And upon seeing his first enemy corpse that absolutism began to fade. Skinny, pale, softly bluing lavender lips and fading color in the cheeks. This was just a foot soldier. Just a dead kid in a muddy ditch.

The world was easier to absorb before that moment. Abe had liked black and white, and he'd missed it when it was taken from him. Down below, the multitude groaned in protest of the weather, their plaint drowned out by the pervasive, ground-shaking thunder. There were no soft-lipped Asian boys down there. Maybe once upon a time, but not now.

They were the enemy.

Us versus them.

Black and white.

But those things down there lacked malice. They were just automated instinct.

As Abe lathered up he missed gray.

At least Ivory was pure.

Mostly.

"*Pretty in pink,*" Karl burbled. His skin felt funny. Not funny ha-ha, but funny. Funny-ish. "I don't even like Psychedelic Furs." He looked at the pill in his palm, pilfered from Mona's stash. Pink. Though the Bible didn't address drug use, there were very clear principles outlined in it that suggested drug use wasn't acceptable. Christians were supposed to respect the laws of the land. But there were no laws anymore. This wasn't recreational, anyway. This was a life-or-death experiment. That made Karl smile. He'd always found the term "experimenting with drugs" disingenuous, but that's what this was. He felt very scientific.

And itchy.

And sweaty.

And cotton mouthed.

"SHE ONLY HAS four toes."

"What?"

"She only has four toes."

"I heard you the first time. What are you talking about?"

Ellen pushed back from the dining table and stared at Alan, who sat there stirring powdered non-dairy creamer into room temperature coffee, his spoon tinkling gratingly with each rotation. Finally, patience exhausted, Ellen snatched the silverware from her in-the-doghouse paramour's hand and tossed it across the room, where it clattered into the sink.

"Mona. She only has four toes on each foot."

"What are you talking about?"

"She was posing for me again today, so I could finish up the canvas I'd started—and please don't give me that look. Seriously. There's no extracurricular activity and I feel bad enough about myself, anyway. Very regressed. So, please. I'm asking we move on." Ellen scowled, but then let her face relax. Alan continued. "I'd painted her with four toes on her feet and was looking to correct that. Not that I need a model for toes, but you know, it was curious is all. So she's sitting there, in the same ..." Alan was going to say *position* but reconsidered, wanting to avoid any undertone of carnality. " ... posture. And this time I scrutinized her feet ..."

"You know how this sounds, right? Pervy."

"Please? Could you please? Seriously? The point is I hadn't goofed. She has only four toes on each foot." Out of Ellen's vision, he pinched a testicle to preemptively suppress any rogue erections that might betray him. Just the thought of those smooth cartoony peds wreaked havoc on his confused libido. He'd once seen a porno where a guy pulled out and came on the woman's foot. At the time he'd thought it was the stupidest thing he could ever imagine. Things change.

"So what am I supposed to make of this little revelation?" Ellen said, unmoved by Alan's news.

"Look, forget I said anything, okay? This is what couples do, right? They sit at the table and make small talk. Only I didn't think this was so small. I thought it was genuinely interesting. It was just another thing to factor into Mona's roster of otherness. Just forget it."

"Consider it forgotten."

Alan excused himself from the table and left the apartment. Better he should spend time alone. Was this some pregnancy thing? The roller coaster ride had been fun—was "fun" even the right word? Fun? Interesting. The sex had been good. Very. Desperate, but explosive. But this? Did Mike deal with this or was this all some cumulative buildup of hormones, grief and immeasurable *weltschmerz*? He'd failed his mother. Or at least that's how it felt to him. Ellen had a husband and daughter to grieve and feel guilt over. When he thought of it that way, Alan figured Ellen was entitled to some appreciable crabbiness. *My empathy needs recalibrating*, he thought. *It's definitely out of whack.* For so much of his adult life he'd excused deficits in his character as being part of the artistic temperament. But really it boiled down to selfishness, often. Inflexibility. Fear.

He draggled downstairs to his apartment and swung open the unlocked door, taking in his plethora of deathworld renderings, the gooey center of which were the portraits of the resident four-toed temptress. Putting aside his putative coupling with Ellen, Mona was a bit young so even thinking of her that way made Alan's stomach knot with self-loathing. He's always regarded men involved with women half their age as creeps. What good were morals now? Perhaps a sociopath like Tommasi had the right idea. Regardless, you had to be hardwired for that kind of thing. Nature versus nurture. Alan was a nice boy, period. A nice boy with a dirty mind, but really, was there any other kind? A nice boy with a clean mind was illusory. But maybe so was being nice. He'd read many articles with variations on the header "Beware of Nice Guys," and, alas, recognized himself, or at least apsects of himself, in all of them. *All creeps think they're "the nice guy." Am I a creep? Am I? Christ, what a late-in-the-day thing to fret about.*

But am I?

He stepped into the kitchen and opened a package of Cheez-Its, scooping a handful into his mouth. Gone was the rationing mentality. He ate on automatic, not even tasting what he shoveled in. As a thick glob of orangey half-chewed mush wedged in his windpipe, hard edges scraping soft tissue, and he began to choke. He grabbed a bottle of Evian off the counter and took a few swigs, lubricating the doughy wad, swallowing hard, forcing it down. Not so long ago he'd have been savoring each bite, picking the crumbs off his shirt and putting them in his mouth, making it last. Now it was back to indifferent fistfuls. Alan walked over to the front windows and admired the crowd on York. The ol' gang.

"Hey, folks!" he shouted, waving as if to oldest, bestest buddies. "Hey! How's it going down there? Same old, same old, huh? Yeah, I know. But look at this!" He palmed another batch of Cheez-Its, Evian at the ready, and rammed them into his mouth. He chewed open mouthed like an ill-mannered child, flecks of fluorescent snack food spattering the sill and windowpane. He spat a gob of the near-glowing processed food onto the bald crown of one of the meatheads below, creating a pulpy yarmulke. No reaction from the target; a reliable disappointment. It was always the same faces down there; having immortalized them in paint, pastel, crayon, charcoal, graphite and ink, he knew their mugs intimately. It amazed Alan that these brain-dead bastards could be capable of locomotion, yet never go anywhere. They milled around, never straying from their immediate surroundings, like penned animals. It reminded him of families he'd observed in the outer boroughs who never ventured into Manhattan, these urban provincial hicks whose entire lives were played out in a square mile radius. The things below were no different. At least veal had an excuse.

Not that it mattered anymore. If anything, the majority of outer borough zombies were probably indistinguishable from their former selves. *Jesus, even in the apocalypse I'm an asshole elitist.* Alan wiped his mouth and watched the same old, wishing he could change the channel. Absently, Alan snatched a newsprint pad off the floor and began to sketch the crowd.

Just to pass the time.

"Four toes. Four freakin' toes."

"This is more like it."

On the sunlit roof of their former building, three north of a loudly snoring Dabney, Eddie grinned, testing the tensile strength of the jury-rigged swivel that anchored the butt of his fishing rod. He pushed his feet hard against the wooden footrests he'd nailed straight through the tarpaper. Dabney had unequivocally stated he didn't want that craziness happening on his turf. But this was Eddie's.

"This is gonna fuckin' *rule*!" Eddie let out a rebel yell and chugged his beer. He'd gotten to like warm beer. Dave sat nearby on a folding lawn chair and kept mum. *Whatever.* Eddie planted his ass in his makeshift fighting chair and prepared for a rousing round of "flynchin'." The rod felt good in his hands. Sturdy. He tightened a maroon headband to keep sweat from running into his eyes. Nothing to ruin his good time. Eddie cast the line—the noose weighted with a brass plumb bob—and jiggled the pole to test the swivel's motility. Smooth. Beer in one hand, rod in the other, he could almost imagine being on the high seas, maybe off the coast of Cozumel. Sweat poured off him and he felt it cool on his skin. *Seabreeze,* he thought.

"I'm gonna ask Mona to get me one a them New Age CDs of ocean noise. Play that while I'm up here to help create the mood. That shit would be sweet, bro."

"Yeah, sweet."

"You bet your ass, *sweet.*" A few gulps of Corona, a light buzz, fishing with a buddy. Things had sweetened considerably recently. Whatever those pills were, they didn't hurt, either. There was a playful, nerve-tickling, electric quality about them, whatever they were. In concert with the beer? Nice. His skin scintillated. It reminded him of coke, only not as buzzy. Even if they weren't Mona's secret weapon against being eaten alive, the pills were okay by Eddie. He closed his eyes and began to hum tunelessly, rocking his head side to side to simulate the motion of a boat. "Dude, make seagull noises," he suggested.

"What?"

"Make some seagull sounds."

"For real?"

"Do not harsh my buzz, bro," Eddie said, a slight edge creeping into his voice. "Just make some gull noises, okay? *Humor me.*"

Dave hemmed and hawed for a few, then let out a series of awful high-pitched squawks.

"Perfect," Eddie said, even though the imitation was far from. "More, but vary the loudness. Make some sound far away."

Dave had done some questionable things for Eddie, but this was pushing it. Still, he obliged, which made Eddie's smile broaden in triumph. *The Comet dominates.* Soon Dave was on his feet, padding around barefoot on the hot tarpaper, fluttering his hands and screeching wildly.

As Dave caromed around the rooftop like a drunkard's cue ball, Eddie's line dipped violently, then bowed as he yanked it upwards into a perfect arc. "Fuck!" he yelled, Dave oblivious, lost in his seabird impersonation. Eddie dug his feet hard against the wooden blocks and pushed back into the fighting chair, wishing he had a real one, secured to the deck with straps and all. The thing on the other end of the line was a fighter, or at least heavy. The line jerked and whipped around, but the butt remained fixed to the swivel.

"Fuckin' bitch!" Eddie growled, loving it.

His shoulders gleamed with perspiration and tanning lotion, each muscle flexed taut, biceps bulging, knuckles glowing white. The rod pitched forward, nearly toppling Eddie, but he righted himself and threw his shoulders back. He worked the reel and slowly the line was rewound, his catch brought ever closer. The exertion burned and it felt glorious. Invigorating. Vital. "Yo, Dave! Dave! Stop bein' a fuckin' bird an' help me out! *Dave!*"

Dave snapped out of his playacting and once again threw his arms around Eddie's waist, Heimlich-style. The two of them fought the rod and over the lip of the roof came two zombies bound together at the throat—a twofer! "*Sweet bouncing baby Jesus!*" Eddie whooped. As the two struggling bodies flopped onto the roof, Dave released Eddie's waist and ran to grab a brick or two. Eddie gripped the rod with one hand as his catches clawed at the monofilament dug deep into their necks. With his other he retrieved from under the chair a meat tenderizing hammer and stalked closer to his prey. "You don't look so tough to me."

Dave hung back, the proximity of the zombies a bit harrowing.

Dabney rose from his slumbering position and shouted, "You boys are gonna get us all killed with that madness! Stop that shit!"

Eddie didn't hear, his head filled with the thunderous rush of testosterone and barbarity. He advanced on the strung-up twosome, one male, and one barely recognizable as female, any feminine characteristics eroded by living death. Eddie now used the line like a leash, jerking the rod to make them sit up and notice their captor. Distracted from their predicament, the zombies, upon seeing Eddie, began to hiss and slobber, thick ropes of opaque grayish drool hanging from their gnashing jaws. Eddie laughed. "You think if I knocked all her teeth out she'd give me a hummer?" he asked, smirking.

Dave was at a loss.

"Maybe I should bone her till she snaps in two. Maybe I should just bust her up into pieces and see which ones keep twitchin'."

"*Dude ...*" Dave's lower lip trembled with dismay and disgust.

Even through the adrenalized fog of ferocity, Eddie could see in Dave's eyes the latent image of the Wandering Jewess encounter. He thrust out a forefinger of censure and shouted, "Don't go harshing my buzz, bruh!"

Eddie stepped directly in front of the zombies. The line had cut deep into the male's throat and thick, nearly black grue seeped out. His flaking, sun-baked skin was puckered around the incision, the edge frayed and ratty. His eyes were gray and hazy, but their direction couldn't be clearer. Both zombies were intensely interested in Eddie and to a lesser extent Dave, who'd retreated a few feet. The zombies dropped their claws away from the line around their necks and recoiled from Eddie. "You see this shit? You thought the drugs was barking up the wrong tree? Look at 'em, Dave. They're backing away. See?"

"Yeah, 'cause they're scared shitless. Doesn't mean you're immune, bro."

"Killjoy," Eddie sneered, then in a graceful swoop swung the hammer and knocked the jaw clear off the female. "Bull's-eye!" He guffawed as the female's hands jerked up to her ruined face. "There goes your modeling career," Eddie scoffed, well pleased. "And so much for that blowjob, too. Although …" The zombie's sandpapery tongue lolled stupidly in the jawless opening between her upper teeth and gullet.

Dave turned away and heaved.

"Fuckin' *killjoy*," Eddie repeated. He stepped over to the female and smashed out her remaining teeth. The male began to fight against the noose again. Braindead or not, it could sense what was coming and it wasn't a tasty meal. Eddie palmed the back of the female's head and jerked it forward, severing the head altogether, giving the male more room to claw at the line. Eddie chucked the female head across the avenue and watched it land on a roof across the street. *Perfection.* Eddie stepped back and watched as the male struggled to his feet and spat and growled.

"I love this guy," Eddie said. "He's a fighter. A fighter who's gonna lose, but still. Props to Uggo."

The zombie stumbled back as it managed to free itself.

"Can't have that," Eddie said, and with a roundhouse kick sent the zombie spiraling off the roof back to its fellows.

"*Yoink,*" Eddie said, flashing his pearlies.

"Promise me you're never going to do that again," Dave said, straightening up from his puking position.

"Why make an empty promise, dude?" Eddie beamed as he twisted open another Corona. "I just found my new regular sunny-afternoon thing."

Glancing at his lean-to and considering the vacant apartments below, Dabney contemplated a change of venue, thinking it might be time to move this party indoors.

"I WANT TO go out with you," Karl said, standing on the landing by Mona's open door.

"On a date?" Mona stared through Karl's neck, her eyes betraying no hint of humor, derision, surprise or even much in the way of general interest.

"No, *no.* Not on a date," he stammered. "My intentions are purely pure. No, I mean I want to leave the building with you next time you go out. On an errand."

A passable facsimile of curiosity flashed across Mona's face. "Why?"

"An experiment. I want to see if your zombie repulsion has enough juice to keep them at bay with a companion, if your umbrella of safety extends beyond just you. Remember the childhood game 'Ghost in the Graveyard'?" Mona shook her head. "Okay, it was like a variation on tag, only there was a graveyard—the playground, your living room, wherever—and a base. The base was a safe zone. So, one kid is chosen to be the ghost. He's out in the graveyard. Other kids are positioned around the graveyard and have to get back to base. If the ghost tagged you, you were the ghost. But the way we played it was if kids locked arms, or even tied clothing together, you could use 'electricity' and leave the base so long as you were tethered to it with a lifeline. The lifeline carried electricity. Not real electricity, you know, just the power of the base. So you could venture into the graveyard safely and taunt the ghost. Sometimes you all were on base and you'd mock the ghost mercilessly until he threatened to quit. Anyway, I want to see if your gift has electricity."

"Bad idea."

"Maybe so, but I need to know."

"More like you need to die."

Karl decided he didn't like when Mona spoke. He felt zoomy and his skin prickled. He actually felt electricity, currents flowing through his epidermis. His hairs stood on end. Maybe it was excitement. Maybe it was the drugs. The drugs. What *were* those drugs? All those years of living a "Just Say No" lifestyle, and now this. Now a lot of things. He, the simple Christian yokel from a Podunk, under the thrall of the irreligious charismatic urbanite. Whilst enticing Karl into this conspiracy, Eddie had let slip he'd attended parochial school, but clearly those scriptural lessons hadn't taken. If Mona was taking speed she sure didn't show it. Karl knew of a family on the outskirts of his town that cooked up meth. Hopped-up farm boys would roar out of that house in pickups and blast buckshot into neighbors' mailboxes and anything else that didn't move—and sometimes things that did. Big Manfred had pronounced them "doomed."

"So, what do you say, Mona? May I come with?"

"Bring your Bible."

"To stop the zombies? Like *The Exorcist*? 'The power of Christ compels you,'" Karl said, doing a bad impersonation of Max Von Sydow. He grinned, though a bead of sweat betrayed his ersatz humor.

"For Last Rites. Yours."

Karl definitely didn't like when Mona spoke. Drugs. The antichrist. Some folks were right, others weren't. Mona fell into the latter category. How were they fixed for staples? To the best of Karl's knowledge, all coffers were brimming. He wanted to put this to the test. Abe had mentioned wanting books. Was that call to leave the nest? Were books essential? Karl felt impatient and Mona's impassivity exacerbated it. He wasn't a violent man but he felt the desire to slap her, if only to see what reaction she'd have, if any. Would she get mad? Would she fight back? It was maddening, her demeanor. He wanted to punch her. Not in the face, though.

In the stomach. He wanted her to wince and bend over. He wanted to force her to her knees and make her supplicate.

What?

If one could physically purge self-revulsion Karl would be the human Old Faithful, spewing from all available orifices. *Young Faithful.* Faith. Was it natural madness? The drugs? Cabin fever? *Space madness?*

"Mona, would you join me in prayer?" He offered his hands, which now trembled. "*Please*?" he implored. Mona looked uncomfortable—*a recognizable emotion.* Not the one he'd been hoping for, but human all the same. "It's just …" he sputtered, "You've *saved* us. I can't help but feel I need to return the act. You need saving. Your …" He looked up at her, not even having realized that in his fervor he'd dropped to his knees. Mona's eyes were open the widest he'd ever seen, though her was gaze cast at anything but him.

"I'm sorry. I shouldn't impose my thing on you, no matter how consequential."

"Mm-hmm," Mona said as she gripped the doorknob, closing the door.

"Yeah. Prayer is a private matter. I'm sorry. I didn't mean—"

Mona shut the door and Karl heard her engage the deadbolt. Those things outside didn't have any effect on her, but he seemed to have. He felt powerful for a moment. *I scared Mona.* He grinned, then winced, then ran upstairs to his apartment and retrieved a belt from his dresser and began flagellating his back. After several savage strokes he realized he was wearing his shirt, paused to yank off the garment, then resumed. *How dare I take pleasure in causing her discomfort? Forgive me, Jesus. Forgive me, God.*

Pill.

Maybe it was time for a pill. Karl dropped the belt and skittered to his kitchenette to poke one from the blister-mat. A small fluorescent pink caplet dropped into his palm and he washed it down with a bottle of Snapple tea. *What am I doing? What am I taking? I need a* Physician's Desk Reference*, that's what I need. Maybe Mona can take me to the bookstore on Eighty-sixth. But how do I justify wanting that book? Why would I need it? Unless I was taking unknown drugs. Has she noticed missing pills? Plus, if I went out with her would* *she take me everywhere she goes? Say her pharmacy jaunts are private? Maybe that's why she's cagey.*

She has guile. And so, beguiles.

As a boy, Karl had chicken pox, his pale, pasty body festooned with constellations of red bumps that blistered and itched like mad. He felt that way now, although his skin appeared normal. Many a saint had suffered. Even non-saints. Look at Job. Was it to be his fate to suffer like that? Old Testament God was always tormenting His faithful flock. Just look at the world. Was this not evidence of a malicious God? God made man in His image, and man was nothing to boast about, really. Flawed, mean, petty, violent, arrogant. Maybe that's why God wiped nearly everyone out. *But surely those who remained aren't the best and brightest.* Karl knew *he* wasn't. And Eddie? *God help us if he's one of God's chosen few.*

Karl laughed at the thought of Eddie being divinely spared. Karl laughed at the thought of God helping them. What a joke. What a blasphemous joke. With renewed vigor he beat his bare back with the belt until it was slick with blood and sweat, begging clemency. A malicious God was not a God to test. As the belt whipped away with each stroke, spatters of blood flecked the beige walls, evoking the chicken-pocked skin of his youth.

"What can I do?" Karl mewled. "*What can I do*?"

"Well don't do *that*," Ellen sputtered. She stared at Karl in utter disbelief, as did Alan. "Have you flipped your wig? Okay, just assuming Eddie's theory about the drugs is right—and for the record, I can't even believe I'm lending credence to anything that ape has ever said—but just to give the devil his due, you've been dosing yourself for what, maybe a couple days? What makes you think you've built up a resistance to zombies? Because your mind is eroding, what, there must be a positive side to the effects of the drugs? Look at the back of your shirt."

"I can't," Karl said. "It's behind me."

"It's stuck to your skin, and that isn't sweat. What the fuck have you been doing to yourself, as if we don't hear?" Ellen made the whip-crack sound with her mouth, adding a wrist-flick for punctuation. Karl plucked at the back of his shirt and sure enough it was a bit stuck to his spine. Ellen widened her eyes at him in challenge.

"Well, anyway," Karl said, wiping his fingers on his pants, then burying the offending digits in his front pocket, "I'm going. *Someone* has to go. Someone has to put this to the test. To prove either that the drugs work for us, or maybe the umbrella of protection from proximity to Mona. That her gift, whatever you want to call it, maybe it spills out and would protect a companion. Think of the possibilities."

"Great. Operation Big Umbrella." Ellen scowled. The little idiot's mind was made up. "Well. I'm not even giving you a shopping list. I told Mona what I want, but you, you I'll say goodbye to. Not farewell or till we meet again, but *goodbye*."

"Thanks for the vote of confidence," Karl pouted.

"You want me to lie? Fine, I'll catch you on the flip-flop, my man. But seriously? It was nice knowing you."

Karl accepted Ellen's remarks and made for the door, accompanied by Alan.

"Have you told the others about your proposed expedition?" Alan asked.

"Yeah. Eddie said he wanted to go first, not a little bad-word like me, but when I said I might get killed, my guinea pig status met his approval. Anything you want from me? Art supplies or something?"

"Just come home safe."

Karl stopped and looked up at Alan, emotion swelling in his chest, which felt corseted. Eddie had been his usual self; Dave had given him a pat on the back; Abe was in a Valium-induced state of apathy; Dabney, drunk as a lord, yelled at him, accusing him of hubris. He'd gotten teary-eyed and then kicked Karl out of his new apartment, 3B, locking the door after Karl had been summarily dismissed. And now Ellen's dressing down. Alan was the only one to wish him well. What was wrong with this world? That was the million-dollar question in a world where a million dollars meant nothing. Alan and he shook hands and then hugged, Alan clapping Karl's back and then realizing as Karl blenched that maybe that wasn't such a good idea. Alan looked at his hand, seeing traces of blood on it, and began to apologize, but Karl appreciated the gesture.

"One thing," Alan said, his tone cautionary. "I don't know if those things have regular senses, but I know sharks are drawn to the scent of blood, so you should really do something about your back. I know it's still hot, but maybe a jacket? Something?"

"I hadn't even thought of that."

Karl ran upstairs and pulled off the shirt, the material stuck to some still scabbing spots, making them bleed afresh. He poured some water down his back. He needed something stronger. If the lash wounds were there to appease a displeased God, maybe something to exacerbate the pain would go over well. In lieu of rubbing alcohol, he fetched a bottle of cheap vodka from his cupboard, stepped into his bathtub, and poured it over the wounds. The stinging pumped tears out of his eyes as if he were rerouting the liquid cascading down his spine through his tear ducts. He stung everywhere, the stench of the liquor overwhelming the room. It burned his nostrils and singed his injured back. Patting it dry with a towel, Karl then bound his torso in Saran Wrap to seal in any scent of blood. He popped a couple of pink pills, pulled on a fresh shirt and his windbreaker, then made his way to Mona's, his body tingling. Hoping it would further mask his potentially delectable aroma, Karl threw scented candles into his knapsack, then slung it over his back. Maybe it was the drugs, maybe it was the booze absorbed through the wounds, maybe it was adrenaline, but his back was numb. He felt no pain, physical or emotional.

As he passed the Fogelhuts's door he gave it a hard knock. "Wish me luck, old man!" Karl shouted. Silence. He drummed the door with palms flat. No reply.

Fine. Be that way.

"Let's do this thing," was Karl's mantra all the way down.

Let's do this.

Let's do this.

MONA PAUSED ON the roof of Dabney's van to watch Karl struggle down the rope. Abe and Dabney aside, the others had all come to see the twosome off and to witness what would happen next. Karl touched down on the roof, losing his footing for a moment. Mona grabbed him around the waist as he steadied himself. Like an overheated radiator venting steam, the onlookers released a collective sigh of relief. Karl's heart pounded so hard he was afraid the zombies might hear it. Gripped in equal measure by terror and euphoria, Karl surveyed the scene around the van: innumerable undead below, friends and neighbors above, the world everywhere. Karl hadn't seen the exterior of 1620 in half a year. How could something so prosaic seem so beautiful?

"Okay," Karl said to himself. "I can do this." He looked up at the sky, which seemed bigger and bluer than it had on their roof, some five stories above. He was eye level with the Phnom Penh Laundromat sign. A pigeon skeleton was nestled between the brick and the sign, a couple of feathers still clinging to the husk. Karl looked away from the tiny carcass to the larger, ambulatory ones at street level. "Oh Jesus," he gasped. Several were looking in the direction of the van, attracted by the activity. "Oh sweet Jesus."

Mona made the shush gesture and then hopped down onto the pavement.

With a soft thud, she hit the ground. The response from the zombies was immediate. They began to shrink away, their hissing more penetrating at this closeness. It was a sound that traveled up and down Karl's spinal cord, lingering for emphasis in the lower colon and upper throat, seizing and massaging both with dead constricting fingers. He could feel sweat collecting beneath his Saran Wrap armor, the brine basting his wounds. His mother used to marinade roasts overnight in the fridge, bound in cling film. He hoped he wouldn't prove to be as tasty to the uninvited guests below. With an iris opened in the crowd, Mona gestured for Karl to join her on the asphalt. *It's now or never*, Karl thought. He released his grip on the rappelling rope and eased himself off the van, first sitting on the edge, then lowering his legs until they were straight, then dropping to Mona's side. The zombies stayed at bay.

"So far so good," he whispered.

Mona nodded and took a step north. Her pace was slow, deliberate—with Karl in tow, slower than usual. She gave the zombies plenty of time to soak up her mojo and make way. Without actually holding onto her, Karl kept close to Mona, walking just slightly behind her. He'd never been this near to the zombies before, and up close, they were even fouler. The countless iterations on the theme of decay were staggering. Some, obvious victims of carnivorous attacks, were little more than haphazard collections of stumps and gristle, barely held together and yet still capable of locomotion. Limbs ended midway. Faces half consumed by rot—or just half consumed, period. Exposed bone. Internal organs that weren't internal any longer. Karl never realized gums could recede so far. Their skin reminded Karl of overcooked fowl, matte, striated, thick and leathery yet translucent. Yellowed, browned and blackened. Most eyes glazed by dull gray cataracts. Some stumbled around, sockets bereft of eyeballs. Cavernous nostrils, just vertical openings, black and rimmed with corrosion.

"They're so horrible," Karl stated. "They're so effing horrible."

"Uh-huh." The response to a comment on the weather. Banal. Noncommittal. But then again, zombies *were* the weather. A constant. Less interesting than the weather, actually. Weather changed. Karl's walkie-talkie beeped and he removed it from its holster.

"Just testing," came Alan's voice. "How's it going?"

"Uh, okay, I guess," Karl said. "They're hanging back, but it's, uh, it's kinda freaking me out, to be honest."

"Of course," Alan responded. "How could it not? But you're out, buddy. You're actually out there."

Karl nodded in response, then snapped to and pressed the talk button. "Yeah, I'm out here. I'm out here. Look, I can't walk and talk. I need to concentrate. Over."

Okay, Karl. Understood. Over and out."

Karl clutched the walkie-talkie to his chest, a talismanic anchor to home. *Ghost in the Graveyard,* he thought. *Base.* His face burned. They hadn't even reached the corner and already he was hesitating. He looked back at the others, still in the windows. Ellen gave a wave of encouragement and Karl felt like he was back at his first day of school, Momma dropping him off, he being brave. *Don't cry,* he thought. *Please don't cry.*

As they headed north Karl gasped as a naked, hunched, gnome-like zombie edged into view. Its pigmentation was almost human and it bore no disfigurements other than its stooped posture and deep livor mortis in its lower extremities. It aimed its nearly hairless head in Karl's direction and he gasped. *Ruth!* She must have fallen from the roof and come unwrapped. Karl stood motionless, staring at his former neighbor. Of all the people he never wanted to see naked, Ruth might be number one on the list. He thought of the late Norman Mailer, *The Naked and the Dead.*

"What's the delay?" Mona asked, not impatient.

"It's Ruth." He pointed.

"Oh. *Oh.*"

Karl suppressed that urge to chasten Mona. It wasn't like he'd just pointed out that the sky was above or that water was wet. This was kind of a traumatic big thing, Ruth ambling around. She wasn't bitten by one of those things. She just came back all on her own. Didn't that portend the same fate for anyone? For everyone? Regardless? How would Abe feel knowing his wife was scuttling around in the raw amidst the unclean? Tidy, persnickety Ruth Fogelhut in her birthday suit—or would that be *deathday* suit—loose amongst the natives. It was an ugly sight made uglier. With not a trace of recognition, Ruth's dead eyes glared in his direction as he felt Mona's hand tug at his arm.

"C'mon," she said.

Opting to not radio back this piece of info, Karl nodded and kept step with Mona, whose pace was deliberate, mechanical. She'd likely have made a fine soldier. Maybe she'd been one. Maybe she was some military experiment gone wrong. Or right. She was immune to the zombies. Maybe she was a supersoldier prototype. Maybe her creators were all dead. Or maybe they were still alive in some bunker, monitoring Mona's progress from a safe distance, a tiny tracking chip implanted within her. Big Manfred used to go on and on about vaccines and tracking chips. Mona's all-black gear was kind of martial. The boots. The haircut. Maybe she was part of some private military company, like Academi.

How did one go about broaching a topic like that and not seem impertinent? Was "I was just wondering" the correct opening gambit? "So, are you some kind of genetically altered superbeing?" *So, am I totally paranoid or imbecilic?* Karl brooded as he trudged in Mona's wake, the euphoria of being outdoors tabled pro tem. The other thought, the one that kept cropping up, was whether or not she was even human. That posed an even trickier question of etiquette. "So, are you an angel of the Lord or a demon from Hell?"

"What?"

Mona stopped and looked at Karl with something approximating interest.

"Huh?" he replied.

"A demon from Hell?"

Karl began to sweat even more, his stomach doing flips. *I said that out loud?* rang through his skull. *Idiot!*

"What?" he stammered, attempting to feign innocence.

"You said—"

Karl cut her off with a wave of his hand. "No, no, no. Not *you.* No. Ruth, I was thinking about. Ruth. Back there. But she's no angel, anyone can see that. Just a weird thing I was thinking. Just wanted to see how it sounded out loud." He forced an inane smile. "Crazy. Not you." He made the loco gesture pointing at himself and shook his head.

"Uh-uh."

Karl longed for his belt to give himself a few savage lashings. The sun seemed hotter down here than on the roof, like it was tuned up or aimed by some giant sadistic kid with a magnifying glass. The air didn't move. Just the flies. Karl's neck skin crawled and oozed perspiration. Between the mortification and fear, his back felt like it was covered with fire ants, the Saran Wrap loosening as it filled with sweat, but hopefully not blood. It stung like mad. Shouldn't it be cooling off by now? No, it was still summer. *Endless summer.* Global warming plus zombies.

Yeah, humanity had somehow done this to itself.

Stupid humanity, Karl thought. *Stupid me. How could I not realize I said that aloud?* He wanted to stop thinking altogether for fear of a repeat bout of honesty Tourette's. He needed to stay in Mona's good books.

The Good Book.

Books.

That's why they were making this expedition.

As they slogged west, Karl was reminded of the annual Puerto Rican Day Parade, which commenced here on East Eighty-sixth. The crowd withdrew as Mona and he trekked up the center of the street, ankle-deep in rotting limbs and rubbish. Okay, this was a little less festive. Karl surveyed the crowd. His mind was jumpy, overstimulated. Their path was serpentine, weaving between forsaken vehicles and countless zombies. Inside one car a zombified child in a car seat thumped its head mindlessly against the window, the glass glazed with coagulated gore. That withered tot had been trapped in that car for nearly half a year and was still animate. Karl shuddered. The seemingly eternal question once again flitted into his head: *How long will it be before these things just run out of steam?*

Books.

Let's do this.

Let's do *this.*

"I need to hit the bookstore."

"Uh-huh."

"Yeah. Abe said he wanted some books to better himself. Yeah. That's something, a man his age. I guess that's kind of admirable. 'Course he could just be bored, but still."

"Uh-huh."

"I need some further scriptural reading, too. To maybe find some answers."

"Uh-huh."

"You really never encountered any other survivors during your travels?"

"No."

"That's so weird. You ever try calling out? Seeing if maybe you got any response?"

"No."

She might be lying. If she were a demon it would be her duty to lie, to please her unholy master. Karl cleared his throat, then hollered, "*Is anyone out there?*" as loud as possible. He repeated it a couple of times but the only reply was increased agitation in the zombies that flanked them. Mona poked Karl on the bicep.

"Don't," she said.

"It's just, if there was anyone out there I ..."

"Just don't."

"Okay. Sorry. I was just ... Sorry. 'You are my refuge and my shield; I have put my hope in your word.' Psalm 119:114."

Mona offered no acknowledgment of the Bible quote. On they trudged, the zombies hanging back, frustrated. The experiment so far was a success. Karl hadn't been eaten. Big success. Huge. This could change everything. As they neared First Avenue Karl felt buoyed by their progress. The sun no longer felt amplified, it felt invigorating. His leg muscles felt purposeful. He looked up at the clear blue sky and felt glorified. He felt closer to God than he had in ages. Or at least fonder. Midway between First and Second the Saran Wrap burst and pinkish brine splashed the pavement. Mona whipped her head around, startled by the wet sound. She stared at the puddle at Karl's feet.

"Your water just break?"

Mona cracking a joke was almost as alarming as the amplified interest the zombies displayed. The scent of his natural soup was like sounding the dinner gong. Though they hung back, their rancor was heightened. The sounds emanating from their cracked, broken faces threatened to void Karl's colon.

"Oh God. Oh Jesus," he whimpered. He wanted to drop to his knees and pray.

"Keep moving."

With stinging liquid dripping from his back, Karl followed Mona's command. The trip back to the building now seemed like miles rather than a couple of blocks. Long blocks. Avenue blocks, which were at least double the length of normal ones. *Abe and his books. Abe.* What had Abe ever done for him? What was he thinking, volunteering for this madness?

Volunteering?

He'd suggested it.

Karl wanted to strangle himself.

Don't blame Abe. You wanted that pill book. You did. Blame yourself.

"Get the fuck offa me!" Alan shrilled, swatting away Abe's palsied hands.

Abe moaned from the pits of his collapsed lungs, pushing up gusts of stale, mucus-scented reek. This wasn't what Alan had expected when he came a-knockin' on Abe's door. Ever since Ruth's demise, Alan felt bad for the old guy, up here all alone. At first, once he'd gotten Abe's door open, he'd thought the old man was just disoriented, the way he was bumping up against the windowsill. Maybe too much Valium. But once Abe had turned around Alan knew he'd joined the ranks of the undead. And now here he was, wrestling with a zombified oldster in a fusty apartment that smelled of mothballs and worse.

Alan managed to knock Abe to the ground, upon which he heard Abe's hip splinter, a sound both dry and wet. Abe grasped at Alan, but like the old commercial, he'd fallen and couldn't get up. Alan felt queasy. This wasn't comfortably impersonal like his relationship to the things below. This was Abe. Abraham Solomon Fogelhut, bearing out the cliché that when one half of an elderly couple perishes the other usually follows in close order—only now, apparently, *they came back.* Alan scanned the room, looking for something to put Abe out of his misery, but saw nothing obvious. With Abe scraping brittle nails against the grain of the rug, trying to rise and failing, Alan reached the door, stepped out into the hall and closed the door behind him. He felt pretty certain Abe wouldn't be mastering the doorknob, let alone getting himself up and about any time soon. Alan gulped some deep breaths, smoothed the front of his shirt, and then headed down to let the others know about Abe's condition.

36

"WELL, THAT'S A putrid development," Ellen said, horror and distaste adding piquancy to tone. "So what do we do?"

"We have to get rid of him, obviously."

"It's come to this. Evicting our senior citizens," Ellen said.

"Well, yeah," Alan agreed. "Postmortem, anyway. Fuck. I liked Abe. He was like a less sour version of my old man."

"Wow," Ellen responded.

"Yeah. But unlike my old man, you could have a conversation with Abe."

"I gotta say, the ripeness of this whole situation is really beginning to wear on me, you know? You die, you come back as one of those. Delightful. Being alive is just the next step to being undead. You think anyone just stays dead anymore? Or is that passé?"

Alan shrugged.

"Some must stay dead," Ellen continued. "They must. I mean it's not like there's eight million zombies out there. The streets are packed, but not *that* packed. But maybe they are. Like I know anything. There are probably apartments all over the city stuffed with zombies too feeble to let themselves out. Fuck. I thought I knew where we stood on this but we don't know anything. I thought it was rat bites or poison gas or some communicable germ or whatever, but it's just how it is now. We come back. *Awesome.*" Ellen took a sip of tepid herbal tea and repositioned her hairclip. "This tea is supposed to calm the nerves." She let out a derisory laugh. "So whattaya think? Is Karl doing great or does Mona return a solo act?"

"Um."

"I'd say that was rhetorical, but it wasn't. Or maybe it was. How could you possibly know? Try the walkie-talkie, would you?"

"Karl said—"

"Just try it. Just get one word out of him. *You alive, Karl?* Done."

Alan depressed the button to broadcast and asked, answered only by static.

"Must be out of range," he said, his voice languid.

"Yeah, well, if Mona makes it back—and I see no reason to doubt *she* will unless Karl's managed to fuck up her good thing—she's bringing me a little something special to take care of my situation. So, maybe I'm a little edgy. Just a little. A tad."

"What situation?"

"Don't be fucking obtuse, Alan. The *baby*."

"Oh."

"Yeah, 'oh.' It's the kind of situation that merits *that* kind of response. And don't worry. I don't hate you. But don't get your hopes up, either. I'm not committing one way or the other. It's called choice for a reason. I just ..." Ellen took another sip, then threw the half-full cup across the room where it just bounced off the wall. "Well, that wasn't cathartic at all. Just another mess to clean up. And speaking of messes ..."

Alan fidgeted for a moment. Abe was one of their own. But Ellen was right: *no zombies allowed.* Eddie would probably relish a go, what with some of Abe's previous remarks at his expense, but Abe deserved better. He deserved to be put to final rest with some kindness. Some dignity, if such a thing was now possible.

"Sure. Let's get it over with."

"He's feisty for a dead man with a busted hip," Ellen observed as she forced Abe's head down with a mop, the spongy pad pressed hard against the old man's windpipe. Abe's arms flailed impotently.

"Maybe we should get the others," Alan suggested, having second thoughts. "Eddie would ..."

"No Eddie. We don't need that throwback to help us."

Alan looked at Abe. It wasn't Abe anymore, but it was. It still looked like Abe. He wasn't some rotting thing. Not yet, anyway. His eyes weren't glazed over and remote; there was rage in those undead orbs. Rage and confusion. Abe caught Ellen's pants cuff in his spastic fingers and tugged, pulling her low riders a bit lower, exposing the waistband of her underpants.

"Uh-uh-uh, you dirty old man," Ellen scolded, but the humor was hollow. This wasn't funny, even in the sickest way. She pushed the mop harder into Fogelhut's throat, the pressure precipitating a volley of excruciatingly thick, wet sounds of strangulation and cartilage being demolished. Alan fought the urge to retch or pass out and grabbed a large towel from the bathroom, which he quickly threw over Abe's face, partly to muzzle him, partly to mask him. Alan didn't want to see that mechanical simulation of life. With the towel firmly secured over the old man's face, Ellen released the mop. Alan blinked away tears. This was so not right. Abe had probably slipped away into a peaceful, Valium-smoothed death, yet here he was, snapping at them. Abe rocked back and forth, his legs useless. That broken hip had hobbled him. He wouldn't even be able to shamble around out there.

"Keep the towel over his face," Alan snapped. "And push down his chest. Keep him still."

"What? What are *you* gonna be doing? Aren't we going to toss him?"

"We are. But in a minute. Hold his arms."

On the floor Abe undulated, the towel affixed firmly over his whole head. He looked like a hostage, crippled and hooded. Alan looked around the room, then spotted a large burnt-orange alabaster ashtray. As he hefted it, feeling its substantial weight and solidity, he remembered his own mom had one similar back when he was a kid, some relic from the seventies.

Alan stalked over to Abe's wiggling recumbent form, hesitated, then lofted the ashtray in a high arc and brought it down hard on the old man's skull, pulverizing it. The sound, muffled though it may have been, was sickening, but to make sure Alan repeated the motion five times until there was only pulp beneath the red-soaked terrycloth. Ellen edged back against the wall, agape, thunderstruck by Alan's benevolent savagery.

Without asking for assistance, Alan lifted the inert body, walked it over to the window and dropped it out. He stared as Abe's body rested for a moment on the surface of the crowd like a body surfer in a mosh pit, before it was absorbed, the new addition sinking to the pavement, lost, soon to be trampled into paste.

No eulogy.

Nothing.

Ellen let some tears escape, not even sure who or what they were for. Alan slumped beside her and both their heads touched at the temples, but no words came. They stared through the room into the void, which offered no comfort.

And Eddie caught a big one on the roof.

Dabney stubbed out his umpteenth chain-smoked cigarette. Eyes watery and throat scorched from the combination of butts and bourbon he'd been consuming since Karl and Mona left, Dabney divided his fogged attention between watching for any sign of their return and Eddie's revolting antics three rooftops away.

Eddie had certainly gotten his recreational sadism down tight. He'd catch one and reel it in with almost no effort, then go to town on it with his trusty assortment of tools. Wrenches, hammers, pliers—the works. Did it count as torture if the victims weren't strictly human or strictly *alive*? Dabney could imagine congressional hearings on that subject. Dave, at one point, had shouted halfhearted encouragement from the sidelines. Now he just sat on the wall, head in his hands, brooding.

Dabney jiggled the bottle by the neck, listening to the liquid slosh around. The bottle had been mostly full when the two had left. Now it was more than half gone. Either Dabney had gone through it fast or it had been a while. He'd check, but his watch had died. He looked over at the other roof. Three dismembered zombies lay in a heap. Catches of the day. Funny way to gauge the passage of time without a timepiece, Dabney mused, too sozzled to take into account the position of the sun or other such time-honored methods. He should have asked Karl to pick up a fresh battery.

Karl.

Would that naïve cracker make it home? Karl was a poor substitute for his own likely dead offspring, but Dabney'd kind of made him his surrogate and he hated the thought of losing him. He remembered ruffling Karl's oily hair. Such a small thing, but he wanted to do it again. When Karl made it back he'd palm that boy's head and mess that hair up good. And now that he'd been bathed a bit, it might even be like white-boy hair ought to be: dry and strawlike, like he imagined Opie's would be. The thought made him smile until his brain converted "when" to "if."

"God *dammit.*"

He tossed the bottle off the roof and, too loaded to go downstairs to his freshly claimed apartment, tottered to his lean-to to sleep it off.

Eddie yanked the last tooth from his catch's mouth and flicked it from the pliers' jaws onto the pile he'd made. He wore a necklace of ears around his tanned neck, having copped the idea from some 'Nam movie he'd seen. He reached over and retrieved a hacksaw from the box and commenced removing the forearm of the struggling wretch pinned beneath his knees. Eddie hoped they felt pain. They made sounds like they did. Sweat dripped off his bare shoulders, the bandana stretched across his forehead keeping his eyes perspiration-free.

"Yeah, like buttah," he grinned, the blade slicing through the skin and muscle straight to the bone, then right on through. These things were seriously malnourished. Sometimes their flesh fell away like well-cooked ribs, not that he had any appetite to try zombie meat. Certainly not since the Mona gravy train rolled in. But it was uncanny how some of these humps had tough leathery hides and others fell apart like nothing. A few shredded to bits while they were still on the line. A couple of firm yanks to get them over the roof's edge and they were gristly jigsaw puzzles. Disappointing.

Eddie held the extremity up and looked into the bones, which were hollow. Wasn't there supposed to be marrow in there? Eddie's pop had been a marrow sucker, which was totally gross. As a kid he'd watch his pop dig this nasty brown paste out of the bones of whatever meat dish mama had made and then suck the bone. When Eddie was hungry he'd feel the acid in his stomach eating away the lining. He remembered hearing something about when you're starving you begin to digest yourself. That's what these humps must be doing, only there was nothing left to digest.

At this point maybe it *was* just a waiting game. The Comet knew facts they didn't.

"Smarter than the average bear," Eddie beamed.

"What? Who?" Dave asked. He took off his shirt and mopped his brow with it, then kept it there to shield his eyes from Eddie's activities.

"*The Comet.* I'm conducting some scientific Frankenstein shit all up in this bitch. Who was onto Mona's drug therapy? The Comet. Who knew the humps were falling apart? Answer: *this guy.*" Sweat escaped the headband and ran right into Eddie's eyes. "Motherfucker," he said with a wince. With one forearm he wiped away the offending liquid, with the other he pulverized the hump's head with a wrench. "That's a solid day's work. Those bitches," he said, gesturing vaguely, "they don't have any appreciation for the work I'm doing up here. I'm breaking scientific ground. Me. *Doctor* Comet. Title honorific, of course."

Eddie looked over at Dave, who wasn't even bothering to mask his disgust.

"*What?*" Eddie beefed. "Anyway, other than Little Miss Spooky, who else earns their keep around here? Who else is proactive? Remember that *proactive* and *paradigm* shit they used to throw at us at work?"

Gaze averted, Dave nodded. "Yeah, I remember."

"Remember that time Staci Kulbertson—Tim McTaggert's assistant—remember when she got *loose* at that company party? That was *ill,* bro. She was shakin' that ass like she was trying to get rid of it. I'd of taken it off her hands, bro."

Dave looked up at Eddie, not knowing what to say.

"Man, I'm sweatin' like a bitch," Eddie said, grinning. "It's hot, man. *It's hot. Hot. Hot.*" He rose and paced, fanning himself with open hands. "Staci was hot. *I* say compliment. *They* say harassment. Fuckin' bullshit '*non-fraternization policy.*'" Eddie lifted a zombie chunk and punted it off the roof. He clenched and unclenched his fists, splaying and extending his fingers as long and far apart as possible, his tendons in sharp relief. "Work was almost kinda like this: close proximity in close quarters. The closest. And even with no fuckin' H.R. narcs breathing down my neck it's *still* hands off. *Motherfucker.*" Another chunk sailed off the roof, this time lobbed. Eddie looked at his zombie piles. "It's man's work wasting these humps. Fuck, I wish it would rain again so I could hose off, know what I'm sayin'?"

Dave nodded.

"Cat got your tongue, Dave-o?"

"No, Eddie."

"So what's the what, bro? Why the long fuckin' face?"

"Wouldn't you rather go downstairs and we could maybe ..."

"We could what?"

"You *know.* There are nicer ways to let off steam than this."

"I don't even *want* that shit," Eddie said. And he didn't. Eddie remembered a dude at work that confided in him that antidepressants had killed his sex drive. The dude had a hot trophy wife and didn't wanna bang her anymore, so behind the dude's back Eddie took care of business at a company party. And then several more times in hotels near work. Eddie the stud. But Eddie didn't feel horny, now. At all. The words were just rote. Staci Kulbertson was hot. Cuckold's wife, too, whatever her name was. But this talk was ... what was the word? *Performative.*

Not being horny upped the angry.

"This is why Spooky's immune, bro. You gotta be a zombie to be off the menu."

"You're not a zombie. Look at you."

"When's the last time I had a boner? I can't even remember."

He brought the wrench down hard on the already pulped skull.

"Let's go downstairs," Dave said. "Put down *that* tool and let's—"

"*I'm in no mood for queer double-entendres!*"

"I can't do this anymore, Eddie" Dave said, tears moistening his cheeks. "This is some seriously repugnant shit. And if you weren't so gaga from those pills—"

"You're takin' the pills, too, bro. *Right?*"

Dave shook his head.

"Fuckin' traitor. Figures. The Comet goes it alone. *Again.*"

Bloodied wrench gripped tight, Eddie stalked over to Dave and loomed. Eddie's eyes weren't right. They danced in their sockets, animated by lunacy, carnage and mystery meds. Dave looked away, then looked straight up into Eddie's eyes, his own resolute. "It's sad," Dave said. "Really sad." He then stood and strode to the other side of the stairwell housing to collect himself.

"Look at you," Eddie said, standing his ground. "*You're acting like a fucking woman.* I was just joking."

Out of view, Dave answered, "Like hell you were."

Eddie looked south, toward the roof of their building to see if the locksmith was witnessing this cringeworthy public display. Eddie was grateful Dabney was sleeping it off. He looked back in Dave's general direction and frowned. *Just like a woman, Exactly like.* Eddie had been through this kind of bullshit too many times to recall. But at least those were for hot—or at least semi-hot—females. This? *Fuckin' drama queen.*

"Day's going great. The fish are practically jumpin' into the boat and you gotta pull this."

Eddie anchored the rod, closed his eyes, inhaled deep through flared nostrils, and strode towards the other side of the housing to settle this nonsense. *It ends nice or it ends ugly, but this shit gets fucking resolved, pronto.* One step from rounding the corner the stairwell door pushed open and out stumbled a free-range shambler, which straightaway sank its teeth into Dave's bare shoulder, eliciting a howl from both him and Eddie.

"Fuck!"

Eddie looked between his besieged bro and the door handle to see the loosened antenna cable drop away from it. *Shoulda paid closer attention to Uncle Sal. Fuck!* Dave wrestled with the undead trespasser and Eddie, hand momentarily palsied, grappled with the hammer in his toolbelt. He freed it, only to have to slip from his sweaty palm. *Fuck!* He snatched the tool up and lunged at his buddy's attacker. One step closer to his target another zombie stumbled out onto the roof, this one groping at Eddie. The angle of his hammer swing wasn't ideal but did the trick, knocking the creature off its pins. It hit the tarpaper with a crunch and began to shudder and emit chalky mewling.

Dave was pressed against the housing, its rough texture abrading his bare back, the zombie expertly perforating his shoulder with its teeth. Eddie body checked the zombie, sending it and Dave tumbling to the ground in a confusion of flailing limbs. Even in shadow, Eddie saw the silver tarpaper coloring bright red. With unchecked savagery he kicked the zombie hard in the side and it rolled off Dave in a twitching heap. With his hammer, Eddie pulverized the skull of Dave's assailant.

"*Motherfucker!*"

Eddie looked at the ground at the spasming second ghoul and bashed its brains out, too.

"Dave!"

Dave did not look good. Blood flowed from the dotted line of toothmarks scoring his rotator cuff. Eddie knelt by his fallen friend's side and didn't know what to do or say other than, "Bro." Helpless, he looked at Dave, who through pain smiled back at him and shook his head. Without animosity, Dave said through clenched teeth, "Tenderness just isn't in your wheelhouse, bro." He then pushed himself off the ground and steadied himself with his good arm against the wall, his left side awash in blood so bright it looked fake. Dave chuckled and shook his head.

"Not gonna lie: this sucks."

"Dave ..."

Dave looked at Eddie with sympathy. "The scorpion and the frog, bro."

"What?"

Dave started walking toward the western exposure of the roof, facing the avenue. The sun was at about five o'clock. Bright. At the ledge he smiled again at Eddie and said, "Look it up."

He then stepped off the roof.

Eddie couldn't even make a sound.

He shuffled past the carnage and looked over the roof ledge, Dave already a shrinking red dot in the ravenous swarm. The hunched backs irised closed and Dave was no longer visible. Just the sounds of the frenzy rose to the roof, and even those faded fast, not that Eddie had any sense of time. Panting, he stumbled backward and slammed into the fighting chair, numbed. *Dave.*

Eddie looked across the expanse of rooftops between this one and theirs. He looked at the fishing gear. At the heap of dismembered gore. Over his shoulder at the housing. No more zombies emerged. He felt dazed. Slow motion. *Gotta block that shit up. Gotta block that shit right up.*

Back on their roof, Dabney snored, having slept through the whole ordeal.

"TYPICAL," KARL SAID, clicking the talk button. Nothing. The walkie-talkie was out of range. His back was clammy and stung.

The exterior of the bookstore was blackened, a fire having badly damaged the establishment. Though the doors were locked, the windows had burst and tiny fragments of safety glass glittered on the sidewalk.

"It's trashed," Karl moaned. "Why didn't you tell me before we got here? You must've been this way before. Did this just happen?"

Without looking back at him Mona shrugged.

"Well, we're here," Karl said, feeling cranky and disappointed. "Might as well go in. Maybe there's *something* salvageable."

Mona advanced toward the gaping maw of a former display window, gingerly poked at the jagged edge, flicking away some loose chips of glass, then climbed into the charred cavern of the store's capacious interior. Karl followed straightaway, wondering if he could just walk along unescorted. He wished he could stop sweating. He felt parched and irritable. His skin prickled. His teeth felt radioactive.

"So?" Mona shrugged.

"So now I browse. I promised Abe legit literature. Plus, I need something, too."

The air inside was heavy with the stench of charred matter, the scab-like wallpaper blistered, scored and scorched. The display tables had either collapsed from the conflagration or stood like crude ziggurats, the books atop them stepped piles of blackened ruin. The floor was skinned with a thick charcoal paste of burnt paper and stagnant water, perhaps from the sprinkler system, and each step was accompanied by a vulgar sucking sound. Street level was a washout, but maybe upstairs was better. Two escalators divided the main room, both leading up into pitch darkness.

"Did you bring a flashlight?" Karl peeped, feeling dumb for not having done so. Mona nodded, and while grateful, Karl resented her for being better prepared. His face flushed as he felt foolish and infantile and intoned, "'Let all bitterness and wrath and anger and clamor and slander be put away from you, along with all malice.' Ephesians 4:31." Mona ignored the recitation and dipped into her Hello Kitty knapsack to fish out two headlamps, the first of which she handed to Karl. She then slipped the other over the crown of her head and turned it on, resembling a miner sans helmet. The beam cut a ghostly white swath through the murk, in which swirled motes of dust and ash.

"Jeez, that's bright," Karl marveled. Flicking his on as they ascended the defunct escalator, Karl asked, "What's something like this cost?" Unlike his scriptural tidbits, which he wished Mona would soak up, Karl was grateful she'd tuned out his question. *Stupid, stupid.* When they reached the landing they stood side by side, doping out the lay of the land. The left side of the mezzanine was trashed, but the right didn't look too bad. The nicest thing was that it was empty, save for the furnishings and merchandise.

"You have any water?" Karl asked, hoping his lack of preparedness was more forgivable than his previous query.

Mona handed him a bottle of water. After a few swigs Karl made to hand it back, but Mona waved it off with a matter-of-fact, "Got my own." That she'd anticipated his absence of foresight made him flush anew.

The bad news was that the "Medicine and Science" section was toast. At least he wouldn't have to explain his need for a copy of the *Physician's Desk Reference to Prescription Drugs* or the like. With resignation, Karl lumbered over to "Literature" and selected a few slightly singed copies of the classics for which Abe had been pining.

Mona stared off into space nearby, chewing something. Karl didn't care to ask. He'd asked enough dumb questions for one day.

"Okay, I guess that'll do me," he said, replacing the full knapsack over his tenderized back with great care. His whole body tingled with pins and needles. Some was pain, some was nerves, some was ... *other.* As they headed back to the escalators he spied on a remainder table a stack of intact copies of the massive hardcover celebrating the fiftieth anniversary of *Playboy* magazine. Pangs of chastity and guilt boomeranged around the insides of his head, laced with regrets over having divested himself of his porn and sexual trophies.

Lourdes Ann Kananimanu Estores—Miss June 1982.

She'd be in there. Maybe even her whole layout, to keep the lonely centerfold in his drawer company. This was almost worse than having to explain away a copy of the *Physician's Desk Reference.* No guy wants to be caught procuring smut in the company of a female. Fresh sweat began to leak. *This is ridiculous,* Karl thought. *Why should I care what she thinks of me? It's only* Playboy. *It's not like it's* real *porn. It's pinups. Why am I justifying this to myself? This barely qualifies as a sin. It was a sin to have thrown away the bounty I had. This is just compensation for my loss.*

With that, Karl snatched a copy of the cumbersome volume off the table. *Oof. Heavy!* If Mona cared a jot, it didn't show. Karl reddened nonetheless as he repositioned the backpack to rest on his chest so he could adjust the contents to accommodate the weighty tome. His back immediately felt better and he felt dumb for not having worn it this way the whole time. Almost to spite Mona, he snagged a second copy. A gift. With Ellen expecting, surely Alan would appreciate a treasury of the finest vixens ever to walk the earth. Or maybe Eddie. Might be wiser to stay in his good graces.

Grace.

This is backsliding. Shame sweat laved his prickly skin. He removed the hefty hardbacks from his bag and, aping Moses about to smash the stone tablets, raised both above his head and proclaimed, "'For sin will have no dominion over you, since you are not under law but under grace.' Romans 6:14!" With arms vibrating with strain, Karl looked at Mona, beamed in triumph over his baser needs and slammed the books to the ground.

Whereupon the charred floor gave way, disappearing Karl along with the books and display table, followed by a shattering crash below. And Mona's face, staring at the hole through which Karl had dropped, actually registered surprise.

Karl couldn't feel his legs. He couldn't feel anything, other than remorse, embarrassment and the near certainty that these were likely his final thoughts. *Typical,* he thought again. He could move his eyes, and aided by the beam of his headlamp could make out that he was upside down. Or at least his head was. The rest of him he couldn't see and apparently moving his head wasn't an option. He opened his mouth and produced a pitiable sound, drool running into his nostril. Above him he could hear the faint creaks of Mona tiptoeing to the escalator, weighing each step, making herself as buoyant as possible.

Once on more solid ground she raced down the long flight of metal stairs and deposited herself directly in Karl's line of sight. Even upside down Karl could see she was upset, and that pressed his panic button. A post-fall dreaminess had temporarily quelled his mounting hysteria, but seeing Mona's semi-vegetative visage register distress was profound and terrifying. She didn't say anything, but as her eyes took in the damage the unspoken appraisal was clearly bad news. The worst.

"Can you speak?"

Karl wasn't sure if she said it or he did. His thoughts were jumbled. His head was his only part he could feel, and it felt like a water balloon full to bursting. He moved it slightly and sensed he was not on the floor. Above it. *Huh?* He tilted his head a little and made out the silhouette of an espresso machine. He'd landed on the barista station. His eyes felt like the pressure behind them would soon propel them across the room. He was panting.

"Can you speak?"

It was Mona. He wasn't saying anything. She touched his face, drying his drool and sweat with a tissue plucked from her silly cartoon knapsack. Upside down, the bag seemed so cute. Mona's face seemed childlike. She didn't seem cold and remote—just fragile and damaged. She's *fragile and damaged,* Karl smirked—or at least thought he did; it was hard to tell.

"Can you speak?"

Karl's vision was dimming or the battery on his headlamp was failing. Maybe a little of both. One from Column A, one from Column B. Karl smiled at Mona. Upside down it's sometimes hard to read another person's expression. "I can't move you," Mona said, her voice thin.

Upside down or not, she was lovely. He pondered how he could have been so judgmental of this otherworldly waif. Mona was no demon. He was certain, finally.

"You're too …" She faltered, searching for the right way to say what there was no right way to say. She sighed and squinted, then looked away from his body, which was twisted in the midpoint, legs pointing east, torso west, the middle bent by some piece of coffee-making equipment. Karl thought about the incinerated medical section. That might have come in useful right about now. *Stay focused,* he thought. *Remain lucid. Remain.* "Broken." She'd finished her thought.

He tried to speak but each attempt choked him, his Adam's apple straining, pressing upwards, crushing the words. The Adam's apple. The *laryngeal prominence.* Little Mister Facty Facterson remembered that from one of those atlases of the human body with the clear overlaid pages. Cross-sections of the various systems. Filet of human. How many parts of his anatomy were broken, as Mona put it? All the important ones? Why was Mona immune? Karl clenched his jaw, then with great effort managed, "Wha moon?"

"Why moon?"

"Wha roo moon?" Mona shook her head, uncomprehending. "*Wha roo moon?*"

"Something about the moon?"

Pointless. "Ah gobba gub," Karl strained, sputtering up fluid, which she mopped away.

"Huh?"

"Imma bag. Ah gobba gub."

"Your bag?"

"Yuh."

Mona opened his bag and felt around. More surprise registered—it was a banner day. With great reluctance she produced the revolver from Karl's backpack.

"You had this the whole time?" Mona was becoming a regular chatterbox.

"Yuh." Big Manfred wasn't about to let his boy head off to New Sodom unarmed. Karl had left it tucked away in its case since he'd arrived in New York, but today seemed the correct occasion to bring it out. He hadn't anticipated being its target, though.

"And what am I …"

"Shoo muh."

"I don't …"

"Peez."

"Can you feel anything?"

"Nuh."

Wanting no part of it, Mona shoved the gun back into Karl's backpack, which rested on his chest. She looked at it, at its straps pinned beneath his immobilized arms. Too tricky to maneuver off him.

"I'll get help."

Karl watched her dark form as it trotted to the blown-out windows, stepped over the threshold, and disappeared from view. Zombies amassed at the lip of the display windows but didn't seem to know how to breach the interior. Climbing was not their forte. Small mercies.

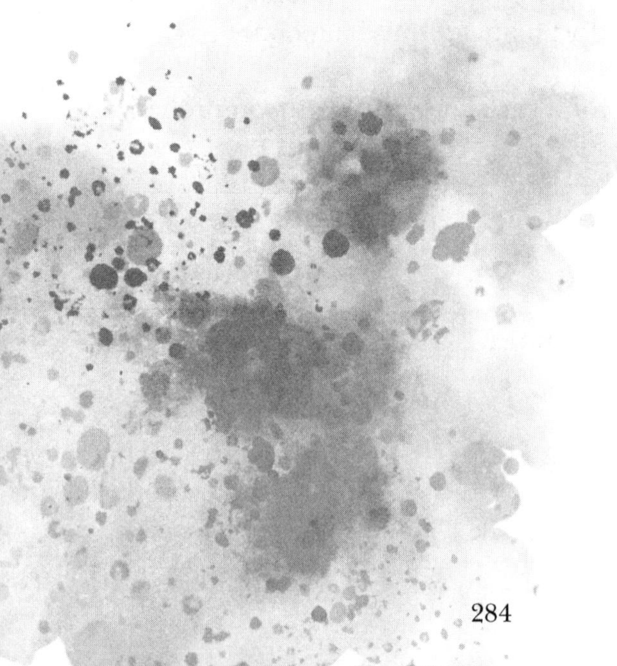

THE POUNDING AND screaming from Eddie's apartment were unnerving. It was like tongues, only occasional swears and Dave's name discernable amid the glossolalia of dark emotion, all set against some muffled generic arena rock. Alan looked up and shook his head. Were it anyone else he'd go check to see if they were okay. But Eddie? Let Dave deal with his histrionics. At Dabney's behest, Alan had once borne witness to the vile spectacle of Eddie fishing for zombies and that one time was enough. Even with Ruth and Abe gone, a building meeting needed to be convened. An intervention. Or eviction. No one would miss Eddie. No one.

Abe, on the other hand.

Alan slumped on his stool and looked at his hand. Arty. *Tammy*, he thought. *Tart-tongued Tammy. Gone. Abe. Gone. Ruth. Gone. Karl?* Alan swirled his brush in mineral spirits and glanced at the canvas. Mona's smooth little four-toed foot. Like a Rubens cherub or Bronzino's foot, as made famous by Monty Python. Pop culture. Once a balm it now kind of sickened Alan. Something so stupid driving a wedge between him and Ellen. Disharmony all of his making. He swirled the brush. "Hey, Arty," he said. He looked at his other hand. "Hey, Wipey." Like a parent not wanting to play favorites, Alan said aloud, "You both do good work. Important work. Essential services, Wipey. Me, though? Mr. Host Organism? *I'm* an idiot."

Ruth had a service. Abe got tossed like trash out a window. Granted, Abe might have laughed in appreciation of such a no-frills send-off. Abe was a kindred spirit regarding faith, but at least he'd made the effort for his wife. Paid his respects. Alan thought about Passovers and Chanukahs he'd attended. How he'd sulked and made plain his atheism. His distaste not just for religion but comforting rites shared by friends and family. He'd shown a complete lack of respect. Been an asshole. What a pointless waste of energy. He'd made people feel bad. What a triumph.

Death always brings on reflection. At least for me, it does.

And now this. This one hurts.

Tears ran down his cheeks not just for Abe and Ruthie, but everyone. His mom. His friends. His exes. Humanity itself. Fresh grief. "Ellen might even love you. You might even love her. So why are you here and she's upstairs, alone? Because you're an idiot. A broken, fucked up, idiot."

Another muffled scream from Eddie, followed by another volley of loud pounding. Then a crash of glass and the arena rock grew louder as it whizzed downwards and then quieter as the boombox was absorbed by the crowd below. But still audible. Def Leppard? Quiet Riot? Couldn't quite tell.

Eddie's on a fucking tear.

And Ellen's upstairs, alone.

I need to fix this.

From the street, in addition to the still playing, albeit muffled, boombox, Alan heard a sharp two-finger whistle followed by the squawk of the walkie-talkie that heralded Mona's return. He tore himself away from the canvas of Mona only to see the real McCoy outside, not looking quite as detached as usual. As the crowd peeled away from her, Eddie's tunes loudened and Alan could see the discarded sound system lying on its back like a turtle. The whole scene was eerier than usual.

Especially as Mona's return was solo.

Barefoot, Alan tore down the stairs and flew into 2B, so upset by Mona arriving stag that he didn't even alert the others. As he dropped the rope for readmittance Mona was just climbing onto the roof of Dabney's van. Ellen appeared over Alan's shoulder, giving him a jolt.

"Where's Karl?" she asked.

"Good question."

Mona's explanation, monosyllabic and fragmented, managed to paint an ugly portrait of Karl splayed on the coffee bar, his upper portion turned this way, his lower that. Ellen fought the urge to ask if this accident happened before or after Mona had managed to score her "morning after" pills. Timing.

"We have to get him," Alan said. "He can't just be left there to die, or worse, be eaten alive. Before he fell, that whole umbrella thing was working out pretty well for you?" Mona nodded. Alan exhaled heavily and pushed back on his chair, the front legs off the floor. He then clunked forward, rose and walked over to the front window to look at the horde. "Right."

"Alan, no," Ellen said, not having it. "Karl wouldn't even be in this fix if he and Eddie hadn't ..." Ellen paused and looked over at Mona, an embarrassed and apologetic timbre creeping into her voice. "Mona, sweetie, those guys—Karl included—have been swiping and taking your pills to—"

"I know," Mona said.

"You know?"

"I can count."

"You *knew* and you let it happen? But they violated your space. Your trust. We're really sorry they did that. And that we kept mum. Like complicit assholes. Eddie's just a piece of shit and Karl ... Karl's just a born follower. But ... we didn't want to keep it secret, but frankly the gorilla in our midst spooks me."

"I know."

"She knows." Ellen felt almost as annoyed at Mona for knowing and not saying anything as she felt about the conspirators' theft. "So why didn't you say something?"

"Like what?"

"Like, '*stop stealing my drugs*,' for starters. What is *wrong* with you? What are they even taking? These clowns have convinced themselves the pills are your secret weapon, you know, against the zombies. And you *knew*? I can't believe it."

"Hard not to."

Alan stepped away from the window, Karl's plight temporarily tabled. "Hard not to what? Notice the theft?"

"Side effects."

"*Ooooh,*" the couple said in unison. Eddie and Dave's rooftop activities. Karl's schizo religiosity. Sweating. Agitation. Side effects. They seemed like natural progressions. Or regressions. But not unexpected. Still. Ellen and Alan felt pretty stupid.

"Severe contraindications," Mona said, eyes downcast, carefully pronouncing the words with a hint of a wry smile.

"So why do *you* take them?"

Mona's smile vanished.

"Mona. Sweetheart." Ellen placed a hand on Mona's, which the girl then withdrew from the tabletop and locked, via interlaced fingers, with her other hand in her lap. Ellen tried to make eye contact, but Mona wasn't up for that, either. "Mona," Ellen said, choosing her words. "A ways back you said you had a theory. Isn't this maybe the time to share it?"

"I'm not supposed to ..."

For the second time in Ellen's experience, Mona looked uncomfortable. Frightened, even. "It's okay, Mona." Ellen was very cognizant of repeating Mona's name. It was a sales technique. Trust building. She remembered an article she'd read about how a person's name connected the most with their identity and individuality. Was it working? Or was it just annoying? Could go either way.

Mona closed her eyes.

Uh-oh?

"When Mama was pregnant." Pause. "With me." Pause. "Mama was. Mama was not ..." Glacial pause. "Mama had ... issues."

Each syllable was like pulling teeth. It hurt to watch Mona struggle, but the time had come. Ellen needed to do something with the tension, so under the table she gripped Alan's thigh. Hard enough to make him wince. "Go on."

"Mentally she was ..." The nearly soundless world seemed to grow more silent and lean forward in anticipation of Mona's tortuously uttered next words. "She always told me to never ..." Another chasmic pause. "There was a clinical trial." *Now we're getting somewhere.* "Mama signed a very iron-clad NDA. Know what that is?"

Ellen nodded and said, "Honey, all the lawyers are dead, now."

"So is Mama." Mona's eyes clenched shut tighter. She unwove her fingers and massaged her forearms over the sleeves. This was agonizing. "I wasn't allowed to … Talk."

"But you sang," Ellen said, trying to make sense of this. "You said you sang opera."

"Singing isn't talking."

Ellen had no argument for that. *Singing isn't talking. No, it sure isn't. Not unless you're Leonard Cohen.*

Mona rubbed her nose and added, "If I spoke, the closet. The hairbrush. The cigarette." She exhaled through her nose. "Mostly that."

"Your mother sounds like a fucking monster. No offense."

Mona hesitated, then pushed up her sleeve to reveal constellations of cigarette burn scars. Ellen and Alan's stomachs seized. Mona traced a finger over the scars, like Braille telling a biography of abuse. "The drug. Maybe it helped her? I dunno. But after I was born, I always took it. They said I needed it."

"So what happens when you run out?" Alan asked.

Mona shrugged.

"You can't let Eddie filch any more of your supply," Alan said. "But someday …"

"No more pills."

Mona slumped, looking drained.

"So it's not going to do anything for them, is it?" Alan asked. "I mean, this is all speculation, conjecture, but …"

"Doubt it. It's in my DNA, pretty much. Like Thalidomide."

"Four toes beats flippers."

Under the table Ellen squeezed Alan's thigh, this time in reproof.

"Mama always said I was a mutant with no superpowers."

Ellen looked at the girl and said, "Guess your mama was wrong."

Mona directed her gaze at Ellen's midriff, then made actual eye contact with her and said, "In that case, if anyone should be stealing my pills, it's you."

Jesus.

"So, Karl …" Mona began, but Ellen's mind was racing.

As Karl lay on the table contemplating his imminent demise, he failed to notice he'd shifted his weight off his no longer numb but now throbbing hips and crossed his legs. From his Dutch angle perspective he stared across the verge, the street choked with undead. He glanced up at the hole through which he'd fallen, hoping to catch a glimpse of Jesus or some angel beckoning him forth, home, but no such luck. He wiped his forehead and started counting off the moments left.

"What a moron!"

Karl sat upright, feeling pins and needles where before he felt nothing.

"What a dope!"

He looked at his hands, flexing the fingers and rotating the wrists.

"What a dummy! Thank you, God! Thank you, Jesus! Thank … Oops."

Not being paralyzed equaled glee equaled lack of judgment equaled shouting. He turned toward the street and saw agitated zombies staring back. "Oh, balls," Karl peeped. The mob amassed by the window frames still hadn't quite figured out how to vault the three-foot wall that separated them from their appetizing quarry, but it was only a matter of time. Even if they didn't have the smarts to lift one leg over, repeat, the shoving from the peanut gallery would deliver the first wave over the hump in a moment or so. Karl massaged his legs, trying to rid himself of the paresthesia needling his thighs and calves. From no sensation to an overabundance. Karl would feel blessed were he not on the verge of soiling himself in terror.

For a moment he felt cross with Mona for leaving him, but she was no medic. She was just a girl. A spooky chick. But she'd gone for help. He couldn't wait for her to return. She'd be pleased that she'd been wrong.

He dropped to the floor, feeling wobbly, but *feeling*. And with a pronounced *clunk* his gun hit the floor, too. Karl stooped forward to retrieve it and for a moment swooned as blood rushed to his head and everything went black for a fraction of a very long second. Half bent, he gripped the countertop with one hand and picked up the revolver with the other. His legs protested, so he jogged in place to get them up to speed. The floor felt solid. Then again, it had felt solid upstairs, too.

The zombies' ingress loomed. But still they hung back. Did Mona's miracle drugs work for him? He didn't want to risk heading toward the street to find out. He tried the walkie-talkie again, to let Mona know he was up. Nothing but static. Karl did a little spastic two-step, but didn't know where to run. The obstacle between them and him was still doing the trick, but once they got in it could be a feeding frenzy. *Head out or retreat? Might Eddie actually be right?*

Karl took a couple of tentative steps toward Eighty-sixth and regret washed over him in an instant as zombies began to storm the castle, the rear guard shoving the first row down and using them as a desiccated flesh ramp. *Stupid Eddie! Stupid me! Why do I have to be so ...* The first wave fell in heaps on the sooty ground, attempting to right themselves as more stumbled on top of them. And then more.

Karl aimed the beam from his headlamp up the escalator. What would the odds be of falling through the floor twice? Tempt fate by fleeing upwards or fulfill the obvious by sticking around down below? Maybe he could make it to the roof. Then what? Jump? One thing at a time. On still unsteady legs Karl limped to the escalator and gripped the handrails in a half pull, half run to the upper landing.

The second-floor restrooms were in the back. Maybe like the movies there would be some air duct he could climb into that would lead to safety. He slammed into the men's room—noting for a nanosecond how funny it was that even now he consciously chose it as opposed to the lady's room—and scanned the dark chamber, aiming the beam this way and that. Drop ceiling, but no grating, no duct. *Typical, typical, typical. Don't have faith in Eddie and never believe what you see in the movies, dummy!*

No lock on the door, of course. He opened it and peeked out. The zombies still hadn't made the mezzanine. *There's got to be a way out of here. Think.* But without a floor plan it was just guesswork. The first wave of zombies had made it to the landing. Karl couldn't see them yet, but he heard them shuffling, moaning, exuding pure need. Did they scent him, like hounds at the hunt? Maybe his odor was masked by the stink of char. His only option was the stall with the bolt lock. If he perched on the toilet and was very quiet, maybe they wouldn't find him. *Cripes.* The moans were hungry. Purposeful. *Oh Jesus.* It sounded like there were a lot of them.

Tons.

Tons.

With a thunderous crash a larger portion of the charred floor gave way.

"'The Lord will rescue his servants; no one who takes refuge in him will be condemned.' Psalm 34:22."

Hallelujah.

"I *have* to go with her," Alan said, voice resolute, though his eyes told a different story.

"Are you strong enough to carry him home, if he's even still alive, which let's face it is pretty fucking unlikely?"

"No, but Mona and I can get him into her shopping cart."

"I don't like it."

"I *hate* it, but we can't just leave Karl out there."

"Fuck. *Fuckfuckfuck.*"

"I don't disagree. But—"

"Fuck!"

Ellen joined Alan at the window and put an arm around his waist, the first affectionate contact they'd shared in a while. That touch, that small embrace, bolstered Alan's resolve. Ellen looked at his face and caressed his cheek. She tilted her head back and he responded with a kiss. For all their sexual encounters, this was the first time either of them felt a deeper connection to the other.

Ellen whispered, "What about Eddie? Why can't he—"

"Have you heard him? I dunno what's eating him, but …"

"Fuck," Ellen repeated, this time with resignation. "You wanna play hero? Is this some latent macho thing?"

"I'd prefer to think it's duty and compassion, but it's probably guilt."

"There's that Jewy New York thing."

Alan smiled. "Right. Which you love."

Ellen neither confirmed nor denied, keeping her eyes on the multitude on York and beyond. Mona sat on the roof of Dabney's van and drummed her fingers and even that little hint of impatience was unnerving. Alan took another hard look at the horde and the small girl on the roof below. *Four toes beats flippers. Idiot.* He then looked at his own bare feet and said, "I can't go out like this."

"You shouldn't go *at all.* Maybe the drugs *are* helping Karl, in the meantime. We literally know nothing. Are you a scientist? Am I?" Alan was about to respond but Ellen continued, "We don't know shit. All we know is Mona is exempt, but the rest of us ..."

"This pep talk sucks."

Alan gave Ellen's hand a squeeze, hoped it didn't come off as patronizing, then disengaged from Ellen and strode toward the open door of 2B.

"Alan!"

Ellen's voice echoed in his head. He knew if he gave her more time she could dissuade him from escorting Mona. *I should have gone home to Mom. I could have at least tried.* Halfway to his apartment to snag his own Docs Alan heard the thunder of footsteps pounding down the stairs from above. *Eddie or Dave.* He hastened his own upward flight and saw the former appear on the landing above, shirtless and so drenched in sweat he seemed oiled. Eddie had substituted his Daisy Dukes and espadrilles for urban camouflage pants and jump boots. He wore fingerless leather gloves and his now trademark headband was tight across his forehead. And that grotesque string of ears. But all that was upstaged by his eyes, which blazed. Alan's chest hitched with nostalgia for malnourished Eddie.

"I saw Tuesday Addams came back. *Alone.*"

"Eddie—" Alan started, but bit his tongue. No pop culture pedantry.

"Bible Boy still among the living?"

"TBD," Alan said.

"By who, you?"

Alan had to admit Eddie looked more the man for the job, wild eyes notwithstanding.

"I was thinking."

Alan stepped forward and as he attempted to access the landing Eddie shoulder checked him into the wall. "Think again." With one foot half on, half off, the top step, Alan stumbled, skidded his arm against the swirled stucco wall, which even under innumerable coats of paint abraded his skin as he lost balance. Alan's arms shot out to grab the bannister or Eddie or anything to prevent him plunging down the stairs backwards and headfirst. Or at all. His fingers only clutched air and down he went, shoulder hitting the wall, then cracking against a stair tread, the aluminum nosing gashing it. His legs flew in a tangle overhead and as he collided with the bottom newel his arm snapped like a dry twig. Alan rolled onto his side and clutched his ruined arm, whimpering. "Dude," Eddie said. "Looks like you're goin' nowhere."

"What—" Ellen began, but Eddie ignored her as he launched himself out the window and rappelled down the rope like a champion. His feet landed on the van roof with a satisfying metallic thud and even more satisfying actual reaction from Spooky.

"Where's Alan?"

"Baby bird broke his wing. Terrible thing. *Terrible.*"

"Broke his wing?"

"Accidents happen. It was just a thing. I'm going this way, he's going that. Look, I'm here to help, yeah?"

"I …"

"A great man once said, 'You go to war with the army you have, not the army you might want or wish to have at a later time.' I am the *best* army, *so let's do this.*"

He looked up as Ellen did a double take between the two on the van and behind her.

"Broke his wing?" Ellen repeated.

"*It was an accident!*"

And with that, Eddie gestured for Mona to lead the way.

ONCE AGAIN MONA created a clearing, then gestured for her companion to follow. With a defiant *just-try-to-eat-me* whomp, Eddie dropped to the asphalt and glared at the retreating skinbags. *G'wan,* he motioned, chin jutting. *Wanna piece a me? C'mon.* Nothing doing. Buoyed by their reluctance to encroach, Eddie stepped forward, following Mona's wide round behind. How long would he follow? Could he take the lead? He felt pumped. Even more pumped than on the roof. This was a major rush. Major.

Flanked by resentful spectators, the duo soldiered west on the main drag, their progress greeted by hissing and keening. Mona didn't look back, just straight ahead towards their destination. Eddie didn't care. She was nothing to talk to. He'd rather divide his focus between the crowd and the cleft of Mona's ample butt. Betwixt those orbs was pure sweet honey. How many months had he spent between Mallon's flat Irish loaves? Mallon. Dave. His pasty potato-eatin' keister, two slabs of lightly pimpled pancake, white as Wonder bread but not nearly as appetizing.

Dave. Fuck. Eddie shook his head violently, like a dog fresh from a bath. *Happy thoughts. It wasn't my fault. If he hadn't of slunk away like a bitch … Nope, still not happy. You're out here, motherfucker. You're doing it. Fuck those other people. Do they even know? They don't.*

"So, you think peewee is still alive?" Eddie said, breaking the silence.

"Huh?"

"Karl. Think he's still alive?"

"Dunno."

"He was getting' kinda weird, there, clutchin' that Bible kinda tight. You'd of thunk maybe he had God on his side. But maybe not."

"Dunno."

Dunno. Pfff. Always a pleasure talking to this one. "You ever see that *Ten Commandments* movie? '*Mmmyaaah,* where's yuh messiah, *now, see?*' That shit's funny, right? That's what I'm gonna say to Karl if he's not … you know." *Like Dave? Shut it, stunod. Happy thoughts. Happy. Smiles, everyone, smiles.* "All *this* …" Eddie gestured at the zombies, not that Mona saw, and continued, "I used to go to church, right? I mean, c'mon. Italian from Bensonhurst? Of *course* I'm Catholic to the bone, because of my moms. But this shit?" Another nod to the undead. "So I wanna ask Karl, where's *his* messiah now?"

Nothing. No reply.

"What? You into God, too? Sorry to offend."

"I'm not."

"Not into God or not offended?"

"Neither."

Even though they were in agreement her response irked him. She probably never believed. It's one thing to lose faith; it's another never to have had it in the first place. That was kind of arrogant. Eddie didn't believe in God, but atheists were assholes. Just as smug as Born Agains, but colder. Like they thought they were better than everyone else. Smarter. Better not to talk. Better to just scope that pear-shaped ass. With each footfall one buttock would jiggle, then the other. It was hypnotic. Eddie started humming, then quietly singing, "*I see you baby, shakin' that ass, shakin' that ass* …" Eddie used to dance like crazy to that song. He'd hit the clubs, make with the gyrations and then bring a hottie or two home for some pelvic mayhem. The more focused his reminiscences the more audible his singing.

"*I see you baby, shakin' that ass, shakin' that ass* …"

Mona stopped walking and turned to face Eddie.

Reverie over, Eddie stared back into Mona's fisheye. She gestured at the shamblers. Even though they hung back they were agitated.

"Don't rile them."

"Oh, sorry. Sorry," he said. "Just singin'. Even a guy like me gets the nerves, can you believe it?" He flashed his best aw-shucks grin. "But remember that one?" Mona shook her head. "It's a good one. Groove Armada. That's whose song it was. Yeah. I used to get kinda nice to that shit."

Mona turned away and they resumed their trek. The second her back was turned Eddie stuck out his tongue. *What kind of underwear does Spooky wear? Probably the most basic bitch full-coverage granny panties. Or maybe she goes commando to go with that dykey paramilitary look of hers. Yeah, that. Maybe that's why I'm just not feelin' it for shorty.* Eddie's mind rewound to his loss of appetite for porn. His increased appetite for destruction. *Dave. Fuck, Mallon. Fuck. Why'd you … Happy thoughts.*

"I see you baby, shakin' that ass, shakin' that ass …"

Mona sucked her teeth in that gross disapproving way.

"Sorry, sorry."

Don't judge me, bitch, Eddie thought.

Dave. Does anyone else even know he's gone, yet? The way he looked at me. He wasn't even mad. It's like he felt sorry for me. Me. He gets chomped and I'm the one he's feeling sorry for? What the fuck, bro? He judged me. She's judging me. My whole fuckin' life I've dealt with that shit.

A fresh rivulet of sweat escaped the headband and stung Eddie's eye. He wiped it away, closed his eyes and then pressed his palm against the cloth to release the moisture collected within. Perspiration cascaded down his forehead, forking at the bridge of his nose. It tasted salty but not bad. Then he realized it wasn't just sweat.

Tears?

Dave.

Who's to say he'd become one of those things, anyway? Who knows shit about anything, anymore? The Wandering Jewess came back. No bites. So did the Fogelhuts. Maybe just Jews came back. Eddie chuckled at the thought. *Jesus was a Jew and he came back. Is that where that Chosen People arrogance comes from? All the Jews Dave and me worked with sure acted like they owned the world. Had the secret knowledge. Dave. Dave pulled a Louganis and there's no coming back from that. Maybe some*

Neosporin would've cleared that shit up. So maybe we weren't getting along so great, there. But bros are bros. We'd of worked it out. Fuck.

He fingered his necklace of zombie ears, vacillating between thoughts of Dave and punishing Spooky's *culo*. Or wishing he even wanted to. *This ain't right. Those pills. But here I am.* But first things first: Karl needed some rescuing, so The Comet was on it. The zombie ears felt like suede. Or did they? Maybe it was his fingertips. His mouth felt like the inside of his socks, the texture of his inside cheeks rough like terrycloth. And dry. So dry. Eddie swigged from his canteen. As the water sluiced down his throat he remembered something from junior high.

"The brain's fuckin' weird," Eddie said to the back of Mona's head. He trotted forward and walked abreast of Mona. "You know? Like, I was just thirsty, right? So I guzzle some *agua* and what comes back to me? This fuckin' book from when I was a kid, with this little baby Mexican or Indian. But I remembered his name: Coyotito. 'Cause as I was guzzling I remembered this line from the book about Coyotito's little tongue lapping thirstily or greedily or some such dumbass shit. That book sucked, but I remember some of it. 'Cept its name."

"*The Pearl.*"

"Yeah. *Fuck* yeah, *The Pearl.* Holy shit, I can't believe you knew that. That book *sucked*, am I right?"

"Mm-hmm."

Eddie grinned thinking about that little brat taking lead in the *cabeza*. The more he thought about it the more that flooded back to him. In zombie movies head shots took care of everything. He looked at the throng as it held itself back, fighting its hardwired desire to tear the two of them to shreds. Eddie popped a finger gun at them, each a rotting Coyotito.

"And you know what else? Wow, it's all coming back. That big Baby Huey mongoloid and his little pal. Or was that a different book? Petting rabbits an' shit. Same guy, right?"

"Steinbeck."

"*Yeeeeaaah.* Him. Dude, he sucked."

"Mm-hmm."

"Steinbeck. Was he a fuckin' Jew? Is that Jewish?"

"Dunno."

"Sounds Jewy. No offense, I mean if you're a Jew. Jews are all right."

"I'm not."

"Not offended or not Jewish?"

"Neither."

"Cool."

Eddie's mouth still felt like felt, dry and scabrous. The water didn't help. He was sweating like a pig. Did pigs sweat? Isn't that why they rolled around in their own filth, because they couldn't sweat to cool off? And dogs. Dogs panted because they couldn't sweat. Did any animal sweat? Sweating was sweet. Eddie wanted something sweet. A bomb pop would be the bomb, but Mister Softee had stopped making his rounds. Mister Softee, with his friendly waffle-cone face and whippy-do vanilla swirl bouffant.

"*Try as he might he can never get hard / his name is Mister Sof-teeee*!" Eddie sang softly to the tune of the old ice cream trucks' clarion. "Remember that?"

Mona shrugged.

"Your loss, honey. Mister Softee was the shit." Eddie polished off the water. Didn't concern him. He'd pick up a bottle or five on the way home. "Yo, I've gotta take a leak. You mind?"

Not waiting for a response, Eddie unzipped, aimed at the zombies nearby and doused them. As they stood there and took it, Eddie grinned and sniped, "S'matta, your mamas never told you to come in from the rain?" No response. Not even wrath. Between the zombies and Mona ... He shook off the last few droplets and tucked himself away.

"There's a whole lotta shit we could steal out here in the world. Fuck, it ain't even stealin' no more. It's just *taking*. Scavenging. It's practically our patriotic duty."

Mona shrugged.

Those shrugs. Spooky was really chafing at Eddie. A woman shouldn't ever come off all attitudinal to a man. Even Eddie's mom had agreed on that point, and when the occasion called for it, she didn't protest a slap across the chops from Pops. Was that was Spooky was begging for? Women liked it rough from time to time. Just a fact of nature. Eddie let himself lag just a little behind her again. He preferred her ass to her face, anyway. Even with his sex drive in neutral.

The scorched bookstore loomed on the left.

With Eddie away on his mercy mission—hard to fathom the word "mercy" in context with Eddie, but there it was—Dabney positioned himself on the northernmost roof, with its clear view up Eighty-sixth Street. He'd cleared away the zombie remains the idiots had left behind and used cinder blocks from that long-forsaken restoration to secure the stairwell door. When—or *if*—they got back, Dabney was going to lay down the law: no more sick nonsense up here. No zombies allowed.

Dabney lit a cigarette from the tip of the one he'd just finished and felt decadent. In his days as a breadwinner he'd savored cigarettes and put some time between them. Last he was paying for this particular vice, coffin nails were going for over ten bucks a pack over the counter. He'd started buying from the Native Americans via the Internet for roughly half that, but still he didn't blow through them like they cost nothing. Now they did, so what the hell. Live a little, even if the living he was doing was sure to accelerate dying. Into a proper weighted tumbler he poured himself two fingers and swished the bourbon around to aerate it. Sophisticated. And again, it was "the good stuff." That's why he wasn't just swigging out of the bottle.

He took a sip, then frowned. Not at the drink, which was a delight, but drinking. Now. At this moment. Suddenly the bourbon burned as it went down his cigarette-scorched throat. He stubbed the butt out on the brick, then flicked it at York. How long had it been since Karl and Mona had gone out? How long since Mona and Eddie? Six or eight fingers ago. Maybe more. Dabney rested the bottle on his thigh as he straddled the low dividing wall separating the rooftops. Even inebriated he was mindful to not perch too close to the edge. But this wasn't a mellow bourbon buzz. Now it was infused by guilt. "Old habits," he pronounced with the exaggerated elocution of someone trying to cloak intoxication.

He looked at the bottle of sixteen-year-old small batch in his hand, then allowed it to join his discarded cigarette over the wall, its muted impact below punctuating his thought: *no more.*

"Giddyup," he slurred, wiping some boozy spittle from his stubbly chin. He dug his heels into the puckered tarpaper and slapped the curved top of the wall. "Git along little dogies." He thought of Woody Strode and began to tear up. Woody was long gone. Everything he cared about was.

Once upon a time his wife had called him "adorable."

Once upon a time small children had called him "daddy."

Once upon a time he'd been his own boss.

Dabney hoisted his ass off the divider and teetered putty-limbed across the rooftop. He tripped and fell, his numbed palms scraped raw on impact. He pulled himself off the ground and dog-tired dropped his leaden keister into Eddie's jerry-rigged fighting chair. It felt good. Better than the wall.

He fell asleep, the hot sun baking his marinated brain.

"THAT'S THE BEST I can do," Ellen said, assessing her handiwork on Alan's damaged arm. A serviceable splint buttressed the broken bone, which fortunately had not popped through the skin or anything that gnarly. He'd taken five ibuprofens and three shots of whiskey but still was in agony.

"It's practically a miracle it was Wipey, not Arty," Alan said through gritted teeth.

Ellen had not been apprised of the pet names bestowed by Alan's ex, so the reference took a moment to land. "Oh. Cute. Yeah, I guess that is lucky."

"I *wanted* to go. I *needed* to go." Alcohol and pain added to the self-pity.

Ellen looked out the window at York, everything settled back to normal.

"She might be immune to those things," Ellen said, "but she's not immune to a Neanderthal like Tommasi. Especially hopped up on mystery meds."

Alan attempted to stand, but gravity, shock and Four Roses voted against it. Ellen looked at him, then back out the window. Her shoulders sagged, then straightened and steeled. "Well, fuck. Okay."

Within the gloom of the bookstore, Mona flicked on her headlamp. She didn't have another to offer Eddie, so she beckoned him to stay close, within the light, within the umbrella.

"If I find any Steinbecks I'm gonna piss on 'em," Eddie said.

Mona chose not to respond and made a beeline for the countertop onto which Karl had fallen, finding nothing but books in his place and some completely kaput zombies, their backs and limbs broken, the last vestiges of unlife gone.

"He was here," she said, pointing.

"He ain't here now."

Mona looked up, aiming the light at the hole Karl had made, which was now many times larger. That explained the wrecked carcasses and additional charred timber. Eddie looked up at the opening.

"That's a big fuckin' hole."

"Mm-hmm."

I'll "Mm-hmm" you, you little bucket of fuck. Maybe the drugs were wearing off, but his mood was souring, the euphoria of being out in the world being supplanted by the claustrophobia of the darkened interior of this bookstore.

"So whatta you suggest?" Eddie said, tamping down pique. "Looks like Karl might've got up on his own steam, no? Them zombies clean their plates, but not so's there's nothing left. There'd be blood or something. Bones. Something *gristly and moist.*" He wiped his sweaty brow, cleared his throat and felt cotton mouthed. In the beverage case he found some bottled water and tossed one to Mona who, much to his surprise and disappointment, caught it. In sync they chugged.

"Think he got up and went on home?"

"We'd have seen him."

She had a point. It seemed unlikely that Karl would have taken a divergent path from the one he and little miss talkative just took, especially if he was all busted up. Then again, if he was immune, he could've gone any way he wanted. Eddie really wanted to know if he needed Spooky to keep him safe. He looked back at the gathered crowd hanging back outside and the stragglers that had invaded the store. Even within their dead eyes he could see the hunger. The ones inside pressed back into the shadows, girding the interior walls. A noise came from the upstairs and Eddie looked up into the gloom at the spot where the hole was. In the murk it looked like a busted mouth, the splintery floorboards like crooked teeth.

"You heard that." Lacking any clear inflection, it wasn't so much a question as a statement. Eddie made a face as he considered Mona's way of speaking might be contagious. He said it again, this time as an obvious query.

"Mm-hmm."

So annoying. With the beginnings of an eyelid tic, Eddie dashed up the escalator and ran onto the mezzanine, taking care to avoid the gaping hole. As his eyes adapted he saw nothing unusual: some chairs, the upholstery roasted away, the springs and foundations jutting out, bookcases, books, books and more books.

"Yo!" he shouted, caution to the wind. "Karl, you in here?"

A soft moan from the back of the landing.

Mona softly touched his bare shoulder and he felt a tingle from head to toe. It was the first time a woman had voluntarily made contact with him since everything went kablooey. Blood raced into his groin. *Dude, now is not the time.* The light from her headlamp bothered Eddie's dark-adjusted eyes and he fanned it away, frowning as she stepped ahead of him. Those dead eyes of hers. Those pointy little A-cups nestled beneath the illegible grindcore logo of her hallmark long-sleeved black tee. Eddie was very hard. This was messed up. He was sweating more than the temperature warranted and again his mouth felt dry. The air tasted like death. He wanted some mints. His eyes darted back and forth and his skin prickled like it was swarming with fire ants.

The moan sounded again.

"Karl!"

"*Shhh,*" Mona cautioned.

"Why? What's th' fuckin' diff'? We're immune, so it's all good." Through his pocket he gave his erection a firm squeeze. He was freeballing, so no underwear confined his jewels and scepter. *Hello, old friend.* Maybe the drugs diminished his libido, which had actually been kind of a relief, but they were definitely fading and the beast was back. The Comet.

"*We're* immune?" Mona repeated.

"*You're* immune," Eddie affirmed. "You are. *You.* But we got the umbrella going on."

Mona squinted at him in a way that made her sexier and more slappable in equal measure. *Did she wear black eyeliner? Nah, just a trick of the dark.* The moan came again. Mona gestured for Eddie to follow. He was sick of this arrangement. *He* was the *man. She* should be following *him.* She should be doing a lot she wasn't doing.

They turned the corner and the headlamp illuminated a group of hunched over zombies polishing off Karl, his torso gaping like a savaged piñata. Vibrant graffito of arterial spray decorated the bathroom wall, fresh blood pooled in all directions and Mona had a bona fide reaction: she threw up. Sensing her presence, the zombies recoiled and retreated deeper into the men's room. Mona wiped her mouth and was about to suggest retreat when Karl moaned again.

"He's … not … dead," Eddie whispered.

Subconsciously, he'd backed away from the open bathroom door, his entire body rigid as his groin. Mona edged past Eddie and inched toward the restroom. As she brushed by him, he felt another emotion seep in: shame. She was going to Karl. *She.* All five-foot-nothing of her. Resentment supplanted shame. *Look at her.* Eddie continued to fall back. The stench of the fresh viscera was playing havoc with his guts, but still his headlamp was directed at the scene before him. Spooky knelt by Karl. And the zombies hugged the wall. It was bonkers. Even in a confined space like that they couldn't get away from her fast enough. He could almost relate.

She pulled a hankie out of her pocket and mopped Karl's brow. She was bent far over and she was talking to Karl, and though Eddie couldn't make out the words he could tell her tone was comforting. Karl's hand feebly groped for hers, which she accepted and clasped. And all to the soundtrack of hampered undead hissing. Unreal. The hero moment. The fallen brother-at-arms. Like he'd seen in countless war movies, the scene played out before him and here he was. Here. Not there.

You fuckin' pussy.

Humiliation followed by the unique sensation of jagged teeth bearing down on bare shoulder meat. His. Eddie's eyes met those of the zombie whose teeth were dug into his upper arm. Eddie's deep brown and lively. His attacker's gummous and gray. The communication between them crystalline: *I am going to eat you* versus *oh no you aren't.*

Eddie shrugged off his assailant and brought his fist down on the bridge of its former nose, now just crusty cavernous slits. Bone splintered and the thing let out a low groan, but didn't lose interest in its dinner. *So much for immunity.* Eddie scanned frantically for Mona. Another zombie fell on Eddie, teeth bared, bony fingers digging into his waist, not quite breaking the skin, but near enough. Eddie batted away at both, shrieking, "*Mona, help*!" So much for pride.

Mona looked up from Karl, whose own eyes glazed over as he passed. She saw in the gore his revolver and hesitated, then picked it up, unsure what to do. She tucked it into her cargo pocket and headed for Eddie, looking less apathetic than usual. The zombies caught one whiff and, like skeeters to deet, backed off. Eddie assayed the damage. A ring of oozing bloody tooth holes limned his shoulder. His abdomen ached.

"*You took your sweet fuckin' time*," he growled.

He felt sickened by his girly plaint for assistance. And yet still he was hard.

"Karl," Mona said.

"Karl was a fuckin' goner already. Best thing you coulda did was stomp him. Make sure he don't come back."

Eddie stormed toward the bathroom to do just that, then caught a fresh gander at the zombies and gore within and froze. Adrenaline pumped hard. He was hard. He stood between the john and Spooky, hoping her mojo spread this far. To be fuckin' dependent on her galled him. Look at her. *Look at her!*

"I don't know how this shit works," Eddie said, staring at his wound. "Do I become one of those things or what? In the movies they always become one of those things. But maybe movies are bullshit. Dave got bit and he just ..."

Dave. Fuck.

Mona shrugged, wiping her nose on the back of her hand. She was gross. Like a little kid, only a little kid with womanly hips and a nice round ass. Open palmed and melodramatic, Eddie swept a whole row of books off their shelf.

"God, that pisses me off," Eddie spat. "That little shrug of yours. You're no mute. You can speak. So what's with the little tics and shit? You got something to say, *say it!*"

Her eyes weren't hooded, like usual. They were open wide. And that was another thing he didn't like about Spooky: she barely ever blinked. She was like a cat. Or a baby. Eddie had no fondness for either. He rubbed his damaged spot, smearing blood. He looked at his palm. It scintillated. He was sweatier than before, his face hot. Burning. Feverish. His mouth felt drier than ever. Maybe it was just adrenaline—his nerves were pretty jangly—or maybe it was infection.

"This could've been prevented," he said, more to himself than Mona. "But I blame *you. You* mislead us. Those drugs ain't worth shit." He rubbed his crotch absently, inadvertently wiping blood all over it. The sweat stung his injury. "Fuckin' drugs." He shook his head, face pinched.

"We should go," said Mona, her voice faint.

"I blame *you.*"

"Really, we should."

"Fuckin' drugs."

"You'll be okay."

"I need a pick-me-up."

Eddie lunged at her and she juked, the circle of zombies on the mezzanine cringing away. As a teen Eddie had been in plenty of street brawls, always accompanied by an audience hanging back to watch the spectacle. Eddie had endeavored to not disappoint and would return home or to the dorm bloodied but triumphant. The zombies opened a gap to the escalator and several dropped through the hole. Eddie laughed. *Idiots.* He grappled at Mona as she fled, snatching a tuft of her choppy hair. She wrenched free, which elicited a satisfying screech from her as a clump of hair remained in Eddie's clenched fist.

"Those shorts are coming down!"

He stormed onto the escalator and stomped down toward her. *Those short little legs aren't gonna outrun The Comet.* On the main floor she headed for the entrance, the floor littered with writhing, freshly fallen, zombies, these not as damaged as they'd landed on their crumpled brethren. Even with her gift it took a few beats for the shamblers to respond and make way. She padded toward the front of the store, the café area where Karl had been injured on her left. Eddie's feet landed hard as he jumped the final six or so steps for effect and Mona spun to face him. *Look at that expression! An expression. Any expression, but this one I like. Fear.* The zombies began to withdraw and Eddie advanced.

A gun.

A gun?

Wait, what?

In Mona's trembling hand was a formidable piece Eddie had never seen before.

"You fuckin' *hate* guns," he said. "You little phony."

He stepped toward her. Uncle Sal, he of the complicated knots, had these DVDs of scantily clad chicks shooting all manner of firearms: pistols, assault rifles, submachine guns, name it. Eddie had cranked it to those many a time on overnight visits, while Sal and Aunt Sheila sawed logs. And now here was Spooky brandishing some Dirty Harry-lookin' hand cannon. What was it? Sal liked guns but didn't know one from another.

"This is a good look for you," he said. "Puts a little life in those dead doll eyes of yours. A little fire. Like you're human or something."

One hand rubbed his wound, the other his crotch.

"Look, relax, I'm not gonna rape you or nothin', I'm just playin'. This is all very emotional, Karl and everything. I'm a little tweaked." Her eyes narrowed. Was she buying it? He was, in fact, very tweaked. And aroused. And sickened. It was a buffet of emotions and impulses. Some chick that had dumped him called him *emotionally illiterate.* Guys like Zotz were loaded with sentiment. Artsy types. *Zotz.* Just thinking about him angried Eddie's blood up. Zotz and the Widow Swenson. He looked at his shoulder. *Why the shoulder? They pulled the same move on Dave.* He set his jaw and looked at the way Mona was holding the gun. Sideways, like a stupid movie. *Gangsta.* He smirked. *So stupid.*

As Eddie stepped toward her a zombie, still recumbent from its tumble from above, snatched at Eddie's leg. Its strength wasn't much, but the ground was slick and uneven and Eddie toppled atop it. *So stupid.* A confederate ghoul joined in and within seconds Eddie was under a dogpile of mangled undead, fighting but with no leverage.

"Shoot!" Eddie screamed. "Shoot 'em!"

Mona hesitated, unsure, then squeezed the trigger and fired a wild shot into the store directory, the combination of recoil, noise and inexperience knocking her off her feet. The back of her head collided with the marble countertop of the barista station and it was lights out.

Yards away the zombies polished off Eddie Tommasi, whose dying wails sounded nothing if not girlish.

"YOU CAN'T BE serious," Alan sputtered, following Ellen past the barricaded vestibule and down into the musty basement. He felt dizzy and gripped the handrail to keep from blacking out.

"Of *course* I'm serious. You think I *want* to be doing this? I have to. If there's no more Mona there's no more us. She's our lifeline. Plus, she's one of us. So, I have to."

"Can't we give it a little more time?" Alan pled. "It's only been—"

"Ages. It's been long enough. It's like Ten Little Indians. We're down two men and Mona. Plus, Abe, Ruth and who knows what became of Gerri? I tried Dave. If he's in there he's sulking or passed out. Dabney's in no condition. Fucking alcoholics in this dump. Who knew? You get a pass. Extenuating circumstances."

Alan ran a hand over his bandaging and looked at Ellen. "Thanks. I mean that."

"I'm not gonna give you shit for getting wrecked. You literally *are* wrecked."

Ellen placed the camping lamp on a stack of crates and looked around the room. In all the months since the pandemic began she'd only been down here once or twice. Even in the better times this dank subterranean space gave her the creeps. Near the boiler there were a couple of cage-style wire mesh lockers for tenants, one rented by the Fogelhuts, the other unoccupied. Ellen approached the Fogelhuts' locker and gave the combination lock a yank.

"Figures," she muttered. "I'd suggest looking for the combination in their apartment, but that could take forever."

"I'd suggest you abandon this, period."

"Yeah, well."

Ellen dug around Mr. Spiteri's tools, which lay in a haphazard array on and about a crude wooden worktable by the stairs. There were several toolboxes, which she rummaged through until she produced a short-handled drilling hammer. She liked the heft. "This'll be a good weapon out there, just in case." She slapped the head against her palm, then took several vicious whacks at the lock, the only result being the bones in her hands being rattled.

"See?" Futile," Alan said, a hopeful, somewhat manic, smile splitting his face. "Okay, you gave it your best shot, so—"

"Not that easy," Ellen rebutted. She tugged on a thick pair of rubberized work gloves and returned to the locker, smashing not the sturdy lock, but the lightly rusted fitting through which it was looped. That broke away after several focused whacks and with a creak the door swung open. Ellen grinned, pleased with her cunning.

"This is the worst idea, ever," Alan said, panic rising. "*Ever.*"

"You were going to attempt it, you fucking hypocrite."

"And you were against it. You. So, who's the hypocrite?"

"Both of us. So shut up, okay? You ever read 'A Modest Proposal'? If we don't get Mona back we're looking at the longest short winter of our lives and a very limited menu." Ellen rubbed her belly for emphasis.

"That's in very bad taste," Alan said.

"No shit, but this is all I can think of. It worked for Abe. How many times did he suggest one of you *young bucks*—" Ellen made air-quotes "—do this? Dozens. 'If an old fart like me could do it, what's your excuse?'"

"You're not a buck."

"Want me to break your other arm? I thought you were more enlightened."

"I am. Maybe. I dunno." Alan sat on the steps and considered his words. "I just don't want you to ..."

"I don't want to die, Alan. I don't." She rubbed her stomach again. "I don't. Really. I've wrestled with that kind of ideation, but

I don't. I want to live and that girl has been beyond good to us. And helped us live. And we let her leave in the company of a creeper I wanted you, *of all people*, to protect me from. Sorry. *Sorry*. But look at you. You're clever, you're talented as hell, but you're just not *that guy*. It worked for Abe."

"It worked for Abe because he did it *before* things got so bad out there. There were countless morsels besides him for the ghouls to choose from. They didn't *need* to pick a well-insulated geezer. You recall anyone else trying this ploy and succeeding?" he added.

She couldn't because no one had. Back in April Paolo from 2B had been shamed enough by Abe to make an attempt and was devoured in plain sight within yards of the building. But he hadn't donned Abe's gear, assuming enough layers of his own would suffice. He couldn't help but stay fashionable and died looking good. Ellen had long ago abandoned stylishness.

She pulled the boxes out and ripped them open. Inside were Abe's improvised armor: the *Baby Sof' Suit®* infant winter onesies and the XXXL pair of *Bender's Breathable Sub-zero Shield® Sooper-System™ Weather Bibs*. Stepping into them and leaving the bib down—as Abe had described in detail many times in the prior months—Ellen began stuffing onesies down the pants, padding herself from the ankles up. When she'd reached maximum density she pulled up the bib, heaved on the matching camouflage parka and stuffed in more onesies and any other rags she saw lying around. With the hood of the giant parka cinched tight around a scarf and a pair of snow goggles, Ellen resembled a camouflaged Michelin Man.

"So," Alan said, a hint of worried derision in his tone, "how are you going to get upstairs now, Stay Puft?"

Ellen cursed under her breath. She should have suited up in the apartment. Already she was self-basting in perspiration. With rubber-gloved hands she gripped the railings and hauled herself up the narrow flights of stairs to 2B, her sides scraping the wall and the bannister. By the time she reached the window with the rappelling line she was soaked with sweat.

"I think we really have something," Alan said. He didn't look so hot. "We could, anyway."

"Yeah, I agree. And we will."

In an attempt to suppress tears, Alan's face contorted in a much more obvious way. The nose wrinkled, the lips compressed, the eyes squinched. Borderline comical.

"Don't be such a drama queen," Ellen said. Shifting the scarf and balaclava and goggles she smiled at Alan and he could see the affection, which made this so much worse.

"Can't you wait a little longer? Maybe they're all okay."

"Alan," she said.

She touched his face with the thick glove, then removed it to touch skin-to-skin. Her hand was slick with sweat, which Alan kissed.

"This may be the last I get to taste you," he said, no longer able to repress the tears.

"No, it won't."

"Okay then," Ellen said, refitting the scarf, balaclava and goggles, then gloves.

With the grace of late era Orson Welles, she positioned herself on the windowsill—barely able to fit through the opening—swung her legs out, gripped the rope and lowered herself onto Dabney's van. The zombies noticed the motion but didn't seem overly riled. Ellen's heart jackhammered her innards. Her ribs ached. Her eyes felt in danger of escaping their sockets, so focused were they on the horde below. With a faint wave, Ellen sat on the van's roof, lowered herself to the ground and disappeared from view.

Several infinite minutes passed and then Alan spotted Ellen's bloated form bobbing up York toward Eighty-sixth Street. Though the zombies didn't make way, they didn't attack, either.

When Alan exhaled it felt like the first time in his life.

It was more than weird to be out among the undead.

Though she couldn't be certain, Ellen felt as though in spite of the temperature and copious garments, she'd stopped sweating altogether. It was unlikely, but she felt a permeating chill. To combat fear she attempted to keep her thoughts detached. Their skin was matte, but with oily patches, the pigment bleached or discolored. The white zombies were pasty yellow, the black ones gray and ashy. Even the matter underneath their shredded derma, the fasciae, peeled to reveal brown muscle tissue and dry bone.

Everything looked desiccated. *What you guys need is a good moisturizer,* Ellen thought. *Some Oil of Olay or some Neutrogena. Something with a high SPF rating. I mean, look at you guys.*

She focused on the path ahead. The bookstore was two and a half avenues west. Even though it had been at a snail's pace, without realizing it she'd already made it to First Avenue uneaten. That was good. That was very good. Were she a person of faith she'd think it miraculous.

Since the zombies hadn't made an opening for her she was rubbing elbows with them—even the elbowless. Though there was generous padding between her and them, each contact mainlined straight into her nerve endings. *Focus,* she thought. *Focus.* She recalled self-help gurus with their "can do" attitude and their mind-over-matter mantras. Ellen had always taken those guys to be con men, though, so conjuring them didn't help. And really, didn't their shticks always boil down to creating wealth? *Not helping. Not fucking helping.*

Condensation accrued on her goggles, the top portion of her view erased by fog. *Great. Soon I'll be blind. Ms. Magoo on a rescue mission.* Something shoved Ellen from behind, propelling her forward a few paces too quick. Her face contorted under its wrappings, her lips compressed, half swallowed to stifle the shriek lodged in her throat, eyes shut, prepared for the worst. She bumped into several zombies, but they responded only by growling and lightly shoving back. *Am I immune?* Ellen wondered. *All this time, maybe I could've gone out. Maybe I don't even need all this gear. Yeah? Don't get cocky,* her brain chided. *Good idea, brain.*

The slog west was interminable. What struck Ellen as odd was that down among them they didn't smell bad at all. Maybe it was all the wadding around her nose and mouth, but they seemed virtually odorless. Did the stink rise? Were they losing their scent or was she merely desensitized? They were ghastly to behold, though, and being in their midst hammered home the improbability of their existence. How did they persist? Some were barely more than skin tarpaulins encasing collapsed innards and strings of sinew. Movement would brush her undercarriage and she'd look down only to see some half-, third- or quarter-zombie inching along the pavement like a semi-pulverized worm. The most natural bit of genetic programming was the survival instinct, but this was so beyond that.

The crowd seemed to swell as Ellen pushed onward, the space between them closing, closing, closing. The material of the hunting parka, the uncounted layers of baby snowsuits, all of it, felt inadequate. The undead's emaciated frames, their pointy shoulders—some ending there, armless—their angular hipbones, all of it scraped against the plasticized shell of her outerwear, injecting amplified echoes directly into her ear canals. Her pulse thudded in her temples and she could hear her heart laboring. She fought the urge to scream. To laugh. To cough. She wanted to choke. Bile rose in her throat several times and she swallowed it back. *How can they not scent me? I must reek of fear. Any second I might shit myself. Does shit sound the dinner gong? Do they still crap?* Though many people did so at the moment of death, defecating seemed likely to be solely the province of the living. But these things ate living human flesh. Once again she thought of Mike and wondered about their digestion. They were so withered, almost mummified. Did the ones missing their gastrointestinal tract still feel the need to feed? Did they absorb nutrients? So many questions.

Ellen felt like the zombie equivalent of Dian Fossey, a scientist studying a contrastive species … only dumber. She and the species.

She looked down at the pavement to check for zombie scat.

Am I insane? I must be. What sane person would be out here in the first place? The padding she wore began to feel like a full-body maxi-pad, because surely Ellen felt sweat must be spraying off her. She thought of the countless commercials depicting absorption, always with innocuous blue liquid. Her liquids most assuredly would not be blue if shit got real. She stood motionless, pondering her predicament and her grip on it. Her eyes focused not on what was happening beyond the fogged lenses but retreated within, her focal depth confined to her own eyeballs. Things moved there: floaters. She watched the transparent blobs swim in the vitreous humor between the lens and retina.

A fly alit on the goggles, its unexpected appearance making Ellen flinch. Her spasm attracted some unwelcome glances and the odd hiss. *Oh shit. Don't let me get killed by a fucking fly.* The insect remained on the lens, grooming or whatever it was they did when they fussed with their forelegs. It was getting more difficult to see, the condensation creeping further down the lenses. Ellen's eyes darted back and forth, making contact with dead eyes in the mob. It struck her that Alan had gotten the eyes wrong in all his studies. Maybe because they'd been done at a distance, but in his zombie portraits he'd made their eyes symmetrical, forward facing, their vision binocular. Up close Ellen could see that in almost all of them—the ones that still *had* eyes—they pointed in different directions, one aimed straight out, the other rolled to the side or pointed inward at the nose. Some rolled back into the socket. All glazed with death, grayed and fogged and yellowed. Flies and larvae crawled in and out of the zombies' various orifices, their hosts organic mobile homes.

The other thing that landed hard at this vantage point was the latent humanity. In the recesses of these cratered faces were vestiges of the people they'd been. Maybe it was just a consequence of the haziness, like how they'd supposedly smear Vaseline on the lens to appease aging starlets whose visages were more creased than they'd like in closeup, but it was so clear to Ellen that these were the people in her neighborhood. She recognized the brooch on one's crusty lapel. It was that lady who'd always sniped at the cashiers at the CVS. And that one was maybe the guy that would borderline harass her from behind the counter at the bagel store.

Takir. Yeah, that's him.

Ellen's head ached.

Something gripped her leg and panic deposited itself directly in her colon. She looked down and saw looking back up at her something tiny and female. From the window it was impossible to see to the pavement, but Ellen was now confronted by a zombie whose stature would be hidden below the sea of adult shoulders and heads. A child, one sad Peppa Pig barrette nestled in its lusterless hair. And what had appeared dark, Dondi-esque, eyes were in fact just hollow sockets. Its mouth hung open, the striations radiating from parched lips. It still had its milk teeth, but for two missing dead center. *Dead.* Through the muggy soft-focus Ellen saw the child this once was. The lavender shirt retained its chroma, shielded from the bleaching rays of the sun as a consequence of her elfin proportions. Ellen looked up and down again at the adults around her. Their lower extremities were less faded. The small hand released Ellen's leg and the wee one shambled off, lost again amidst the sea of rickety legs. More moisture clouded her vision as tears joined the condensation. She wanted to just collapse to the ground and let what passed for nature take its course. *Why bother? Why anything, anymore?*

Mona.

Hold it together.

These aren't the people in my neighborhood. They aren't. They're things. That wasn't a little girl. That was a thing. Just things. That's all they are. Things that if they scented you would …

Her legs were moving of their own volition. Zombielike.

When in Rome. Not much farther. Mind over matter, mind over—

Another snag, this one lower, at the ankle. Through the miasma Ellen saw a legless zombie with only one arm hitching a ride, its clawlike, almost fleshless hand digging splintered nails into her thick rubber Wellington boot. *Oh fuck. Oh Jesus.* Ellen didn't dare attempt to shake it off for fear betraying her humanity—her edibility. Step after mired step the freeloader was dragged until Ellen found herself stuck, unable to impel that leg forward. She looked down again, straining her eyes to fathom the hindrance. Another zombie had trodden on Ellen's passenger. Ellen tried to disengage her leg from the bony hand. Nothing doing. In death—or would that be *unlife*—was rigor mortis the status quo? Until her hitchhiker's hitchhiker stepped off, she was anchored to this spot.

The other zombie stumbled off the back of her passenger and Ellen moved forward, wondering how long the ankle-gripper would hold on.

Situated in a large apartment building, the bookstore was midway between Second and Third Avenues. Wading through the crowd it struck Ellen that zombies didn't really walk. The ones that could stood upright, sort of, but they just kind of shuffled around aimlessly, their movement dictated by the group rather than the individual. They were like plants impelled to move by a breeze. The only time Ellen saw them propel themselves with purpose was when it was feeding time. *Like with Mike. No. Don't. Don't think about Mike. Don't think about the way they shredded him like pulled pork. Don't think about the sounds he made, not quite dead until he was. Don't think of an elephant. Just move. Move.* It had to be scent. Were there scientists anywhere working on answers? Some underground bunker somewhere? If so, was that even a comforting thought?

As she cleared the southwest corner of Second Avenue, Ellen's passenger again snagged on something, this time accompanied by the sound of fabric tearing. She looked down and scarcely visible through the haze saw the culprit: not the hanger-on, but a rusty detached bumper. Ellen's guest's detached hand, however, was still hooked onto her boot, the rest of it lost in the profusion of spindly legs. Then she noticed a splotch of something pale and pinkish. *Paint? Chalk?* Her own pale skin exposed in the perforation. *Fuck.* The bumper had torn the material. Ellen transfixed on a small blossom of red dripping down her upper calf.

The adjacent zombies' postures stiffened a fraction, as did hers.

Inches away one canted its head at an angle that telegraphed its intent: to begin the beguine. *Fuck that.* Faster than she'd have thought possible the zombie lunged and snapped at Ellen, burying its teeth in the surface of the outer layer of the parka near the shoulder. The padding was thinnest there and Ellen felt a pinch. Not skin-breaking, but piss-inducing. She punched her attacker hard and it fell away, leaving behind a couple of embedded teeth.

Nonetheless, the word was out: *dinner is served.*

Scent.

Violent motion.

The zombie's associates heaved toward Ellen, their need raw, guileless. She swatted at them, punching and shouldering. They were weak but plentiful. She was practically blind, but her goal was within yards. More teeth and limbs bit, pawed and clawed at her. She heard more material tearing. One arm penetrated the outer parka shell and she felt it groping at the bib of her overall. If she started hemorrhaging *Baby Sof' Suit®* infant winter onesies she'd soon graduate to actual hemorrhaging. The image of her own entrails boiling out filled her forebrain. *No, no, fuck no!* She twisted side to side and the perpetrator's arm snapped off with a sickening pop, still twitching within her coat, its bony digits grazing her right nipple, which stiffened inappropriately. *Oh god, oh god, I'm being me-too'd by a fucking severed arm!*

Ellen drew her own arms in, making herself as compact and missile-like as possible, then, bulky as she was, tore ass toward the bookstore. Skeletal hands snatched at her, as did stumps. Her hood got yanked down, snapping her head back, material cinching around her throat. She gagged, but kept on. The goggles pulled sideways across her face exposing one eye, blocking the other. Terrified as she was, the sudden rush of air on her wet face felt refreshing. *Don't readjust. Keep moving. Keep moving, you fucker! Do it! No blitz, no fucking blitz! Please.* She rammed forward. Another pair of rotting arms attempted to detain her. *I'm not a huggy person! Get off of me!* She wrenched to one side and broke away. Half-blind Ellen saw her objective loom ahead. *Make way for Stay Puft!*

Even if Mona's not in there, even if they're all perished, I'll— Ellen couldn't think of anything encouraging. *I'll be stranded here and die. So be it. Maybe I can find some duct tape and mend the rips, provided they don't eat me alive in there.* Ellen vaulted over the broken window, palmed the scarf off and with her teeth yanked off the glove. Dexterity restored she pushed up the goggles, fished a flashlight out and clicked it on. The zombies were right on her ass, tumbling into the confines of the store. Ellen whipped the light left and right, up and down. The floor on this level was clear. She saw the hole in the ceiling above the barista station. *Okay.*

"Mona!" she shouted. "Mona!"

No reply.

Ellen bounded up the escalator, casting the beam of light in every direction. She was a goner, but why make it easy for them? Stumbling over piles of burnt books and ruined standees Ellen tripped and cracked the goggles on a bookshelf. She removed them, feeling her forehead welt where they'd impressed into it. "Okay," she wheezed, dazed and short of breath. "Okay. Okay." Staying on her knees, she crawled behind the bookcase and ventured deeper into the store's upper level. From below she could hear the inarticulate jeremiads of her pursuers.

Edging out of the aisle, her bare palm made contact with something moist and sticky. She aimed the beam of light at the floor, which was coated with a well-trodden glaze of semi-fresh blood that led to the men's room door.

"Fuck."

Alan was right. This was a stupid idea. Foolhardy. Dumb. Not concerned with what killed cats, curiosity compelled Ellen toward the restrooms, each movement forward accentuated by the tackiness of the coagulating blood. Pushing open the door she saw what remained of Karl, his death expression open-eyed, gape-jawed, anguish. From the shoulders up he was almost intact, but from the upper ribs down it was like a bomb blew him in half, his soft bits mostly gone, just flesh shrapnel slathered over the floor. Ellen threw a hand over her mouth and swallowed back the sick. *Not morning sickness. Mourning sickness.*

"Karl. You fuckin' …"

Why not puke? Who am I holding back for?

More tears came, instead.

"Bible Boy. God *damn* it."

Her head slumped forward, the crown resting directly in the mess. On hands and knees in the remnants of Karl she ugly cried and despair laughed, then rolled into fetal position. In her compromised fat suit armor, smudged with tacky blood, she resembled a crippled engorged tick.

"Fuck," she moaned, then shrieked, "*Fucking fuck this fallen fucked-up world!*"

Her sobbing increased in volume and she didn't care. Let them come.

"Ellen?"

Ellen?

Through a smaze of tears and snot, Ellen saw a figure in the doorway. Speaking to her, not lunging to devour her.

"Mona?"

"Uh-huh."

Ellen started laughing. "*I'm here to rescue you!*"

"I can see that."

Ellen rose from the floor and flashed the beam at Mona's face, which sported a bruise on the jaw.

"Did Eddie do that to you?"

"This did." She showed Ellen the revolver. "The kick, anyway." She rubbed the back of her head. "But he would've …" She trailed off, enough said.

"That motherless fuck." Ellen reached for Mona, then hesitated. "Do you mind if I?" Mona shook her head and Ellen felt a large knot on the back of Mona's cranium. "Were you downstairs?"

Mona nodded.

"Jesus, I must've run straight past you to get away from the mob."

"I was out cold, but your screaming—"

Ellen smiled. "Glad I'm not much for stoicism."

Mona returned the smile.

"That's a lot of blood," Mona said. "On your … outfit."

"Not mine."

"Still, might be safer to …" She pantomimed stripping it off.

Ellen peered down over the mezzanine railing at the crowd that awaited them below. This ridiculous getup got her here, but rolling over in Karl's fluids probably hadn't been the best idea.

"I hadn't thought of …" Ellen began. "I kinda gave up, to be honest."

"I noticed."

Ellen peeled off the outer layers, leaking baby onesies. With the oversized shell gone, she stood there barely dressed, wearing just cotton shorts, a tank top and the Wellingtons. She shivered a little.

"Not gonna lie, I feel a tad vulnerable."

"The umbrella works."

As they descended the escalator, Mona pointed out some freshly excarnated bones and loose gore that trailed off beyond a display unit. Ellen aimed her light at the mess and saw some recognizable accoutrements. *Eddie.* Neither commented as they ventured out of the store, but Ellen thought *good.*

On Eighty-sixth, with the retreating crowd creating a concentrically widening berth, Mona took a few moments to stretch and get her land legs, readjust her clothes, then fished a folded piece of paper out of her pocket and, with a slight limp, started walking with purpose.

"What's that?" Ellen asked, keeping pace.

"The list."

Ellen was flabbergasted.

"Are you kidding?" she stammered. "After what you've been through? Take the day off."

"Can't."

"I don't understand. You might be concussed. Eddie nearly—" Ellen stopped herself, unable to complete the sentence. Just the thought of it filled her with rage. "He …"

"Failed. He failed."

Ellen had to keep pace to avoid getting eaten, not that Mona would leave her to the zombies. Mona was on a northward course, up Second Avenue. Ellen opened her mouth to question this, then stopped herself. As they neared a small pharmacy her face flushed. It was already maybe too late for that to curtail her pregnancy, but as they neared, she was certain she didn't want to. What was this whole rescue attempt about? Once a mother, always a mother.

"I don't want it," Ellen said. Before an audience of chagrined ghouls Ellen, star of the grimmest Lifetime Channel movie ever, clarified, "The mifepristone."

Mona looked at her. "Okay. But I haven't hit this one yet."

In the dark interior Mona strode straight to the dispensary counter and vaulted it with athleticism Ellen hadn't expected. Headlamp on, Mona knew right where to look and within seconds filled her cartoon knapsack with her quarry. She slung Hello Kitty behind her, adjusted the straps and went back over the counter like a pro.

"Your pills," Ellen said.

"Yours, too. If you want. Not for you, but …"

"Can you spare them? What'll happen when you run out?"

"We'll see, I guess."

Epilogue. October, *Now.*

It seemed early for snow, but there it was: a light flurry stippling everything a stark white. Chilliness seasoned the air, but it felt good after months of oppressive heat. Still, it gave pause. Winter was coming. Ellen turned away from the window. Though the horde was still plentiful, their numbers seemed to be thinning. Maybe she was kidding herself, or maybe was just a matter of time. She'd seen them up close. Ellen sat back down at the table and contemplated her next move. Buying hotels was always risky.

"Dude," Mona said, agitating the tiny top hat.

Ellen looked at her. She, too, had changed a bit in the months since "The Karl and Eddie Incident." She'd likely never be Miss Personality, but she'd come a long way since her debut. She managed a smile now and again and her sentences, though short, were mostly actual sentences.

Dabney, with the change of weather and subtraction of neighbors, had abandoned his rooftop shack altogether, settling into Gerri's old place. He's also lightened up on the booze, though he still enjoyed a dram on occasion. He entered the living room opening a jar of salsa, the chips already on the table. He took his seat and dipped a chip.

"So," he said. "Tick tock." He smiled.

Constructed of more salvaged duct parts, Dabney had rigged a small indoor fireplace, which warmed the immediate area nicely. Alan wouldn't have managed that on his own, but he'd helped. They'd done some other home improvement projects together, like fortifying the corroding vestibule barricade, which helped them bond. Still, at some point the collective might need to move on.

Ellen rubbed her belly, feeling her passenger within. Maybe it would be another girl. By the gameboard lay a half-empty blister pack of Mona's pills. Now Mona's and hers. Unlike Eddie and Karl, she seemed to be experiencing no adverse psychological effects. And her dry mouth? Ellen popped a lemony lozenge and rubbed her belly again, wondering if lightning would strike twice. Was the theory correct? Would Baby Swenson have Mona's gift? Would she also have her muted persona? Like Mona had said back in the drugstore: *we'll see, I guess.*

And with those thoughts filling her head Ellen laid her cash on the table, said, "Fuck it," and bought a hotel.

Afterword: Why a Redux?

THE IMPETUS TO do a revised edition of *Pariah*, my second published novel, at first stemmed from the many conversations I've had over the years with my manager, Matt Kennedy, regarding some plot points he felt needed fleshing out. In collaborating with screenwriter Ryan Ederer on a screenplay adaptation of the novel more and more not just solutions, but complete deviations from the original came to mind. And to my thinking, improvements.

Not gonna lie: reworking this novel was way more emotional than I'd counted on it being. It forced me back into a dark headspace I'd very happily left behind when I abandoned my post as a lifelong New Yorker for a brighter spot on the West Coast. Don't get me wrong, New York City is a great place. One I look forward to visiting again. But living there, not so much. The toll it exacted on my psyche both forged my creative voice but also chipped away at my mental wellbeing. Both my parents were, to some degree (in my dad's case, a higher degree), pessimists. Negative. That also influenced my outlook greatly, more nurture than nature, it turns out. Although I certainly have moments where I "return to form," much to my chagrin. Like this book, I, too, am a work in progress. I hope.

Anyone that's familiar with my work knows I have a proclivity for monkeying with it upon each new release. From my perspective it's another chance to get it right; to better it. To others it might be indulging Quixotic perfectionism. To yet others it may be what

I've dubbed "Lucas-ing" and taking perfectly good work and making it worse. I certainly hope that's not the case. Sometimes director's cuts are improvements. Often, they're not. But I've always sympathized with that urge *to make it better.*

Pariah's origins go back. *Way* back. The original pitch was for a graphic novel for the then-new Vertigo line at DC Comics. Their creator-owned, edgier, more adult line. Zombies were not yet enjoying a renaissance, let alone oversaturation, so pitching an undead graphic novel was not fashionable, even with the full support of an ascendant youthful editor. For whatever reason, everything I ever pitched at Vertigo was met with rejection by the head of the imprint. A clash of sensibilities, I suppose. So be it.

Regardless, *Pariah* lay dormant for a number of years.

When Dark Horse Comics launched its *ZombieWorld* title in 1997 I unearthed the *Pariah* pitch and sent it to the series editor and got a provisional "yes." The caveat being that *ZombieWorld* was following a loose timeline, and even if the stories were self-contained and didn't even follow a cohering mythos, I needed to write a prequel for *Pariah* set at the beginning of the zombie pandemic. Then, later, we could do *Pariah* as a serialized GN. Illustrated by the great Tommy Lee Edwards, "Winter's Dregs" was that prequel, and the only character to carry over from it to the novel was Abe Fogelhut, making his way home in his cartoonish bib overalls and onesies-stuffed "armor."

In addition to the aforementioned conversations with my manager, I cannot overstate the impact listening to the book-oriented comedy podcast *372 Pages We'll Never Get Back*, hosted by RiffTrax's Michael J. Nelson and Conor Lastowka, had on tackling this revised edition. Without naming the names of some of the books they rightfully roasted, just listening to these two gents week after week pinpoint some truly dire writing traits made me acutely aware of things I needed to address in my own work. I didn't lean too heavily on pop culture references, but the podcast highlighted for me not only how obnoxious this can be, but also how badly it dates. And making a character an avatar to spew your own petty and pointless predilections and prejudices doesn't necessarily make for compelling reading. Especially if it doesn't move the plot forward or really make any impact whatsoever other than, "There, I said it." Great. Who cares?

Over the years I've mined my own life for material, particularly the comic series for which I'm probably best known, the quasi-autobiographical *Minimum Wage. Pariah* is a work of fiction—duh—but for some reason rereading it in preparation for this edition, held more personal connection than my more obvious romans à clef. It put me very much in the very personal headspace in which I'd resided when writing it back in 2009. And that was not a happy place. One thing that was a surprise was how my sympathies had shifted since that original '09 draft. Alan Zotz, when first written, was the character to whom I related and empathized most. But for the revisions I found him often judgmental, condescending and somewhat infantile. I beefed up Ellen, feeling she was more worthy of the hero's journey, which had originally been Alan's. She had greater motivation. The relationship between Eddie and Dave needed work. Dave finding his truth in the apocalypse. Eddie, an emotionally illiterate a-hole, more conflicted about his feelings.

I've experienced life events I think have given this draft more gravitas. Experienced the loss of both parents and some good friends. A marriage. Seismic events that shaped the person I am now. My experience with grief was more limited when I originally wrote *Pariah.* And some things, alas, you really must inhabit before depicting them accurately. *Pariah* is so much about loss. Everyone has lost so much in this book. That said, a book wallowing in grief would be a slog. I wanted just enough to inform who these characters are, but not so much to drag the reader down into the pit. Balance I hope I've achieved.

On a deeper level, working on this edition made me confront an angrier, darker, more rigid version of myself. What I now call *New York Bob* (because everyone knows it's healthy to think of yourself in third-person). For the longest while I defined myself by skewing toward negatives. That popular thing? *I hate it.* I used the word "hate" far too freely. What I really meant was dislike, or don't care for. But the default was "hate." Particularly in recent years one can see how cancerous that word is and all it contains. Hate tears apart nations from within. Hate alienates friends and family. It's also not much fun to be around someone like that. I always used humor to mitigate my negativity, and often it worked.

I was a pill, but a funny pill. Still, at a certain point that novelty wears off. Part of moving to California was to reboot. Not just transplant myself but work on who I am. Who I could be. That *better* version.

It's a more emotional draft, for sure.

Someday, perhaps, I will write a sequel to Pariah (I have one plotted), in which some of the cast of "Winter's Dregs" might connect with Mona, et al. Time will tell.

To the readers for whom this is their first and only experience with the book, thank you for taking the plunge. I hope you found it rewarding and entertaining. And if there are any readers that also read the previous edition, thank you doubly.

Stay safe and healthy.

Bob Fingerman
Los Angeles, April 2021

P.S.: When Alan goes into lecture mode with Ellen he talks of plague and SARS. I could have updated to Covid, but who knows how that will all play out? This book is set during a vague mid-2010s. I've always set my books a few years earlier than written because we never know how things are going to pan out. And big horrific events like 9/11, Covid, Trump, well, one needs some time to gain perspective to fold them into fiction. Working on this revision during the pandemic has been another wrinkle. When I wrote this, originally, I speculated—pretty accurately, I think—on life during lockdown. The bunker mentality. Decades of working from home prepared me better than many, I'd imagine.

Bonus Stories

The Summer Place

I'M LOOKING AT the red ring of fresh shiny tooth marks on my right palm, some highlighted by small dots of blood. Not a lot of blood; in fact quite little. But enough to have me concerned. It's times like this I get nostalgic for tetanus. Remember tetanus? When you were a kid and you'd go tearing around a vacant lot, some future construction site or some such, and you'd catch your tender young dermis on a rusty nail. Tetanus! Adults had warned you! You'd get visions of lockjaw and freak out. The grownups had cautioned you that infection with tetanus would cause severe muscle spasms and that those would lead to "locking" of the jaw so you couldn't open your mouth or swallow. It could maybe even lead to death by suffocation. Tetanus! Ah, the good old days.

Tetanus is not transmitted from person to person.

I wish I could say the same for this current unnamed affliction.

That part also sucks. I don't even know what to call this. The scientists and doctors hadn't come to a consensus by the time the broadcasts had ceased. So, what's the official classification? What's the name? I never understood the concept of naming a disease after yourself just because you discovered it. Why would you want your name associated with pain and suffering evermore? What was Parkinson thinking? If I was a doctor and I chanced upon some terrible malady I'd name it after someone awful—Hitler's Syndrome or Bush's Complex. At any rate, what would you call this latest—and likely final—pathosis? *Zombification* sounds kind of stupid. And if it's brewing, if you're infected but zombification hasn't blossomed into full-blown zombiehood, what then? What do you call its period of gestation?

I'm not man enough to go all Bruce Campbell on myself and lop off the offending extremity. Not yet. But why bother? It's in there, doing its thing, circulating. I guess. I remember hearing about this guy who was bitten on the ankle by some totally poisonous snake, in South America I think it was. Anyway, he knew he had about three minutes before the poison killed him. The guy was a lumberjack or something—maybe he was decimating the rain forest. Maybe the snake was protecting its turf. I can't remember that kind of detail. But he acted decisively and took his chainsaw to his leg and cut it off at the knee. And he lived. The guy lived. He cut it off before the poison could reach his heart. I couldn't do that. I can't. So I'm a-goner.

Why should I be any different?

Still, I feel so stupid.

I bandage the bite, more for the psychological comfort it provides. I just don't want to keep staring at it. Still, there goes my sex life, not being one for ambidexterity. I step out onto the porch and look down at the asphalt walkway. I'd call it a road, but no cars were permitted here. Sure, the occasional emergency vehicle was allowed—they didn't call it *Fire* Island for nothing—but no civilian automobiles. During the summer, just a few short, endless months ago, this road was teeming with the pasty and the tan, the fit and the flabby, all making their circuits to and from the beach, most of the guys toting coolers and cases full of cheap, low-octane suds. I never saw anyone with food. All of these beachgoers, the rare quiet ones and the common boisterous types, seemed to sustain themselves purely on beer and greasy wedges from the local pizzeria.

I'd kill for one of those mediocre slices right now.

The walkway is mostly obscured by slushy sand—just patches of buried blackness showing through here and there. I used to sit on this porch, reading—or at least pretending to read—and scoping the hotties. Right before the current, ultimate, nameless pandemic came and ruined everything, the *Girls Gone Wild* epidemic had swept the nation. Formerly normal girls, ones with a modicum of propriety, would suddenly whip off their tops and bounce up and down. All it took to loosen them up was massive quantities of alcohol, a bit of flattery and the materialization of a video camera. How many parents cried themselves to sleep at night because of those DVDs?

Guys with oversized Dean Martin fishbowl snifters of frozen margarita would chant as these local girls made bad would frown, then giggle, then comply and let their boobs out to Neanderthal choruses of, "*Whoo-whoo-whoo*!" Maybe that was a portent of the looming bestial decline of mankind. Nah. But it's amazing how fast a sexy girl can become an abject object, all desirability drained away in mere moments.

I don't know.

I thought coming back to Fire Island would be a good idea. Isolated, especially in the off-season. I liked the whole no cars thing. Back in the city, when it was really beginning to get soupy, the maniacs in their cars were more dangerous than the zombies. The roads were choked with panicky motorists attempting to flee, causing all kinds of mayhem along the way. What did they expect? Light traffic? Idiots. Of course all the roads were clogged. And every poor pedestrian schmuck one of these amateur Dale Earnhardts nailed would rise as one of the undead. Brilliant. Broken dolls peeling themselves off the pavement to wreak havoc on the ones who struck them down. Or whoever was convenient.

I used to be a bike courier, right after that movie *Quicksilver* came out—but not *because* of that movie. Never let it be said I was influenced to take a job because of a movie. Remember that thing? Kevin Bacon as a hotshot bike messenger, for the like five minutes Hollywood was convinced such a lame-ass job was cool. All those dumb movies about urban iconoclasts. Anyone for *Turk 182*?

Anyway.

Even after I moved on from that gig I remained an avid cyclist. My legs conditioned for endurance, I avoided the main arteries and biked all the way from Elmhurst to Bayshore, Long Island, which is a pretty long haul. I don't know how many miles—my odometer fell off somewhere along the way—but a lot. Especially when you consider the meandering back roads nature of the trek. None of that "as the crow flies" convenience. En route I could see things worsening citywide, the zombies increasing their numbers at a dizzying pace. *Be fruitful and multiply,* I thought, ever the heretic. Even taking this shunpike route I avoided many a close call and witnessed many horrific sights. Amazing how many variations on the themes of evisceration and dismemberment there are. I splashed through more than a few puddles, and I'm not talking water. Having learned the hard way how to avoid hitting pedestrians, getting doored in traffic and other hazards of the bike courier's trade, I managed to eschew ensnarement by the hungry undead.

At least the zombies are slow.

And can't ride bikes or drive cars.

Yet.

When I got to the marina—actually, that sounds a bit grand. The wharf? The dock? Whatever. Where the ferries left for the island, I realized there wasn't exactly going to be regular service. What was I thinking? Panic doesn't make for cogent planning, but you'd think on that interminable bike ride I'd have flashed on the notion that maybe ferry service to the island was terminated. Oddly, the ferries were still docked. Empty. No one was around, which was rather eerie. *Not a creature was stirring, not even a zombie.* Forgive me, but Christmas is coming. Call me sentimental.

Anyway, I boarded one and got as far as the bridge before I realized I had no idea how to pilot such a craft. I don't even know how to drive a car. And I had the brass to think those anxious drivers idiotic. Here I was, way out in Long Island, not my bailiwick, with no plan and nowhere to go. I was exhausted, too. I walked over to the vending machine to score a refreshing beverage. I'd earned that. The machine was dead, not accepting currency, paper or coin. I kicked the machine, shook it, then basically beat the hell out of it. I needed to vent. As it lay on its side, its front came undone and it spilled its innards in a cacophony of tinny—or would that be aluminumy—clanks. I chugged three cans in a row of Ocean Spray cranberry cocktail and felt better. I then stuffed a bunch in my backpack and as I was about to check the grounds for more comestibles I spotted some interested parties dotting the periphery.

Not human.

The ruckus I'd made was the clarion, the dinner gong. I might as well have shouted, "Come and get it!" while tinkling a comical outsized triangle. If I'd entertained even fleeting hope that these callers were reg'lar folks, their herky-jerky locomotion quashed it in a trice. I gathered up a few more cans—delicious refreshment could double as solid projectile, if need be—and mounted my bike. But I wasn't sure where to go. I made a few quick figure eights around the parking lot, then made for the private boats. Many of those were missing, but a shoddy-looking motorboat was moored to the jetty. I stepped down into it, and when I didn't go straight through the bottom decided I'd be a seafaring boatnik after all. I grabbed my bike and loaded it into the dingy little dinghy, then tested the motor. A few yanks on the cord and it sputtered to life just as the lifeless approached. *Mazel tov*!

I'd never steered a boat of any size before, but for a first-timer I didn't do too badly. I managed to follow the basic course I'd remembered from all our trips on the ferry and within, oh, maybe two hours or so I made it to Ocean Bay Park, the dinky community we'd rented in.

We.

I remember the concept of "we."

"*We*" was pretty sweet. I was part of a "we." I had a wife. But guess what? She became one of those things right at the onset. On her way home from work she got bit. Well, more than bit. Consumed. I got a call from a cop who kept pausing to vomit noisily on his end of the line. He vomited, I wept. Then she came back and tore into the officer. Or at least I think that's what was going on. It sounded crunchy and wet. He kept screaming until, well, until he stopped. It was a really moist call. I'm being flippant, but sue me. It's all I have left. If I'm not flip about losing her I might just…

Anyway.

I might just what?

Kill myself?

That's a laugh.

All I know is I heard her moaning before I got disconnected—moaning and chewing. I got the picture, even without the benefit of a camera phone.

So after ramming into the side of the dock—starting it up I could work out, stopping not so much—I got out of the boat, dizzy and nauseous. I lay there for a while gasping, trying not to hurl. I must have looked like a fish out of water. It was mid-October, still not too bad temperature-wise, but drizzling. A good alternative name for Fire Island would be Rust Island. Back in the day people would ride their bikes all over, but always these ratty, rust-speckled wrecks, and here I was with my almost top-of-the-line mountain bike. Like it mattered. But at the moment I felt annoyed that my precious bicycle was going to be ruined by the elements. Priorities, young man, *priorities.*

Fog was rolling in, obscuring everything. If there were zombies afoot I wouldn't see them coming—or hear them. I hastened my pedaling and raced to our house. I say "our," but really it was just a rental. And now that I was no longer part of a "we," "our" seemed moot, too. I approached the dwelling that was little more than a shack and slowed as I heard footfalls.

Not human.

Deer.

Fire Island is rotten with these skanky, tick-encrusted deer. They're not beautiful, cute or charming. They're the animal kingdom's answer to skid row vagrants. Dirty, infested with chiggers and lice and all manner of parasites. Their ears look like warty gourds, festooned with ticks so engorged they look fit to burst. These deer root around the trash, knock over garbage cans, mooch for scraps when you're eating outside. Where's Ted Nugent when you need him?

I got inside, locked the door, checked all the windows and then collapsed onto the naked mattress and into a nightmare-rich slumber, assuming the island to be pretty much deserted.

I was almost right.

The next morning I checked the pantry, though why I can't say. At the end of the season we cleared out all our edibles so I kind of knew it would be empty, which it was. I guess it was wishful thinking. Maybe cupboard elves had left something to gnaw on. Whatever. What else is life but hope? What would propel us forward but the inborn combination of hope and masochism? After hydrating myself with tap water I snatched up a blackened iron frying pan, cracked the front door and took a gander. Still drizzling but the coast was clear.

I tiptoed down the short flight of creaky wooden steps to the dirt path and stepped onto the sandy asphalt. Sandy Asphalt. Sounds like the name of a third-string stripper of yore. I digress. To my left was the beach followed by the ocean, a mere hundred or so feet away, to my right the ferry dock and the bay. The island's about thirty miles long, and at its most expansive only about three-quarters of a mile wide, just a long strip of sand. I mounted my bike and bay-bound made for the general store, a weathered gray clapboard number that had overcharged for everything. Ocean Bay Park—what in its heyday I'd referred to as Lunkhead Central—was silent apart from the patter of rain. Granted, even before this apocalyptic turn of events off-season would have been pretty calm, but this was different. The store's screen door hung open, not swaying on its corroded hinges. Even a rusty creak would have been reassuring. The silence was unnerving. Unnatural.

I jiggled the doorknob. Locked. A swing of the frying pan through the window later I was inside, stuffing my face like a little piggy with beef jerky, chips and lukewarm Pepsi. I filled my pockets with snacks and potables and hit the road in search of I don't know what. Other survivors? More food? A gun? Yeah, all of the above. Inland, such as you'd call it, the roads were much clearer so biking was easy. The fog was burning off so visibility wasn't bad. I cut through Seaview and approached the larger—in relative terms—town of Ocean Beach, relishing the pleasure of riding my bike where the town ordinance had been "no bicycles allowed." The jolly scofflaw in a world where law is passé. Fun. I did a couple of laps around the center of town, checking out the spoils: general store, hardware store, a couple of shops devoted to souvenirs and beachwear, a disco, some eateries, bars and ice cream parlors. And the old movie theater, a wooden structure I'd avoided, something churchlike in its mien that had kept me away.

I broke into the hardware store—funny how natural looting becomes—and selected a few lethal objects: a small, wieldy ax, a 12-volt battery-operated nail gun, and plenty of ammo, namely nails. I also grabbed a heavy jacket and rain slicker that were hung on a peg behind the counter. What can I say; I packed light and forgot a few things. After knocking on doors and shouting, "Is anyone there?" till my throat was raw, I rode back to the crib and charged the nail gun. It would have to do until I found a real gun. If I found one, that is. At least the power was still on.

As I ate a dinner of processed foodstuffs I heard a noise outside. The indicator light on the battery charger was still flashing, so I grabbed the ax and snuck up to the front door. Even with the porch light on I couldn't seen anything. I heard the noise again. Something was moving out there. Had my light attracted it? Likely. I pulled on the heavy jacket and opened the door a hair, casting a focused beam from my flashlight into the hazy darkness. This fog was getting tiresome. The crunch of underbrush drew my attention and straight ahead was a ratty stag, one antler broken and dangling, the other an elaborate six-pointer. Listen to me trying to sound like the great outdoorsman. The deer on Fire Island were a protected species. They were completely unafraid of humans, so certain were they that they'd remain unharmed, like city squirrels.

It was a little early in the season for this buck to be shedding its antlers. Maybe it had gotten caught on something or been in a fight over a doe. Satisfied it wasn't a zombie I closed the door and resumed my repast, savoring each salty morsel of dry beef and chips. Amazing how salty American snack foods are. Stomach full of delicious garbage, I fell asleep easily, legs sore from all the abuse I'd heaped on them.

Over the course of the next few days my notion of retreating to Fire Island proved both a prescient blessing and shortsighted curse. It was indeed quite empty, but *too* empty. I was hoping to find *some* other refugees from the world. A young or even not so young widow. A couple with the swinger ethos. Maybe just a guy to hang with. I rode southwest through Robbins Rest, Atlantique, the aptly named Lonelyville, Dunewood, Fair Harbor, Saltaire and Kismet. I stopped there because I didn't want to get too close to the Robert Moses Causeway, the bridge linking the island with the mainland—or at least Long Island proper. I was afraid that where there were cars there might be problems. Zombies and people in quantity.

I felt like Charlton Heston in *The Omega Man*, Vincent Price in *The Last Man on Earth*, both mediocre adaptations of Matheson's *I am Legend*. Tooling around like a tool on my ten-speed I was nobody's legend, that's for sure.

As a boy I'd been pretty self-sufficient, at least in terms of my ability to have fun alone. Often I'd play games like I was the last person on the planet. I'd deliberately choose routes to and fro bereft of people. I'd walk beside the tracks of the Long Island Railroad or along the traffic islands down the median of Queens Boulevard. Sure there'd be cars whipping by, but for miles I could walk without encountering another person in the flesh. My dad accused me of having a morbid fascination. I liked horror movies too much. Now, looking back, I reckon it was all a rehearsal for what was coming. Look at me, the Nostradamus Kid.

The loneliness was eroding me from within.

I tried heading in the other direction, which proved tricky. Point o' Woods was fenced off from Ocean Bay Park—no doubt to keep out the riffraff, of which in its day OBP had been densely populated. Unable to negotiate my bike over or around the fence, I climbed over and made the rest of my slog on foot. I'd never explored any of the other parts of the island back when it was alive. Sunken Forest was just that. Pretty, but creepy like everyplace else. Sailor's Haven wasn't. The super gay Cherry Grove was a bust. Hell, not that I'd have made a lifestyle change, but I craved camaraderie and so long as it was platonic I was up for anything. Anyone. But nothing. No one.

I was so tired and dispirited I didn't bother schlepping to The Pines and points beyond. This was a ghost island, and I suppose as crushing as that fact was, ghosts were less harmful than zombies—at least *physically*. I'd managed to evade being literally consumed only to end up consumed by crippling melancholy. This was living?

There was no television, not even a test pattern.

Radio was fine if you enjoyed static.

I embarked on a house-to-house search for reading matter. I needed something with which to keep my mind occupied. Crossword puzzles. A Gameboy. Anything. The problem with summer rentals is that people don't leave stuff year-round. Sure I found some romance paperbacks—which I read, I hate to say—but nothing edifying. I found a cache of techno-thrillers, you know, Tom Clancy garbage. I read those, too, but stultifying doesn't begin to describe them. The bodice-rippers were better. I was in and out of almost every house between OBP and Robbins Rest before it dawned on me that I didn't have to stay in my trifling little shack. What the hell is wrong with me? Seriously. I had the run of the land and I spent my first three weeks in that drafty dive.

What a goon.

I took up residence in a sturdy and significantly more comfortable five-bedroom ranch-style number. The little pig had wised up and abandoned his straw hut for the brick palace. There was even a stash of porn in the master bedroom. I'd found my roost. With the power still on I kept my drinks cold. There was booze, and though I'd always been pretty much a teetotaler I began indulging. I'm not saying I became a drunkard, but every night after sashaying around my new demesne I took the edge off. And if that sometimes meant ending the night flat on my back, the room spinning like Dorothy's house on its way to Oz, so be it. Sobriety had lost its charm.

On a ride back from the market in Ocean Beach my front tire blew and I wiped out, spilling ass over tit into a shallow ditch opposite the ball field. Maybe I was a little hung over. It's possible. Not being a seasoned inebriate I was still defining my limits. For the first time in weeks the sky was cloudless and the sun was blinding. Even before the tumble my head ached. Now it throbbed, my palms were scraped raw and my vision was impaired. Even behind dark glasses I squinted against the glare, sprawled in the dirt angry, and even though there were no witnesses to my slapstick, embarrassed.

But there was a witness.

Hiding behind a water fountain near the bleachers was a zombie. How could we have missed each other this whole time? I scrabbled to my feet, groping for whatever weapon I could find, but in my pie-eyed complacency I'd left them all back at the ranch. All I could manage was my tire pump, which was pretty impotent.

The thing is, the zombie just cowered there, maintaining its position. Still wobbly from the fall and residual spirits I stumbled backwards against a staple-riddled lamppost, gauzy remnants of weather beaten notices for past community events clinging like scabs to the splintery surface. We stared at each other for what felt like eternity, neither of us doing anything. I began to wonder if this was a zombie or just a hallucination. Maybe the spill had given me a concussion. But it wasn't. My vision cleared yet the zombie remained, staying put. Not attacking.

"Hello?" I asked, feeling stupid for doing so. "Can I help you?"

It recoiled at the sound of my voice. The zombie was female, and had been fairly young when she was alive—maybe a teenager or slightly older, judging by its apparel more than anything else. I'd never gotten to study one up close, most of the ones I'd seen a blur as I'd whizzed by them in transit. Her facial epidermis was taut, not slack as I'd pictured it in my mind, and the color of raw chicken skin, only the yellow wasn't quite so robust. Her deep-set eyes were filmy and lacked focus—in my present condition I could relate—yet her gaze never drifted from me. Her mouth hung slack, her breath slow and wheezy. Two things struck me: one, she was breathing, and two, her teeth were toothpaste commercial white. In the movies zombies are always snaggletoothed, their enamel grossly discolored. This undead chick had a movie star grill.

She also seemed impervious to cold, considering her bare feet and midriff, low rider relaxed-fit jeans and thin tank top. I could see a pink bra under her low-cut white top. She had cleavage. Was I appraising this animated corpse's sexual attributes? Yes. Yes, I was. I was wondering if sex with a zombie constituted necrophilia. Who could say? The definition of necrophilia is an obsession with and usually erotic interest in or stimulation by corpses. But what of ambulatory corpses? What then? Though her body skin was a bit loose—relaxed-fit skin?—she was well preserved. Was it loneliness or madness that motivated these thoughts, not to mention a surge of blood into my groin? Both.

"Uh, hello? Can you, uh, you know, uh, understand me?"

She cocked her head like a dog, her brow creased in concentration. It was almost adorable in a sick kind of sad, macabre way. Against my better judgment I took a step in her direction and she flinched, then began to back away. I took this as a sign to curtail this insanity and make tracks. I righted my bike and walked it home, looking over my shoulder at my hesitant new companion who did likewise.

I didn't drink that night, but I must have jerked off a half dozen times.

I know, I *know* ...

The next day I replaced the inner tube, grabbed my nail gun and hit the road. The weather had turned much colder over night and the gray misty gloom had rolled back in. As I pedaled it began to drizzle. Soon snow would come. I considered gathering wood for the fireplace but was focused on finding the zombie girl again. I tried the ball field, of course, but she'd vacated the area. Still, I thought, slow moving as they seem to be, how far could she have gotten? Was she a local? Did she retain knowledge of her surroundings? Was she capable of anything beyond rudimentary mentation? Or even that?

As I approached Lonelyville two does broke through the brush and blocked my path. They looked unwell, to put it mildly, even by Fire Island standards. Their fur was patchy, the bald spots scabby and oozing. Tumid ticks, as per usual, enshrouded their ears. In the rain they steamed; the smell was not good. I slowed, hoping they'd clear the way, but they just stood there looking unsure what to do next. I didn't have some fruity little bell to ring at them so I braked and shouted, "Hey, clear the road! Go on, beat it! Scram!" I made those nasty noises through my teeth that shoo cats away, but no dice. They tottered, looking drunk. I felt a flash of envy, then yelled at them a few more times, but the filthy beasts were unyielding.

I didn't feel up to a hassle with nature, so I made a U-turn and wended my way back home, zigzagging the streets up and down, looking for you-know-who to no avail. That afternoon I emptied a bottle of vodka, polished it off with a variety of mixers, then disgorged the contents of my stomach into the kitchen sink. Thank goodness for the garbage disposal. I managed to clean up before passing out on the linoleum floor. Flashes of *Days of Wine and Roses* and *Lost Weekend* flickered behind my throbbing eyelids. When I awoke it was the middle of the night and I was disoriented as hell. At first I thought I'd shrunk—*The Incredible Shrinking Souse* or *Honey, I Shrunk the Drunk,* to keep up with the movie theme of this bender—my sightline being that of a man whose face is stuck to the floor.

I literally peeled myself from the sticky surface, rubbing my face, which had been imprinted with the texture of the linoleum. I felt like crap, but upon seeing my pattern-scarred *punim* in the mirror began to laugh until the choking curtailed my mirth. Symmetrical red striations etched the right side of my face. What a boob. I stumbled into the bathroom, urinated painfully, then gargled away the sour booze-vomit aftertaste. It hadn't been *that* long. Why was I falling apart like this? Could it be something to do with the death of humankind, especially my family, and most of all, my precious wife? Could it be because I was pining for the company of a female zombie I thought was passably attractive? Yeah, maybe that justified this rotten uncharacteristic behavior. There have been worse rationales for hitting the sauce.

I managed to get to the bed before surrendering to dormancy again.

I dreamt of a threesome with my late wife and the undead girl. Both stripped me naked and led me to a bed in the middle of the baseball diamond. The sky was black. Not nighttime dark, but black. A void. Eyes glowed from the bleachers accompanied by a chorus of chirping crickets. The two women began to run their tongues up and down my body, my wife working my upper portion, the living dead girl south of the waistline. The thing is, both of them were in that zombified state, but it was blissful—until they started devouring me. I didn't wake up. I just lay on my back watching them consume my flesh, opening my abdomen and pulling out my innards. I was paralyzed. They looked so contented.

I woke up and, goddamn if I'm not king of Mount Perverse, I had an erection.

In spite of my hangover I managed to eat and keep down a reasonably healthy breakfast, determined to find the girl. I don't like being haunted but she was doing just that. What would I do when I found her? Would she still shrink away or would the native hunger zombies seem to have—hey, I'm no expert—present itself? If so, would I flee or just let it happen? This whole survive-just-for-the-sake-of-survival thing isn't that great. It's only been weeks and already my *joie de vivre* is pretty well kaput.

I mounted up and hit the dusty—well, moist, actually—trail. The mist was icy and I had to keep my eyes squinted tight to prevent ocular abrasion, but I was resolute: I would find this zombie girl and either court her or exterminate her, depending on her receptivity to my companionship. Maybe she just wanted a tuna sandwich. Maybe this human flesh eating was just a phase. Again, I'm no expert. Maybe she needed a hug. I know I did. I'd just like to spoon again. Be in bed and feel the small of a woman's back against my stomach, my crotch nestled against her tush.

As I pedaled I felt more and more conflicted about this loopy notion of bedding down a zombie. And it wasn't even a sex thing at the moment. I just wanted to snuggle. What man just wants a cuddle? A crazy, lonely one, that's what.

Calling out would be a no-no, she being the shy type, so I just kept my eyes peeled and pedaled slow. I skipped Point o' Woods and beyond. I just couldn't envisage the zombie girl lofting herself over the high chain link fence. So, block-by-block I explored Seaview, pausing only to pick up a few provisions, including a visit to the liquor store. In each town I dismounted and checked the nearby beach. Nothing. Well, nothing but skanky deer. At each encounter I mused it was a good thing for them I wasn't fond of venison.

Yeah.

The first frost came in early December. Maybe my zombie heartthrob had succumbed to the elements or starvation or decomposition. I had no idea how long an undead individual lasted, with or without sustenance. How often did they eat? Could they subsist on grubs and squirrels? I hated not knowing. I hated that I couldn't log onto the Internet and Google "zombie, feeding habits, lifespan". I needed to Ask Jeeves, but couldn't. Like everything else, the 'net was down. I never realized how addicted I was to outlets of mass communication. I missed TV, radio and the web as much as I missed human contact. Sick. Books and backdated magazines were not cutting the muster, no sir. My nights were a debauched stag party for one, the time split between drinking to excess and masturbating when I could manage it.

It was while walking my bike through that town whose name I loved so well, Lonelyville, that I stumbled upon—literally—the undead object of my desire, but now she was just plain old dead dead, her stiff supine body glistening with ice crystals. I knelt down beside her and stared, my grief indescribable. Her tank top had disappeared, and her bra was torn, one cup shredded revealing a pale, translucent yellow breast. Her face was angelic, at least to me at that moment, and I felt shame for having fostered lust for this creature. Not because it was unnatural—you can debate that all you want—but because she looked above such secular desires. Tears began streaming down my cheeks but I didn't wipe them away. I felt more loss here for this stranger than I had for my own wife, maybe because my wife's demise was in the abstract. I hadn't been there for it. I'd also been in a blind panic like everyone else.

Now, in this tranquil wintry setting, I had the luxury of time to grieve. I let it all out for this strangely captivating zombie girl, for my wife, for all of humanity. I bawled and right there in the road, lay on my side and spooned her, my body shaking not from the cold but from previously unimaginable loss.

And as we lay there a grizzled stag stepped onto the road, staring at us, its eyes black and unknowable. Steam pumped from its craterous nostrils and it grunted with bestial authority, like we were trespassing. *We*. I so badly needed to be a part of "we" again. Does that make me codependent? My vision blurred by anguish, my mood black as pitch, I glared at this four-legged interloper. It grunted again and scraped a hoof against the pavement. The effrontery was too much. It was this goddamned filthy animal that was trespassing on this scene of human loss.

I disengaged from the girl's cadaver—and that's all it was now, just a plain old regular garden-variety corpse—and stood up, my fists vibrating with barely contained mayhem. I wanted to hurt this threadbare excuse for a deer, its antlers cracked and collapsing, its fur a mat of mud and grime and abrasions. I stepped toward it and it shook its head back and forth, its right antler threatening to drop off with each motion.

"I *hate* you miserable bastards," I hissed. "I've always hated the deer on this godforsaken island, but now you, you really *put it in italics*. Can't you see this is a private moment? I know it's beyond your feeble peanut brain to show any goddamn respect, but so help me if you don't get the hell away from here I'll bash your skull in!"

It stood there, steaming away in the sleet.

So I took a swing at it. Not the brightest thing I've ever done, but I was a tad overwrought, shall we say? Open handed I made to slap it right across the muzzle and it bit me. And then it hit me why these deer looked so spectacularly putrid: *they were dead.* Undead. Whatever. They were animated corpses. Humans aren't the only ones circling the drain. It's all life. All of it.

So now I'm looking at the fresh white gauze wrapped around my right hand, a ring of small red dots seeping through. Not a lot of blood; in fact quite little. But enough to have me concerned.

And back on that road lays the undead girl of my dreams. I didn't bury her.

I guess I'm infected.

HE FOUND HIMSELF in the unlikely position of drawing cartoon bunnies. Dewy-eyed Disney cuties, cotton-tailed and adorable. He hadn't even thought himself capable of such a thing, but here it was, manifesting all over two-ply Bristol, sweet as you please. And as purgatives went, it wasn't that effectual.

Ink-stained fingers were poor preparation for the actuality, it turned out. Not the actuality of rendering floppity-hoppities; *the actuality outside.* Years of grinding out horror—imagining, then depicting, every manner of freak, ghoul, gore-soaked act of depravity—had left Chuck stymied by his new reality. He found himself haunted by interviews he'd given. All those glib answers that he'd either 1) be better prepared than Joe Average because he'd envisaged it all, or 2) that he'd know better than attempt to survive in such a cataclysmic eventuality. He knew that humanity, when and if the time came, would be well and truly screwed so why bother staving off the inevitable? He'd pop the muzzle of his Glock into his mouth and fellate some death into his noggin.

But he'd been wrong in both cases.

He wasn't better prepared and his desire to live was stronger than he'd ever imagined it could be. Oh, his dad had told him time after time that all living things are hardwired to want to survive, but he'd argued humans were smarter than that. "Smart's got *nothing* to do with it," Dad had countered. "It's just there, in the *blood.* In the primordial jelly. When shoved up against death you're going to shove right back. '*Not today,*' you'll shout. Not if there's any chance to put it off until tomorrow. Or the day after that." It seemed so ridiculous. "No," Chuck had said, "I know better. If the ghoulies ever actually rose up, I'd put one in the brainpan. *My* brainpan. Game over."

Well, they had and he, dainty art lad that he was, had no gun at his disposal.

And that hardwired survival instinct kicked in as strong as Dad had said.

Holed up in the studio he'd shared with five other ink-monkeys—*Der Bunker,* they'd dubbed it—he'd pored over all their collected horror comics for previously overlooked insight. The Warren mags, *Creepy* and *Eerie.* Reprints of E.C. classics from the Fifties—*Vault of Horror, Tales from the Crypt, Haunt of Fear*—and not-so-classics from lesser imprints of the Eighties and beyond. All the others they'd collected, including ones from Italy and Mexico that none of them could read but with art that needed no translation. Domestic garbage like *Haunted Thrills, Witches' Tales, Tales of Voodoo* and so on. He and his studiomates had amassed quite a collection of portrayals of every conceivable horror. They'd marveled at the mastery of some contributors and laughed at the ineptitude of others. Artists used to have to pull a lot out of their asses before the Internet came along. Websites devoted to gross anatomy—the grosser the better—made illustrating horror easier than ever. Forensic pathology websites; sites devoted to every awful way to die. Innumerable videos and JPEGs. So, Chuck and his confreres were experts at delineating every snapped sinew and spilt innard.

But reality always trumps, so even in a world of "Two Girls, One Cup" and *Human Centipedes One, Two,* ad nauseam, seeing your friends set upon bangs a different gong. Their innards now *out*-ards. Chuck had boasted a cast-iron stomach. He'd dared associates to unsettle his gut with the worst they could find. His email inbox was often choked with imagery of such a vile pedigree he marveled the Feds hadn't come to drag him away. The funny thing was, he hated the trend of Torture Porn. He liked his horror with monsters from beyond. Torture was just human-on-human evil. He craved escapism, so even though he'd executed one or two torture yarns, they'd been bummers.

Zombies.

They were Chuck's jam. He never tired of them in all their myriad incarnations: voodoo, Romero, fast, slow, somewhere in between. Big ones, small ones, rotten or fresh, he loved them all and had his best hours at the board and tablet immortalizing them. He'd seen every movie but none ever got down to the real nitty gritty. He'd pondered and wanted answers. With all that fresh human meat in their rotting guts, did zombies defecate? How long did unfed ones last?

Now life was one long crash course filling in those gaps.

Zombies shat. As if their stench wasn't bad enough, zombie scat had a bouquet that needed to exist before anyone could fathom how horrid it was. "Two Zombies, One Cup". Chuck might have found that funny, once. Now, not so much. His more squeamish associates had borne the brunt of his geeky machismo. He'd lambasted them for pussing out during movies, averting their eyes at gore porn—or *gorn,* as he'd dubbed it—from the Web. They'd been packed into this studio like sardines and he'd been cock of the walk, bullying them with his consequence-free bravado.

Now.

Now he was alone in this massive building. A place that used to be a hub of industry, back when they actually made stuff in Gowanus. The stink of chemicals and glues and solvents would be an earthly delight compared to the sweet 'n' sour pong from beyond the windows. This big building, partitioned into art cubbies with art nerds crammed in. That was a kind of manufacturing. Now *no* form of industry existed here. He'd founded this studio because he hated working alone. Being alone. He thrived on interaction.

All the action was outside.

On the street.

Even the canal was clogged with writhing bodies; ones that had toppled in and now couldn't squirm their way out of the blackening goo. It was like the La Brea Tar Pit, only the exhibitions were still animate. Or re-animate. They wanted out. They wanted to be with the others, stumbling around. And the sounds they made, all of them. That was another thing they'd gotten wrong in their preconceptions of the ghoulish horde. They're not quiet.

They warble and wail and make sounds the likes of which you wouldn't think the human vocal mechanism capable. Not even Diamanda Galas. Unearthly land-based whale song, only the opposite of soothing. Not white noise. Black noise? Blood noise?

Spore noise.

The shamblers formerly known as people sported antler-like racks protruding from their cracked skulls, the tips of each branching prong festooned with bulbous blood red "fruiting bodies"—*sporocarps* sporo-spewing fungal loads, infecting others. The money shots of airborne particulate matter bursting from these orbs as they asexually propagated had diminished of late, but that left Chuck no less stranded. Freeze-dried fruit, fruit rollups, all manner of jerky and nitrite-laced meat stick. Cheese crackers and tortilla chips. Bottled water and juice and warm beer. Comic artists like to snack and for that he was grateful. But much as he was glad for all the provisions squirreled away in pantries, lockers, desk drawers, he yearned for something fresh. And besides—*tempus fugit*—the provisions were almost gone.

He also yearned for some company.

Stacy Bendix.

She of the full-sleeve tattoos and thick black nerdframes. She of the unnatural hair color-of-the-week and enticing muffintop and occasional whale tail. She who knew she could outdraw her studiomates without breaking a sweat and not just because she kept them slightly addled with barely suppressed, definitely borderline harassment-type thoughts all day. Bendix, fresh from New Hampshire, raised by hunters, knew the ins and outs of guns and katanas and all manner of armaments.

First sign of trouble, casual as you please, she produced from her locker a sticker-covered black plastic case—Chuck, et al, had assumed it to be a paint box or some such—keyed it open, retrieved a couple of pistols—

"You have guns *in here?" Jerry had shouted.* "Guns? *You didn't think that was worth mentioning?"*

"S'my business," Bendix said, unruffled.

"B-but they're guns. Why here? *Reference? That's what the Interweb's for! We don't do guns here. That's not cool."*

"Reference," *she'd jeered.*

"But why here?"

"Because my boyfriend doesn't like 'em at home. Not gonna throw 'em away," she'd said. "Jesus."

Jerry, Tony, Steve and Chuck had all died a little inside, that being the first mention of the boyfriend they'd all wanted to be. Position filled, so to speak.

—and vamoosed. Oh, she'd invited the others to join her, but they'd demurred, choosing the safety of the great indoors. From the sooty studio window they'd watched her slam into her junker, fill the air with exhaust and rumble, peel out and not look back. She bounced several off her hood before disappearing around a corner.

Bendix.

Chuck's swagger was a put on, a coping mechanism. Hers was so real she didn't even use it. But *she'd* been the alpha. The one that played it close to the vest until shit got real. *Bye, Bendix. Yeah, she'd survive this.*

The cartoon bunnies stared glassily up at him. Was there something accusing in their eyes? The twinkles of light he dappled into them? Maybe it was just his darkening mood, but the cute seemed tainted. Not that cute was ever his forte. Whenever called upon to draw children, Chuck's always looked off. Like middle-aged midgets, their features too mature, their expressions too consternated. Even his happy kiddywinks looked like they'd been shouldering *weltschmerz,* Atlas-style. But the bunnies. The bunnies were a letdown.

"I'm drawing you creeps to put some smileage on my face. Hoppity-hop and—"

Clank.

Not a loud clank. Not echoing thunder. But audible.

Clank. A door opening. Downstairs. Then the compressed whoosh of it being forced closed against the pneumatic door closer's will.

Someone else was in the building.

The coat-racks hadn't worked out how to open the doors, so maybe it was her. Maybe she'd come back. One by one the others had fled, proving Chuck most un-alpha of all. Plus, he'd had nowhere to go. A depressing living situation he'd kept mum. "Dude, you're *always* here," Steve had teased. "*Always.* Go home." This *was*

Chuck's home. Rent on his apartment had gotten too high. There was water here, heat—sort of—electricity. A communal refrigerator. Why pay two rents when his one-sixth share of *Der Bunker* was only three hun' a month?

They didn't need to know. Sure, they were buddies. But studiomates weren't privy to everything and as his dad had taken every opportunity to remind him: "Don't kid yourself, these are *work* friends. *Friend* friends are a whole different ball of wax."

The fact that only on the day of Bendix's departure had they learned of her private life kind of put Dad's words in stark relief. If she'd been a *friend friend* they'd have known she was involved.

Chuck listened to the silence that followed the breach. Though he could now hear nothing he knew he was no longer alone and his colon began to undulate. Fresh sweat prickled across his brow. In every horror movie the idiot called out, betraying his position. That's what got you killed. In every videogame he ever played, stealth was never his strong suit. He was a barge ahead guns blazing type. Not like Bendix. Not real deal. But here. Now. He knew stealth was his friend. His *friend friend.* Because friend friends keep each other safe.

Work friends?

Work friends bug out and leave you behind.

And get slaughtered while you watch.

Pummeled, not eaten. Beaten down by fucked-up antlers that gouge and scrape. Then bukkake toxic loads onto their victims to propagate. And eyes went blank and drawers got filled and the air stank and the situation reeked even worse.

Footfalls.

Uneven footfalls.

He was not alone in sucking at stealth.

And though an ardent gamer, his modding skills sucked, too. He'd attempted to pound nails into the one passable weapon, a softball bat, only to split it. Cheap wood? Likely. But that had been his only line of defense. He crept along, hugging the wall with his back—*because that's what you do, right?*—keeping mum.

"*Chuck?*"

Male voice. Bruised. Diminished. The coat racks didn't speak. He wrestled with the urge to respond. But it was someone who knew him. Someone who knew he was still in here. So, in spite of what his guts were telling him—

"Yeah? Who is that?"

"Steve."

Steve!

Chuck bounded down the stairs, landing on the nonskid surface with all-caution-to-the-wind thuds. And there was Steve. What was left of him, anyway. Last to leave, first to return, Steve. Steve, lying in shadow, rim-lit by soot-filtered sunlight, glossy insides now taken up residence outside his skin, a little. Organ meat protruded in a way that photos of accidents and war casualties and medical texts had ill-prepared iron-stomached Chuck. *Jesus.* And poking from his forehead, two adorably disturbing nubs. The beginnings of spore-antlers, like a fawn. Steve had always been the most hyper-sexed. A priapic satyr known for taking long "bathroom breaks" to "purge the system." Especially once Bendix had joined the ranks.

And she knew. They all knew.

So, Steve, with the baby antlers. Pan incarnate. So not cute. *Like the most recent bunnies.*

"You *do* live here, don't you?" Steve said. His face managed a smile, even.

"Yeah."

"But not just now. Like for a whiles, yeah?"

"Pretty much. Fuck, Steve."

"I know, right?" Steve fingered his nubs. "S'crazy."

"I don't even…"

"S'okay, man. S'okay. Doesn't even hurt. Upside to the downside: once it's in you it's like mondo THC-ville. You feel… *I* feel … *baked.*"

"But they eat. They bite and gore—"

"*Ish.* But the tradeoff is not without its charms, amigo. I am tripping balls. I bring glad tidings. I come bearing news of the Word and the Word is *get spored.*"

"Bendix—"

Steve's smile faltered. "Bendix." His hand casually glanced his crotch. Even in whatever state he was in, Steve was Steve. "Yeah. Bendix didn't get far."

"No?"

"But she got with me. I got with her. Not necessarily the way I wanted. The way we *all* wanted. It's different for girls. You ever notice that? Anyway, *something. I* got what *she* got on accounta her getting it first."

"She's infected?"

Steve scowled, but stoner-softened. "S'ugly word, *infected*. In-*feck*-ted." Stoner inflected. He giggled. Chuck's eyes wandered. He saw it wasn't so much a collection of externalized innards as bulbous, bladder-like, sacs. Something moved within, coursed, liquid-like, insect-like, too, like a hive. Life within these reddish, purplish, translucent, Portuguese man o' war-like polyps. Tendrils wriggled, pushing up from between them and Steve's exposed bellyflesh. "Bendix is happy. You ever look at the faces out there? Scary? Not up close. Take a closer look. Up close and personal."

"I'm not going out there. Look at the state of you, dude. Your guts—"

Guts?

"No guts, no glory. The pneumatophore's a metaphor: *smooth sailing awaits, Chuck*."

Chuck winced. Stoner philosophizing. *Not on my watch*, he thought. *But yeah, on my watch. Totally. Because this is happening.* Some tendrils trailed, flailed, flowed like liquid over Steve's thighs, downward. Chuck eased back and haunch-waddled a few paces back from his supine studiomate. The activity in the sacs surged. A couple more waddles back. The antlers pushed out further, accompanied by rivulets of blood at their bases, trickling down Steve's forehead and into his open eyes, dyeing them red. "I'm not gonna lie," Steve said, the smile, though strained, not leaving his face. "This hurts a tad bit. Just a little. Just a wee little—" He broke off into a reedy, high-pitched keening mixed with small hiccups of giggling. "If this isn't your *sceeeeeeene*," Steve singsonged, "I'd bolt that *dooooooooor*."

"I'd like to invite you leave," Chuck said, gesturing.

"Help a brother out," Steve said, voice strained. The keening increased in pitch and diminished in volume. The sacs were at full-flutter, pulsing, their ill-defined contents flowing, rushing, racing …

Upwards.

The antlers cracked out of Steve's skull with a stomach-churning wet pop, spattered small fragments of bone and skin on the cement floor, the battleship gray now festively dappled in oxygen-rich red blood. "*Stings* a little," Steve panted. "But oh. *Oh.* There it goes. *Endorphins.* I dunno. Something. Some … *thing.*"

Without having noticed his migration, Chuck had retreated a full twenty feet from Steve, whose face was beatific as a lama having reached satori. Chuck's mind, on the other hand, was making Warner Brothers' cartoon *homina-hominas. Sweet Mary Mother of Fuck* this was no place for him to be. Visions of demonic cartoon bunnies hippity-hopped through his think meat. *Is this how they get you?* He managed that cogent thought. *Dazzle the shit out of you and render you paralytic with jaw-dropped wonderment?* Made sense. He envisioned a crowbar between his hands and the floor and forced his digits up. His knees sang protest songs in a language unnamed but they complied, too.

Feet?

Your turn.

To move.

Now!

What was this? Chuck was rethinking the whole zombie thing. *Steve wasn't dead.* Those things on him… in him. He'd been occupied. Something or things had taken up residence. He remembered about those man o' war. He'd visited friends in Florida, during what looked like an alien invasion. Thousands of them bobbed on the ocean's surface, their potentially lethal tendrils drifting deep below the surface. His friend, an ardent amateur scuba enthusiast, regaled Chuck with firsthand knowledge of getting stung by one. How his body had felt on fire. How he'd been paralyzed and in agony. How his stepdad had mitigated the anguish by pouring on meat tenderizer and then pissing on him, both ingredients supposedly neutralizing the venom, though Chuck had later learned the urine remedy to do more harm than good.

Is there any meat tenderizer in here?

Chuck didn't think so, and anyway it seemed a little late in the game for Steve. But for the first time since middle school Chuck felt a frisson of science curiosity. *Bendix!* Though it was totally against the building rules, Bendix kept a hibachi on the roof to grill brats, chops, steaks and so on. "You jackasses can subsist on ninety-nine cents-a-slice pizza," she'd sneered, "But a *real* woman eats *real* food. Fuck the landlord." Ever the scofflaw, Bendix.

Chuck raced up the stairs taking two, three at a time, his heart hammering. He'd used that grill on the last few wieners in the fridge. But her gear in the cabinet, the tongs and so on, in the condiments, did she—

Adobo Meat Tenderizer. There it was.

Chuck's stomach growled. Just the thought of a steak, even a cheap cut. The memory of the ocean surface dotted by thousands of Portuguese man o' war. Aliens didn't have to come from outer space. Inner space. The canals below. Clogged. Like a public pool on the hottest day of summer. Maybe he'd been wrong. Maybe they didn't want out. Maybe they were happy. Maybe it was a birthing tank, all those bodies keeping it warm. Bobbing up and down. That horrible whale song. Maybe to them it wasn't horrible. Nature in revolt. A change. Mutation. Whatever it was.

Adobo in hand, Chuck reached the ground floor and found Steve, who now sat up, back to the wall. The blood had already begun to coagulate on the floor, darkening at the edges as it dried. Steve looked up at Chuck, eyes unfocused. Chuck removed the lid and advanced a few tentative steps towards his buddy. The sacs were still and looked empty. The air slightly hazy. Chuck's nose tickled, like allergy season. His eyes stung a little. He squinted at Steve's rack and the antler tips were open, hollow.

Motes hung in the air, the fading sunlight of the day filtered through the grubby chicken wire laminated glass.

Motes?

Spores.

"Wha's wi' th' seas'ning?" Steve said, voice thin and high.

Chuck looked at the jar in his hand and felt stupid. "Nothing."

"Bendix's grill," Steve said. His eyes smiled, though his mouth was not quite in sync.

"I always thought that would be a cool name for a comic."

"A noir," Steve said. His eyes closed. But his chest rose and fell.

"A noir," Chuck echoed. Agreeing.

Chuck contemplated pulling his shirt over his nose but what was the point? He'd inhaled. A couple of sacs dropped from Steve.

Now opaque they looked exactly like organ meat. He thought about how he'd thought people were stumbling around with their guts hanging out. Not. He collected them from the floor and walked back to the stairwell, all urgency gone. Up he went, one flight, two, all ten, and pushed open the door to the roof.

With the sacs on the grill, Chuck tapped on a little Adobo, just because. It wasn't dried fruit he thought. Or jerky. Something fresh and weird. But fresh. Maybe it wouldn't be so bad. It was alien, so this wasn't even cannibalism. Some unclassified taboo.

Conform. Join the herd. The new normal.

Steve had looked happy. Fucked up, but happy.

Maybe they all were.

He'd inhaled.

Bon appétit, Chuck thought.

AFTER A SEMI-HEAVY READ LIKE ***PARIAH***, MAY WE SUGGEST SOMETHING LIGHTER AND FLUFFIER, LIKE ***DOTTY'S INFERNO***, A COMIC STRIP COMEDY SET IN HELL, ALSO BY **BOB FINGERMAN**.

MEET DOTTY.

IN LIFE SHE WAS A CALL GIRL. IN DEATH SHE'S BEEN DAMNED TO WORK IN HELL'S NEW MALE ARRIVALS DIVISION ASSIGNING WAYWARD SOULS THEIR CRUMMY AFTERLIVES. FOR ETERNITY. ALL THE SAME, DOTTY SPENDS MORE TIME AWAY FROM HER DESK ON ODD JOBS AND ADVENTURES, BE THEY FETCHING CERBERUS FROM HELL'S DOG POUND TO LICKING PSYCHOTROPIC TOADS' HEADS AND TRIPPING BALLZ. FOREVER IS A LONG TIME, SO MIGHT AS WELL MAKE THE BEST OF A HELLISH SITUATION.

FROM THE PAGES OF *HEAVY METAL* AND *SOFT WOOD*, AS WELL AS SEVEN NEVER-BEFORE-SEEN STORIES, ***DOTTY'S INFERNO*** IS A ROASTY ROMP BY *MAD* AND *MINIMUM WAGE* CREATOR BOB FINGERMAN.

AVAILABLE NOW, FROM HEAVY METAL/VIRUS!

FIND OUT MORE AT HEAVYMETAL.COM